THE EDUCATOR

For Tracey, Ribh and Finn

1

In the silence, and all alone, Reena Singh lay on her side, and as a single tear found its way downwards and onto the floor, she closed her eyes, and died.

Earlier, as she had walked homewards through Bloomfield, with an almost unbreakable smile on her face, she thought about the evening meal ahead. Her four sons were sure to arrive for their meal, and probably bring their wives with them. She enjoyed cooking for them, she mused. It really gave her a sense of purpose these days. With one thing and another, she was beginning to see less and less of her sons, and Javed, her husband, was working awfully hard in the Warehouse just outside of town, near the airport. He worked long hours, and highly unsociable ones at that. The fact of the matter was that Reena was lonely. In fact, she longed dearly for her family to visit, and when they did, she was only too willing to look after them the way that she used to, day in, day out.

As she walked, she began to sing. Not a traditional song, but a tune she had heard on the radio that very morning. It had a lovely melody, she thought to herself, and almost deserved to be sung aloud by everyone. People think curious thoughts when alone, and she was suddenly visited by an image of the whole country singing the tune to themselves. At breakfast, walking alone like herself, or in the bath. She chuckled in mid-note, and glanced at her watch. At nine thirty in the evening, with the nights drawing in, she made a mental note to avoid getting out by herself. There were so many stories on the news about women being attacked and assaulted, and she was just as much a target as any youngster, she thought. She stepped up the pace, as she had frightened herself slightly into doing so. Besides, if she was going to cook this meal, she contemplated, she had better get her skates on.

In her haste, Reena had not noticed the quiet footsteps behind her. They drew ever closer, with an unnatural lack of sound for people who were moving so quickly. Reena, oblivious to the rapidly advancing shadows, continued to sing her song, in time with her own footsteps now. The two dark silhouettes to her rear began to part slightly, and draw alongside, placing the short, weather-beaten sixty-year-old between them. Reena looked around, sensing that there was someone in close proximity, resembling a scared animal when a predator approaches. Just like that animal, her initial reaction was to freeze. She was immediately drawn to the fact that the shadow had piercing blue eyes, which seemed to stare right through her. That was all she could focus on, for the rest of the face was masked by a jet black balaclava, and when she turned to face the other follower, she was met with another pair of peering eyes, only this time she could not help but notice how glassy the eyes looked, almost like the eyes of a child's soft toy.

It was unfortunate for Reena that she was approaching a sparse patch of wasteland, which stretched out almost as far as her own back garden. Once used as a public sports ground, the stands had long since vanished, and had been replaced by stinking piles of household waste, dumped at will by members of a community with as little respect for nature as they had time to dispose of their waste properly. Suddenly, rough, rasping hands grabbed her at each arm, and Reena began to scream. Her eyes opened wide as a muscular arm was forced around her neck from behind, and a hand was placed over her mouth to stop the screams from sounding any alarm. With very little effort, she was lifted off her feet and walked almost comically into the wasteland. Reena twisted and turned, and suddenly her mouth was free from the stifling palm. She pleaded with her assailants.

'Please, don't hurt me. You can take my handbag, anything I have. Just don't hurt me.'

'Shut your fucking mouth, Paki!' Came the reply. Reena immediately understood the motives these people had for attacking. In a fraction of a second she had realized. All these people wanted was to hurt her. They hadn't a clue who she was, or where she came from. She tried again.

'What have I done to you? Please, leave me alone.'

'I'll tell you what you've done, you fucking bitch. You came over to our country, stole our jobs, our homes, and you walk the streets as if you have the right to. Well, Paki, we're going to teach your lot a lesson. We're going to teach you that you don't rule the manor, we do.' Reena was immediately hustled to the ground, and her arms were pinned to the floor. The smaller of the two attackers, who up to this point had been silent, spat venomously into the woman's face, inciting a cry of disgust from her.

Reena writhed and twisted, but it was all in vain. A torrent of blows began to rain down from the two men, and as she became weaker and less able to stand, they turned into kicks and stamps. Finally, as her own blood-stained twilight closed in, she began to murmur. A murmuring that carried on, until the last hammer blow that stopped her heart. She was humming the tune she had heard, her sweet melody. As she gasped her final note in a crimson symphony, she was greeted by a comforting white light, and a multitude of people, all humming the same tune. The night fell silent.

2

'Now then, children. We've been doing a lot of work on measurement lately. Today we're going to talk about some exciting measurements that we don't usually use.'

From his Year Three class, total apathy was the response. Matt continued regardless. 'Can any of you tell me what a cubit is?'

'Yes, Mr. Greaves.' Chirped a tiny voice from the back of the class. Matt smiled. It was Ashleigh. It was obviously going to be good. His dark green eyes twinkled as he encouraged the waif-like snippet of a girl to enlighten the rest of the class with her pearls of wisdom. 'Well, sir, it's a kind of angel, and when two people are in love, he fires an arrow and it makes them love each other more. That's what a cubit is.' She smiled. Of course she was right.

'That's a really good guess Ashleigh, but I'm afraid it's not quite correct. I'm hazarding a guess, and it's a long shot, but I feel that you're talking about Cupid, the mythical being who has entwined many a couple in his web of love.' Matt Greaves loved the sound of his own voice. There was something in the Welsh swell and cadence that reminded him of a great schooner tripping over the waves of a far-off ocean somewhere. To others it was simply a chance to tell jokes about buggering livestock.

A minuscule voice at the back of Matthew Greaves's consciousness began to speak. It often spoke to him at times like these. It told him that this was as good as it was likely to get. It told him to accept that this was his niche in life. And he accepted it. The days had started to blur into one. He was keen at one time, but after eight years as a primary school teacher the novelty had begun to wear off. It was no longer a thrill to hear the gems from the children. He had heard it all before. There was no thrill these days from parents emptying their hearts out. There was nothing that they ever said these days that remotely surprised him. He was slowly becoming more and more convinced that this was not what he had entered teaching for. A mass of paperwork, constant inspections (or threats of), and what he called 'a torrent of daily shit' from parents were becoming a millstone around his neck. If only there was something to defeat the monotony, he thought.

He delivered his lesson, and the children went home. He sat alone at his desk, bothered by no one. This was his favorite part of the day, when he got to kick back and relax. His marking done for the day, he was just wondering whether to stop for a drink on the way home, when his question was answered for him. The almost perfect silence was shattered by the sudden appearance of a blitz of a man, wearing a faded pair of Levi's 501 jeans and a T-shirt emblazoned with the slogan '*Jesus Saves with the Credit Union.*' It was Nick, his brother.

'Wotcha.'

'Hey,' was all that Matt could muster as a reply.

'Grab your stuff. We're going out. Pay day, remember?'

'Yeah. Okay, where to?' Matt knew what the answer would be; only he elicited the response just to be sure.

'Well,' Nick motioned, 'we could head down to The Arthur, then on to a club after that. We haven't done that for a while.'

'That's because you're always skint after a fortnight. Honestly, Nick, I don't mean to sound like Mum, but I don't have a clue what you do with your money. You earn more than me. Where does it all go?'

Although Matt was only kidding his brother about his interest in his brother's financial affairs, there was an element of truth in what he was saying. For one, he *did* earn more than Matt. There was an abundance of money in computer programming these days. Especially for those as gifted as Nick. While reckless, Nick had many strong qualities that his thin frame and sense of humour hid well. Qualities that Matt wished he too possessed, although he would never tell his brother that. He was dependable as a friend, and there had been many times over Matt's Thirty two years that his younger brother had bailed him out of trouble, when it should have been the other way around. In the family, Matt was renowned for not having the longest of fuses, and his brother was thankfully around as a calming influence when he let his temper get the better of him. Admittedly, this was usually after around nine pints and a few whiskies, but nevertheless he was grateful. He was a good friend, and the two men shared everything. Matt felt that there was more than just the everyday brotherly relationship going on between them. They had hardly ever fought whilst growing up, and although they would never admit it, they both knew why. They simply loved each other too much. Losing their father when they were twelve and ten respectively had magnified this love, and they were both happy knowing that they could count on each other, no Matter what.

Matt stared at his brother, expecting a response to his query about Nick's money. His brother averted his gaze and chuckled.

'Look, are we going to sit here and muck around all evening, or are we going to get pissed?'

Matt smiled and reached for his coat. 'You're right. Life's too short to waste time working. I need a little excitement in my life. A few drinks is definitely the way forward.'

It was not long before the door to The Arthur stood before them, its creaking sign sounding like distant screams. Named after the famous king, that was where the resemblance ended. Matt had contemplated this on many occasions, and he was still none the wiser as to any similarities the public house could possibly have to the greatest of warrior kings, according to folklore. There was no mystery about the place for a start. What you saw was what you got, and that was not much at all by anyone's standards. The interior told a similar story. Smoke-beaten walls and a sticky nineteen seventies carpet gave the pub not so much a lived in feel, but a lived-in, moved-out of, moved-in-by tramps and then demolished feel. Despite its idiosyncrasies, the beer was cold, smooth, and strong (much to Matt's agreement), and the Prince Arthur had become an important part in the complex jigsaw that was Matt's life.

Time seemed to have no meaning when the brothers were out together, and inevitably, after a few pints of something cold and fizzy, plus the customary whisky chasers, the conversation wove its way round to their childhood. On this occasion, it was Nick's temper that was the topic of conversation.

'Bollocks,' grunted Matt, 'Your temper was far worse than mine. Always has been.'

'Like when, smart arse?' came the reply.

Matt pondered for a short moment, then retorted. 'Do you remember Alice Payne? There you go. Prime example. You couldn't let it lie with her, could you?'

'Listen, the only reason she wanted to go out with you and not me is that you had a paper round. One sniff of your filthy lucre and all she wanted to do was suck you dry, quite literally. No thirteen-year-old could compete with that.'

'I can't believe you got so wound up though. That was the first time you had ever come at me with such malice. I remember thinking that I didn't mind the run-of-the-mill fights, but this was something different. You had a look in your eye that I hadn't seen before. You really meant to hurt me.'

Nick laughed loudly, attracting the attention of a group of teenagers at the end of the bar. He clearly remembered the events that followed.

'That first punch,' he mused, 'really connected. The next one was the one that got you good, though. Right in the chops. It was like something out of a Rocky film.'

'Yeah, but it wasn't the punch that did the real damage, was it?' Matt thought ahead in the proceedings, and after the attack by his younger brother he, too, had lost control of his temper. After a volley of punches that made Nick aware of the strength his brother possessed, Matt let go of Nick, allowing him to put some space between them. Nick moved into the garden, whereby Matt had chased him relentlessly, still blinded by the white mist that had descended upon him. He was brought kicking and screaming out of the blind rage a moment later, after standing on the garden rake, which had been left out the previous night. It took four and a half hours to be seen at the hospital, and after copious vomiting (Matt had a phobia about hospitals), his broken nose had been mended.

Matt found himself rubbing the slight curvature in the bridge of his nose, and needed to be brought back to reality by Nick. He almost jumped, lost in thought about the incident, when his younger sibling smiled and nudged him, saying, 'Come on you, there's women out there to be shagged. Time's a-wasting.'

Matt looked at his brother, smiled, and looked into the bottom of his glass. The amber liquid stared back at him, beckoning him to drink another, then another, and then another. Matt was on the verge of becoming depressed, and Nick sensed it. He gave Matt a friendly punch on the arm, as if to re-iterate his last statement. He looked up from his glass, and for a brief moment the two brothers locked eyes, as if looking deep into each other's memories. There were no barriers. There never had been any between them. Without saying a word, they held a silent conversation, asking and answering questions in a way that only family could. Within the space of those few seconds, Nick had felt Matt's anguish, shared in his pain of losing his father, and relived the memories of a bleary winter's day when William Greaves was laid to rest, forever shrouded by the blackness of earth. The cries of two brothers seemed far off and distant now, just echoes in the past.

It was Matt who broke the silence between them. 'You're right. Time's a-wasting.'

3

The smell of frying onions filled the air. It was a comforting smell. The kind of pungent, lasting odor that acts as a reminder of days gone by, when winter teas were relished upon returning from school.

John Selleck sat in a worn, musty chair, a remnant of a three-piece-suite discarded many years ago. As he sat, letting the images from his video streak across his face, he could not but wonder how many others there were like him, right now, relaxing in the comfort of a worn out, battered chair they did not have the heart to get rid of. That's what we do in this country, he thought, we keep rubbish. The things we don't need seem to stick around, and the more valuable things always seem to be forgotten. Maybe one day that will change, he mused. His thoughts had wandered from his video. He re-focused his attention to his subject Matter. As the old footage of Hitler ranting at a Nazi rally pummelled its way into his consciousness, John became absorbed, and instead of The Fuhrer exciting the masses, it was he. It was a thought he often entertained. Since his Comprehensive days he had been interested in the Second World War, and he had developed a keen interest in all things relating to that particular period. In the last ten years, in fact, he had made quite a tidy living on the quiet, buying and selling memorabilia from the war era. Anything really, from newspaper cuttings to original medals and even original military clothing (when he could get his hands on it), he bartered and traded until he got the right price. Anything could be bought at the right price. Money was no object. In fact, to Selleck it was not always money he used to ply his trade. He did favors for people. Small, large, it was of no consequence to him, although one thing remained constant. They were always repayable in full.

A hulk of a man, he stood six foot four inches in height, although his muscular frame made him look much, much taller. Hair cropped almost to the scalp, he gazed through deep blue eyes that betrayed his personality. Usually an attractive symbol of warmth, his shrouded a spirit as cold as polar ice, unrelenting, unforgiving. Set deep into his skull, they radiated a chill that penetrated the deepest psyche. Often, he got what he wanted with only a look. One gaze was enough to scare some.

He did not consider himself a domineering character, though. He considered the subservient nature of others a weakness, an irreparable fault that he was only too willing to exploit. He never asked for favors. That would be too unbecoming of a *real* man. To succeed, you had to ask, and if that didn't work, you got others to take for you. He never classed himself as a gangster. Gangsters got caught. They were notorious, open, fiendish caricatures, who ran from what they were in a way he abhorred. He simply kept a low profile, did favors for the right people, and asked them to repay them at convenient moments, relying on his stature when they refused. In the space of a few short years he had gained the respect of some, if not all, of the locals willing to call themselves hoodlums and crooks. He was surprised that they left him alone. His small band of cronies was no match for the local pushers and thieves' guild, but they somehow recognized the potential in him.

Selleck smiled blankly at the screen, images of the Third Reich drowning him, overwhelming him with promises of power, wealth, and the good of the Master Race. One day he would walk down the road unhindered, without the shadow of the foreign demons behind, in front and above. Soon, he would look around his beloved surrounds, and revel in the glory of one race. Pure, untouched, untouchable. One day, he pondered. Amidst his delusions, he opened his hand, revealing a lock of jet-black hair. Freshly cut, he thought of the look in her face, as he stood over her, dominant, triumphant. He had no thoughts of reprisal; he knew only too well any investigations in his neighborhood would lead nowhere. He was simply not thought of as someone who could do something like *that*. He was simply too quiet a man for *that*. He let the hair fall through his fingers as easily as her life had ebbed away, and allowed his feet to rub it into the carpet. He had never been one to dwell on yesterday's news.

'Those onions must be done by now.' He thought aloud. With a saunter that highlighted only the faintest trace of arrogance, he walked to the kitchen.

****

When the alarm rang at six thirty the next morning, Matt lunged at it with considerable vehemence. It was not that he hated getting up. It was merely the fact that he saw himself as above it all. In his mind's eye, he was relaxing on a beach earning twenty per cent, sipping margueritas and enjoying the company of scantily clad women. The reality of it all, however, was much, much bleaker. Between the divorce, his prospects and his hangover, there was nothing much to get up for. He reached for the telephone, and his medical encyclopaedia. This was going to be a tough one. He had overdone it lately on the sickies, and he was going to have to come up with something special if they were going to take him seriously. He scanned the pages, and began to laugh at the prospects. Anal warts, cancer, tonsillitis, he could just imagine Mrs. Pilkington's face as he gave his prognosis to her. It was not that she hated people who so obviously were clutching at straws when it came to legitimate excuses. In fact, it was quite the contrary. Although regarded as somewhat hard-nosed and unforgiving (hence the nickname Satan amongst staff, including the head), she had developed a soft spot for Matt. Whether it was his cheeky approach to her and every other female member of staff, or whether she fancied him in a menopausal fashion, without her covering for his indiscretions, he would have been down the disciplinary road a very long time ago.

With this in mind, Matt replaced the medical bible, and the telephone receiver. 'Bugger it. It's my assembly anyway today.' With this, he jumped out of bed, and started his daily pre-school ritual of shit, shower, shave and shampoo. Always meticulous about this, he believed that he would not be able to function without adherence to these four tasks upon rising each day. Some had jogging. Others masturbated. Matt had the four 'S' things.

The throbbing 1.3 litre engine of his 1979 Talbot Sunbeam roared into life, the choke pulled out to the maximum as it always suffered in the mornings. Once the windscreen had cleared, he was on his way. Not too fast, not too slow. You never knew when the police would be waiting for you to blow in the bag, he thought. It would be an enormous blow to him if he were to lose his car. Although it sported mostly gold colour, the white wing and blue door gave the car a lived in, comfy feel, and the interior, although smoke stained and worn, always gave an impression of comfort. Matt could afford more, but he was not interested in cars as status symbols. He was more interested in a machine that moved when it was supposed to, and stopped in a likewise fashion. He was a teacher after all, not a racing driver. Besides, his father would turn in his grave if he knew that he had given the very car away which he himself had driven before he died.

****

Matt couldn't help but notice that the staff room was a little more animated than usual when he arrived for his cup of coffee. Instead of the usual laughter and banter associated with staff rooms (and locker rooms), there was some serious conversation taking place. It was not long before Matt caught the gist of it all, when one of the Year 6 teachers, Dave Poole, made his contribution.

'Whoever did this should be shot. If I could get my hands on the scum that did this, I'd bloody kill them.'

'What's happened then? More graffiti on the walls this time? Not shit on the toilet floor again?'

Everyone stopped and stared at Matt. He was clearly missing something here.

'You mean you don't know?' Poole questioned over his spectacles, his eyebrows threatening to spill over them at any time.

'I'm sorry, no. What's the news?'

'I thought you'd have known. Sunita Singh's mother was killed last night. Her body was found in the wasteland behind Chesterton Street this morning, by some kids playing over there before school. Beaten to a pulp, the rumors say.'

Matt sat down. His previous remarks no longer existed. Despite all his misgivings it was common knowledge that to Matt, teaching wasn't just a job. He really did care for the children and their families. Some had bothered to question him on the Matter, although he was always a closed book on the subject.

The truth was, Matt knew where these children came from. Not in the physical sense, but from a psychological standpoint. He knew what it was to want more from life, but to be held back by factors out of his control. He had always envisaged himself working in the city, taking the tube every day, a bona fide member of the rat race. That wasn't to be, though. With the death of his father at the start of what he counted as his truly formative years, and with what he considered very little support from his secondary school, he was doomed from fulfilling his dream from the very start. By his admission and that of his peers, teenage children were just about the cruellest creatures in creation, and in order to avoid being the subject of criticism, he fell into line with his fellow students and kept his nose clean, although not too clean.

Greaves blinked, and reality set in. One of the parents of a child in his school was dead, laid out, cold and alone, while the rest of the world went about its business. That, to Matt, was simply not on. He felt sick. Sick enough to approach the head teacher, Mr. Baker, when he entered the damp, somewhat pathetic staff room.

'Can I have a word in private please, John?' asked Matt in his best professional voice.

'Sure. Do you mind if I say what I've got to say first? I'll ....'

'It's about Mrs. Singh.'

'So's this, Matt. Please.' He gave Matt the look which said 'I understand' without patronizing him. For his sins, John Baker was a very good people person. He took center stage and waited for the staff to be quiet, rather than ask them to listen. He commanded respect, and it was not long before the coffee-swilling machine ground to a halt, all eyes on the slightly greying, lean figure about to speak.

'Good morning everybody. I'd just like to say a few words, if I may, about the horrific news which has undoubtedly reached you by now. I've never had to deal with anything like this before, so I thought I'd better tell you what I'm about to do, and you can tell me if you think it's right or not.'

A few people looked at each other quizzically. The throng did not, it seemed, know what to expect.

Baker continued, 'In circumstances like these, we must all spare a thought for not only the direct victim, but also those left behind. I have tried to do this to the best of my ability, and as a sign of respect I am going to make it public knowledge that the school will be closed for the rest of the week. Those of you who knew Mrs. Singh will remember her as a supporter of the school, who in her role as parent stood ahead of most in the interest she showed in the progress of her child. With reference to the funeral, I am told it will be held in three days' time, at the Sikh temple in Bloomfield. Mr. Greaves, I'd like you to accompany me with Dave Poole as representatives of the school. You will all need to make it clear to the pupils that they will not be attending school from tomorrow until next week. I will ask Mrs. Pilkington to make the necessary phone calls to parents, and I shall be issuing a letter of course. If you have any questions, please see me later.'

There was silence. That is, until Matt spoke up. He could not understand why Baker had required his presence, and not one of the senior teachers.

'No offence, John, but why me? I know that Dave should go, being Reena's teacher, but shouldn't one of the more senior staff go?'

'I can understand you're pretty confused. I know lots of you were involved with the family through Reena in one way or another. However you, Matt, were probably closer than most due to your involvement with Reena as coordinator for more able pupils. I thought her family would appreciate having as many friendly faces as possible around in their time of need. Wouldn't you?'

Matt nodded his agreement. There was no argument. He was going to have to attend and that was that. It was at that precise moment that realisation hit him like a thunderbolt from above. His reasons for piping up weren't due to lack of understanding on his part. He thought of his father, William, and the hole in the ground waiting for his coffin. He thought of the noises cutting the silence all around the chasm dug in the ground, and he thought of the smell of fresh earth put aside to cover his mentor once he was to be inhumed by the earth, ashes to ashes and so forth. It was simple. He was still haunted by the death of his beloved father, and to see it all over again was going to be hard. He wondered whether the rest of the teaching staff were breathing a collective sigh of relief at that particular moment in time.

Making his way back to class, he was confronted by Mrs. Pilkington. *Oh Christ, not now*, he thought to himself. *Just fuck off and leave me alone in my little world of ignorance.* Unfortunately, that wasn't to be.

'Matt, I'm glad I caught you on your own. It's about your tea money and school dinners.'

'Sheila, can't this wait? I've got to get to class. I'm going to be late. The Literacy lesson waits for no man you know.'

'It won't take long. Listen, you don't have to be a bloody genius to know that I've got a soft spot for you. Heaven knows I've done you enough favours since you've been here. In fact, if it wasn't for me, you'd have been down the capability road a long time ago. But you owe me some serious money Matt. Now, do I have to get the tea police around, or are you going to be a good boy and cough up for Auntie Sheila. Don't make me angry. You wouldn't like me when I'm angry.'

Greaves thought for a moment. She was, of course, right as usual. The capability code was a little scheme that schools had up their sleeves to keep teachers in school and inhibit them from having too many sick days. Basically, after a certain number of days off, alarm bells rang at County Hall and the Head Teacher received a nice little reminder that Johnny X was being a naughty boy. This led to lots of hassle, namely interviews with the Head, and for persistent offenders the setting of targets and warnings, culminating in medicals with moustached female doctors and possibly disciplinary action from the school. Sheila had forgotten on many occasions to log Matt's little indiscretions formally, thus the comment about favours. The other point she was trying to make, and succeeding in doing so, was that Matt's current outstanding bill for tea and school dinners was eighty three pounds and twenty pence. He was convinced that this was some sort of record, but he chose not to mention that as it was likely to send her into overdrive. Before he answered, he looked long and hard into the eyes of the school secretary.

As far back as he could remember, Sheila had worked at the school. People had always spoken of her in revered tones, and had always considered her the fulcrum upon which the day to day success of the school balanced. Like many other school secretaries (or administrators, as they liked to be called in politically correct circles), she had many roles. Nurse, social worker, accountant, banker, confidant. Each role of equal importance, and each done to perfection. She was truly one in a million. Widowed, with two grown sons and one grandchild, it seemed as if life was merely something that got in the way of her job, an inconvenience. Nobody really knew her outside school. She never attended social functions, and enjoyed a little anonymity. What people didn't see was the charity work she did, or the paintings she frequently churned out in the attic of her house, expertly converted into a studio where she could unwind and express her emotions in the only way she knew how. Her eyes burned with a flame that would be a long time in dying, and Matt knew that he wasn't going to be able to work his charm on her in the same way that he did with other women of her age. He smiled charmingly.

'For you, anything. I'll get my cheque book out at lunchtime and I'll settle in full. Until then, parting is such sweet sorrow. Adieu, my dear. Farewell.' He took her in his arms, and she chuckled.

'Get off me, you great oaf. Mind you don't forget, okay?'

'You know me, Sheila. As if I would ever forget.'

He made his way to class, and before long the multitude of familiar faces came in to greet him in their own way. For some it was a grunt, for others a lengthy recollection of the previous night's antics. Today, though, it was different. For obvious reasons the fizz had been taken out of their champagne, and it was evident that even at the age of seven, these Year Three pupils were no babies. Many had seen hardship, violence, and some war in different countries. Many had seen plenty more besides. One thing struck Matt though. Wherever you taught, wherever you were, it was never the children who were the problem. It was the adults who brought them up who ruined them. Behind all the bitterness, frustration, angst and passion, there were real human beings inside these children who were gasping at the chance to be let out. All he had to do was channel them into finding the door for them. It was going to be hard work today. He could feel it.

He sat them down, took the register and looked around. There it was. The expectancy that always came, only this time the children wanted Matt to make it better, make everything all right. He couldn't, and deep down they knew it. However, they wanted him to say something and he felt obliged to.

'Listen, you lot, judging by everyone here, you've heard that one of the Year Six girls lost her mother last night.'

'It was Reena's mum.' One of the class remarked.

'Yes, it was.' Matt responded blankly. 'This is a very sad time for all of us, and I'm sure that many of you are wondering why someone would do such a terrible thing. Well, I can't answer that question, but what I can say is that there are many bad people out there who are willing to do many bad things, and if we need to learn anything it's that in order to stop these people, we need to set an example to them. The best way we can do that is by getting on together and realizing that we're all the same, no Matter who we are.' The children contemplated this, and then a voice broke the silence. It was Ashleigh.

'I heard my dad talking to my mum before, and he said that it serves her right for being out all alone on her own that late at night.'

Matt looked at Ashleigh. That was pretty straight for her.

'Well now, I don't think anyone should be saying things like that to anybody else, Ashleigh. Everyone is free to go out whenever they feel like it, and we should all feel that the streets are a safe place to walk, no Matter what time of day.'

'But.......' Ashleigh continued.

'But nothing, Ashleigh. Just because it's late, it doesn't mean we should all be inside. If there's one thing that we've all got, it's freedom to come and go as we please.' Matt felt that he was getting too serious with the children, and that this one comment from Ashleigh was opening a can of worms.

'But she's not free any more, is she Mr. Greaves?' replied Ashleigh blankly.

'No, Ashleigh, I guess not. Now, let's get on with something else, shall we?'

4

That evening, Matt decided to keep himself to himself. He didn't much feel like going out, despite some serious badgering by his brother. There was no melancholy overtone to his refusal. He simply felt that he could do without the alcohol and the company of others. He occasionally withdrew into his shell. Sometimes for hours, sometimes longer. It was his way of dealing with things. Whether it was the right or wrong way, he neither knew nor cared.

He sat in his favourite chair, that occupied the only window in his two – bedroomed flat with anything like a decent view. It was not sprawling fields and countryside that made him gasp when he looked out. It was the concrete vista that made him realise his own insignificance in the grand scheme of things, and when he saw the thousands of people shuffle by each time he looked out, he realized the futility of getting animated over anything much. Or so he thought. As he fingered his glass of tequila, and felt the liquid warmth work its way down through his chest and into his stomach and beyond, there was a different feeling tonight. He could not stop thinking about the young girl's comment at school that day. Ashleigh's words had somehow stirred something deep inside him. *But she's not any more, is she Mr. Greaves?* Her comment prior to that, about her father's reaction, also stirred him into a more pensive frame of mind. He thought about what made this man tick, and what would prompt him to say such a thing. You must have hated people to have wished that on someone. What a complete prick, he thought, as he downed his glass, and reached for a refill.

Matt now felt bothered. There he was, quite happy to feel sorry for himself, when up crept this rogue thought, generated by a seven year old girl, and ruined his night. Thanks a bloody lot, he mused. He couldn't even wallow in his own lethargy without someone ruining it. It was no good. The moment was lost. He screwed the cap onto the bottle of tequila, grabbed his jacket, and headed out of the door. There was no way that he could stay in now. He needed a walk, just to clear the cobwebs out. Maybe he'd take a walk round to the scrubland where it all happened. Matt wanted to see for himself whether the streets really were a safe place to walk alone at night, or whether Ashleigh really did have a point.

****

The fresh air actually seemed fresh that night, instead of the high octane trash that normally filled his nose when he set foot outside. Maybe it was the clarity of his thoughts at that precise moment that was making the putrid stench of two million cars seem cleaner than it actually was. He looked up. He still couldn't see the stars. Just a reminder of the times that they were living in. Man's reliance on the car was killing them, and they didn't care. As long as it didn't do it in their lifetime.

Matt walked faster. He liked to feel his lungs filling and emptying, he realized. He enjoyed the physical sensation of respiration. Pretty soon he was walking at what he assumed would have looked a very strange pace. Like the children when they were caught running down the corridors and asked to walk. He smiled, and relaxed his pace. Besides, he was now only a hundred metres or so from the spot where Reena Singh had been killed.

All around, the air seemed still. It was as if nature had understood that a terrible atrocity had taken place, and it was waiting for something, or somebody, to readdress the balance of things, to right the terrible wrong. No birds seemed to sing in the evening air, and it became evident that there were not even the sounds of the late night revellers on the way home from their drinks, smokes and kebabs. The neighbourhood was completely devoid of any normal sounds of society at all. In fact, if it were not for the fact that he could hear his own breathing, Matt would have sworn that he had gone deaf. The silence was almost deafening.

Suddenly, without warning, a hand touched Matt on the shoulder from behind. He spun around, his fist clenched as if to strike. It was an instinctive reaction, fuelled by his current location and the recent events. He realized that a noise was escaping from his lips. Not a word, or phrase, but a simple noise. It wasn't a scream, he realized in slow motion, merely a vast exhalation brought on by a sudden shock, which in turn had rattled a few of his vocal chords. Either way, whoever had touched him knew that they had frightened him.

'Relax, mate. Jesus, I was only going to ask for a light.'

'You frightened the shit out of me. Don't creep up on people like that. You almost gave me a bloody heart attack.' Matt retorted to the fresh-faced, jeans and leather-clad youth in front of him.

'Sorry mate.' There was silence, and Matt looked at the young man in front of him. There was nothing to distinguish him apart from the others in this area. Burberry baseball cap, jeans and white trainers. The unofficial uniform of the masses. Matt was expecting him to say something, but he just continued to stare at him, which he thought was a little strange. It was at that moment that he felt the presence of somebody else close by. Somebody behind him. He looked around quickly, and in a split second realized that something was seriously amiss. Matt's next course of action took nanoseconds to realise itself in his consciousness, however in undertaking it, it seemed to take forever. The thoughts read as follows:

1. I appear to be in trouble.

2. There appear to be two of them and only one of me.

3. As I am probably going to be mugged or worse, and as I am in an area where a terrible crime has been committed, I will therefore try to eliminate any chance of a similar fate by getting my retaliation in early, and therefore increasing my chances of survival.

The punch landed as squarely on the young assailant's nose as it possibly could. The effects were immediate. The uniformed attacker went down immediately, with a shout of excruciating pain. There was to be no retaliation from this one, Matt thought. The tears streaming down his face would have half blinded him, and the fear of another, heftier blow would also be playing on this guy's mind. He turned to the second man. True to his intuition, he now stood before him with what appeared to be some sort of cosh in his hand. From the look in his eyes, though, it was clear that he either had no previous experience of using it, or Matt's early retaliation had prompted to re-evaluate the importance of this line of work. Matt knew he had to capitalize on the indecision.

'Right,' Matt said in a very matter-of-fact, even tone, 'one down, one to go.' He motioned towards the second attacker. He took one look at Matt, another at his partner in crime, and ran for it. It seemed that there was going to be no further cause for concern from that guy tonight. Unless he was running home to get his bigger, uglier brother with an even bigger, uglier cosh than the one he had just seen.

Matt bent down quickly, and grabbed the bleeding youth by the lapels of his Ben Sherman denim jacket. They were stained with red, and Matt felt good about that. He couldn't afford clothes like this on his wages. He was satisfied that this guy was at least going to have to spend some of his ill-gotten gains on a new jacket if he was going to pull women on a Friday night again.

'What's your game then? Still want a light, do you?' he asked in a slightly menacing tone.

'Leave it out, mister,' came the reply, 'we were only having some fun. Fucking leave me alone.'

'Leave you alone? LEAVE YOU ALONE?' He pushed, almost threw the youth down the road, to where he imagined his house to be. 'Now fuck off, and go home and read a book.'

Matt ran for it himself. He didn't want to hang around here any longer. He had made his mind up. As his pace quickened from a jog into a sprint towards his own house 2 miles away, he realized something serious. Ashleigh had been right. It really wasn't safe to be out alone on your own here, and it wasn't automatically his right to be free to come and go. Not according to these people, anyway. As he disappeared, the street became as deathly silent as it had been before. Somewhere, a curtain twitched and returned to its original position.

5

As Matt climbed out of his car at the crematorium, he realized that his hands were shaking. He was very clear as to why this was happening; a mixture of sadness in relation to the sad loss of the girl attending school, but at the forefront of his mind was the recollection of what funerals entailed. He remembered attending his father's funeral, and the wailing and screaming that went on amidst his relatives and family friends. His father had said that there were only two times in your life when everyone who mattered was in the same room. He also stipulated that during one of them you were usually present, in order to celebrate (or commiserate) your wedding, but for the other it was uncommon for you to attend and enjoy it. He was, of course, referring to the funeral.

Matt smiled to himself, and as he locked his car he heard a familiar voice, which at that precise moment in time seemed very welcome.

'Matt, glad you made it mate. How are you feeling?' It was Dave Poole.

'Not bad mate. You know.' Dave knew about his feelings for his father. They had discussed this over a beer a few times. Dave had lost his own father some years back, and was very helpful in helping Matt to understand his feelings of loss and grief.

'Where's John? Is he not coming? I didn't see his car, Dave.'

'It's parked out the front mate. John said something about making a quick getaway to a meeting after this has finished. He's probably inside already. Come on, let's get into character.'

They didn't have to try too hard to get 'into character.' The crematorium was packed, and there seemed to be representatives of a thorough cross-section of not only the school community, but the wider community as well. An array of local dignitaries, including the mayor of Bloomfield, had turned out to pay their last respects. There was no huge pomp about this ceremony. From Matt's limited knowledge and understanding of other cultures, he had an idea that at Sikh funerals it was a tradition to not allow demonstrations of sorrow to intrude upon a peaceful entry into the afterlife. In fact, the temple, or Gurdwara, was unnaturally quiet, given the circumstances surrounding Reena's death and Matt's own feelings towards the events that had taken place. Looking around, Matt didn't need to hear crying or wailing to notice the sorrow painted on the faces of those present. It hung around the attendees like a sour odour, dragging the faces and spirits downwards like an anvil around their shoulders. It was almost unbearable, and on more than one occasion Matt found himself wiping silent tears from his eyes. The same, soundless tears that he remembered crying at his father's funeral. This was all compounded by the fact that there was nothing that anybody could do about it. This selfless, caring woman, who was wife to a husband and mother to children, had been bludgeoned to death for absolutely no reason whatsoever. Somebody, somewhere was walking around, breathing and wasting good air, while this poor family had to rebuild their shattered lives, not that they would ever be the same.

Matt suddenly caught the eye of Sunita, Reena's daughter. She did not avert her eyes, and raised a faint smile at the sight of a member of staff from the school. He had taught Sunita, and unbeknownst to him, he was actually her favourite teacher. She raised a thin hand, and the shadows around her eyes told the truth about exactly how much crying she had done. It was too much for Matt. He arose from his seat, and made his way to the exit. Dave Poole and John Baker made no effort to restrain him from leaving. They understood only too well what this might have been doing to Matt. Indeed, as he was leaving, Matt even thought that John had asked him to attend deliberately, to exorcise his own personal demons. That image became shrouded very quickly though, and as he pushed the door to the crematorium closed, he began to quicken his pace, just as previously he had quickened his pace on his evening stroll.

This time, though, he was in an entirely different frame of mind. He envisaged an imaginary man, kicking and punching. Maybe two, even three. In his mind's eye he saw himself as the avenger, committing violent acts of retribution against the cowards who had committed this crime. As the rain began to fall on the empty street, and as Matt's tears mingled freely with the falling droplets, all he could think of was exacting his revenge on whoever did this. He knew the likelihood of realizing this was more than slim, but everyone had to have a dream. This was his.

Matt's anger and focus on his thoughts meant that he walked straight past the towering figure leaning against the bus shelter, his cap pulled low over his forehead. He missed him staring in the general direction of the crematorium, with an almost equal focus on the building as Matt had demonstrated as he walked past just seconds earlier. And thankfully, he missed the almost untraceable smile that had spread across his face, as he thought of the favour he had done the white population of Bloomfield and Britain in committing the murder of that insignificant speck of a woman. He, too, turned, and began to saunter slowly homewards, indistinguishable from the masses he mingled with on the way.

6

Matt's mood lifted slightly as he strolled into the Prince Arthur and ordered a pint of lager. He paid for it using some change he'd accumulated over the past few days, and was relieved to get rid of it. He felt that he had enough weighing him down, without the load of his silver as well. Keith, the long-standing landlord of the pub, took the penny change and inserted it into the charity box upon Matt's command. He brought his own drink back to where Matt was seated on a tall stool, and for a moment, Keith said nothing. He knew that Matt was out of sorts, and besides, he was aware that he hadn't brought his dickhead brother around for a session for a few days now. Keith had guessed that maybe they'd had another falling out. God only knew how many they'd had in the past. He was just contemplating on how to broach the subject, when Matt did the dirty work for him, and started to get things off his chest.

'I'll tell you something, Keith. I don't think I've been this pissed for a long time.'

'But you've only just got here, mate. Now you know what I've told you about drinking in other pubs, mate. It just hurts my feelings.'

Matt smiled weakly. 'I mean pissed off, you idiot. This business with this murdered woman. I was at the funeral today. I saw the hurt in her family's eyes. Whoever did this must have had a heart of stone mate. I bet they didn't even know the woman.'

Keith looked at his most faithful patron and close friend and gave him as honest a reply as he could.

'I'll tell you something, Matt. I've been around the block, and I've been in this game for a few years as well. But one thing's the same. Wherever you go, it's always the same. People never stop surprising you in the things that they're capable of. Just when you think you've seen it all (and he had seen quite a bit, as it turned out), something comes along and just blows you away. I'm sorry to disappoint you, Matty my friend, but round here, what did you expect? Just take a look around.'

Matt did just that. He normally gave Keith a modicum of abuse, as they had developed a relationship sound enough to be able to do that to each other. They often ended up in tears, unable to control their laughing, after a good character assassination from both. It was never ill-meant; they had far too much respect for each other for that. However, they fed off each other like a couple of second-rate comedians, and they were often not even that funny to the rest of the crowd, but they didn't care.

Tonight, though, was different. Matt knew that neither he nor Keith were in that frame of mind. He took the landlord's advice and scanned the bar, taking in every conceivable detail. There certainly was a real cross-section of the community in tonight, he mused. In one corner, a group of lads in their early twenties, still in their football kits, ribbing each other about a game they had just played. In one of the snug areas, a couple who were clearly arguing, but trying to hide the fact from everyone. Matt wondered what the argument was about, and whether they would make up later, if the formula for relationships stood true to form. At the bar, the toothless rollie-smoker who supped no more than three pints in any one session, and had creases in his face that not even the newest Teflon steam iron could get rid of. And finally, around one of the larger tables, the suit brigade, who faithfully passed by and drank a very quick five or six pints, interspersed with mobile telephone calls, as they contemplated going home for the evening. It was staggering how they all managed to stand shoulder to shoulder without tearing each other apart. On one level, it was what he imagined heaven to be. Everyone getting on without fuss. But on the other hand, it could also be hell. Matt couldn't remember the literary piece he was thinking of, but he was sure he'd once read a play about a bunch of people who wake up in a room without doors, and no way out, to eventually realise that they despise each other and that maybe this was their hell. To be trapped forever with those that they hated more than any other for eternity. Matt decided that the first image was better. He'd much rather that the cup was half full on this occasion.

He was suddenly interrupted in his thoughts by the realisation that somebody was standing next to him at the bar. He turned his head, and there in front of him was a face, a familiar face, but he just couldn't put his finger on it. Inwardly, he groaned. That could only mean one thing. He was looking at a parent. This was most definitely not what he was after tonight. There were three things that he dreaded hearing. Number one, 'It's about your tea money.' Number two, 'Can you use your release time to cover Reception Class?' Worst of all, number three, which normally comprised of 'How's Johnny doing then?' or worse still, 'Johnny thinks the world of you. Buy us a drink, will you?'

All women say that men are incapable of multi-tasking, which is, performing two tasks at the same time. The reality of this concept, however, is quite the opposite, and Matt subconsciously proved it as soon as he saw who was looking at him. On the one hand, part of him was desperately trying to figure out who the unknown face was. This slim, nicely proportioned woman with a rather engaging smile, was definitely in his bank of faces somewhere. Even the sleek, figure-hugging leather jacket that she was wearing (rather nicely, he added to himself) seemed familiar. Another department of his brain was equally as desperately moving down the male pulling checklist, namely hair, breath, flies and sufficient money for drinks and cab fare home in the morning.

She smiled at him, and Matt was overwhelmed by the warmth that he saw. There was no pretence in the smile, no falseness, and definitely no insecurity. She spared matt the awkward task of initiating conversation.

'It's Mr. Greaves, isn't it?'

'That's right. Listen, I'm really sorry, but your face seems familiar. Where is it that I know you from? I've definitely seen you before. Are you a parent of a child at Bloomfield Primary?'

'That's it,' she replied, 'Ashleigh Parkes. The name's Sara, by the way.'

'Matt.' He replied without hesitation. 'She's a nice kid. Loads of energy.'

'Yes, you're not the only person to have said that. She may not be the sharpest tool in the box, but she's made from the sharpest steel.'

Matt was taken slightly aback by her honesty about her daughter. No school report that Matt wrote, or any other teacher for that matter, would be as blunt as that about a child's ability. It was true, though, and he found himself hoping that Sara wasn't in too much of a rush to return to her seat.

'I wouldn't put it quite like that,' he offered diplomatically, 'she's a real star. Can I get you a drink, by the way?'

'I'm really sorry, but I'm with my friends.' She pointed to a group of women sitting around a circular table in the far corner of the bar. Matt's spirit sank momentarily. Although he usually made it a habit not to get personal with parents at the school, there was something about Sara that made him want to know more, to keep talking to her. He was genuinely disappointed that she was not going to be paying him any attention once she had received her drink and returned to her friends in the corner.

What happened next surprised him though. He'd been around the block enough times to know when he was getting a positive sign from a woman. He'd noticed the occasional flick of the hair while he talked to her, and the way in which she seemed to move just ever so slightly closer to him as she talked, invading his space just fractionally.

'Erm.......listen, they're going on to a club from here. You know Archers on The Parade? They're talking about a late night tonight, but I've got to work tomorrow. I'm not really up for it. Are you going to be around in about half an hour? I'll come back then for a chat if you like. You can buy me that drink then if you fancy it. I promise I won't quiz you about Ashleigh.'

'Yeah, okay.' Matt tried his best to play it cool, but he couldn't really pull it off. 'If I'm around, that'd be great. See you later Sara.'

As Sara made her way back to her friends, greeted with a smile and gentle teasing, Matt prayed that he would get the chance to buy her that drink. For the second time, he went through his mental checklist.

7

The next hour seemed to drag on forever. Matt stared into his pint, watching the contents disappear slowly. It was like sipping treacle as he watched the hands on the giant wall clock trudge their way towards closing time. Despite Keith's best efforts to keep him motivated in a drinking capacity, his mind set was totally focused on one thing; namely to make sure that Sara came back to talk to him. There was something that had worked its way under his skin, and he couldn't put his finger on it. Maybe it was her confidence. Despite his bravado, deep down Matt knew that he wasn't always the most confident person around the opposite sex. He even thought that if he had been just that little bit more confident when he was married, the he maybe wouldn't have let his marriage slip away from him.

He pondered his ex-wife, Andrea, for a moment. As if he hadn't had enough on his plate when his father passed away, he had been in a position where he was forced to deal with her affair and the feelings of inadequacy that went hand in hand with it. He didn't know the guy; there was at least one forgiving factor in the proceedings. As a personal assistant to a busy London executive, he could understand that there were times when she would have to have been away for the occasional night, it was expected and assumed that this was going to be the case. But to sleep with someone totally unrelated to work or social life was just so totally unexpected, it virtually devastated any self-esteem and male pride he had at that precise moment in his life. It was as if someone (or something, for he regarded anything that could provoke such a thing to happen as a beast of some kind) had reached into his soul and wrenched out everything that he felt happy about. His father, his wife, his security with his partner, all screwed it up into a ball and discarded like an empty crisp packet. And salt and vinegar flavour at that.

His musings were interrupted by a tap on the shoulder, and a friendly voice that he recognized immediately as Sara's. 'Hello,' she said simply, 'me again.'

Matt instinctively looked at his watch. A whole hour had passed while he was mentally regurgitating the past. My god, he thought, that's how quickly your life slipped away from you. He brought himself back from his ponderings, and politely moved his chair aside for Sara to sit down. She willingly obliged by doing so. Almost too willingly, Matt perceived. Things were definitely looking up tonight. His spirits brightened immediately.

'So,' he started awkwardly, 'where do you work then?'

'It's nothing special really. I work in town for Grimley's. You know, the department store?'

'Yes, I buy my underwear from there.' Matt replied, immediately regretting his statement.

'Really? Are you a briefs or boxers man then?' She giggled as she asked him. Matt caught on to the levity of the situation, and played along. 'Well, it depends really. I work weekends as a relief Chippendale dancer, so that requires briefs. Usually though, I wear Y-fronts, patterned more often than not. I'm into paisley at the moment.'

They looked at each other momentarily, both formulating a mental picture of Greaves in his Y-fronts in front of the mirror, and her also picturing him as the Chippendale dancer. They burst out laughing, with a squeal of delight that broke the ice totally, and bypassed any squirming that both Matt and Sara would have thought was customary under these circumstances.

Things took off from there. With the help of a few more drinks (lager for him, whisky and coke for her), they sat and talked for the next two hours about books, television, films they'd seen, and most surprisingly to Matt, sport. She was a keen

Chelsea fan, and was quite keen to discuss the intricacies of a squad rotation system versus the more traditional methods of team management. Matt realized that for the first time in ages, he was actually enjoying a night out without the alcohol taking priority in his thoughts as a means to an end. He also realized that although breaking his own rules about fraternising with the proverbial enemy, sat in front of him was an intriguing, beautiful, thoughtful woman who was able not just to stimulate his intellect, but other parts of him as well.

Matt looked up at the wall, and then looked around the rest of the pub. It was empty, apart from Keith sitting in the corner cashing up a till tray, and the pair of them still at their table. The clock read eleven twenty five. They had missed the bell indicating last orders, and had missed the out flux of patrons onto the street. Matt was usually among these, unless asked by Keith to stay behind and chew the fat with him over something that was bothering him. He guessed the fact that he had not been turfed out was Keith's little present to him, given the rigours of the earlier funeral that day, and his mood before bumping into Sara. Oddly, he had forgotten all about the funeral, and the misery that surrounded the tragic circumstances of Reena Singh's death. He looked across the table at Sara, and prayed to himself that she longed for the night to carry on as much as he did.

'Christ, look at the time. We really got carried away there.' She said, almost apologetically.

'I know. Good company does make time fly though.' Matt detected a faint blush on Sara's face at this point, and decided not to lay the cheese on too thick, in case he frightened her away. She seemed too worldly wise to fall for any of the pulling-line bullshit, he thought, and would prefer a much more honest approach. Besides, he told himself, he didn't know if sex was what he was after. After a slight pause while they finished their drinks off, he spoke first to avoid a pregnant pause.

'Listen, I'm really glad you came back tonight. It's been really good to talk to you. Tell me if you're married or whatever, but I'd love to go out again if you were able to.' Sara's face darkened slightly at this. Matt sensed the change, and began to apologise for embarrassing her about it. She pre-empted his comment by getting there first.

'I'm not married. I used to be, but things didn't really work out. After Ashleigh was born.......'

'Hey, don't feel that you have to tell me if you don't want to. I've only just met you Sara.' Matt threw in.

'It's okay, I don't mind. I was going to say, after Ashleigh was born her father seemed to lose interest. He was more interested in his friends than his family. I couldn't live like that. Simple really.' She clearly didn't want to say any more. Matt thought she'd said enough already anyway. He was also in a quandary now. He didn't know whether it would be appropriate to ask Sara back to his place for a coffee, or whether he would appear too pushy. The Prince Arthur wasn't exactly the most romantic of settings, but in the dim half-light of the bar, he couldn't help but think that she looked sensuous, and extremely inviting. He'd been around enough women to know that her chosen perfume was Cabotine de Grés, and he drank in its exquisite aroma with every breath. Fuck it, he thought. I might as well ask her. The worst she can say is no. he didn't get a chance. Sara looked up from her drink and made a statement, with a sense of calm and openness, that was quite unexpected to Matt.

'Before you beat yourself up about it, we should leave now if you'd like a coffee. Is yours okay though? I've run out of milk I think. Ashleigh's round at my mother's until tomorrow, so I've no rush to get back. Can I call a cab from yours? I'd love to carry on the evening if you would.'

Matt reached for his coat. When Keith looked up from his cashbox, the bar was quiet. He smiled to himself, and resumed counting once he had bolted the door behind them. You couldn't be too careful these days.

8

As Matt and Sara exited the Arthur that night, they both shivered in the brisk night air. It was hardly winter, but nevertheless it was cold enough for them to walk a little faster, and pull the lapels up on their jackets as they walked. Bowing their heads to avoid the chill wind, they did not notice Elijah Omoku passing them on the street, despite his six-foot frame. With a crop of thick black hair, just growing into what he perceived to be an ultra-cool seventies afro cut, he towered above his peers, and the beginnings of a moustache on his upper lip belied the young, enquiring mind underneath the adult exterior. To his friends at Broomfield Comprehensive, his appearance often laid him open to ridicule, but anyone who knew Elijah soon realized that he was far too amiable to receive the sharp end of adolescent wit and sarcasm. Teenagers were evil at times, however even they were able to show compassion for the compassionate, and generally left Elijah to enjoy a wide circle of friends.

Returning from one such friend's this evening, he hastened along the desolate pavement, staring at the cracks and mentally counting the number of steps he was taking down the street to pass the time more quickly. Underneath his black puffer jacket he had stowed away one of his many computer console games, that he had collected back from his friend that night. A generous boy, he did not mind sharing his possessions with others; his father's success in the city, and his divorce with Elijah's mother, ensured that he would never have to go without any of the luxuries that others his age thought were their right. His sensitivity, however, prompted him to remain extremely modest about his material wealth, and it was a slight sense of guilt, coupled with pity for his poorer school colleagues that pushed him to share the things he was given on a regular basis.

As Elijah neared his home, he thought about his future. His father had made it clear on many occasions that if possible, Elijah should follow his father into the corporate sector in some fashion. He was constantly reminded of the benefits, every time he was given a lift in a new sports car somewhere instead of getting the bus, or any time he was taken to a restaurant by his father and one of his many lady friends. What his father didn't know, however, was that Elijah's real love was not finance, but music. Having been bought an acoustic guitar on a whim one weekend about 3 years ago. His father had quickly forgotten about the purchase, and his time away from his son during the early part of the evenings betrayed the amount of practice that Elijah had actually been putting in on a daily basis during the time since the guitar's arrival. Elijah had plans all right, but not to make his money in the city. As a seventeen-year-old, he was more than familiar with MTV, and his real idols constantly pushed himself to better his skills and dexterity with the guitar. He had to admit to himself that his lead guitar, in only three years, was pretty good. The hours of listening to BB King and Hendrix and emulating their licks and riffs had paid huge dividends. There were not many songs now that he couldn't play, and he was determined that by this time next year, he was going to be part of a band. He knew he would have to start small, but once he'd been spotted, who knew? He smiled to himself as he turned the corner three streets from home.

He suddenly looked up though, knowing instinctively that something was off beam. He had made this walk many times before, and he had become extremely familiar with the sights, sounds and even smells along this particular stretch of road. It was his nasal passages that were bothering him now. He could smell smoke, but that was not it. There was something else, something more pungent in the air. He turned the final corner, and was greeted with a sight that made him forget everything that he had contemplated on his way home. And when he had pushed his way past the crowds of neighbours and onlookers outside his home, the image outside his house burned itself onto the inside of his skull, never to be removed. His mind refused to accept the images at first, and his ears refused to listen to the police as they tried to bar him from entering his driveway. He became immune to the feel of the restraining hands on his clothes, tugging him back from the images before him. And eventually, he was oblivious to the tears cascading down his cheeks as the police extinguished the flames billowing from the brand new Mercedes SLK, next to the charred body of his father, his Jamaican-born father, lying face down in the middle of the gravel, his blackened, crispened flesh hiding a secret. A secret that would eventually be discovered by somebody who had no business trying to unearth it.

9

Far away from the horrific scenes outside the Omoku household, a different smell permeated the air. It was the smell of freshly brewed coffee. Brazilian, fresh-ground coffee, newly percolated and delicious. Matt cut many corners, but he knew good coffee. He was not a snob; anyone who knew him would concur. However, when it came to his morning drink, only the best would do. When asked on several occasions about this, he gave the same answer. *When working in an environment where stress is at a maximum and time is at a minimum, if you can afford yourself a small luxury, then go for it. Life's too short.* And right now, the blissful look on Sara's face as she sipped her cup was worth every penny that he had paid for the ground coffee that very morning.

'So tell me, Mr. Teacher, do you enjoy what you do? There must be times when you want to do something else eh?' Sara enquired.

'Now there's the sixty four thousand dollar question. Do I enjoy what I do? Jesus, how do I answer that one?' Matt had been asked this before, however he had usually avoided giving a straight answer by simply saying yes or no, or by feigning a heart attack. That usually worked in the right circles.

'Promise not to laugh if I tell you why the answer's yes?'

'Guides' honour.'

'Well, I do, but it's a bit cheesy. Every day I see the parents of these children shuffle in, and shuffle out of school at the end of the day. The children that the majority of these parents take with them have nothing to look forward to in the evenings really. Television, PlayStation if they're lucky. By the time the turkey twizzlers are cold on their laps in front of Neighbours, they've lost the will to live and are asleep, ready for another thrilling instalment the next day. That's a generalisation of course. Present company excluded.'

'Of course,' Sara smiled and stared into her cup, 'go on.'

'Well, what keeps me going every morning is the fact that I get a chance to put a smile on their faces. Even if it's for a second, if they smile while they're in my classroom and under my care, then I'm happy. I know that the likelihood of me seeing any of the children on University Challenge is pretty slim, but as long as they're happy, that's enough for me. I know, it's cheesy, but you asked. And now you know.'

'I don't think it's cheesy at all. In fact, I think it's very honourable.'

'Don't know about that.' Matt shrugged.

Moving around the coffee table, Sara had already made her mind up about her next course of action. She slowly knelt in front of Matt, and with great care, moved forward to him. Matt leaned into her from the sofa, and with the lightest touch, their lips met. Matt would never brag, but he had slept with his fair share of women before, but the anticipation of the kiss that they were having had been immense. He couldn't put his finger on it, but there was something about Sara that was impossible to resist. Maybe it was her honesty. Maybe it was her ability to seem natural despite the fact that they had only met a couple of hours ago. He didn't know. All that he knew was that he wanted her desperately, and the way she was pressing herself into him was an indication that she felt the same way too. While kissing, more urgently now, he placed his hand in her hair, and felt the velvet through his fingertips. She moaned in appreciation, cupping his face in her hands as she sank deeper into him. Matt could stand it no longer. He broke away from the kiss, and stood up. There was no protest from Sara. She was fully aware of where Matt wanted to take her, and she felt completely at ease with the situation. Holding hands, they walked to the bedroom and stopped at the door.

'Are you sure about this?' Matt asked Sara.

'Stop being such a gentleman and shag me, you idiot.' She replied. For what was not going to be the only time that night, they burst into squeals of delight and shut the door behind them. Outside, in the distance, a fire engine blared its siren as it sped towards a fire.

10

As Sheila Pilkington arrived at school the next day, she was intrigued by what was waiting for her on her desk. It was unusual to see something so clearly for a start. Under normal circumstances, her workspace was often covered with old receipts dumped there by teachers, in order to claim the cash back for small purchases, usually cookery resources and batteries when there were none for the plethora of remote controls that were used around school on a day-to-day basis. That, and the daily invoices from stock orders, window cleaners and the ICT technician. Today, though, she was greeted by something quite unusual. On the desk, in a space that had been deliberately cleared, was a small white envelope. With a calligraphy pen, someone had taken painstaking care to write her name, the slant of the handwriting masking the author beautifully.

'What the hell?' Sheila thought aloud. She looked around sheepishly, as if the culprit might be lurking somewhere in the office. Nobody there, she realized. The other odd thing, she noticed, was the strange, intoxicating odour that was permeating the air around her. It normally smelled of a mixture of her own perfume and Pritt Stick, but this was a stronger, fresher smell. It then dawned on her, like a sledgehammer falling. Smiling, she picked up the envelope and sniffed it. After shave, but not just any after shave. It was Davidoff, and she had only told a handful of people that it was her favourite brand of splash-on for men. Indeed, it was only five people that had managed to glean from her that it was also her late husband, Tony's, favourite as well. Sheila felt herself blush, and a rush of memories rise to the surface. Happy memories, of the two of them laughing and walking in the Welsh hills around Pembrokeshire. That was always their place, the great outdoors. She smiled to herself, and wiped a tear away from her right cheek. 'Silly sod.' She said to herself, taking a silver letter-opener and slicing through the top of the sealed white letter. She removed the contents, and gazed at the two pieces of paper lying flat on her hand. The first, and most surprising, was a cheque for eighty three pounds and twenty pence. The second was a handwritten note, with each word painstakingly crafted using the same calligraphy pens that had been used to write her name on the envelope. She read each word carefully, the smile growing on her face with each word.

Dear Sheila,

What a wonderful world we live in, where you can come to work, and where the smiles on everyone's faces around you make each day worthwhile. I hope that you find the contents of this letter useful. You know as well as I do, it had to happen sooner or later. I have reached a turning point in my life, and I have decided to make amends for my inadequacies of the past. Please accept my offering, along with my undying love.

With all my eternal love

A secret admirer.

xxxxx

p.s. I hope you liked the scent I applied. My guess is it had the desired effect. It was either that or Windolene.

Sheila looked at the letter, and then at the cheque, and then back at the letter again. She knew, of course, by the amount on the cheque that it was from Matt.

'Stupid bastard, he's getting worse. He must have spent ages writing that this morning. He must have been awake all night even...........' She stopped her soliloquy, and her eyes narrowed as she thought of what could have possibly kept her favourite surrogate grandson awake all night. The penny dropped a fraction of a second later, and she shook her head.

'Oh my god,' she exclaimed to the same invisible person she had been conversing with in the mornings for the last ten years, 'he's got a girlfriend.'

****

'Morning, you lot. Thanks for being so quiet during the register. Now, anybody do anything nice last night?' Silence ensued. This was the time of day that Matt cherished. He loved the gossip. Deep down, although he abhorred the rumour mill that was the school playground, his regular self-assessment told him that he was just as bad as the cockle women who regularly preyed like vultures on the weak, stirring the pot until it overflowed with untruths. This was where he could really get to grips with what was happening in the community. If you wanted to know the truth, then you had to get it from the horse's mouth. Admittedly, you often had to lead the water to drink first, but more often than not the little cherubs were just dying to spill their guts. Especially, he thought, if the subject matter was juicy. Hatches, matches dispatches and the occasional hooch-fuelled catfight were commonplace in the locality, and Matt loved it. A hand rose quietly from the back.

'Yes, Robbie, what is it?' Matt enquired, a hint of intrigue in his voice. Robbie Murphy was a wire-haired, ginger explosion of a boy, once a traveller, now settled in one of the more spacious and luxurious council houses on the local estate. He was, however, one of the quietest children in the class, and the one least likely to say anything during any communal times. *It'll probably be nothing, Matt thought, but never mind, at least he's getting involved.*

'I heard my mum and dad shouting in bed last night. My mum must have been angry with him because she said he was a dirty bastard and that he was going to get it.'

Matt froze. On one hand, it was quite possibly the funniest thing he had ever heard. On the other hand, it was hideous. He was not a particularly religious man, however right now he was praying to anyone that no child would ask him to explain what that meant. Nothing but silence permeated the classroom. You could, in fact, cut the silence with a knife, and a blunt one at that. Another hand went up, a familiar, small hand, belonging to Ashleigh. Oh God, thought Matt. I don't need this. What if her mother has been talking to her about last night? Oh please, *please,* don't say anything about it. At least, not like Robbie did. He bit the bullet.

'Yes, Ashleigh, what is it?'

'Don't worry. My mum said that to my dad once and when they got up in the morning they were all happy with each other again.'

'Assembly time, you lot, let's go.'

****

The playground is a terrifying place for those unaccustomed to it. At set times, the peace and tranquillity of the neighbourhood is shattered by the sound of doors being flung open, screams, eager conversation about television the night before, footsteps, screams, the occasional expletive, screams, laughing, crying, arguing, and screams. And then the children come out and meet the teachers on duty. Matt, today though, was having problems concentrating on important matters like how many beers he had at home in the fridge, whether his coffee would last him for the next fifteen minutes, and what would happen to him professionally if anyone found out he had been sampling the local produce, and enjoying it at that. And boy, had he enjoyed it. He was of the firm opinion that sex was excellent, but it was magnificent when there was somebody else there to enjoy it with him. As far as he was concerned, there were not enough superlatives to describe the time he had spent engaged in sexual congress last night. It had seemed ages since he had done that with anyone, but a large part of him felt extremely pleased that it had been with Sara. When he left for work this morning, slightly earlier than usual, she left at a similar time, in order to collect Ashleigh and avoid prying eyes in the neighbourhood. Upon parting, he remembered how she grabbed him by the lapels of his jacket and pulled him close, kissing him deeply on the mouth. Matt had not hesitated to ask her if he could see her again, and she wasted no time in replying to the affirmative. They were going to step out that Friday, and the fact that it was only Wednesday was beginning to eat at Matt. *Jesus, keep a grip on yourself. It's only been a day, he* thought to himself. *Just don't mess it up. Act normal, and she won't see you for the freak you are.*

Matt felt a tug at his jacket sleeve. There was a little girl, pigtails swishing as she jumped up and down, waiting eagerly to tell Matt her news.

'What is it, sweetheart?' Matt asked her. He liked the term sweetheart, especially with the little ones.

'Mr. Greaves, It's my friend Cassie. She was in the millennium garden having some quiet time with me, and we had a bet.'

'What sort of bet, my love?' he replied. He didn't know whether he was going to like this or not. From behind the little girl stepped a little girl, who could only be Cassie. She was grinning from ear to ear, and she would have been the most delightful child ever, had it not been for the piece of gravel that was currently stuck in her right nostril.

'What's your name, my darling?'

'Jessica.'

'Be a love and get the bell, would you. Playtime's over I think.'

11

As Jim white pulled out of the yard, a fleeting thought passed through his mind. *In the not too distant future my son, we'll be obsolete. A thing of the past. We'll be a picture on a museum wall somewhere.* He decided to throw caution to the wind, and went as fast as he possibly could down the street for about a hundred metres. His legs finally gave way, and he had to resort to pedalling his pushbike at a more sedate, leisurely pace. His uniform pristine, apart from the regulation bicycle clip, he began his daily circuit of the streets of Broomfield. Like the day before, and the one before that, and like each day for the fifteen years before that, he pushed himself along the streets, avoiding the potholes, and familiar obstacles that had now become his friends.

Born James Whitaker White, in Partridge Lane, Broomfield, in 1965, he had lived in the same town all his life. Others had often criticised him for his lack of ambition to see the outside world, had used adjectives such as 'blinkered,' 'insular,' and 'uninteresting.' This never raised a response from Jim. He had grown up as a very happy child, the son of a policeman and secretary in a time when police were respected and traditional family values were commonplace in many more houses than today. His love of the law had blossomed from the age of ten onwards, shunning the occasional game of football to stay in and watch his cop shows. Van der Valk, Z-cars, Starsky and Hutch, and his favourite, Columbo. He would never admit it, but he even to this day tuned in to the occasional episode of Midsomer Murders, although why anybody chose to live there was beyond him. He had always proclaimed to his wife Julie (much to her annoyance after the twentieth time or so) that no-one in their right mind would even entertain buying a property in Midsomer, with the number of deaths each week that occurred there.

It wasn't necessarily the thought of catching robbers red-handed, and it certainly wasn't the chasing that he craved and loved as part of the job. Unlike most boys with a similar interest, he liked the actual thought processes that his favourite stars used. Methodical, unbending, uncompromising, and of course humorous when they needed to be. He loved it all (apart from the one with the old lady who always reminded him of a librarian, he could never watch *that* one). He managed a wry smile at the traffic lights as he dismounted for a second to wait for the lights to change. What was confusing, to others more than himself, was if he was so desperate to be a great policeman, then how come he'd remained a constable for the whole of his career? He knew the reason why, and was not ashamed of it. To him, the small-fry that he rounded up on a daily basis for petty crimes such as shoplifting, drunk and disorderly offences and minor affrays, were enough for him. He didn't need to be bringing down million dollar drug rings for policing to be worthwhile to him. Here, in Broomfield, he could put something into the community on a regular basis. Let the super cops take care of that side of things. Here, on the streets that he had been cycling each day for a small eternity, he felt at home. His arrest rate was high, and the criminality on his 'patch' was on the decline. He felt a real sense of pride about this achievement, but was nowhere enough as conceited to think that it was all down to him. Someone, after all, had to tell him where to go and what to do. He merely saw it as a gift in terms of his ability to interact with others. Consistently, fairly, humanely, and on a daily basis. Despite the fact that his epaulettes only held his number and nothing else, and despite he had seen countless of his friends adorned with stripes and in some cases pips on theirs, he knew what meant the most to him. His work on the streets, his family, and his love for the job over money. The lights changed back to green, and he began his ascent to Gallows Hill, the highest point in Broomfield. Panting a little, he glided along effortlessly, his lean body only breaking into the slightest of sweats. Conditioned by his regular half-marathons and the occasional triathlon, he was more than equipped physically for the daily ride, and more besides. Offenders half his age would marvel at his stamina when a chase was underway, and to this day he had never been shaken in a foot pursuit. He was strong in body, and generally strong in mind, however today there was a slight chink in the armour that was annoying him. So much so, that he stopped when he saw one of the reasons for his perturbance. Outside one of the many newsagents in town, reports of the deaths of Reena Singh, and a local businessman named Saul Omoku, were playing heavily on his mind. As if one fatality wasn't enough, there had been two within a fortnight. This was almost unheard of. One, a murder on the street, probably a mugging gone wrong. The other, potentially a car theft gone awry when joy-riders were told no for the first time in their lives. Jim was confident that the culprits who committed this awful duo of atrocities would eventually be caught. If Columbo taught him nothing else, it was that eventually all criminals make mistakes. These would be no different. It was just the severity of it all, and the impact of these events on the local community. Jim knew Reena Singh. He met her from time to time outside the school when he was talking to children there. Lovely woman, he thought, and such a shame to be taken so early in her life.

Realizing that he had lost concentration, he looked around, regaining his focus on the task at hand, namely keeping a close look-out for anyone transgressing in any way, or in need of help. Nothing to report, however something did catch his eye. On a bus shelter, on the opposite side of the road, was new graffiti. He knew this because of two things: firstly, the sheen on the paint showed that it was forty eight hours old, maximum. Secondly, this was nothing like the usual stuff. The adolescent population of Broomfield regularly invested time in honing their artistic skills on bus shelters, freshly painted walls and the suchlike. However, they usually resorted to more colourful sexual metaphors and statements of their undying love to the last person to drop their pants for them under the park slide in the early hours of the morning. This, he surmised, was something entirely new. A new kind of town art, which was more disturbing, potentially more sinister. Checking that nothing was coming towards him on the opposite side of the street, he turned his cycle and freewheeled across the road and over to the dilapidated waiting-station for the town's public buses. In the tree above, a finch sang gaily, in a vain attempt to attract attention to a mate, and failing that, anyone who would be bothered to listen. White failed to hear it though. He was paid to notice things, and he was certainly seeing this now. He had become totally engrossed in the symbol before it, and the slogan that had been written underneath.

Superseding any previous graffiti stood a perfect square. Not just a square, but a *perfect* square. Each side exactly the same as the one adjacent to it, each pair perfectly parallel to its counterpart. An amateur geologist in his own adolescent years, White had no trouble in recognising the pair of rock hammers, crossed at the handles and unusually double headed, completing the symmetrical aspect to the symbol. Brilliant white, they sat inside the square, which was painted claret red. Or blood red, White allowed himself to say aloud. He also realized correctly that someone had gone to great lengths to paint this. It was not simply a time filler for one of the local street kids. This had been put here to serve a purpose, as an advertisement to others. In large black letters, surrounded by white paint to accentuate them and draw the reader's attention, was the message. 'CLEANSE OR BE CLEANSED. THE NEW DAWN IS ARRIVING.' White immediately delved into the dirt bag underneath his saddle. From it he produced a digital camera. He took it out of its nylon padded case and turned it on, a light hearted chime sounding to signify that the camera was ready for action. For the next ten minutes

James Whitaker White took upwards of twenty photographs, from as many different angles as possible. When he had finished, he re-mounted his bicycle and carried on down the road, the image burned onto his memory. He was going to have to think about this one. He was going to have to think very hard. Behind him, the finch gave a final chirp and flew off to find another home. With his greying hair starting to glisten with effort of cycling, Jim continued on his tour of his beloved town, and as his six foot frame began to power the bicycle along again, he smiled to himself, feeling lucky that he had found a vocation that he truly loved.

12

As Matt waited outside Grimley's that Friday evening, he felt extremely odd. Although he would never tell Sara this, the feeling was quite reminiscent to his early courtship of Andrea, his ex-wife. The waiting outside in the cold, just for a chance to hold hands and talk together. The time spent shaving properly, grooming carefully just in case the evening took an unexpected turn and he needed to smell nice in all the right places. Although a distant memory, Matt couldn't help but smile to himself for feeling like a teenager about to get his hands on his girlfriend's breasts at a party for the first time. He took some time to remind himself that he had already done this, and that there really was no need to allow his digestive tract to behave in this fashion, but it was no use. No matter how he tried to disguise it, he was extremely excited about meeting Sara, and to top things off, he was going to introduce her to Nick at the same time. *Kill two birds with one stone*, he had thought to himself earlier that day. He'd made the call and instantly regretted it. Receiving the responses he had known deep down he would receive from his brother, he relived the moment once more.

'Hi Nick, it's me, Matt.'

'Hey, what's happening there mate?'

'Just wanted to see if you were out tonight.' He thought he would wait another few seconds before dropping the bombshell.

'Sure mate. Usual place?' Nick enquired, not that he had to. It was always the Arthur. Without fail.

'You know it bro. By the way, I'm going to be bringing a friend. There's someone I'd like you to meet.' There was silence for a fraction of a second. Matt knew that Nick had put the pieces together, and was just thinking of a response.

'A girl?' *Here we go.*

'Yes, a girl. Her name's Sara.'

'Is she pregnant?' *He's such an idiot.*

'No, mate, she's not.'

'Do you love her?'

'See you tonight then you cretin. I'll meet you on the corner outside at about half eight, okay?' Part of him now wished that his brother would say no.

'This, I wouldn't miss for the world.' He was gone, not even a goodbye.

Sara was on time leaving work, and was as happy to see Greaves as he was to see her. So much so, that she didn't hesitate to plant a firm kiss on his cheek before he started getting anxious about whether he could or not. Once again, she explained that Ashleigh was at her mother's, so the night was theirs to spend as they wished. Trying to avoid thinking of the connotations of that statement, Matt announced that she would be meeting his younger brother for the first time too. This went down well. Sara was keen to know about Matt's family, and he had been considerably guarded about it during their post-coital moments. He had filled them in on the members (and ex-members too, including his father), but had left it at that. She had felt that was enough for the evening's interrogation, and although genuinely interested and unashamed of asking, she felt that if she pried any more, she might put him off wanting to see her again. Although they had shared their bodies with each other willingly, they would both be true in admitting to each other that they had shared much more than that. Although early on, she felt an instant attachment to Matt, and she was shocked to admit to herself that his apparent vulnerability, which hid behind the sarcasm and wit, mirrored her own. As naturally as if they had been together for years, they instinctively reached for each other's hand as they began the stroll to The Arthur. Realizing their meeting of minds on this point, they looked at each other briefly, shared a knowing smile, and made their way down the pavement, chatting furiously as they went.

As planned, Nick was waiting on the pavement outside the pub. His breath condensing in the cold night air, he turned when he heard his brother and his escort arriving. Sara immediately realized that they looked extremely similar physically, although Matt probably filled his shirt a little more with muscle than his younger brother. Reaching him, they stopped, and Matt made the first move.

'Have you been waiting long? It's a cold one tonight.'

'Actually, I'm quite hot.' Smirking, he removed his denim jacket. Underneath, he wore a black t-shirt, the front of which was adorned with the words 'MATT'S GOT A NEW GIRL.'

'Sara, this is Arsehole. Arsehole, this is Sara. Let's get a drink.' Matt was doing his best to keep a straight face, but it was too much. All three burst into peals of laughter. The ice firmly broken, they pushed the door open and made their way in. As the first of many drinks that night were passed over the bar, Nick looked at his brother and caught his eye quickly. Although he was the first to ridicule his sibling, he loved him dearly, and Nick had noticed immediately the change in his brother. With so close a fraternal bond, it was impossible not to notice. In the few seconds that they had while Sara took her first sip from her pint, Nick took the time to mime his approval to Matt.

'Nice one.' He mouthed quietly. Matt, appreciating the reaction, winked and put his arm around Sara. To round off the introductions, Nick also put his arm around Sara, and proposed a toast.

'To friends.' Simple as that. They echoed his sentiment.

'Now,' Nick began, 'has Matt told you about his rash?'

'Yes, actually, I rubbed some cream into it last Wednesday. He hasn't mentioned it since though. Must have been embarrassed that I had to open a second pot of cream.'

Nick laughed aloud, glad to see that apart from being loads of fun, she would be able to take Matt's crap without even thinking about it. He suggested that they grab a seat, and they moved into one of the snugs to enjoy the evening. It was Friday, and Sara was going to be in for a treat tonight, Nick mused. For tonight meant live entertainment. Wondering if Matt had warned her, he thought of the usual two-piece outfits that graced the lounge. The brothers had seen more than their fair share of these groups, usually given exotic names to sound more enticing. 'Two's company', 'Domino', and one of his personal favourites, 'Sexual Cocoa.' He remembered almost peeing himself with delight in anticipation of that particular group, knowing full well that they were probably going to be made up of a half-decent part-time plumber and his girlfriend, who had been to too many karaoke evenings and had decided that this would be the first step on the road to stardom. They didn't let her down either. He recalled with a smirk that after three numbers the female element sprained her ankle doing some sort of spin, and had to have a surgical support bandage applied by Keith, who had recently attended the first-aid at work course on offer from the brewery. Whitney Houston's 'I wanna Dance With Somebody' had never been the same again.

Tonight's turn was right on track too. 'Astral Fountain' were, according to the poster outside, 'SEMI – FINALISTS ON TV'S 'STARSEARCH'.'

What rapidly became evident, however, was that the reason for them making the semi-final must have been some sort of tragedy occurring the night before. This pair, Matt thought, were probably the worst they had seen to date. After a shaky start with a below-mediocre rendition of 'Light My Fire' from The Doors, the set went rapidly downhill, with a range of artists covered from Mariah Carey to Lindisfarne. The crowning glory though was the closing number, an extremely poor rendition of 'The Greatest Love Of All.'

'The greatest tragedy of all,' Nick mused aloud to Sara between shots of Jack Daniels, 'is that one of them hasn't died during the course of this evening.' Sara shrugged, and while they laughed, she turned to the bar, where Matt waited to take his place in what she thought must have been the third or fourth round of beers and chasers by now. His back was turned, but as if by some invisible connection, he turned almost at the same time that she affixed her gaze on him, and let his gaze linger admiringly on her. She felt herself blushing, and fought the urge to look away. Instead, she found some inner confidence, and smiled what Matt would later describe as 'A smile that would melt the ice caps.'

A strange thought crossed her mind. She thought of the two brothers, and wondered what they must have been like growing up together. With a fraternal relationship as strong as theirs now, she figured that they would have been almost inseparable as children. She also felt a slight tinge of jealousy, gently stinging her inside as she thought of her own family upbringing, and the dreadful nights waiting for arguments to erupt downstairs while she tried her best to complete homework that she would never be able to ask for help with.

Avoiding melancholy, she roused herself sharply from her thoughts and moved to the bar, where she unceremoniously placed her arms around Matt. He made no effort to pull away, and the feel of his arms reciprocating, holding her close, stirred animal thoughts in Sara. She wanted to tell him how he was making her feel inside, how much the time she was spending with him was making her wish it was more permanent, and how his outlook on life was making her feel that she could accomplish anything. She was beginning to float on air, and although scared witless at the prospect of another serious relationship after the last time, she was secretly hoping that this was going to be the one. She wasn't after the dream. She was a pragmatist, and what she craved deep down was someone to confide her dreams in, to share her hopes with. Someone who wasn't the dream, but rather someone who could help her decide what the dream was. She didn't, however, share this in words. She turned to him and gave him what she thought would be, under the circumstances, the next best thing. 'Make mine a double, will you?'

As the night began to draw to a close at the pub, and as alcohol began to tighten its grip on the three revellers, the conversation began to meander in ways that all three had experienced at some time in their lives, but tonight's conversation piece was a topic that all of the participants felt very strongly about. A topic that stirred passions greater than any argument on religion, politics or money ever could.

'Look here, you're all talking bollocks. The most memorable thing about the fucking eighties is the shoulder pads. You've only got to watch re-runs of Dynasty to see that. They had to widen the bloody doors, for fuck's sake.' Nick was in full flow.

'You have a point, but it's got to be the films that made the eighties. There will always be iconic films, but it's the eighties that hold many of the most memorable.' Sara retorted. She was really enjoying this.

Matt's ears pricked up at this point. He spotted an ideal opportunity to liven the evening up a bit, and didn't think for one moment would mind.

'Hang on,' he said, 'hold that thought, I'll be right back.'

Nick and Sara looked at each other, and Nick, pretending that he didn't know what was just about to happen, raised one quizzical eyebrow and in a perfect Leonard Nimoy Voice, 'Most illogical.'

Matt returned a few minutes later, with a tray. Placed upon the tray were a selection of alcoholic shots, ranging from what turned out to be peach schnapps to a rather disgusting Czech speciality called Slivovitch, which apparently was made from plums, but tasted more like the sweat from his own. He placed the tray onto the table, and smiled the drunken, twisted smile of a man who was about to potentially ruin someone's night, even his own. This, he decided, was going to be the acid test of his relationship with Sara. If she happened to lose, and managed to take the punishment without crying or having to go to hospital, then she was definitely long-term material.

'Right then film buffs, the game is 'Eighties Film Alphabet Roulette.' We'll draw straws to see who starts on A. The rules are quite simple. If you fail to name a film beginning with your letter, you drink. If we get all the way back to A without missing a letter, I'll drink the lot. Whoever drinks the last drink, should we reach that eventuality, chooses the next five.' He turned to face Sara, who was grinning with a mixture of dread, excitement and glee at the potential outcomes of this game. Matt was not to know, but she was quietly confident that she would do quite well, and that it would be her, not he or his sibling, who would be walking home in the straightest line that evening.

They decided, in best sporting tradition, to decide who started by a mature, sensible method. For many aeons ancient civilisations have let the gods decide their fate. For the Vikings, they used stones carved with ancient runes. For the ancient Egyptians, they would tumble coloured sticks onto the floor and let them decide. The game of 'Ip Dip Doo' however, for some strange reason, had been completely ignored by the societies of years gone by. To Matt, Nick, and surprisingly to them, Sara, this was immediately the fairest and most reliable method that they could think of. All three, upon Nick's mention of the use of this poem, immediately were cast back to their childhood, and the playground in particular. For Matt, it was used to decide who would be the cops and who would be the robbers. To Nick, it was the method employed to choose who would stand in the middle for a game of Bulldogs. To the unacquainted, this simply involved one person starting in the middle, and then hordes of his (or her) peers charging between two fixed points whilst the hapless middle man tried to catch them. For Sara, her memory was of herself and four of her closest friends using Ip Dip to decide who was to ask the new boy, Jason Daniels, for a kiss.

Sara drew first blood (which incidentally did come up under 'F') with 'American Werewolf In London.' Matt followed quickly with 'Beetlejuice.' And so it continued. Each of the trio seemingly unperturbed by the array of drinks lying at the hub of the table, awaiting one lucky recipient to partake in a shot of the elixir of their choice. Nick, stumbling on the letter O, was the first to relieve the table of the burden it carried. Sara chimed in with 'On Golden Pond,' not really knowing whether it had hailed from the eighties or whether it was the nineties. She didn't care though. She was having way too much fun. Fun that she hadn't seen for such a long time. She found herself smiling at Matt uncontrollably, and unashamedly at that. He returned the favour, and under the table stroked her leg absentmindedly. Sara, noticing his display of affection, turned and faced him while Nick struggled with Z and helped himself to another drink.

'You enjoying yourself?' Matt asked above the racket around them.

'Yeah. Very much. You?'

'You bet.' Came the reply. 'In fact, I'm having the nicest time I've had out in ages. You know it's because of you, don't you?'

Sara blushed at Matt's very open and candid statement. That was the first time during their brief relationship that he had said anything that heartfelt or touching. She wasn't used to men telling her things like that, but plucked up the courage to respond in kind.

'No, but you bring out the best in me Greavsie. You're a bit of all right.'

'Listen,' he quickly interceded, 'you don't have to worry about flattering me. I'm a sure thing.'

Sara looked away to stifle a laugh, a look in Nick's direction. He had finished his drink some time ago, and had witnessed the exchange between the two. He was smiling, partly in amusement at the mileage he would have at a later date with his brother regarding his sentimentality, but more through a genuine happiness at seeing Matt smile with a good reason for doing so. They had been through much together, and although, despite his faults, Nick had done his best to support matt through their father's death and his divorce, he had always felt that His brother was in need of the company of a good woman. Not just in a sexual sense, but in the sense that he needed somebody to share his feelings with other than his brother. Although he didn't often show them, they were there, buried deep down underneath the shroud of humour and bravado that he used to keep outsiders from learning the truth about him; that he had a heart, and a big one at that.

The game proceeded, and it came to the letter N for Sara after what seemed an eternity of rounds. All three, to an outsider, would have been content knowing that they had all given a decent account of themselves, demonstrating a sound understanding of the subject matter. They had all by this point had an extra drink or two, and were beginning to feel it, but they had all succeeded in some difficult contributions to the game. Sara, through what was developing into a drunken haze, stared slightly vacantly into space while she thought.

'Come on,' demanded Matt, 'it's your round next. Hurry up and get 'em in.'

'I know, I know. I was just thinking. Give me a break. I know, 'New Dawn'.'

Nick interrupted with a pseudo buzzer sound. 'I must contest that, as I think the title you are looking for is 'Red Dawn.'

'No, I'm sure it's New Dawn. Patrick Swayze, some other eighties bimbo, and a plot about some shitty revolutionaries somewhere. Yep, New Dawn.'

Matt squinted at her through his own alcoholic veil. He hated to admit it, but he was in agreement with his brother on this one. 'I think he's right, you know. It is Red Dawn.'

Sara stood firm, and her conviction was enough to make the brothers stumble in their quest to prove that they were correct and she was wrong. They had reached an impasse, and it was decided that it was a natural end to the game. Nick, sensing that they were reaching the end of the evening, pointed out that there were still three drinks left in the centre of the table from the last round that was bought for the game. They looked at the options. One rather congealed advocaat, one neat gin, and worst of all, one dark rum. Matt almost gagged at the thought of the rum. There had been many occasions with his brother where Nick had suggested that they play various games with rum. That wouldn't normally have seemed so bad, but it was the fact that he always chose Woods' Navy Rum. He was almost sure that there were many people out there who really enjoyed it, and he would never deign to cast any aspersions on the drink itself, for he was a firm believer in the adage 'Each to their own.' However, when he thought of the word 'Navy', he automatically thought of distinguished men in uniform clinging to the mast as their ship descended to the bottom of a savage, unforgiving sea. However, if they were all drinking this shit, he mused, then it was small wonder that the ships were sinking. He couldn't even walk straight after half a dozen of those, let alone steer a boat. He snapped out of his delirium, and thought of his choices. Advocaat, hideous in texture and guaranteed to curdle the moment it hit the stomach after mixing with the other spirits he had drunk; Gin, whilst lovely mixed with tonic water, was slightly reminiscent of WD-40 when drunk on its own, and finally the rum. Hobson, he reflected, had a lot to answer for.

His angst was cut short by Sara, who had, it seemed, sensed Matt's hesitancy and had decided to help him along. Almost in slow motion, her hand, moved toward the centre of the table, and equally as slowly, the boys turned their heads to see which drink she would take. She went straight for the rum, saluting the brothers quickly before downing it in one. Matt gazed with a mixture of wonder and horror, expecting the inevitable delayed reaction and convulsions after imbibing what he perceived to be the naval equivalent of brake fluid. The reaction never came, and Sara simply turned to him and said, almost with a tinge of guilt, 'Love the stuff. My Nan always has a bottle handy. Can't get enough of it. Hope you don't mind me taking it.'

'Nah,' Matt replied, 'I'll get over it somehow.' He reached for the advocaat, and prayed to the Roman god of wine, Bacchus, for clemency.

They grabbed their coats, and after saying a quick cheerio to Keith, who was clearly enjoying the busy hum of the Friday night revelries, they stepped out of the cocoon warmth of the pub into the harsh, unforgiving arms of the night outside. After warmly saying how nice it had been to meet Nick, she and Matt went their separate ways from him, with a promise that they would repeat the night out very soon. Turning to Matt, she looped her arm into his and they strode off towards his flat. They didn't even discuss the matter; both wanted it to happen, and whether it led to anything of a sexual nature or not, Matt was glad that tonight he would not have to sleep alone. Besides, he was going to need someone to rub his back while he hugged the toilet after drinking the advocaat.

As the two embraced the cold and made their way down the street, they were blissfully unaware that not too far away, under the very ground that they were walking on with such happiness, that there were such despicable and unforgivable acts being committed, by people who took their happiness in different ways altogether.

13

1964 was a very good year. In a converted church in Manchester, television engineers worked industriously and fastidiously to ensure that every possible eventuality was covered in readiness for the first ever broadcast of the new pop music show for young people, entitled 'Top Of The Pops.' Backstage, a group of young, carefree musicians collectively named The Rolling Stones got ready to come out and perform their recent hit 'I Want To be Your Man.' Only commissioned for six shows, the concept was to be a resounding success, dominating the youth culture for the next four decades. Its presenter, Jimmy Saville, attired in what was to become one of his many trademark garish outfits, steadied himself and went through his numerous fill-ins. He also practised a yodel which was to be emulated by many, but mastered by none.

Elsewhere, other equally important events were occurring around the globe. Events that would be sometimes iconic of the era, and sometimes be forgotten as easily as a teenager forgets what their attire was the previous week. For example, the Sun newspaper saw its first edition printed, under the watchful eye of editor-in-chief Sidney Jacobson; the head of the world famous Little Mermaid statue was inexplicably stolen, sawn off and taken hostage, an event which baffled police and speculators for the next thirty three years. Only when the artist Jorgen Nash confessed to the crime did the truth surface.

Closer to home, crimes of a different sort were being committed, sparking the real birth of gang culture, an ugly precursor to street warfare that is still rife in most major cities today. The Mods, attired in their customary green Parkas and transported on the eternally cool Vespa moped, traversed the countryside, converging on Brighton beach to clash with the Rockers. Throwbacks to the decade before, and emblazoned with both hair and motorcycle grease to add effect, they participated freely in savage attacks on each other and holidaymakers, repeating the acts in similar seaside resorts such as Hastings and Margate. Soon to be revered images of smartly dressed and well groomed men brutally beating each other were to adorn the newspapers like trophies of their bloody and sometimes fatal battles, with locals and holidaymakers running for cover on nearly every weekend in selected beach hotspots around the south coast. Young men of various backgrounds, joined as in most crusades by a unifying hatred of anything other than what they were used to, chased each other around the streets and into alleys, breaking bones and laws as easily as the wafers on the ice-creams they ate afterwards.

Whilst the mods and rockers continued to escape to the seaside, another type of escapism was making the news. Revolutionary escapism, in the form of a fantasy film. A cinematic piece that was to capture the hearts and minds of children and adults for decades to come, and which was to be hailed and ridiculed both at the same time for avant-garde animation and spurious accents. The film, of course, was Mary Poppins. To make an almost unheard-of clean sweep at the Oscars, winning eight in total, it was paraded by its producers as a modern-day masterpiece and triumph of technology, unifying the media of live action and cartoon drawing in a way that was to prove the gateway to film makers of the future.

Compared to the people involved in all of these acts, Brian Sedgewell had received no accolades for his work. He had never been to an awards ceremony, and he had never mixed with anyone of importance in the arts. He was, however, an extremely important man. It was his guidance and expertise that ensured that the inhabitants of Broomfield had adequate water to drink, bathe and water their suburban gardens each weekend. It was his knowledge and understanding of his subject matter that allowed kettles to be filled without ensuing illness, for toilets to be flushed during commercial breaks in the population's favourite soaps, and for window cleaners to fill their steel buckets every Saturday. Brian was currently waist deep in water, in relative darkness, and approximately twenty feet underneath ground level. Most men in that situation would turn white, and eagerly look to remove themselves from the situation. Not he. Brian loved his job, and having helped to build the labyrinthine collection of underground inspection tunnels, his pride in the finished article encouraged him to forget the potential dangers of working in such conditions and to revel in the opportunity that such a facility allowed those who treaded the floor above to live their lives because of his efforts.

Simply called I-9, the complex had been an enormous feat of engineering and forethought from the start. When the National Water Board, or NWB, had modernised the water supply due to expansion of the population in Broomfield, it had been decided that the normal inspection tunnels accessed by manholes be closed, and a new, more efficient system be introduced that would make remedial work and routine inspection easier and more labour efficient. With expert engineers, geologist support and construction specialists, the end product was a complex which not only held the inspection access points, but held separate observation stations, its own independent power supply in the form of three enormous diesel generators, rest areas for workers undertaking sizeable jobs and even storerooms for electrical and other power equipment, should the necessity to store such equipment for any length of time be necessary. It was remarkable in every sense.

Brian Sedgewell, full of admiration and affection for the tunnel system, was able to look on with love on his underwater domain for only a short while longer, and as he admired his handiwork in his subterranean hideaway, another kind of darkness was hiding. Deep within him, it spread quickly, and soon Brian was reduced to a shell, a carcass of his former self. A non-smoker, he believed himself to be ahead of his time in abstaining from tobacco, fearing the damage to his body that the tar and smoke was likely to induce. Smug as he was, he was blissfully unaware that the smoke that he breathed in at weekends, passed through the lungs of others, was doing an equally powerful job in starting his final journey. After a brief illness, and a trip to his doctor for treatment for what he believed to be nothing more than a viral infection, he was eventually given the one thing that all humans should not be given; the knowledge that they are truly dying, and a speculative guess at their longevity. He died soon afterwards. The sanctuary of the curved walls, his beloved life's work for many years, lived on in his memory, harbouring the darkness and keeping the silence company until one day someone would stumble upon it, shattering it forever, abusing the place that he loved so dearly as his ashes mingled with the other detritus beneath people's feet.

****

The sound of dripping water cut the silence like a scythe, and the breath of nearly thirty men could be seen in the dank air. Energy saving light bulbs swung from white electrical cord overhead, the only testament to modernity, an anachronism which stood like a defiant finger to the past. The group of men were unremarkable in their everyday lives. Plumbers, painters, office workers, waiters, all men who undertook their duties with alacrity and a smile, hiding the darkest of secrets as sand on a beach hides its treasures. Here and there, faint scratching and the occasional squeak could be heard, as the rats gorged themselves on whatever they could find, feasting on the flotsam and jetsam of everyday life.

In the centre of the group, stood a young man. As unremarkable as the rest of the men that filled the room. There was but one subtle difference. The man in the middle had fear in his eyes. Fear of the unknown. The fear that only a truly frightened man can feel, when he knows for certain that for whatever reason, a foreboding fills the air around him, its stench permeating everyone and everything in the immediate vicinity. Samuel Kettering was extremely worried. New to the organisation, he had wanted to make his mark, had wanted to prove his manhood by daubing the walls of this tainted and poisoned town with a warning that change was in the air. He had wanted to tell them all that he and his friends were going to rid the town of its problems. He had been summoned to the meeting two days later. A personal call from Selleck. He didn't sound too happy either. When asked for the reason for his summons, the reply was simple.

'Well, Sam. Let me see now. You've been a busy boy I see. You're quite the artist, aren't you? I saw your handiwork for myself. Let's have a chat about it in two days' time. You know the place. Don't be late please. You know how it displeases me.'

Not showing was not an option in his mind. He had always had the best intentions, and if he was going to get his wrist slapped for a bit of graffiti, then he would take his reprimand without getting bitter, and learn his lesson. As the time passed though, in the back of his mind he felt a growing sense of unease. He had heard the stories about Selleck. About the way in which he would punish people for the smallest of things. One time, he recalled in a completely inappropriate reverie, how one of the members was punished for making Nazi salutes in the middle of town. It became apparent from two other such incidents that Selleck found something deeply offensive about any such actions, and from the rumours that he had heard, it was the tainting and supposed dilution of the actions of the Reich that was the main bone of contention. It was as if the principles were good enough for Selleck, but not good enough for those who worked to fulfil his vision. Which, at that particular moment in time, was not actually very clear. It involved ridding Bloomfield of a few individuals who were not conducive to the strength of the white population, but the long term aims were not really talked about. Was it him, or was he the only one who had suddenly seen this minute flaw in the grand design for the New Dawn Movement? Whatever his feelings on the matter, he was brought back to reality by the opening of what seemed like a metal door someway down the central corridor, its ferric protests informing everyone that something was about to happen.

From his prime position, Sam Kettering could make the blurred, gigantic shape of Selleck against the grey walls that enveloped the crowd. The shape became bigger, and silence ensued. As if exuding the foulest of smells, the gathering formed an automatic and almost perfect circle around Sam, however each of the individuals closest to the inside made every effort to be just the right distance from the epicentre of what might possibly be something significant. Kettering's eyes widened, and were he able to loosen the tape over his mouth, and were he able to move away from the two assigned unofficial guards, he would have immediately begun to protest his innocence of all crimes he had ever committed, and then run for it. In Selleck's right hand, glossy and sleek with polishing and gun oil, was a gun. A gun that, although unusual in appearance, appeared to be able to inflict some serious damage.

Selleck did not look at Sam. Not for the first three minutes and twenty five seconds. He firstly addressed the masses, beginning with the greeting. Strictly members only, this was never uttered outside the confines of the I-9.

'The new dawn is coming.' Began Selleck.

'And we are the instruments.' Came the reply.

'Throughout the centuries, leaders have often promised much and not delivered to expectation. Hitler, the numerous leaders of Rome, and so on. The problem? The ideas were sound, but the staff were not always able to perform to their job descriptions. Well, we are different, my friends. We are here to stay, and I would personally like to thank you all for the hard work and effort you have made in undertaking your duties over the last few months. Some of the tasks have been necessary, but dangerous, and you have been prepared to follow your instructions very carefully indeed. All of you but one, it seems.'

It was at this point that Selleck's gaze fell on Sam. He moved closer. The stench of sweat was overpowering from Selleck, and Sam's eyes automatically fell to the ground when the two males, Alpha and Beta, came within inches of each other.

'The thing is, everyone, that one person does not follow their job description to the letter. One person likes to daub the walls of the village with our crest, and draw unnecessary attention to our collective. This cannot be allowed to go unpunished. I have brought an item to share at tonight's meeting. You know it is a gun. But do you know what is significant about it?' Silence. 'I'll tell you then. This is a Parabellum Pistol, commonly, and incorrectly, known as the Luger Pistol. It is a toggle-locked, recoil operated, semi-automatic pistol. The design was patented by George Luger in 1898, and produced by German arms manufacturers D.W.M. starting in 1900. It was made popular through its use by Germany during World war One and Two. The name Parabellum refers to the cartridge it used, which was increased in size over time.'

Selleck looked around, and although he didn't care, he was sure there were some impressed faces staring back at him. Maybe he had let a little too much of his knowledge out there. He didn't like people knowing too much about him in any way really.

Especially his family. He didn't like prying at all into that area, even in the usual small-talking way that minions often seem to think is impressive at these meetings.

'Anyway, the relevance. It has served for many years as a weapon of choice. But the reality is, like many things, that it was not good enough at first to do a decent enough job. They had to throw the first version away and replace it with something better. Which is where you come in, you worthless piece of shit.' Sam's eyes met Selleck's, and the fear was clearly visible, invoked especially by the gun moving around. Sam wondered whether it was loaded briefly, then forced himself to focus on a way out if he could. He was truly terrified. Terrified that he might never see daylight again.

'You may think you were proving your allegiance, but the only way to do that here is to do as you're fucking told. If you can't do that, I may as well put this gun to your head and pull the trigger now. Do you understand what I am saying?' A rapid nod came back. All eyes were transfixed on the lone member in the centre, and although the individuals there were mostly either too scared or too interested to look anywhere else, they all chose to do so. Selleck followed his comments with a decisive action. He raised the gun and rested the end of the barrel against Kettering's temple. Sam Kettering was, of course, unable to restrain himself from crying, and relieving himself in front of everyone. A large pool of urine flowed freely down his leg and onto the concrete floor. The tears blinded him, but he would gladly have accepted blind for what was coming. He was suddenly filled with hate, and his eyes turned a little more resolute under the saline shroud. He wished that he could take his revenge on this man, a bloody and painful revenge. He knew that this was not going to be the case, and he was soon to become a cautionary tale.

'Goodbye Sam. Say hello to Hitler for me.' Sam screamed a muted protest, and Selleck pulled the trigger. The blackness that Sam was expecting to accompany those final words lingered, but vanished when he heard not a brief explosion, but a dull, mechanical click. The silence still ensued, but the faces of the crowd were now either showing feigned expectation that this was always going to have happened, or disgust at the sight before them of the man reduced to a shell. The magazine had indeed been empty, but Selleck may as well have pulled the trigger. To the collective, he had become as worthwhile as a corpse.

'Never let me down again.' Selleck barked. He ripped the tape from Sam's mouth in one motion. Through adrenaline soaked vocal chords the whisper came back. 'I promise.'

Selleck made his way back into the darkness of the tunnels. This was the sign that the meeting was over. Sam's hands were untied, and his guards dissolved into the crowd. Without a thought for anything else, Sam Kettering made his way out with the others, realizing fully that if he ever talked of this with anyone, the chamber would be loaded next time. As he broke the surface and entered the night air, he forgot his pride and ran home to the same bedroom he had slept in since he was born. As he lay awake that night paralysed by the memories of what had happened, and as his parents and his younger sister slept soundly in the adjacent bedrooms, he knew that only two things would come of this episode. As surely as the tears were cascading silently down his face, he would never breathe a word to anyone, and as certainly as he would be scarred emotionally for the rest of his life, he would one day take his revenge. Outside, a bird began to mark the arrival of the sunrise.

14

Nick Greaves sat alone at his laptop, munching on a Mexican-style wrap that he had bought from the garage, and chuckled to himself absentmindedly. The closest that this would have come to Mexico would be the faint possibility that one of the slaves who worked in the factory might have had a tequila slammer the night before. He had the munchies though, and this was the sort of crap that could save a man's life under the right circumstances. He cast his mind back to endless university nights, sitting around in circles with his classmates (not that he saw many classes though) smoking pot and commenting on how everything was heavy. In fact, things were so heavy, it was a miracle that the world didn't implode on itself and create some sort of black hole. So heavy that it was equally miraculous that people managed to move about freely. Which was, admittedly, often a minor problem for Nick and his friends. It wasn't necessarily a vicious circle, more of a non-violent and giggly circle, which nobody really wanted to step out of. The more socialising of this kind they seemed to do, the more sociable and perceptible to real talking points they became. It was as if the paper cylinders they shared together were conversation lightning rods, channelling discussion topics from some hidden ether out there. Or, alternatively, they were happy to avoid the bars and clubs in favour of a more sedate and less costly pastime. It was safe to say that if it came down to a choice between beer and pot, their little collective would always favour the latter. And the cash they saved by drinking and smoking at home always came in handy for the customary fourteen Kit Kats per person that served the same purpose as the faithful Mexican wrap.

Nick brought himself firmly back to Earth with the realisation that those days were long gone, and that if he were ever to return to his chemically enhanced days, he would be a dinosaur, having been superseded totally by the ever expanding volley of super-drugs that were encouraging more and more children to kill themselves each day. Having just turned thirty, he felt that many of the things that he felt were synonymous with growing up, were being cast aside in favour of what he now called 'Experience Light.' People not only wanted the highs, but they wanted no effort on their part, they didn't care whether they were alone or not when they got them, and they wanted them for next to nothing. What was the world coming to?

Finishing his wrap and casting the wrapper aside, he returned to the task at hand. He had come in from the night out with Matt and his new squeeze (very nice too, he thought) having thoroughly enjoyed the company and the laughs, and that was mostly always the case. However, there was something that had leaped into his consciousness whilst making a late-night coffee that had begun to erode away at his psyche, and had continued to do so until he had decided to let technology prove him right or wrong. Sara had mentioned the title 'New Dawn.' Great film, lots of big names, slightly farfetched story about teenagers who join a group of freedom fighters or something. However, Nick and his brother had both insisted that it was 'Red' not 'New' and deep down he knew that he was right. His brother, not wanting to ruin his chances of a long awaited liaison with a woman, did not contest the issue, but Nick decided to check it out, as a future talking point and as a little bit of ammunition against Sara should he ever need to be fined with something horrible next time they were out. He was good at that. He stored little nuggets of information up until they were needed, and then popped them in there when nobody was looking or able to defend themselves.

Nick looked at his laptop screen. His university time had not been totally wasted, and despite his attitude to socialising, he had been naturally receptive to information and had sailed through his degree. It had not been very long before he was taken on by ActCorps, one of the biggest names in technology manufacture, and when

Nick was head hunted by this firm, they were willing to pay handsomely for the right person. It turned out one of his senior lecturers was taking a nice back hander in pushing names their way, and they were only too happy to snap up any rising stars who could dent their future profits. Starting out as a junior programmer specialising in systems security, it soon became apparent to both Nick and his employers that he had surpassed expectations, and he rapidly rose through the ranks, swiftly overtaking those who had sometimes been there for years. This did not, however, seem to make him unpopular, due to his ability to get on with everyone and his knack for getting people to perform tasks whilst thinking that they suggested them in the first place. A highly marketable skill in today's climate, and his superiors recognized this. He was better than well paid, and was able to have the car, the nice flat and a supercharged social life. A life so rich in diversity that it needed constant fuel in the shape of money, and Nick needed to keep the proverbial car running. He did this in a singular fashion. He simply utilised his skills to provide additional security for the right people. This could mean digitally enhanced pensions, or simply an additional nought in a lesser bank account here and there. Not many people knew it, but Nick was comfortably able to hack some of the more secure areas of cyberspace without really breaking a sweat, and more importantly, without any chance of a trail leading to himself. His kit was state of the art, and his laptop was undoubtedly capable of causing mayhem with only a few keystrokes. Nick never considered this though, as he knew two things; one, that should he insert his own e-killers into the ether, not only would society come to a virtual standstill, but so would his additional income. A no-brainer, really. So he plodded on, adding bits here for people, and taking bits away in other places, and maintained a healthy lifestyle. Which tonight had included the Mexican wrap.

Nick tapped into his search engine the words 'RED + DAWN.' Immediately he was given thousands of results, all pointing to the fact that Sara was going to be drinking a few more shots of navy rum the next time they met. He knew it. He would gloat for a little while, of course, and enjoy seeing her get drunk, but he kind of liked here, and decided that he would not force this to continue, as was his wont on previous occasions, much to his brother's distaste.

Not wanting any serious accidents, he leaned away from the machine and opened a can of lager. Sipping the bubbles from the opening, he continued to take a healthy slug before setting the can down on the glass coffee table in front of him and looking at the screen. Even though he knew he was right, he entered a new search, 'NEW + DAWN.' When he looked closely at the results, he saw lots of references to song lyrics, some advertisements for religious publications, and some vague references to sites offering royalty-free pictures of the dawn from various locations around the world. There were others, and Nick flicked through the pages one by one, not really interested but interested more in the fact that the topic of Dawn could be so important to so many people. He laughed aloud. He wasn't even there to see it on most mornings (and he made a mental note to ensure that he didn't see it when it blazed into existence in a few hours' time). He couldn't see what all the fuss was about.

It was then that a solitary link caught his eye, due not to its promises, or to its enormity, but due to the fact that if he had blinked, he would have missed it. The first few words underneath were understated, and in plain font. Nick blinked his rapidly blurring eyes clear and read:

Join us today. Protect tomorrow............

Nick became instantly intrigued by what was being said there. Protect tomorrow? How? Why? He clicked on the link, but was disappointed when a message informed him that he did not have permission to view the requested page, and that it was only grantable on request. Nick understood that there were some sites which were only for members, but they usually gave people a chance to join. He was annoyed by the fact that **he** was not allowed in, and he was always allowed in.

'Hmmm, we'll see about that.' He defiantly whispered. As if worried that he was being spied on, he checked left and right, then looked straight ahead. He began to break down the electronic walls that surrounded his prize. As it would turn out, they were not very strong, and a few well-placed lines of code proved too much for the site's feeble attempt at fortification. As soon as the last defences crumbled, his face was showered in a red glow, as a very strange icon appeared in the centre of his screen and sat there, pulsing. He scrolled down. Nothing else, just the icon. Nick studied it closer, as if the minutiae would give away a secret as to what it stood for. Nothing leaped out at him. He saved a copy, and decided to have another look in the morning. He was way too tired to be playing Columbo. And besides, it was probably some spotty teenager's attempt to form a gang, who would probably cause mayhem terrorising the tearooms of Bloomfield with their incessant giggling and leaving of crumbs on the tablecloths. He shut his laptop down, and after finishing has lager, tumbled onto his bed, where he would remain until exactly one thirty eight in the afternoon the next day, his mission accomplished.

15

Matt was convinced that there were only two things that were completely reliable in life. Firstly, that any piece of toast dropped at any given time would always land face-down, ruining any chance of salvage. Secondly, that no matter the situation, no matter how grave the circumstances, ice-cream cheered you up. As he walked along, he quickly pondered the moments shortly after leaving the cemetery when his father was buried. He was upset, that was for sure. However, as a twelve-year-old boy the strawberry cones that his mother bought as they strolled slowly back to their hired black dirge-chariots were always going to be memorable. He brought himself back to the present, and to his walking companions that day. In Matt's life, this was a big day. Not only was it the first real solo date that he and Sara had ventured out on, but she had asked politely if she could bring her daughter along too. The daughter who was currently sitting opposite him every day, as an empty vessel, waiting to be filled with knowledge. Ashleigh was delightful, and he really liked her for her ability to say the right thing when all hope as an educator was lost. Not necessarily (and not usually) the correct thing, but always the right thing. Matt despaired sometimes, knowing full well that there were a large percentage of his children who were never going to be able to utilise their mathematical knowledge to any dizzy standard, but who could be relied upon to strip an engine, or in the future just strip, without blinking. Now knowing Ashleigh's mother, he could see a possible future for the young girl. Hairdresser, shop assistant, flight attendant. Who knew? But not senior V.P.

The first thing that he had insisted, in order to break any ice that may have formed in Ashleigh's mind, was that she call him Matt while they were out, but in school it would have to be the usual 'Sir,' or 'Mr. Greaves.' She saw the logic in this suggestion, and went about being a child without any further comment. This pleased both Matt and Sara, who were slightly nervous about how Ashleigh might take the whole 'New Friend' scenario.

Matt tried to hedge his bets on a first venue, and had suggested the fair that had come to Bloomfield some three days earlier. This was welcomed warmly, and as far as matt was concerned, the outing couldn't have gone any better. Candy floss, dodgems, air rifles, and teddy bears. And Ashleigh had enjoyed the stalls too. They had laughed loudly together (when the gypsy had estimated Matt's age at ten years too many), had screamed appropriately on the waltzers, and had clung on to each other for dear life on what was unquestionably the sorriest Ghost Train that any of the party had seen in their entire lives (a little traveller boy who shouted 'Boo!' in the dark was as scary as it got).

As they made their way through the park, just before Sara's house came into view, Ashleigh decided to run ahead. Matt seized his chance to catch Sara's hand, and also her eye, before they had to make their farewell for the evening. Sara spoke first, before Matt had a chance to communicate how much he had enjoyed the day out together.

'Listen, and don't say anything, Matt. I just wanted to say that we've had a terrific day out with you today. I really mean that too. I don't……..'

'Don't what, Sara? You don't have to thank me for anything. You're both terrific. Why wouldn't we enjoy ourselves? I just hope that we can do it again. You'd like that, wouldn't you?'

Sara rolled her eyes. 'Of course I would silly. We both would. I just felt that I needed to tell you how happy I am at the moment. I know that we haven't been seeing each other long, and that you're probably just as worried as me about where this is going, but meeting you and seeing you like this, its…..it's …different to what I'm used to. And Ashleigh too. She's been through a lot, with the divorce from my ex and everything. What I'm about to say right now could end everything between us, and I wouldn't be surprised. But I'm going to say it anyway. This one day out today, this one trip to the fair, may seem a small thing to you.' She stopped walking briefly, and they turned instinctively to each other, their eyes meeting directly, honestly. 'However Matt, for Ashleigh, it's the closest thing to having a dad that she's had for ages. You don't need to be an expert on children to know how good it is for her to have a man and a woman in her life, even for days out. So thanks Matt. Now you tell me that you're scared, right? Here's where you……….'

She didn't have time to finish her sentence. Matt pulled her close, bent down slightly, and kissed her in a way that would not have looked out of place in a Cary Grant film. Slow, gentle, and summarising exactly how he felt. He was apprehensive about the personal and professional issue that others may or may not see with his relationship, but because of what she had just said, coupled with his own feelings on what having a father meant, he had been made to feel that he could only be doing good by being there, with no expectations. When their lips parted, he opened his mouth as if to speak, but Sara stopped him. They both knew that he didn't need to say a word. He put his arm around Sara unashamedly, and she reciprocated.

'So, chips tonight then? What's on T.V.? A cup of tea would be nice. Any chance?'

Sara looked up and smiled the smallest of smiles at him warmly. 'Yeah, o.k.' It's only P.G. Tips though.'

'What did you think I drank? The sweat from a maiden's thighs? Jesus Sara. I'm a teacher, not the Sultan of Brunei. P.G. Tips is fine.'

Their laughter, and the sound of Sara calling after her daughter and telling her to slow down and watch the busy road, carried some way across the playing field. Far enough for a tall figure in a denim jacket and faded jeans to hear. Far enough for him to slowly turn purple under his collar, and just far enough for him to make a decision that as soon as possible, that avenue of pleasure was going to be firmly closed off for Sara, and the new man in her life. With a purposeful stride, the long legs began to carry the hulking frame of John Selleck homewards. His head hung low, he began to formulate scenarios in his head. Future scenarios that first involved pain, but then worse fates for the man who clearly didn't know when the time was right to leave another man's things alone. He reached for his mobile, flipped it open, and began to dial.

16

Jim White sat at a plain communal desk and sighed. He lifted his eyes from a stack of papers that adorned the space and rubbed them. He was completely frustrated by the whole series of events that had been transpiring in Bloomfield over the last few weeks. Death, and especially suspicious death, was almost unheard of. Despite being a social and cultural boiling pot, what some might say was an accurate reflection of the United Kingdom as a whole, Bloomfield was almost devoid of serious crime. Jim was quite proud of that fact, as it gave him a sense of himself as a protector, a super-hero with the power to deflect violence and mayhem to other places more deserving of it. Despite feeling so smug about his part in the lack of serious violent misdemeanour, his annoyance was steadfast; and the cause was lying in front of him. He, like his idol Columbo, had a hunch. Usually, when the man in the Macintosh had a hunch, he was seldom proved incorrect. Jim was seemingly no different. On the rare occasion when his minor-league investigative skills had been called upon, he had tended to be right on the money with his feelings, intuition and outcomes. On this occasion, his hunch was relating to something a little more sinister than a lying publican who had been serving drinks to underage children, or a drunken husband trying to avoid prosecution for disturbing the peace. This was murder. Well, in his eyes anyway. The recent spate of sudden deaths in the town had been completely out of character for the place and its occupants, and although the potential was there, things rarely spilled over into anything more serious than the occasional street brawl.

Jim redirected his gaze back to the pictures and paperwork related to the two recent deaths. The first, the poor Asian woman mugged (although there was no proof of anything ever being stolen) and beaten to death. Jim did not know this Reena Singh personally, but if his experience of most other Asian families was correct, he could well imagine her down to a tee. Family orientated, polite, hard-working, intelligent. The photographs taken at the crime scene showed her in a different light. Victim, weak, defenceless, amongst other labels, sprang to mind. Here was a woman who had not only died suddenly, but without the dignity that was, to Jim, everyone's right in death, irrespective of the life they had led to that point.

The other set of photographs showed a fifty-two year old man, of African descent, who had again died suddenly, and equally as painfully as the previous subject of the photo shoot adorning his desk. Saul Omoku had left behind a wife, two children, and a charred black circle where his remains had been scraped from his drive. Until the forensic evidence was returned, it would have to remain as his own speculation that petrol was the accelerant in his demise. There was not much to distinguish him as the family man who resided at the address written down on the stark, white piece of paper in front of Jim. Dental records and jewellery were the giveaways, although some of the lighter pieces of gold and silver had melted into his skin due to the intense heat created by the fire and could not be removed. The rest would be examined, of course, but Jim did not hold out much hope that any additional evidence would be forthcoming from the reports returned on the jewellery, apart from the chemical makeup and possibly their place of origin if any hallmarks were left to identify the pieces with. He would never be able to explain why, but Jim prayed quietly to whomever that they were not from Argos. It was another dignity thing.

Jim looked over his shoulder; he was, technically, not allowed to view these files as he was not CID and had been involved only in a very superficial way, being assigned to protect the crime scene while interviews and forensic checks were being carried out. He was strangely drawn to dig a little further though. Partly out of a morbid curiosity due to the otherwise mundane existence he led on a daily basis. But also due to the fact that in his heart of hearts, he felt that in a community as small and incestuous as Bloomfield, it was a strong possibility that the two crimes were connected. Jim looked at any similarities between the two crimes. Firstly, no witnesses. Both crimes had been committed in relatively deserted conditions, while all neighbours, pedestrians and other potential witnesses were too busy trying not to be noticed. Secondly, neither of the victims were white. He filed that one away to be brought out at a later date. Racism was a very strong motivator in many cases of violence, usually carried out by perpetrators whose own experiences in life had never taken them further away from home than the local post office. Thirdly, neither of the deaths were made to look like accidents of any kind. They were plainly and simply results of extremely violent and aggressive attacks. We could, he mused, be looking at one killer. Alternatively, we could be looking at two or more killers, united by a common reason for wanting to carry out the attacks. There was a third option to Jim, that the deaths may actually be totally unconnected, and that they could even be the work of a psychopath who doesn't need an excuse like racism. He didn't dwell on that for too long though. There was not enough evidence either way to make him discount options one and two, and in his experience there was usually motive. He rubbed his eyebrow absentmindedly, and stared out of the window at a grey lifeless sky while he turned these thoughts over in his head. The silence enveloped him, wrapping him in its cocoon warmth while he tried to look at any minute detail that might help shed some light on proceedings.

He jumped, and laughed loudly when the telephone split the noise vacuum with its old-fashioned twitter. The Trimphone was the eighties' way of saying that technology was the key to the future, epitomised by its shape and distinctive tone. He liked to answer calls after one ring only, as a sign that he was alert and ever ready. He just made it in time, and the voice on the other end of the line made him sit up instantly.

It was Jessica Quinn, the senior forensic pathologist. Jim was a modest man; he cared very little for networking and the antiquated systems which often saw lesser policemen and women elevated above his rank far more quickly than others. He went about his work, and devoted much attention to the one element that he felt was far more important than being merely a presence. He interacted with people. He spoke, laughed, and sometimes cried with everyone he was sworn to protect. He did it not for recognition, but for the sole reason that he felt it mattered. Therefore, it completely passed him by that he had some powerful friends. He believed in the adage that 'Nice things happen to nice people.' What he didn't ever bargain on, though, was the fact that other nice people had very long memories, and that meant favours when he needed them. Jessica Quinn was more than willing to repay Jim. Old school friends (and once lovers in his pre-married days), they had remained close from the moment they left for university together, through their brief relationship, and then into their own married lives. Sharing regular family outings, trips, barbecues and dinners, they were the very best of friends, even more surprising when they had been physically close as well in the past. It also helped that Jim had caught a burglar who had stolen a priceless silver locket that had once belonged to Jessica's Mother, after she had reported it stolen. Jessica was clearly a star in her own field, and although she would never mention it, she knew that her name was being brandished around for bigger and better things in the not too distant future. Until then, though, she had sworn to herself to remain dedicated to her science. She spoke first.

'Jim, it's Jess. How's it going down there?'

Jim looked around to check whether he could speak freely. 'You know, Jess. Same barrel of treacle to wade through. What can I do for you?'

'Listen, Jimmy boy. My guess is you've got one eye on the two killings that have taken place. One, Black African male, the other Asian female. Am I right?'

'You know me too well Jess. CID are keeping a very tight lid on things here. It was everything I could do to even get a peek at the photos. It's terrible though. Poor buggers. I'd love to get my hands on whoever committed these terrible crimes. I'd give them a bit of Jim White justice, I can tell you.'

Jessica's tone quietened, as if she was trying to talk with someone else present. The reality, however, was that she was more frightened about anyone hearing that she was about to aid a non-critical player in the investigation in obtaining pertinent information. 'Well,' she whispered in almost seductive tones, 'get yourself down here pronto. I've got something you might want to see. Come later though, after the mortuary is closed. There's something. Only small, but it may be useful to you. And bring chocolate.'

****

When Jim arrived later that evening at the mortuary, he showed his ID at the door and made his way to the sterile, harshly tiled rooms where Jessica did most of her work. Unbeknownst to most people, the forensic pathologist spent most of their life performing post mortem examinations (or autopsies if you were a fan of Quincy M.E.) on people who had died of natural causes. This was usually due to the fact that a treating medical practitioner would not always be available to sign a death certificate for any number of reasons. What most people were also oblivious to was that whilst the principles of pathology were similar in both clinical and forensic pathology, the latter looked more closely towards the end-point of the forensic investigation, which was the judicial process. The highest levels of knowledge and understanding were required not only in forensic pathology, but also cytopathology (dealing with diseases on a cellular level), neurobiology (study of cells of the nervous system), and microbiology (study of unicellular micro-organisms). Coupled with legal knowledge and ability to communicate to a massive range of agencies when performing their duties, they were an extremely marketable commodity, and held in very high regard by all who needed their services.

Jessica Quinn was no exception, and was in fact regarded as one of the most thorough in her field. Her ability to juggle the demands of the role, a young family, whilst still remaining extremely amiable, was often the wonder of her superiors, and was also the main reason why she it was thought she would make the coroner's post her own very soon, and then continue on her journey upwards, to wherever that might be. A keen sportswoman, her athletic curves made men want her, and women jealous of her, however this was not of concern to her. She loved her work; it was her driving force along with her family. And as Jim entered, he noticed the spark in her eyes which was purely down to her belief in herself, medical science and whatever she was about to reveal to him.

They kissed as old friends would, and then got down to business. Jessica initiated the conversation in as clinical a fashion as befitted her role.

'Jim, talk to me. What are you thinking?'

'Well,' he said, breaking off a piece of seventy percent free trade chocolate and popping it in his mouth, 'I've been thinking. I've been thinking that maybe something wasn't right about all this. I'm presuming that we're off the record here so I don't mind telling you, I think that maybe the murders are connected. They're both from different countries, they were both from respectable families with no dodgy connections as far as I'm aware, and they were both subjected to horrific methods in terms of departure. It's pretty thin at the moment, but I feel that this isn't over yet. This is Bloomfield, for god's sake. I know we're the global village and susceptible to the same idiots as anywhere else, but we've been protected by this invisible bubble for so long.' He sighed, and cleared his throat of the smell of formaldehyde and chocolate that was beginning to stick in his throat. 'Maybe I'm too naïve. Maybe I need to wake up and smell the coffee.'

Jessica came back quickly with her response. 'You're a good policeman, Jim. Everyone knows that. Don't beat yourself up about it. Arseholes are arseholes wherever they are. They're usually born and just grow bigger each day, until they do exactly what society is expecting from them.' Bloomfield is quaint, I'll grant you that. Hell, that's why we live here, to be protected from the real world. But occasionally, Jim, some of the real world gets through, and then it's down to people like you and me to stop them if we can. Which brings me to these murders. I'll tell you straight that there is no DNA evidence here. Circumstances were either not conducive to traces being left, or the murdering bastards were too careful. But there is something that leads me to believe that whoever did this may have wanted to have sent a message out to the masses. Come with me.'

'Let me guess. This is where you show me a corpse, right?'

'Right.' She smiled. She knew it was not the first time he had seen a dead body, but the range of reactions to observing death in its rawest form was wide. Laughter, sickness, even diarrhoea, she had seen them all. She figured he would be all right though if he had tried to lighten the mood a little.

They walked together to the cold storage facility, where bodies of the deceased were kept for their examination until they were released for burial, cremation, or whatever religion or personal request dictated. Stopping outside one of the horizontal, aluminium faced coolers, she looked at Jim as if to check again that he was okay with what was going to happen next. He nodded silently, and then braced himself. Jessica opened the door, and slid out the shelf on which Saul Omoku's body lay. There was no body bag; this had been dispensed with at the earliest opportunity. A sterile sheet adorned the shell of the person formerly known as father and husband, and this was pulled back. Jim was a tough guy, but even he blanched when faced with the sight of the blackened, charred corpse, teeth bared in defiance of the grim reaper due to the absence of lips, and burnt beyond recognition to anyone. Through the charred flesh, Jim could make out the Y incision, through which organs and stomach contents would have been examined. Jim shock was suddenly replaced with sadness, and he shook his head slowly, trying to imagine what would motivate someone to perform such an act.

'You were saying something about something unusual you'd come across?' He offered to Jessica.

'Hmm. Listen, Jim. The signs are obvious here that this guy's been burnt to a crisp. But I want you to look at this. She took a pair of tweezers, and prized Elijah's eye open at a point where there had clearly been an incision made horizontally.

'Your handiwork?' Jim enquired.

'Yep. The eyes were fused together in the heat. You won't believe how the body changes in these circumstances, apart from in the obvious ways. A normal examination is sometimes not always possible due to the effects of fire. Not so this time though. We were quite lucky here. His face, although subjected to third degree burns, was caked in mud as he fell forward. This instantly cooled the flesh in his face, and that meant that the eyes were saved underneath. Tell me what you see.' She held the lid open, and Jim looked closer. There was nothing that he could see that told him anything. Jessica sensed that she needed to augment the explanation for Jim.

'Look at my eyes first. Then look back. It's not difficult to spot, Jim.'

'He did as he was told. There was something staring back lifelessly at him, come to think of it. He hadn't spotted it earlier, as he didn't have anything to compare it to. But there it was.

'Bloodshot. Those eyes looked bloodshot. Mind you Jess, you don't have to be a bloody genius to see that this was probably quite stressful for poor Saul here. Dry air to the extreme was the cause of this?'

'You're good, Jim, but there are many other causes of bloodshot eyes. You might know this, but it's due to blood vessels being dilated near to the surface. The thing is though, notice the patches? Not uniform spread, is it? It's more like little patches of blood that have collected. Want to know what happened?'

'I'm all ears Jess. Fire away.' Jim sat on a nearby stool with one eye on Jessica and one on the corpse. He didn't know why, but he couldn't keep his eyes off the charred remains. It was as if they were a reminder to him about the person that used to reside in the body.

Jess sat herself, and began her recount of events as lightly as if she were telling a child's story. 'I thought at first that this was going to be pretty straight forward, even if it did exactly what it said on the tin. Man gets attacked, roughed up a little, petrol goes on, man lights up. However, when I uncovered the eyes they led me to believe that something different was afoot. I know people are constantly banging on about how resilient the human body is, and how we are forever seeing or hearing stories about human survival. Cliff Richard is living proof of that one.' They laughed together, and this lightened the mood. 'The reality is, though, that it doesn't take much to kill a man. You've just got to know how to do it right.'

'What are you saying Jess? What do you mean by 'do it right'?'

'If you were going to make sure that you killed someone, how would you make absolutely sure that you did the job? If no-one was ever going to know it was you?' She waited for an answer. She wanted to hear this.

'I don't know. Probably slice jugular or carotid artery I guess. I'm no killer though.'

'I know you're not, Jim. But believe it or not, you're not far off. In layman's terms, even in the lovely specimens with the largest percentage of body fat, both of the blood carrying vessels you mentioned are only around a quarter of an inch under the skin. It's not hard to damage them really. Anyway, I digress. You've seen what Saul's eyes looked like, Jim. But it wasn't dry air that caused those marks. I peeled back his eyelids and there were additional red marks under his eyelids. The fire had been hot enough to seal his eyes shut, but when he toppled over the mud had cooled his face sufficiently to ensure that the underside of his eyelids didn't burn. His own skin performed very well in exercising its duty to protect the organs. His skin and flesh, although messy, had preserved his eyes underneath. I'm sure he would have been blinded anyway, but there were round, smooth marks visible. They're called petechiae, Jim. Consistent with pressure on the jugular. Enough pressure to induce unconsciousness and brain death. It only takes just over four pounds of pressure to be sustained for ten seconds to induce blackout. These petechiae aren't visible when the carotid is occluded though.'

'Occluded?'

'Completely closed. Sorry. After four minutes of that, he would have been brain dead.'

'Were there any other signs?' Jim probed. He sat as if carved in stone. This was astonishing news.

'Yes, there were. Once I had spotted the petechiae and the subjunctive haemorrhage in the eyes, I decided to take this line further. The thyroid cartilage was damaged, indicating some sort of pressure hold, such as the sleeper hold favoured by the military or something similar like a reverse headlock. Also, what was left of his tongue was badly swollen, which is also a sure sign.'

Jim looked absent for a fraction of a second, as if trying hard to digest this information slowly and methodically. 'So what you're saying, Jess, is that....'

She stared him down. 'What I'm saying is that Saul here was definitely strangled before he was set on fire. He was dead before he burned. The burning was, possibly, a sign to someone. But they knew they were going to kill him. Nobody keeps someone in a sleeper hold long enough to cause brain death if they want their victim unconscious. Jim, whoever did this definitely knew what they were doing. And what's worse, they wanted everyone to know that they had killed this man.'

17

John Selleck's considerable frame swayed as the train side-stepped from one track to another on its pre-determined path. As it did so, he wondered whether the people on board the train realized that their own lives were maybe as pre-determined as the method of travel they had chosen. In fact, he believed his own life mirrored a train journey almost identically in parts. Firstly, a product of someone else; he was certainly that. His father's influence on his development had been considerable, and although he fully realized that he had not been subjected to the same developmental influences as many of his young friends at the most crucial times, he was in some ways happy that his father had treated him the way he did. He rubbed his arms, remembering the spots his paternal role-model used to favour in his more violent moods. Through his black leather jacket he felt hardness, scar tissue from one of the more memorable times when he was forced to shelter himself from the brief onslaught of belt buckle, fist, or whatever came to hand. He remembered the words thrown at him, in particular the reinforcement that any physical conditioning from his father would only serve to make him tough, and able to defend himself. He diverted his stream of consciousness back to his previous comparison before the deluge of memories forced its way to the front.

Secondly, the pathways were very clearly mapped out for both the train and himself. To veer from the path would be certain disaster for the train and its passengers. That struck a chord with him too. He knew his destiny was to send the unwelcome home, in any condition that suited them. This was a path he was only too happy to traverse, and he took comfort in the fact that there were now many who had been willing to join him in exercising his grand schemes. He chuckled at their weakness. They may have disagreed with some or more of his principles, but give a collective a catchy name and a clandestine meeting place, and you could get them to jump off a cliff if necessary. They were most definitely his followers, and he was the leader.

The train juddered to a halt, just outside the Oxford Circus Tube station in central London. The subterranean train system weaved its way I and out of daylight, depending on the station being travelled to, and Selleck looked at his own reflection in the window, augmented and slightly distorted by the shape of the window and the darkness outside. He looked at the tired eyes, and his relative height to those around him in their seats. Nobody was looking out of the window, and this was an ideal opportunity for him to scan his fellow travellers without drawing unnecessary attention to himself. The mix of people and backgrounds around him was staggering. He physically winced at the sight of the foreign contingent, as if stung in pain by their very existence. This changed to an almost unnoticeable smile, as he remembered his destination and purpose for the visit, and how his actions over the next few days would be on the lips of these people for some considerable time afterwards.

Exiting the tube station via the labyrinthine tunnels and escalators, he emerged into the light and immediately felt the tension rising as he was surrounded by the smells, sights and sounds of seven and a half million people jostling for their own piece of private space. He realized in an instant that although he would enjoy the anonymity of a city this size, the daily routine and lab-rat existence would soon become tiresome. He made his way through the crowds of ticket sellers and tourists, onto the central island, where the statue of Eros, the Greek god of love, watched over the throng in cherubic poise. Selleck looked at the two-pound map he had purchased at the station. It was a short walk through the streets from here, and when he had his bearings, he began the trudge through the greyness of the day towards his destination. Ignoring the cars and buses that were pulling away at the pedestrian crossing, he shuffled across the road onto

Oxford Street, and onwards in the general direction of Soho Square. He had travelled into London many times, and despite his distaste for the crowds and cosmopolitan feel, he did relish the opportunity to pound the streets. He very rarely took his car anywhere, preferring to walk. Another remnant of his upbringing, with his family having barely enough money to put food on the table, let alone afford such extravagances as a car.

Selleck's arrival at his destination awoke him from a sobering thought. He realized that he had been walking for about forty five minutes, and he had completely tuned out of his surroundings. He noticed that in that short space of time, he had inadvertently become as comatose as the slaves to society surrounding him. He had been assimilated into the flowing masses, with all oblivious to each other's purpose and feelings. The city may indeed have a pulse, he considered, but it would have been more apt to have had Lethe, the river of forgetfulness in Hades running through it than the Thames, its lifeless counterpart in this particular hell.

What stood before him was a café. Nothing special, just a few square metres of bolted-down tables, alarmingly strong tea and fried food. The clientele were remarkably varied. Small groups of painters, plasterers, bricklayers, all laughing and sharing jokes about the weekend's football; a barrister with his silk tie and gown still adorning his shoulders; students enjoying another afternoon of subsidised beer followed by a cheap meal; and nigh-invisible civil servants, snatching a quick break before climbing back onto the giant hamster wheel which they helped to turn on a daily basis. Selleck checked his watch. Twelve fifty-five. He smiled. Perfect timing. He climbed the two worn steps and entered the café.

His instructions were very clear as to how the meeting was going to work. The excitement of what he was about to do almost overflowed, and he forced himself to follow his instructions to the very letter, in order that he would not jeopardise anything.

This had taken a very long time to arrange through a variety of contacts that he had, and he was not going to see his hard work torn to shreds by a stupid mistake now. He checked his props. Newspaper under his arm, check. Wristwatch on his right hand, check. And New York Yankees baseball cap on his head turned backwards, check. He felt the last one was definitely a test of resolve as well as anything else, as the only possible reason for that being requested was to make him look silly.

'Cup of tea, milk and sugar.' He ordered the waitress behind the counter flatly.

'Right you are, love. Where you sitting? Over there?'

Selleck nodded and moved to the table in the very corner of the café, adjacent to the kitchen door. It was a busy time of day, and he realized that this was deliberate. Busy place, therefore no ability to cause a scene if anything went wrong. He ordered a bacon sandwich, as directed, and when it arrived, opened it up and sprayed it with ketchup. Selleck looked round. He suddenly realized that if this was part of the plan to recognise him, his acquaintance would have to be here in person. His heart quickened, and he looked downwards, not wanting to seem too eager. He bit into his sandwich, mildly surprised at how tasty it was. His tea arrived shortly after his sandwich, plonked with apparent disdain on the table, though not by the waitress. The hand which almost completely enveloped the cup was even bigger than his own, and covered in black hair. Selleck looked up when the hand did not remove itself from the cup. The eyes that greeted him were lifeless, cold, and seemed to pierce his skin.

'Come.' A raspy voice whispered. It was uttered by a man in a filthy apron, drenched in sweat and whose hair hung limply over what appeared to be Mediterranean eyebrows which had reached the end of their travels and met in the middle of his face. The uni-brow accentuated the dour complexion, and Selleck did not speak. He stood, and followed the shadowy figure down a narrow corridor, past the toilets and into what seemed to be the café's storeroom. He was still holding the mug of steaming tea, and realizing his mistake, he motioned to return to the table.

'No. Bring tea.' Came the grating voice again. Selleck nodded and walked on. Despite his status in his own home environment, and despite his ability to look after himself, he felt scared. This was real, and he felt adrenaline surge through his veins, not just because of the purpose of this meeting, but because of the potential repercussions on him if he did not meet the seemingly high standards of his new temporary business partner.

He was led through the dark store room, right to the far recesses of the building, where a dead end beckoned. Selleck looked around, and realized there was truly no way out apart from the way in which he had entered. He looked at his tour guide, who smiled, revealing a set of rotten teeth, blackened by years of smoking filterless cigarettes and drinking over-proofed vodka.

'Stay. Wait here.' The voice cut the damp air like a machete.

'Okay. Where will I go? Is this where I'll meet…….'

'Look up. Don't worry. Meeting soon.' The man turned without another word, and made his way back to the café area, to resume whatever duties he had. Slaughtering live animals, by the look of his garb, thought Selleck.

Selleck looked above his head, and noticed the smallest of security cameras eyeing him suspiciously, a lone red light blinking slowly above the lens. Selleck had not noticed the camera, and wondered whether his images were being recorded. He was uneasy with this, and determined to ask his associate should the opportunity arise. As he stood, the sound of bolts being drawn back suddenly became audible through the floor next to him. Whilst looking up and from side to side to see where he might possibly be led next, he had not thought to look downwards. The noises stopped, and the darkness of the room was carved in two by a bright white light, which had excised itself from behind a trapdoor in the floor. It was a seamless join, and Selleck would never have found the door in a million years. Whoever had built this was desperate not to be discovered. Selleck thought again of what he was doing, and immediately understood why. The door opened fully, and when his eyes had adjusted, he noticed the wooden staircase leading downwards in to the light. A shadow painted the floor, and a voice seemed to drift through the air and up through the open hatch.

'Mr. Selleck? Please, don't waste time. Come down the hatch. You wish to see me? Please. I'm a very busy man.'

'Er…yes. Sorry. I didn't mean to keep you waiting.' Selleck's unnatural politeness betrayed his usual demeanour. Moving down the staircase, he entered the space below. A lone white corridor stretched before him, with a single door at the end. Blocking the path was a man who could only be described as a man-mountain. Standing at six feet five inches, and with shoulders which dwarfed Selleck's own, he almost blocked the sight of the far doorway. Grey hair cascaded down over the gargantuan shoulders, threatening to spill further should the man move. But it was the eyes that drew Selleck to his face. They were of the most piercing shade of blue that he had ever seen. Cobalt in colour, they gazed at Selleck without faltering. Selleck broke the stare first and looked away briefly. He waited in deference to the man before him. He was relieved when he was spoken to once more.

'You are Selleck.' A statement, not a question.

'Yes.'

'Good. I am Pitov. Alexander Pitov. You wish to make a purchase. Come through. I will give you the details and we can talk further.' He turned, and walked to the subterranean doorway at the end of the white corridor. Selleck followed. As he walked,

103

the trapdoor closed with an almost silent whisper, entombing the pair of them under the busy streets of London, for as long as it was going to take.

18

'Please, Mr. Selleck, sit down. Would you like some more tea? Maybe something stronger? You look like you might need it.' A smile forced outwards from thin lips. This time though, the teeth were white, and perfect. Here was a smile that had been paid for handsomely.

'That would be fine. Whatever you have going would be great.'

'Vodka, Mr. Selleck. Okay?'

'Okay.' He felt it wasn't an option. Two glasses were taken out from behind a mahogany desk, followed by a bottle of vodka, its lack of label indicating that it was the real stuff, not the commercial rubbish that was sold over the counter in the United Kingdom. Selleck took the opportunity to look around while his drink was poured. The room was almost bare, apart from two cupboards in the corner (each protected with digital locks), a larger than average safe, also with a digital keypad adorning the front, and a lone workbench in the corner. The mahogany desk seemed an anachronism, as if left by the previous owners of this room and too big to be taken apart. The giant blotter was well used, and Selleck wondered what type of communication was coming out from here that warranted such use of the blotter. He took the offered glass. Pitov raised his glass. 'Salut.' He downed it, and looked at Selleck to do the same. Not wanting to offend Pitov, he did so. He was determined not to cough, and fought the urge as the heat flowed through his chest and into his stomach, creating a slowly spreading glow. 'Cheers.'

Pitov looked calmly at Selleck, and evaluated him from across the desk. Anyone who knew of him was probably well connected, therefore he should not be underestimated. Probably someone who could clearly handle himself, so he mentally made a note that his Beretta 9mm pistol was available in the top drawer, should anything start. He knew, though, that he was in the stronger position. All comers needed his services, and were usually only too willing to pay any price asked. He smiled, and began discussions. 'How did you hear of me, Mr. Selleck? Dimitriy, whom you were guided by to here, tells me that he has checked on you, and you are a bit of an enigma. You are not Mafia, and you do not have any Mafia connections. You do not have any police connections, so you are not a threat that way. Believe me, if I thought you were, you would have been in the Thames by now. You are of no consequence around here. So, if you please, where did you learn of my services?'

It was a long time since Selleck had been threatened. On this occasion, though, he had no doubts that to protest in any way would end the meeting, and possible worse, his run of good health. 'I have many connections in London, due to favours that I have done in the past for others. I heard of you through an associate of mine named Michaels. He once made a purchase from you also, around two years ago. He said that your work was very professional.'

Pitov narrowed his eyes, and thought about the name mentioned. He recognized it, and connected the purchase to the name. This seemed to be enough for him, and he smiled. 'Very good, I remember. I was particularly proud of that one. Michaels was a good customer. Paid immediately. I like that. Will you do the same?'

'Of course. Name your price.' Selleck was not going to blow this. He'd do whatever it took. It was new territory for him and he was prepared to play by the rules of the game, however one-sided.

'Let me tell you something about me, Mr. Selleck. I, too, am very well connected, and very powerful in my own way. I have made a tidy living in this country since the collapse of my own, and the U.S.S.R. unfortunately were not able to pay my kind of prices on a regular enough basis to persuade me to remain there. There is too much confusion there these days, with the balance of power shifting almost daily from the Mafia, to the government, and then back again. This will go on indefinitely, and it unfortunately means that there is no home for me there until this issue is resolved. However, there are many like myself who use their previous military backgrounds to good use, and fortunately for me, there will always be people like you who rely on my skills to get what you want. And even though you may or may not feel my price a little excessive, I have no doubt that you will be happy with the product.'

'I'm sure I will.' Echoed Selleck. He was sweating profusely, and needed to move things along. 'So, what is your price?'

He did not answer immediately. He put his fingertips together and touched his lips. 'Firstly, let me show you my handiwork. You may, of course, feel that my services are not exactly what you are looking for. That would, of course, be a shame. We would have to decide where to go next if that were the case.' He smiled again. Selleck did not have to think too hard about the fact that he was being told that he had come this far and was now obligated to proceed.

'Of course. Be my guest.' Selleck offered courteously.

'Da. Let me see. Ah, I know....' He moved from his desk in a fluid movement and arrived at the locked cupboard in two strides. With hands which were capable of immense strength, yet also delicate manipulation of the smallest items of machinery, he tapped in the code to the digital key pad, whilst out of habit covering the numbers with his other hand. A single beep sounded, and he opened the metal door with a clang as it banged against the adjacent cupboard. Reaching high onto the top shelf, he brought out a metal briefcase, and returned to the table, placing it very gently on the blotter. No thicker than a laptop case, it gleamed in the ambient light of the room, as if powered by its own energy source. This was, of course, going to be the case inside, but not outside.

Sitting back down, Pitov entered another digital code into a keypad next to the handle, and both clasps popped open. He turned the briefcase around, and motioned with his hand for Selleck to open it. Selleck obliged, and his heart rate quickened to almost threatening proportions when he saw the contents. It was just as he imagined. No, better than he had imagined; the stuff of his recent dreams was about to become reality. He suddenly felt the large amount of money he had brought with him begin to metaphorically burn through the satchel it was carried in, and he eyed his prize carefully. Densely packed into the briefcase were two cuboids of C-4 explosive, around the size of a tissue box apiece. He could see miniature protrusions just under the surface of the explosive. Ball bearings. My god. This was a bomb capable of some serious damage. Selleck had done his fair share of homework on explosives, but this was way beyond his idea of a bomb. His efforts at best would have been very crude, and he realized that if he wanted the best, he was going to have to pay for it. It was an extremely complex piece of machinery. Three sets of wires led from the control console, yet only two were visibly going into the explosive as far as he could see.

'Why three sets of wires and only two entering the explosive?' He enquired.

'You are very astute. One is redundant. Should it be recovered, anyone wanting to manually diffuse this bomb will have their work cut out. Should they have enough time to release the control panel from its mounts, the road to the explosive is complex. Also, an additional failsafe facility is built into the bomb which will detonate it if the circuits are not cut in the right order. It can, of course, be armed and disarmed remotely via this remote control device. It is effective within a radius of around five hundred metres.' He looked squarely at Selleck, and waited for a response.'

'Amazing, Mr. Petrov. Absolutely amazing. What will the effects be?'

'With this particular type of explosive, a shockwave which will take out anything within one hundred and fifty metres, vaporising anything at ground zero. As far as incendiary effect goes, there will be a considerable amount of heat. Enough to annihilate anything within roughly a hundred metres. This can be changed according to your wishes, of course.'

Selleck thought about the upcoming Festival of World Culture to be held in Bloomfield at the weekend. There would be thousands of people at the Arena, the open show ground that was widely used by many organisations. The festival had been arranged by partner councils, and long, drawn-out meetings had ensured that maximum exposure was given to publicising the event. In promoting racial harmony and peace, Selleck thought, they were setting themselves up for a horror so vile that ripples would travel far. Maybe far enough for all foreign nationals to be denied entry to his beloved country.

'I want this one. This will do just fine. How much is it?'

'It's not as easy as that, my friend. Firstly, the price will be twenty thousand pounds. Materials and labour are included in this price. I do not want to know your motives, and I do not care. However, I must tell you that your price also buys you the guarantee that should my name, location or involvement in this escapade of yours become apparent, you will be contacted, and asked to answer some very difficult questions. I am yet to find anyone who has managed to answer all of the questions I am capable of asking. I am sure you understand the situation.' Selleck nodded. He understood the implications. He would not survive any interrogation.

'Also,' Petrov continued, 'the device has been built from scratch. I make a habit of constructing all of my devices in completely sterile environments. That way, all risk of detection by sniffer dogs and other detection devices is minimised to the full. I want you to get the most for your money, Mr. Selleck. Now, if you understand and agree to this, we will part here, and you will leave me the money as a gesture of goodwill. I assure you, my word is my bond.'

Selleck's brow deepened. Would there be time enough to both pick up the device and plant it? 'What about timing? I need it by next weekend.'

Petrov curled his cheeks into something resembling a smile. 'Today is Tuesday, and you need it a week on Saturday. Okay. I will do this for you, despite needing longer usually. I will complete the task and fulfil my end of the bargain. Now, the money if you please.' He sat back and waited for Selleck to move. He did not have to wait long. Selleck reached up, and swivelled his satchel around to the front of his body. He had worn it on his back like a school child during the course of the whole conversation. He undid the front flap, and slowly moved his hand inside. Petrov's eyes opened wider, as if realizing that he had made a mistake. His guard was down momentarily, and if Selleck had a gun, he could dispose of him as quickly as he liked. What materialised, however, was a pristine envelope, bulging slightly from its contents within. Selleck opened it, and poured out a stack of notes, neatly arranged into bundles of five thousand apiece. Gleaned from sales of various goods on the black market (mostly innocuous goods such as DVD players, CD players and the such like), this was relatively small change to Selleck. He was probably worth twenty times that much in stock he held, acquired from places frowned upon by the usual consumer. He counted out four bundles and slid them across the desk. Petrov did not move. As if by telepathy, the door opened and Dimitriy entered slowly. Picking up the bundles from the desk, he retired, leaving the meeting to conclude.

'Now, Mr. Selleck. You or a named associate will return here on Saturday Morning. Nine Sharp should be fine. I hope this will give you time enough to do what you need to do.'

'Many thanks, Mr. Petrov. I'll see you on Saturday then. Would you like to count the money before I go?'

'My dear friend,' he cut in, smiling, 'I trust you. Besides, if you were one English Pound out, you would be talking to Dimitriy right now.' He stood, to indicate that the meeting was over. As Selleck took his cue, and opened the door, Petrov called him back briefly.

'Mr. Selleck.'

'Yes?'

'Please remember, I am merely a supplier of goods. I do not buy into any religion, or become emotionally involved in causes. I am a ghost to you. Do you understand? If you do not, there may be a case like the one you have purchased waiting somewhere nice for you.' This drew Selleck's gaze to the table, where he stared for fractionally too long at the bomb.

'I understand.'

'Good. Dimitriy will show you the exit. Travel safely.'

Selleck made his way up the steps, and into the storeroom. The darkness made him blink briefly to adjust his eyes, and then he navigated his way through the boxes and cartons, out through the bustle of the café and into the street. There were no pleasantries from Dimitriy; just a nod, and he turned his back in an outward display of disdain for the desperate purchaser. Selleck began to walk, but he couldn't feel the floor beneath his feet. It was as if he was gliding ethereally over the pavement, powered by his thoughts on what lay ahead for him. Later, as he sat on the train and as the world passed him by like missed opportunities, he pictured in his mind the devastating impact that his act would have. Whatever he had done in the past now paled into insignificance; he knew that he had just taken the embodiment of his vision up to the next level.

19

Matt looked up from his desk, and stared at his empty classroom. During the day, the sounds of a school are unlike any other; laughing, crying (usually the teachers receiving their pay slips), and the busy hum of children learning. Even while the teachers were drinking coffee and talking about television they saw last night, or more burlesque topics, the noise was there, outside, permeating everything. Teachers were able at will to immediately tune out of this noise, and Matt prided himself on his ability to do this while the children were still in the room; however, after school, it reminded him of a graveyard. Not because there was any morbidity about the place. It was an uplifting sight, with the children's work and certificates emblazoning the walls in bright colours. Colours which often betrayed the home circumstances of many of the children he taught. If he were celebrating those, he would be the first person to use different shades of black. He remembered walking into the graveyard shortly after his father's death, and realizing that despite the busy traffic outside, how it was unable to penetrate the hedges that surrounded it. How the inhabitants somehow protected the sanctuary of sleep with an invisible shroud, impermeable to everything but the noises of lament. The school was identical to this after normal school hours, with a similar shield protecting it, allowing only the sounds of cleaning to enter, and the occasional scream from a teacher in his cell somewhere.

Matt was busy marking some assessments. Each year, the children from age seven through to eleven sat tests. These results were taken, inwardly digested by staff, and used to inform where future gaps needed to be plugged. *Testing at age seven,* he thought to himself. *As if life at that age wasn't testing enough for some of these children.* He was quite conscientious these days about the paperwork. He had not always spent as much time on such matters. He smiled to himself as he remembered his first few years of teaching, used purely to fuel his social life. He had absolutely no idea that this was a career, and that there was actually a point to it. As his invincibility to alcohol and late nights had worn off slightly, he had gradually devoted more and more time to the role of the teacher, and less to the role of the drunkard, and was now satisfied with the outcome. He knew he was nowhere near the finished article; he felt that anyone who saw themselves as such should give up teaching. There was always a reason to learn in his book, and the humility needed to recognise this fact sometimes missed many of his peers totally. They were the ones who usually ended up leaving early, or being invited to, anyway.

The half-mountain of assessments had worn him out. He needed to switch off, and he rubbed his temple to relieve the tension that was beginning to mount there. He looked at his watch. It was unusual for anyone to remain at school longer that seven o'clock, unless there were functions or meetings they were required to attend, usually with the school's governing body or parents. There were no evening classes tonight at the school, so Matt would be kicked out soon anyway, he realized. He kicked his chair back, and stood up, allowing his limbs to gain some feeling before grabbing his coat and keys and heading out into the Victorian corridor outside. The stone assimilated heat like a sponge soaked water, and despite the central heating in school, the corridors remained cool. Listening to his shoes tapping on the age-old floor tiles, he made his way into the twilight and took a gasp of fresh air into his lungs. The evening was overcast, and a heavy downpour had just finished, having washed away the grime and angst that had previously hung in the air. Matt pulled open the door to the Sunbeam, and forced the engine to give up its slumber in order to take him home. It grudgingly agreed. The ride home was a blur of eighties' music, with the radio DJ droning between tracks about nothing, giving his opinions to listeners who neither cared nor wished for them. The monotonous tone of the engine wearied Greaves, and he opened the window to revive himself. He thought about his tea, and the merits of pizza. That sounded good. He pulled his car into a free space outside the entrance to his flats, and climbed the stairs to his door on the first floor. He stopped at the top of the flight of recently polished steps, and looked down the corridor towards his front door. He knew, even from the acute angle, that the door was open. It had even been deadlocked that morning. Matt put down his briefcase and took off his jacket soundlessly. The tension began to mount in his body, and he forced himself to think coherently. He should, of course, have made his way downstairs and telephoned the police, so that they could possibly catch anyone doing anything untoward in the act. However, the little voice in his head started talking in the most persuasive of ways, telling him in whispers that he needed to punish anyone who had invaded the privacy of his home, which he paid for each month and which was his, and his alone. Ignoring the pleas of reason from the rational part of his persona, he crept forward, his shoes making no sound on the freshly carpeted landing. He made it to the area immediately outside his front door; nothing could be heard from the inside apart from the ticking of the wall clock in the landing. The atmosphere could be cut with a knife. He rephrased that mentally. He did not want to think about anything being cut with a knife. He weighed up the options briefly, One, he could storm the room and rely on surprise to outwit anyone who might be in waiting there. Controlled aggression would be the key to that. He had read that in one of those SAS stories that had begun to be popular some years ago. Two, he could rely on stealth, and creep in keeping a low profile, ready to charge at the sight of an unwelcome guest. There was certainly enough adrenaline flowing through his veins right then to maintain an aggressive outlook. That was for sure. He opted for the first of the two options, ignoring the most sensible third completely. It just wasn't in his nature.

He peered through the door. It was deathly silent. He waited another second or two, then gently pushed open the door an inch. Its creak sliced through the silence like a sword. It seemed to hang in the air, an invisible finger pointing at Matt. *Fuck it,* he thought. He charged into his flat, expecting to be confronted by a hooded menace. When he reached his living room, though, he stopped dead in his tracks and stared around the room, in utter shock and disbelief. He was statuesque; trying to assimilate what was there in front of his eyes, invading his senses completely. It was the smell that shook him into consciousness, back to reality. It was so offensive, that he ran to the kitchen and vomited profusely, expunging the bile from his stomach until nothing remained. He dashed into the living room, and having the sense to cover his hand with his sleeve to not disturb any possible fingerprints, he opened every window in the flat. The cold air from the twilight outside was welcome, and began to dilute the horrific smell. The smell of what could only be human waste. God only knows, he had often felt like running from his own bathroom from that smell. The odour that was staining the air within his living space was overpowered, however, by something else.   The perpetrator of this act had emptied his bowels whilst at the flat; matt could see signs of that in the bathroom. The faeces had then been taken, and smeared on the walls. There, across the wall, in as large a font as could humanly be mustered with the materials available, was the word 'CEASE.' Matt was surprised to find that his first reaction upon reading it was to glean that it was spelt correctly. *I really need to switch off,* he almost said aloud. He tried to make sense of what he was staring at. Someone, either alone or with help, had come into his house, evacuated their bowels, and written this word on his wall. There did not seem to be anything missing, and there were no signs of forced entry, so whoever got in knew what they were doing with locks. It was the motive that was more puzzling than anything else, though. Matt tapped his head with his finger subconsciously. *Think, god damn it, think. If these guys have got the right person, what on earth is it that I'm supposed to have done that they want me to stop doing?* He checked the sofa for any debris, dismissed the likelihood of the visitors having sat on it for a cup of tea, and sat down himself, hoping that inspiration would come to him. He stood up again immediately, his anger turning his face almost crimson with fury and agitation. He thought about the attempted attack on him a short while ago whilst he took a walk in the neighbourhood, and swore to himself that if he caught the arseholes who did this personally (realizing that this was not likely in the least) he would not show as much self-restraint as he had done previously. As he made his way to the kitchen to check it out, he snatched the cordless phone from its cradle. He dialled and asked for the police.

'Emergency services. Please state which service you require.'

'Police, please.' Silence, briefly, then a business-like voice asked for the details. He listened to the instructions, and gave his address. He was told that someone would come around immediately. He left the flat, and stood in the corridor. Just as he had expected, nobody came out onto the landing form any of the adjacent flats to ask if he was all right, or if they could help in any way. He stood, alone, and waited. And as he did, he tried to think of his own acts which could have warranted such a response. There was nothing new in his life that was different from his established modus operandi. In fact, if it wasn't for the fact that he had started seeing Sara......... He tilted his head to the side, processing that last fleeting thought. Sara. She was new. Could she be the key to this act? Thoughts cascaded through his mind like water through a sieve. Was she with someone else and not telling? If so, she surely gave no sign. Maybe she was good at hiding things from others. He was. He shook his head, dismissing those thoughts immediately. He was a very good judge of character, and she was the only person he had let close to him in a very long time. Her sincerity was the key that had unlocked the door to that Avenue, and he knew he was not misguided.

He was relieved to hear the gravel crunch outside under the weight of the wheels of a car. It was the police, and he raised his eyebrows in surprise at their efficiency. He was not expecting that to be the case, based on his previous knowledge and understanding of how stretched they were. From the car stepped a constable, his grey hair betraying his years. He strode with purpose to the front door, his helmet under his arm, and pushed the doorway to the entrance lobby open.

'Hi. Up here.' Matt called.

'Sure thing. You all right?' The police constable called up as he mounted the flight.

'Yes, okay thank you. Just surprised and really pissed off, if you'll excuse my French.'

'Don't worry,' he replied as he came face to face with Matt 'Je parle Francais. I'm Constable Jim White. Can I take a look? When did you find that someone had come in?' The two men locked eyes, and they made their own immediate evaluations of each other. One as an officer of the law, the other as a victim needing support.

'Just now in fact, no more than about twenty minutes ago. You won't believe what you see though.' Matt motioned in an 'after you' gesture.

'Okay. Try not to touch anything if you can. Our scene of crime people will need to give the place the once over.' He came into the living room. 'Jesus Christ.' Well, if they've got some unusual eating habits, we'll soon find out I guess.'

'I did touch the windows with a covered hand to make sure that I could get some fresh air in here. It stank worse earlier than it does now, and that's saying something.' Matt looked at Jim, wondering what the next move would be.

'There is, of course, a plus to all of this mess, especially the wall, Mr. Greaves.' Jim chipped in with more than a hint of optimism in his voice.

'Really, do tell. Call me Matt by the way.'

'Well, their chosen media has given us quite an edge over them. They seem to have forgotten that in today's day and age, DNA evidence is extremely powerful. I'll give you a point of example.' He looked around the room briefly, and pointed at a stool that was underneath the table in the living room. 'Was this under the table originally?'

'Yeah.'

'Okay.' He pulled it out and sat down on it. Matt sat on the floor against the wall next to him, where there was very little chance that the invaders had settled. 'A while ago, I was called to an incident not far from here, where some burglars had been very creative at night time. Believe it or not, they had drilled out the window from a downstairs lounge while the occupants were asleep. '

'No way.' Greaves was astounded that anyone could get away with it.

Jim chuckled. 'Way. Cheeky buggers. They went through the downstairs office in a flash. Credit cards, the odd bit of cash, bank statements for identity fraud, they took the lot.' The family were devastated. I remember they were saving for a holiday in Florida.' Jim shook his head quickly to bring him back on track with his train of thought. 'Anyway, everyone thought that was that because there were no discernible fingerprints, and there was no other evidence to point the finger at the culprits. Until, that is, someone noticed a cigarette butt underneath a stone in the garden. The scene of crime team took this away, and from around the filter managed to get the DNA profile of a man named Chester Barnett. Shouldn't really tell you his name but there you go.'

Matt piped up immediately. 'But he could argue that he was just walking past and threw the cigarette over the hedge, couldn't he?'

Jim admired Matt's sharpness, and smiled. 'He could, and did. However, it wasn't a coincidence that there were two other butts found at two different houses some miles away, where those families had also been subjected to burglaries on the same night. Now, he's either the master of magic and can walk in three different places at the same time, or he visited those houses in the middle of the night at different times and chuffed away at each one.'

'Wow. You wouldn't think that was possible really, would you?' Matt was genuinely impressed with the story, and he would certainly be regaling that one at the first available opportunity.

'You'll be surprised, my friend, what those guys can come up with. Now, excuse my colourful metaphors here, but if they can catch a man using DNA from a cigarette, surely they can come up with something positive from ten tons of human crap.'

Matt laughed to hear a figure of authority using such language. He imagined how well he would go down in school talking to the children like that. He didn't fancy his odds of further career enhancement should he decide to go down that route.

'So what happens now?' Despite wanting to clean the waste from his walls, he knew that would not be immediately possible.

'Well,' White replied, 'The techno guys will be here shortly, given that human waste is involved. The sooner they get their samples and let you clean up, the better it'll be for everyone. Don't hold your breath for any news immediately, though. There would be quite a quick turnaround if a murder had been committed, but it can sometimes be a few days or more when it's a domestic like this. CID will be informed, and then they'll want to speak to you. At your convenience, of course. Until then, though, I'll take a few details down. Try to be as specific as you can, and that'll help a great deal.'

Matt began recounting the tale of how he found his flat, and once he was done, Jim rose to leave. It was fully dark outside, and there was much work to be done on the place to be sure that he wasn't going to catch anything vile from the waste. Hepatitis,

Toxoplasmosis, and Polio sprang to mind. Greaves sighed. He just wanted them to arrive, do what they had to do, and let him erase any sign of their existence. One thing was for sure, though. If he ever caught any one of the idiots who were responsible for this, he would most certainly let them know who he was. He began to recount his amazing tale of the innocent man who came home to find his walls covered in the most serious warning, without any idea as to who was responsible or as to why they had made such a request.

20

There were two things wrong with Friday nights. One, it led to Saturday and Sunday, which inevitably led to Monday, and for many people, getting back onto the perpetual hamster wheel which provided them with luxuries like taxes, heartburn, traffic jams and the occasional fling at the office Christmas party with Marjorie from Accounts; the other was that as one grew older, the ability of old friendship groups to be able to commit to social activities became more and more diminished, with each passing week. To Nick, this was his own private purgatory. Despite not being disposed to settling down and spending his Friday nights on the sofa watching 'All Star Mr. And Mrs.' Or something equally mind numbing, he envied those who did, because they had the ability to tolerate that sort of lifestyle. He wished he could, but it simply wasn't going to work for him at that particular moment in his life. He often wondered whether he had some sort of attention deficit disorder, which failed to allow him to become rooted to any one person or place for any significant length of time. The reality was, though, he had a picture in his head of the type of girl he wanted to settle down with, and so far they had not visited the Prince Arthur on a Friday night. Not while he was there, anyway.

Nick had decided not to exercise his social muscles that evening, preferring to 'enjoy' his own company at home. Besides, there was something he knew that he needed to do. It was the website that he had stumbled upon whilst trying to solve the whole argument about the eighties' movie title, Red Dawn. He knew for sure that he was correct now, and nobody would deny that. He was looking forward to the next meeting with his brother, and curled the corner of his mouth into a small smile at the thought of what he was going to make them drink. It was the site itself though. When the red icon had flashed up before him, and he had read the words 'Join today, protect tomorrow,' he had gone to bed smiling at a teenager's attempts to revive the BMX bandits. However, when he had fallen into slumber that night, he had been troubled considerably by the cinematic dreams which unfolded before him fleetingly. He saw the same red icon, with the twin hammers crossed in the middle in black. The crimson, however, represented blood in his vision, and the hammers were not static, but were moving, dipping and rising together, relentlessly. It was unclear as his head turned gently from side to side, and as his eyes flickered beneath their closed lids rapidly, who was the recipient of the hammer blows, but when he awoke only a short time later, the darkness was of no comfort to him, and he was left with a foreboding stirring in his stomach, and a need to dig a little deeper into what had now become darkly intriguing subject matter.

He moved over to his laptop. Switching it on, he waited only a few seconds for it to power up, having purchased a model with very high technical specifications. Sleek, and glossy black, the wide screen stared at him waiting to show his every command. In the nineteen eighties and nineties the mobile phone was hailed as the new weapon of mass destruction, where all major deals were forged and the hub around which everyone centred their lives, both personal and working. Now, his time had come. The computer chip was here to stay, and he saw himself as one of the leading pioneers in getting true value for money out of the capacity of the microprocessor. Children had their games, but he had more. The ability to search deeper, faster, and more secretly than anyone else could fathom. Sure, there were maybe a handful of people who had the same, if not better, skills. However, most people did not have the ability to open as many doors as he could. He almost winced at the idea of what Matt would say if he found out that his brother was responsible for hacking into some of the best protected servers in the world, as mere personal favours for friends. He had cleaned driving licences, scrubbed out overdrafts, and had even reduced mortgage payments on several occasions. All for a tidy fee, of course. He was sensible enough to know that simply to break into a bank and create new accounts for himself was suicide. There were too many things that could go wrong. However, there were always people motivated by money who wanted to see their assets grow, or their debt shrink, and he was more than happy to reap the rewards of the fees he charged.

He was not one for saving; he would rather live fast and die young, and so on. However, he was not bothered by this. When the cash was scarce, he simply did another favour, and hey presto, there it was. Instant gratification and spending power. It was an addiction that was difficult to kick. The risks were small for him compared to the rewards, and he was determined to continue, at least for the time being. He did wish that Matt would let him help him too, but he knew in his heart that he was too idealistic, and too straight to gain in any other way than through hard, honest work.

But it was not monetary gain that was on Nick's mind tonight. He was going to take a closer look at the New Dawn site and see if his dreams were substantiated at all. He logged onto the internet, but not until he had set up a pathway through three or four different servers, to make it more difficult for anyone to trace his actions. He employed many tactics and programmes to help him conceal his identity, and this was merely one of them. It was an automatic gesture, and one which was not really needed as he was not doing anything overtly illegal, but he felt he could never be too careful.

Finding the site was easy, as it was still in his history folder, which kept a log of the pages he had visited. When he clicked on the link, he was automatically faced with the password request, which he duly obliged, having written it down after breaking it previously. Once again, the logo covered the screen, showering his face with a crimson blanket momentarily. Not as mesmerised as before, Nick clicked on the logo. He was suitably unimpressed by what happened next.

'Hmmm. Not one for pomp and ceremony, are you mate?' Nick said to himself out loud. There, in front of him, was a plain white screen. At the top of the screen were some numbers. Nick looked at them and pondered for a moment. Nothing else, just numbers, arranged in sections. Nick looked at them harder, as if staring without even blinking would make them give away their meaning. They defiantly stared at him, unblinking also.

0-340-79631-6

Underneath, the many rows of numbers were arranged slightly differently.

65,12,8

Nick thought they could have been coordinates, but usually they only represented horizontal and vertical axes. No, these were different. They were something else. There was something that had niggled Nick as soon as he had seen them, a question which compounded his worries about his previous dream after being introduced to this conundrum of a website. Judging by the simplicity of the layout of this site, it was most likely only serving one purpose. And probably a simple one. It was a code. And it had been posted on a bulletin board for the users to retrieve at their leisure, away from prying eyes and without fear of anyone decoding what was being written down. This was not definite, of course, but he had seen bulletin boards before in many guises, and the creators often used codes to keep their usefulness for only those who really needed to see them.

Nick was sure of one thing. Off the top of his head, there was absolutely no way that he was going to know what these numbers were. But there might be someone who might. Or rather, *something*. He went to one of his drawers and pulled out a plain looking CD with the letters 'NRS' written on the case in waterproof marker. He opened the CD drive, and placed the disc inside. Closing the drawer, the laptop took a few seconds to recognise that there was a disc present, and the auto run feature started. N.R.S. actually stood for Numerical Recognition System, and when Nick was doing favours for his friends, he often came across numerical obstacles such as account numbers, coded messages, and the such-like. This piece of software was designed to cross-reference a given series of numbers against a vast database, thus making recognition of its origin much easier. It had come in very handy in the past. He would never divulge where he had obtained this database and software from, however he knew he would be answering some pretty difficult questions if the fact that it was in his possession ever became known. Nick loved that though; the feeling that he was sailing close to the wind gave him a real adrenaline rush, and he felt alive even thinking about the possible consequences of many of his actions.

He entered the series of numbers into the required field, and started the program off on its mission. Sometimes the results were instantaneous; sometimes they took a little longer. There was no quick answer this time. Nick watched his progress meter (a red bar increasing in length) become longer as the minutes went by. He soon became bored, and, scraping a palm across his stubbled chin, turned his attentions to a particularly irritating fly which had become trapped in between the window and his Venetian blinds. Slipping his fingers through the slatted wooden bars which had acted as a barrier from the outside world on many occasions, he deftly flicked the latch to the window. Automatically, the fly caught the glimpse of freedom and rushed out into the breeze, continuing its quest to find a mate, propagate the species, and die accordingly.

Nick returned to the screen, to find the software had completed its cycle, with no results showing. He was aggrieved at this. He had paid a pretty price for this piece of software from an American colleague, and did not expect to come up with nothing. This was going to be a little more difficult than anticipated. As the room darkened, and became illuminated only by the screen and its contents, Nick's mood darkened in parallel. He hated not getting his own way, and this was a character trait that Matt would most definitely concur with should anyone offer it. Nick took a pad and paper, and copied the numerical conundrum onto it. He would post it into one of his many message boards, to see if the cyber-community at large really were as intelligent as they sometimes made themselves out to be. Navigating away from the New Dawn page, he entered one of his community pages, where he often chatted with invisible friends from all over the globe. Within seconds he had posted a question to them all. He did not bother to wait for a response, but repeated the actions a further four times on different sites until he was confident that he had a wide enough spread to illicit a response that would be either partially or completely useful to him.

'Okay, fuckers. Let's see what you come up with then.' The screen's glow cast long shadows on the room, which seemed to increase the suspense of waiting for a response in some way, shape or form. Nick's patience ran out after a matter of minutes, and he realized that it would be agonizing to wait in this way, when there was not even a concrete chance that someone would be able to help him. He looked at his watch. Straining his eyes, he pressed the violet light button, which illuminated the whole face for him to see how late it was. He had no work in the morning, so that would be it for tonight. He would check again tomorrow, when enough time had passed to allow for time differences around the world to become relevant. Everyone, after all, had their own lives to lead, and it was arrogant to assume that his question would take precedence over anything or anyone.

Nick reached for the television remote control. He flicked channels for a minute, until he chanced upon an old episode of 'Airwolf,' the classic eighties action sitcom about a pair of helicopter pilots, one an ex-Vietnam veteran, who managed to get themselves into a scrape each week, always against someone who could fly a plane or lesser flying machine. Always climaxing with it being blown out of the sky, it was seminally regarded as an equal to the other pinnacle of boys' television of the era, 'The A-Team.' Ernest Borgnine was animated about something, wearing a white jumpsuit, which was so tight Nick was certain he could see the glans of his penis through the shimmering shell suit material. He laughed aloud. Jan-Michael Vincent's shiny helmet was not the only one on show, it seemed. Nick jumped up and went to the fridge. Prizing a can of ice-cold beer from the fridge, he cracked it open, sipping the resultant froth from the opening as he made his way back to the sofa. He settled down with his feet up. This was going to be a good night in.

21

It was late, and Matt and Sara were drunk. Having decided to go to the Arthur together for 'A couple of quiet ones,' the evening had degenerated into a full-on drinking session, complete with chasers of varying sizes, colours and textures. Matt loved the impromptu nature of sessions like this, and he firmly believed that they were of more worth than contrived sessions where everyone knows from the start that they are only out to achieve one thing.

They had decided to forego the taxi ride to Matt's newly cleaned flat, opting instead for a kebab and short walk. As they sauntered along, their walking not too dissimilar to horses' dressage, Matt looked at Sara, heartily tucking in to her lamb kebab. Not a romantic image by any stretch of the imagination, he thought, but he suddenly realised that he could be watching her peel potatoes and she would still fill him with a mixture of sexual desire and something a little deeper.

'You want to watch that chilli sauce, you know.' Matt offered.

'Why's that then, macho man? Too much for a girlie like me then?'

Matt smiled, trying hard not to show his food. 'I didn't say that. All I know is that if you read the bottle that it comes out of, there's a government health warning on it. Me, I'm a garlic mayonnaise man myself.'

'Are you now? Well, it's a good job I fancy the pants off you, and also a good job that I've had a skinful of beer. Normal girls are like vampires you know. They hate the stuff. Can't stand kissing blokes after they've been eating it.'

Matt retorted immediately. 'It's a good job you're not normal then, isn't it?'

They laughed out loud, enjoying the banter. Matt's front door appeared, and they squatted on the front doorstep momentarily to finish their kebabs. As usual for Matt, he had ordered way too big a meal for one man, and he could not complete the task. He felt that a kilo of reconstituted lamb meat was enough for any mortal. Sara, however, had adopted a more logical approach to eating, and was able to crumple up an empty pile of greaseproof paper and drop them in the outside litter bins. The temperature had dropped slightly, and she hurried Matt inside, remonstrating against the length of time he was taking to finish. He took the hint, especially when she took off her jacket, slung it over her shoulder and slapped her rear as an incentive, pulling on the lobby door to the block of flats as she went. Matt didn't need any more persuading.

Reaching the front door quickly, he jammed his keys into the front door lock. Her hands were on him even before he had finished entering the flat, pulling his t-shirt off hungrily. He grabbed her around the waist, and pulled her close to him. Their mouths met with considerable force, and both knew that they were desperate for sex. Matt's hands moved to Sara's breasts, gently squeezing. He felt her nipples harden underneath her own t-shirt, and hearing her moans of approval to his touch, he moved his hand around to her bottom, feeling the hardness of the toned muscle underneath. Sara opened her eyes briefly, and looked directly at Matt.

'What's wrong?' Matt enquired, hoping that she was willing to continue.

'Is that a mars bar in your pocket, or are you just pleased to see me?'

'King sized, baby. Help yourself.' He picked her up as if carrying her over the threshold, and moved them into the living room. They stretched out on the sofa, and Matt eased Sara out of her jeans. In the dim light from outside, as her jeans fell onto the floor, he saw the curvature of her waist, accentuated by the tantalizing white lace panties that she was wearing. He kissed her stomach, and she squealed with delight as he moved upwards, kissing her chest, her breasts, and then her lips hungrily. She reached down, undoing his belt and using her legs to slide his own trousers down. Matt's body was in top gear, and she could feel his hardness pressing into her. She opened her legs slightly, allowing him to touch her entrance with his tip after he had removed her underwear, savouring the moment. He could feel her open slightly, and her heat beckoned him to push harder.

Matt got up quickly, and they removed the rest of their clothes. Sara shifted while Matt was up, and beckoned him to sit on the sofa. Both naked now, he did as he was told, enjoying her ability to ask for what she wanted. She straddled him, and they both gasped gently as she lowered herself onto him. They began to move in unison, loving the sounds that they made in pleasure as she rose and fell, bringing herself closer and closer to her orgasm. Matt pushed her away slightly, and closed his mouth around her nipple as she moved. He felt his own climax approaching, and tried to make sure that he did not go too fast. He wanted Sara to enjoy this too. Sara anticipated this, and this seemed to drive her on, not wanting to miss the train. Matt could hold on no longer. He felt the first throes of his own release, and he groaned loudly. Sara clamped her arms around his shoulders, and let out a muffled, guttural moan as she too came, closing herself around his girth as she did so. They panted together, and when their eyes met, they exchanged warm smiles of understanding and feeling, without any need for explanation.

They remained like that for some time, until Sara gently climbed off Matt's lap, and lay on the sofa next to him. He stretched out next to her, and they stayed like that for some time afterwards, holding each other without saying a word. The moonlight spewed in through the exposed window, and illuminated the room, turning everything a lucid grey. Long, dark shadows extended across the room, grappling with the furniture as if trying to remove it into the night. For Sara, it felt exactly right; she was with the person she was really beginning to feel she could trust, and the last fifteen minutes were a testament to that. She was completely content, and was loving the fact that she was in Matt's arms, despite her understanding that in terms of his employment, it was unethical.

For Matt, though, he was silent for a different reason. He had deliberately not told Sara about the break-in, as he did not want her to feel that she was in any way responsible, which of course she wasn't. Deep down though, the fact that someone had asked him to desist in any way at all was gnawing away at him, and he felt that he needed to find out whether or not some element of his relationship with Sara had touched a nerve with someone. He knew how territorial men could be, especially in the socio-economic context of Bloomfield. He didn't think it was the right time to be doing this, especially after what they had just shared, but he didn't know if he would have another chance again soon. He decided to bite the bullet and say something. He broke the silence.

'Sara?'

'Yes honey. What is it?' Sara's friendliness wasn't helping Matt.

'I need to tell you something. It's about the flat. I was burgled a few days ago.' Matt turned his head and looked at Sara, who looked genuinely concerned.

'My god,' she responded, 'were you hurt? Was anything taken?'

Matt gave her a hug, as if to thank her for her concern. 'No, I'm fine, and nothing was taken. There was something else, though. Something that happened. Listen, What I'm about to say, please don't be offended by any of it, okay?'

'Er...okay. Are you going to offend me then?' This wasn't going well for Matt. He sat up, and took a deep breath.

'Whoever broke in left me a message. I didn't understand it.'

'Sara's face creased into a frown. 'What sort of message, Matt? What was so special about it?'

'Well, it was written in shit for a start, which is not what I'd exactly call normal behaviour. And then there was the content. The message simply said 'Cease.' The thing is, I'm not entirely sure that I know what it is I'm supposed to be ceasing. I'm as boring as it gets. I haven't changed anything about my life for years. The last big thing to happen to me was my divorce, and that was ages ago. The only thing I can think of that's different right now…….'

'….is me.' Sara sat bolt upright, but not in a defensive way. She automatically understood what Matt was trying to say. Her feelings of closeness to Matt were strong enough for her not to want him to feel any more awkward about things as they were already. 'You think that maybe our relationship together has brought this on you?'

Matt looked away, ashamed that he was having this conversation now, and having it in the first place. 'It doesn't matter to me, Sara, but do you have any baggage that I need to know about?' They faced each other, not caring about the fact that neither of them had any clothes on. This really was the naked truth. Sara looked away briefly, and when she looked back, she had the beginnings of tears in her eyes. Despite Matt's sometimes brash exterior, he was a sensitive man, and the fact that she was upset began to mist his own eyes over. He was suddenly racked with guilt, and he quickly wanted to free himself of the anvil weight of this conversation and the pressure he was putting on the only woman to have shown any real interest in him in a long time. 'Look,' he began, 'it's ok. Forget it. I didn't mean to upset you, my love.'

'I'm not crying because of you. The fact is, you're right. There is something you may need to know.'

'You're married? Jesus. Why didn't you……'

'No, you idiot. I'm not married. Like you though, I used to be. Ashleigh's father.'

'What about him?'

Sara arose from the comfort of the chair, and took the plaid throw that was on the sofa. She wrapped it around her shoulders and went to sit on the chair adjacent to the window. Stark and wooden, it was the complete contrast to the sofa. It was as if she did not want to afford herself any comfort at all while she told Matt what she was about to say. 'My ex-husband's name is John. John Selleck. He still lives in the area. We don't see him anymore, and he certainly doesn't see Ashleigh any more. It was some years ago that we separated, and she barely remembers him even being around.'

'She's never mentioned a dad at all in class.' Matt chipped in.

'There you go. That's why, Matt. She's never had one.' Sara looked briefly out of the window, as if something hanging on the night air would offer her some support. 'The thing is, we didn't separate amicably. It was extremely acrimonious. But not without good reason.'

'Sara, you don't have to.....'

'I want to. Please let me finish.'

'Of course.'

She continued flatly, as if telling the story in the third person. A third person might help her forget, she thought blankly just before she opened her mouth once more. She stroked her cheek as she spoke, and that same hand then began twirling her hair, as if a regression to childhood. 'It all started out well at first. He had a good job, he worked every day, and before Ashleigh came along we got on just fine. He drank a bit, but nothing too serious. We had the occasional tiff, but then who doesn't? Anyway, I found out I was going to have Ashleigh, and from that second when I gave him what should have been the greatest news of all, it was as if the shutters came down on me, and eventually Ashleigh as well. The drinking got worse, and there was one time when I was ready to go into hospital, when he came home from the pub, and he had been arguing with some Indian guy about something to do with work and money or something. They were working at the airport at the time, and there was a baggage handlers' strike. He was different. There was something about the way he was describing the argument that was really vicious. I asked him to stop, but he turned on me. I didn't see it coming at all.'

Matt realised that her breathing had become heavier, and much faster. He could see that she was getting really animated, and motioned to go over to hold her. She held out her hand in a stopping motion, with her palm facing him. She didn't want any traffic moving her way at that moment.

'He beat me unconscious that night, and I hadn't even done anything apart from try to be a good wife to him, and calm him down. I was rushed to hospital. I remember coming around, and my first thoughts being that I had lost the baby. I remember my hands travelling down to my stomach, and the tears rolling down my face as I felt nothing there. My baby had gone. I was hysterical, and I thought I was going to have to be sedated, until a nurse told me that the baby had been delivered prematurely and was alive. I saw her shortly after that. She was the most beautiful thing that I had ever seen. Those fingers, toes, and her hair was like the finest silk threads.'

She arose, and came back over to the sofa. Matt put his arm around her shoulders, and it felt good to her. He felt dependable.

'I've got to ask, Sara. What happened then? I take it you didn't leave straight away?'

'No. Foolishly, I do what many women do in that situation. I believed it was a once-only thing, and told him that it was over if it happened again. He wasn't there, you know.'

'Where?' Matt replied, having lost the thread of the conversation.

'At the hospital when Ashleigh was born and when I was unconscious. I came around to an empty room.'

Matt could feel the anger building up inside him with every sentence that was being uttered. At this moment in time, he sincerely hoped that it was this guy that had broken into his flat. 'Is he the jealous type, Sara?'

She snorted. 'I'll say. I couldn't even look at another man by the end without him losing his temper. In the end, I had to get a restraining order put on him just to keep him away from us. He's not allowed within a hundred metres of us. Thank god. Listen, if you're asking me if he's capable of breaking in here and scaring you off, I can't imagine that he would do that personally. Don't rule it out though. He was hanging around with some pretty dodgy characters by the time we had split up. They seemed to do whatever he wanted though. It was as if he had them under some sort of spell. God knows what they saw in him like that. He's no leader. Although, if you call Hitler your role model, what do you expect?'

Matt squinted in the semi-darkness at Sara. 'Hitler?'

'He was, and still is, into memorabilia. World War Two, and all that. Short of dressing me up as a fucking storm trooper, he couldn't get enough of it. He made a tidy living out of it as well on the side. As far as I know, that's how he makes his money these days.'

Matt didn't know what to think. From the sound of it, Selleck was a fruitcake for sure. But whether after a few years he could still bear a grudge against his ex-wife for seeing another man he had never met, it was pretty thin. It could also be just another burglar, who was disturbed before they had a chance to take anything, whose idea of fun was to scare the living daylights out of their victims. One thing was for sure, though;

he would pass Selleck's name onto Jim White, the police constable who came around earlier in the week. He might also call on Nick, and ask him to help paint a clearer picture of this guy for him. Matt had never asked his brother for anything like this before, but he really cared for Sara, and he was surprised to feel that he wanted to protect her and Ashleigh against any more heartache. God only knew they had seen enough of that. Worryingly, though, he knew that in a very short space of time, the desire to pay this man a visit would be as painful as it was to have had this conversation with Sara.

'Come on,' Matt finally said to Sara. I've had enough of this heavy shit. Let's go to bed. I'm knackered.'

'I bagsy the window side.' She replied meekly. They made their way into the bedroom, and flopped down onto the comfort of the plush eider down duvet. Sara snuggled into Matt, and her head rested on his chest as cosily as it possibly could. They were just thinking separate thoughts on how perfectly they fitted together as a human jigsaw when Matt's voice softly dented the night.

'I don't know how many there may or may not have been, Sara, but I'm not like them, you know. As long as you're with me, I'll always take care of you.'

'Do you know what, Greavsie? I believe you.' They were asleep within minutes, and as they slumbered, their minds continued to paint images of intrusion, and pain, and for Matt, retribution.

22

Matt sat at his desk, and surveyed his domain. The children were hard at work, and there was a real industrious hum about the class this morning. Everyone seemed to be getting over the events of the past few weeks, and normality (if there was such a thing) was returning to the classroom that he loved being in. Monday meant one thing: news time. Although not compulsory, he liked to give the children a little time to extend their writing, as he felt that they didn't get enough time at present to really cement the skills in writing that they should have at that age. The Play Station had a lot to answer for. The other reason for asking the children to write about their weekend, of course, was that he got to see what *really* went on in their houses when they weren't in school.

He was currently reading through the news book of one of the boys, Michael Palmer, and he was surprised to see him having written so much. It was obviously a good weekend. He read excitedly, making the odd scribble here and there to correct a spelling or give a pointer, as per the school's policy on marking (they had a policy for *everything*). He liked what he read:

......and then I went to sainsburys shoping and mummy gave me a twix for being a good boy. I went to nana's in the afternoon and I played there with her dog sultan and we had a good time. he only bit me once I had beans and sausages and nana gave me twenty p for being a good boy and for scratching her back when she was watching tv. And then I went home again and when I was in my pyjamas I heard my daddy say to my mummy that if she opend her legs for him he would buy her a new fridge.

Matt looked up from the child's book and turned to face the young Mr. Palmer. Michael looked back at him, and smiled, his two front teeth missing. Matt realised that he genuinely had no idea that what he had written was either as hilarious or inappropriate as it actually was. That was why he had gone into teaching. He remembered watching a street magician on television, who had said that he didn't 'Do tricks' for children, as they lived in a world of magic. He had dismissed it at the time as someone merely trying to be really deep and mysterious on camera, but he actually understood that now. The children in his care did live in a world of magic, and he remembered his own reactions to things in school that he would now regard as mundane and tedious.

'Sit down Michael. Nice work, mate. Now everyone, finish the sentence you are writing, and close your books.' Putting Michael's book to one side in order to photocopy it for the staff room wall at break time, he stood up from his desk (it was the first time in around six months that he had sat at his desk. It was seldom used.) and moved to the front of the class. The children were very good at tidying away, and it made life much easier as he didn't have to waste too much time preparing for the next lesson. 'Now, after play we're going to be doing some fun work in maths, and you're going to be measuring time. We're going to be going outside and timing ourselves doing different things, and when we're done, I'm going to be introducing you to the wild and fantastic world of bar charts. Have a good break time please, and there have been several children in school being very silly and stuffing stones up their noses outside. Please don't do this. If we want green stones for the pond area we'll buy them.' The children understood this toilet humour and giggled.

Matt dismissed them in his usual way by asking them general knowledge questions table by table, and as he was leaving, he made a point of picking up Michael's book. The rest of the guys would love that one. It was a popular misconception that the school staff room was a dour place, where overworked teachers sat around drinking low-grade coffee in silence marking books and occasionally crying and randomly swearing. This was not the case. There were, indeed, schools that Matt himself had seen where there wasn't exactly a 'laddish' culture evident. However, it was clear to see that the staff at his present school neither took themselves or the pressures of their job too seriously, and this made for a highly pleasant working environment. He had lost count of the number of times that uproarious laughter had emanated from the staff room, and morale was at an all-time high, despite extreme pressure to meet targets and conform to requirements of the latest government fads.

Matt's train of thought was interrupted by Sheila Pilkington, who poked her head around the door with a cheery smile.

'Hello gorgeous. Before you ask, I can't take you to the pictures tonight. I've got plans. Besides, I know the circles you move in, and swinging parties aren't really my thing. Nobody wants to pick the keys of a nineteen seventy nine Talbot Sunbeam out of the bowl, it seems.'

'Idiot.' She replied, suppressing laughter well. 'I'm just passing on a message from John Baker that he'd like a quick chat with you at lunch time if that's okay. He said it won't take long.'

Matt's eyebrows raised at the summons from the management. He got on with John very well indeed, so he wasn't necessarily worried about the meeting. He towed the line, and was a staunch advocate for John's vision for the school and the policies that were in place. He got on well with the parents, and his marking and assessments were always up to date. He was truly puzzled.

'Okay Sheila. Tell him it's a date. I'll bring the spam fritters.' Matt knew she would tell him this too. She disappeared with a friendly wave. Matt went down the Victorian staircase, and down the tiled corridor to the staff room, in readiness for his refreshing cup of coffee (milk, two sugars). He was cut off, however, by two of the children from the next class up from his own. They seemed quite agitated, so he quickly calmed them down and asked them what was troubling them. One of them, a girl named Alexandra, looked extremely worried.

'It's Sam Jackson, Mr. Greaves.'

'What about Sam Jackson, Alex?'

'He keeps putting his hand down the front of his trousers and then chasing us around the playground.'

'How long has he been doing this for?' Matt enquired, hoping for the best.

'All playtime, Mr. Greaves.'

'Well, why didn't you come to see someone earlier?'

'It's taken him this long to catch us.'

Matt sighed heavily, not knowing whether to laugh or tear his hair out. His coffee was going to have to wait. He turned, smiling, and followed the girls out into the relatively fresh air of the playground.

****

Lunch time soon arrived, after an energetic and productive session out in the playground, where the class did indeed spend the session timing themselves performing different activities. A mixture of physical education, mathematics, and science, this was the type of lesson that inspectors loved due to the crossover between different subjects (the term 'cross-curricular links' is the one usually brandished around in educational circles), and the clear commitment to creativity in the curriculum. Matt collected their work for marking, dismissed the class for lunch, and made his way to the Head Teacher's office. He smiled at Sheila as he took a seat outside the door, famously painted blue by John Baker as an homage to his favourite football team, Chelsea. He was a surprising fellow, and never ceased to amaze the staff and wider community as he reinvented himself, or as he let slip little secrets about his personal life and achievements.

The door opened after a wait of only two minutes, and Baker smiled warmly at Matt.

'Come in, Matt. Sorry to have kept you waiting. Do you want to grab a cuppa before we have a chat?'

'No thanks.' Matt replied as amiably. 'I'll have one later.' They made their way into the solace of the inner sanctum. Pictures of John's family adorned his desk, while the walls were a mixture of trinkets and pictures that he had accumulated on his travels over the years. John was a firm advocate for making the most of the time he was given to spend on Earth, and he certainly did that. Completely devoted to his family, he enjoyed as many luxuries as he could afford, usually enjoying these luxuries with his wife and two teenage children.

'Now then, Matt. I bet you're wondering why I asked you to come and have a chat with me, aren't you.' Matt actually found himself holding his breath, and he exhaled silently to stop himself from making himself any more anxious than he already was. Even though he was a good boy and did as he was told, there was always an in-bred fear of all teachers of being summoned to have a 'chat', irrespective of the relationship that they had with the school's number one in charge.

'I am, yes. Do I need to worry, John?' Matt was not going to beat around the bush. He was not one to play games, and besides, he was extremely hungry, despite still being able to taste that morning's rushed breakfast on his tongue.

'Well, for starters, don't panic. Everything's all right. I just needed to ask you a question. And, I'd like an honest answer if possible.'

'Er, okay. of course, John.' Matt had absolutely no idea where this conversation was heading.

'Well Matt, I, er...don't know quite how to put this, so I won't dilly-dally. It's come to my attention from my spy network that you may have a lady friend in your life at the moment.' Matt's face changed almost imperceptibly, but enough for both men in the room to know where they stood in this conversation. John had found out from somewhere, probably Sheila, that he was seeing Sara. He thought quickly about which way to steer the conversation. He could become defensive, and play the wounded and love struck kitten. He could become aggressive, and tell John to mind his own business. Or he could pretend to have a heart attack. Option three sounded good at that moment. He knew that the adage 'Don't screw the crew' was one that all teachers understood and followed almost religiously, due to the need for a positive working relationship in a profession that was hard enough already. However, there was another of 'Mums' buns are no fun' which was equally as powerful.

'Your spies don't disappoint, John. I'm seeing Sara Moyes. We've been seeing each other for a couple of weeks now.' Matt waited for the retribution. It didn't come, however.

'Hmmmm. I see, Matt. Is it serious?'

'Serious enough. She's lovely actually, and we're getting on famously.'

John came out from behind his desk, and sat on the comfy chair adjacent to the one that Matt was seated at. He turned to face him, and when he spoke to Greaves next, the seriousness on his face was crystal clear.

'You know I've got plans for you, right Matt? I've had my eye on you for a long time now. You're slightly different to the other teachers here. You strike me as the type of person who sees teaching and education as a career, not just a means to an end. Am I right?' John was incredibly astute when he wanted to be. He really knew his staff well.

'I guess so, John, although if you had made that statement some time ago I might not have agreed with you.'

'Thanks for your honesty. I said that because I don't want you to take offence by what I'm about to tell you. Be careful, Matt. If you're serious about this woman, then good luck to you. I hope it all works out for you. But, and I mean this, if you bring the name of the school into disrepute in any way, I'll have no option but to impose any disciplinary measures that are appropriate at the time.' He stopped speaking. Matt took up his cue to respond.

'Okay John. Message understood. You know I'll do my best by you and the school.'

'I'm not without a heart, Matt. Keep this to yourself, but my good wife Marcie here came to be the current Mrs. Baker when I met her at a previous school. She's been married before, Matt, and has another child. She was a parent too. I trust that you understand where I'm coming from now?'

Matt most certainly did. He was extremely grateful that John had been this honest with him, and it put his warning into context. It was not out of sheer worry about the reputation of the school that he had spoken out. He genuinely cared and empathized with Matt, and therefore felt the need to make sure that he didn't make any mistakes for anyone's sake, including Sara's. John immediately went up a couple of notches with Greaves. It also cemented any doubt that he might have had that he was going to try his hardest to make the relationship work. There were more stakeholders in its success than he could have believed.

'Have a nice lunch, Matt. And keep up the good work, my friend. You're doing well up there. They're not an easy class, that lot.' John arose, ending the interview.

'Okay John, and thanks.'

'By the way Matt, do me a favour, will you?' John smiled briefly with a twinkle in his eyes.

'Of course. What?'

'If you see Michael Palmer's mother at the end of the day, tell her that Dixons are having a sale at the moment. She might be able to get a good deal on a fridge there.'

Matt laughed aloud. 'I will, John. I will. If she's been good she might even be able to pick up a chest freezer.'

23

In a sterile environment, with bright light destroying the hope that any shadows had of forming, Alexander Pitov sat at his workbench, silent and industrious. There were few men in the world, he believed, who did what he did with such enthusiasm for their work. He knew that there were zealots with amateur skills in bomb-making who might argue with him over the fact that they, too, were enthusiastic about their work, but there was one fundamental difference between himself and those people. His only cause was financial improvement, and religion or politics did not matter in the slightest to him. He was not a vindictive man. He had a family of his own, and he would die trying to protect them. In fact, he had almost done that on several occasions, after falling foul of the Russian Mafia. They had made the unfortunate mistake of trying to default on payments for services rendered, believing them to be above any such rules of the trade. Pitov, however, was a firm advocate for straight business. If you receive the product, you eventually pay, one way or another. Once it had been established that they would rather kill him and his family than pay their debts, he realised what he needed to do. He was due to leave the country anyway; in his line of work there were better financial prospects abroad.

The Russian Mafia soon learned about dedication to work, and why it was more acceptable to pay one's debts. Pitov always looked back on that time with regret. If he had thought it out carefully, he could have contacted the CIA or similar organisation, and offered his services in getting rid of the Mafia leaders to the highest bidder. He was going to do it anyway. One by one, they began to fall, and it became a personal crusade of Pitov to become more imaginative each time in the way that he despatched his victims. Simple car bombs were no good. They can only work once with the element of surprise before security becomes too tight to repeat the process. Bombs were placed under toilet seats, in food trolleys, and in one instance, even in a telephone receiver. In another life, he had been a military sniper, and stealth was one of his most formidable strengths. He put this to good use, blending into the background when necessary, or when in need of a quick escape. He was aware of surveillance techniques, which were not always state-of-the-art when it came down to the Mafia. They were arrogant enough to believe that most problems could be averted by better firepower. He proved them wrong, circumventing their systems to plant his devices and steal away undetected on every occasion.

When he eventually moved to the United Kingdom, he knew that he would soon be in demand. His connections abroad were many, and he was not short of referrals. His reputation grew quickly, and so, after many contracts and successful transactions, he found himself with the financial means and credentials to remain completely anonymous, whilst living in the lap of luxury. The café was simply a front. There was much more to his empire than met the eye. A luxurious house in the trendy Notting Hill district of London, a Mayfair flat, and more than enough of his share of luxury cars and material goods.

He was made. And, looking down, at the bench in front of him, he realised that so was his latest creation. The silver briefcase package for Selleck. It was being picked up tomorrow at eleven via the usual means. His minion would collect it from one of the left luggage lockers at Waterloo Station after Midday. As Pitov sprayed a clear liquid, derived from the coffee bean, over the seals and crevices of the case to ward off any scent of explosive (detectable by sniffer dogs), he smiled with admiration at yet another successful completion. Whatever the outcome, he had the money in the bank, and that was all that mattered. That, and of course making sure that he stayed away from Bloomfield for the next few weeks at least. You couldn't be too careful.

With a spring in his step, he jumped down from his high chair, and took off his head-mounted magnifier. He closed the case, and set the numerical password on each lock. He carried the package carefully, and placed it into the far corner of the room. From there, it would be taken to its hiding place, ready for collection. Pitov knew that he was untouchable. Nobody would ever trace the package back to him. And if Selleck ever told anyone of the origins of the package without his consent, he would meet the same fate that everyone else had who had dared to jeopardize his business and decadent lifestyle. He switched off the light, and opened the door. Bathed only in the swathe of light from the outside corridor, he swept his gaze quickly over his pristine laboratory, and exited. The sound of Pitov's footsteps could be heard briefly receding into the distance, then everything became silent. His job was done.

24

It was a rare treat for Matt to gamble, and he had way too much respect for money to fritter away his hard earned cash so frivolously on a regular basis. However, Thursday night at Windsor Race Course was something he occasionally did, whether with colleagues at work, or whether with Nick and other friends outside of his work sphere. He had inherited from his father an uncanny knack to spot the occasional winner, and although he would never rely on such enterprises to bring in the bacon, he knew that he seldom came away broke from the races. His philosophy was sound; know how much you are prepared to lose, and stick to that. This was usually a five pound bet per race for him. Study the form, and don't rely on a 'System' to win. And finally, don't chase your money if you've lost a gamble. In the end, he knew that gambling was a mug's game, but occasionally he wasn't averse to being a mug. There was something about the sights, smells and atmosphere at the races, especially the smaller meetings, which appealed to him. There was a real cross-section of the community here, and when he scanned the crowds, he saw the complete spectrum of society there. Affluent businessmen, showing off in front of their clients, gambling huge amounts of money from their expense accounts; groups of young men and women on pre-wedding 'Stag' or 'Hen' parties, hoping to finance the rest of their evening's entertainment with a couple of wins. The invisible proletariat, who relied sometimes far more heavily on their successes at the races to provide for others, despair and hope written in a painful mixture across their faces.

Matt took a bite out of his sandwich, and lay back on the blanket on the grass, which he had set out for himself and Sara. It had been his idea that they came to the races that evening, and Sara's mother had been only too willing to look after Ashleigh, having enjoyed seeing the change in Sara since her relationship had begun with Matt.

He had taken the opportunity of packing a small picnic, all handmade, consisting of sandwiches, a half-bottle of crisp white wine, a variety of cheeses, and some fruit to refresh them after the rest of their banquet.

They cuddled for a while, enjoying the late sun on their backs as they stretched out on the grass. Other revellers, with similar plans, either finished their food away from them on the grass verges, or sat around on their own blankets or folding chairs, waiting for the first of the night's eight races to start. Matt felt that he could have spent the whole evening on the blanket with Sara, and if she suggested that they do so, he was not going to object. When he had picked her up after school, she was wearing jeans, a black leather jacket which showed off her curves very nicely indeed, and a plain white t-shirt. He was not dressed any differently really, the only difference being that his jacket was suede and not black leather. He simply loved the understated way in which she exuded her beauty. She was way too modest to admit that she was attractive, and he felt that sometimes she was a victim of her own past in the way that her self-esteem prohibited her from allowing herself to feel completely happy in who she was. To him, she was stunning, and he felt very lucky indeed to be holding here there right now, with exclusive rights to her time and attention.

'Having a nice time then?' She enquired, as if she had read the grin on his face which seemed to be permanently painted there at the moment.

'Mmm, you bet. Enjoy the sandwiches? I made them with my own fair hand. Straight off the bone, that ham. Best I could find. I love it.'

'Yeah, delicious. Not as delicious as being with you right now though. I could stay here all night.' Matt sniggered to himself. She had to be psychic.

'Listen, the races are starting in a moment. Shall we have a look then? You don't have to go bananas if you're betting. You can bet a pound over there, and with the guys right next to the track, the minimum bet is a fiver.' He didn't want to pressurize her into gambling, as he didn't really know how much money she was prepared to lose.

'Tell you what, gambling man, why don't we pool our resources, spend twenty pounds each on the gambling, and either way, we'll have enough money between us for a drink on the way home then. Sound good to you?'

It did sound good, and Matt liked her inclination to share in the excitement. If they both had a stake in the races, it would double the fun. Also, in doing it like this, he didn't feel guilty about asking her to gamble any money she had. They packed up their picnic, placed it in the boot of his car, and then made their way over to the track. Picking up a programme of events, they huddled together and studied the data available on each horse, including past results, the state of the ground they were running in, and the weights they had been carrying. They chose the first horse together, and Matt learned a very valuable lesson in humility, when Sara proved her own understanding of the horses and racing. As it turned out, it was not the first time she had been, and she also came from a family of men who liked horse racing. She admitted that her own father probably spent a little too much time in the bookmaker's, and as she grew up, she spent much of her 'Quality time' with her father at either the horse races or one of the many dog tracks in London. They placed their bet of five whole English pounds, and made their way to the enclosure, in order to take a look at the horse that they had put their trust in, a novice (a horse that had not previously won a race) aptly named 'New Departure.'

Upon first sight, they smiled at each other. He was visibly smaller by at least two or three hands than the rest of his peers, and they laughed at the prospect of seeing a return on their investment. They made their way to the track, and stood behind the white protective fence, as close to the finish line as they could. Holding hands, they waited patiently for the horses to line up together in the stalls, and as the doors flung open, a huge cheer rang out across the stands and viewing areas. As the horses charged together around the first lap, Matt squeezed Sara around her shoulders in silence, but as the second lap unfolded, they realized that their horse was actually in with a chance of winning. Sitting back in third place, they both began to scream, along with the other interested onlookers, as they saw the throng of four-legged athletes blast their way around the final bend.

'Come on, you bastard!' Sara suddenly screamed, fractionally louder than the ambient screams of the other men and women egging their own investments home. Matt turned to look at her, a mixture of surprise and amusement on his face. He took his eyes off the horses, and instead decided it was much more interesting to watch Sara. Her eyes sparkled in the twilight, and he did not notice the thunderous crowd rush past him, amidst the almost hysterical screaming of those around him. He was mesmerized. She turned to look at him, and she broke into a gleeful smile. She flung her arms around him, and kissed him wildly on the mouth. He reciprocated, and for a fleeting instant, they were lost in their kiss, focussed only on each other and sharing that moment.

Sara broke the kiss, and pushed Matt away. He feigned sadness, only to be replaced when she waggled their betting slip in his face. Matt had completely forgotten about the outcome of the race, and looked up quickly to the electronic scoreboard for the results. They were unconfirmed by the race steward, but their horse had won. Not only that, but he had won with odds of ten to one.

'Jesus Christ. That's fifty pounds plus our stake back. Bingo.' He gave Sara a friendly punch on the arm in a 'One-of-the-boys' type way.

'Never mind bloody bingo. There's seven more of those to come. Come on, you, let's have a look at the form.'

They galloped off towards the bookmaker's stand, to claim their winnings and place their bet on the next race. They, along with many others, were to enjoy winning a few more times that evening, just as some were to experience the bitter taste of defeat. They had plenty of money left over for their drink at the end of the meeting, and as an extra surprise, Matt managed to keep Sara from noticing the stage set up in the racecourse entrance grounds. As a fan of the nineteen eighties, he knew she would be impressed with what they would see on the way back out towards the car. As they passed, he stopped her within twenty metres of the stage. Others stopped next to them, and Sara realised that somebody would be coming out very soon. They were not let down, as a few minutes later a disembodied voice chimed over the very powerful Tannoy system, with some very exciting news for Sara. 'Ladies and gentlemen, would you please put your hands together for the attraction this evening. In a one-off performance, please welcome LEVEL 42.'

Sara turned to Matt, with a look of complete incredulity on her face. She had divulged to him just a few days earlier, when they were reviving the discussion about the entertainment that they enjoyed in the eighties, that Level 42 were her favourite band. Matt liked them too, and was the proud owner of several of their albums, both on vinyl and on C.D. Iconic in their time, they had written some fantastic music, and as their lead singer, Mark King, came onto the stage, Matt could not but feel awash with smugness at the feeling he had invoked in Sara with this surprise ending to the evening. True, it was fortuitous that they were playing that night, but it could not have gone any better. Standing at the back of the crowd that had accumulated, he picked her up under the arms, and like a child, hoisted her onto his shoulders. She squealed with delight, and as the opening bars of 'Lessons In Love' started, she held her arms aloft and moved to the music ecstatically. With his hands on her legs to avoid her falling, Matt looked at himself, unbelieving that he could be enjoying the company of this beautiful woman. He was immediately transported back in his memories some considerable years, to school discos and house parties with lights down low, and his hands inside various items of girls' apparel.

In too short a time, the short set had finished. Sara climbed down from Matt's shoulders, and she rubbed them as a way of thanking him. 'Don't worry,' he said to her cheekily, 'you can rub me elsewhere later.'

'Not tonight, Josephine. I've got to get back to my mother. Ashleigh will have forgotten who I am. I'll see you at the weekend though, eh?'

Matt nodded in agreement. Just try and stop me, he thought. They moved together, back to the car, both hoping that it would start. They were both beginning to realise how temperamental it was, especially in the damp. The evening dew would not help, especially with it parked in a field, and they were not looking forward to one of them having to push if it decided not to cooperate.

In their enjoyment and anticipation of the journey home, they walked straight past the tall, lean youth manipulating the keypad on his very impressive mobile phone. What they would have seen, had they stopped to look, was him selecting around six photographs of them that he had taken with his phone, and preparing to send them via SMS to a contact in his phone directory. Under 'S' he flicked deftly through the contacts until he came to the one he wanted. 'Selleck.' An icon flashed briefly as the images were sent into the stratosphere, where they were bounced through a satellite and back down to earth. A fraction of a second later, they were picked up by the recipient, who happened to be watching television whilst waiting for his supper to cook in the oven. He picked up his phone, and began opening the pictures, one by one. When he had finished looking at them, he moved into the kitchen, and opened the oven to check on his dinner. Tonight, he had an enormous appetite that was going to take some quenching. When he had finished eating, he was going to be using his phone again. There were some people he needed to talk to about something that was beginning to bother him.

25

As the digital images downloaded into Selleck's phone, across town Nick was looking at his computer screen blankly. The series of numbers on the New Dawn web page were slowly driving him insane. His number recognition programme had come up with nothing, which surprised him as he was sure that it would have done the job it was designed for. He made a mental note to have a word with his contact about this, in order to save him from any possible embarrassment with his own superiors in the future. He was nothing if not loyal to his friends and close associates.

The fact that the true meaning of these numbers was eluding him was eating away at him, bringing him ever closer to the explosion he could feel boiling away under the surface. He looked away from the screen, letting his eyes wander across the room, willing the answer to pop out from the walls that were beginning to close in around him.

Nick sighed. 'Bloody thing. What the hell do you mean?' He laughed, realising that he was talking to himself. He had seen enough for one night. He took one final look at the screen, and turned it off. It would have to wait a little longer until he had the patience to see this through till the bitter end. If he tried tonight, he knew that he would only upset himself, and that would be counter-productive to the task at hand.

Moving away from the computer, he retrieved a fresh can of beer from the fridge, and stretched himself out on the sofa. He turned on the television, in the hope that there would be something on that would not only justify the licence fee he paid for the privilege of receiving the signal, but would also take his mind off the fact that he was being slowly undone by what appeared to be a random series of numbers. After five minutes of channel surfing, he switched off the television, having seen nothing that inspired him to leave it on. He drummed his fingers on his chest, noticing as he did so the height to which his chest rose and fell with each intake and expulsion of breath. He closed one eye, and then the other, whilst looking at the ceiling, allowing his vision to switch from left to right sided angles. *God, I am bored*, he thought.

It was then that he noticed the paperback on the coffee table. He had pleasantly surprised himself a few months ago by buying few classic novels, and it was a small known fact to his family that Nick had become an avid reader over the years. His mother had struggled to encourage him to read as a child, and it was not really until he had left school and started work that he had found interest in reading books that he believed would motivate him to read further. After all, he believed that most people were best motivated when they were doing something that they *wanted* to do.

He was currently reading *Nineteen Eighty Four* by George Orwell. This was far and away the best book he had ever read. As per his normal way of operating, he had read the text once, and was now re-reading it in order to get a better personal perspective on things. He thought that people would take him for a basket case if they found out he was reading each book twice, but he had forced himself to do this in case he was missing something fundamental to the author's purpose or to the general storylines that were in place.

Written in nineteen forty eight, the bleak vision of the future described in the novel fascinated Nick, and with every word he read, he became more and more amazed at the differences and similarities between the envisaged future and the reality of what it had actually been like. Originally written as an indictment of the government of the time, the idea of one omnipotent 'Big Brother' who watched everyone to ensure that they towed the party line, was easy to compare to the present, ever-monitored by camera, and ever-keen to keep people's identity and actions close to hand. The doomed principal character, Winston, who embarks on a secret affair with another of the proletariat, Julia, was completely enthralling to Nick, and his eventual downfall and submission to his superiors rang true to Nick's own sentiments on the machine that drove him to work and earn his living each day.

Having flicked through it, he decided he was not in the mood. He turned the book around, and admired the cover. The publishers had encapsulated the ethos of the book well, and had not, he felt, overdone the commercial appeal of the cover illustration. It was definitely eye-catching, but not to the extent as to mislead the reader. He scanned the blurb on the back cover, and he smiled at the creases on the cover that confronted him. It was like a vinyl record to him, where he knew each scratch and crackle that accompanied the music. Every crease, every grease stain on the pages where he had turned then after eating crisps, was as personal as his opinion of the book.

He loved this book, there were no two ways about it. However, he suddenly felt the pangs of tiredness creeping up on him, and if he were going to enjoy this book any further, it was going to be from the confines of the cocoon warmth of his duvet. He returned to his computer briefly, and once again looked at the numbers on the bulletin board, screaming at him in a language that was frustrating him, as it was one he understood as a language, but in this case, the particular dialect was eluding him. He hated this, and it was in his very nature to now try and find out more. He took a scrap piece of paper, and scribbled the sets of numbers down, using a pen that he had been given at a recent training event. Its ergonomic design appealed to Nick, and he wondered in a brief dream as to how much one would receive for inventing such a product. He returned to the job in hand, and placed the paper atop the coffee table. He initially placed it on top of his book, but he soon realised that it was going to accompany him to bed, so it was eventually left in the middle of the table, with his mug on top of it to stop any rogue draughts sending it into the worst place possible, the black hole under the sofa. There they were again;

0-340-79631-6

65, 12, 8

Nick arose, stretched, and bending over, turned his computer off. He could go no further with his mini-project that evening; he decided that enough was enough that evening, and carrying both his can of beer , and his copy of Nineteen Eighty Four, he moved to his bedroom. He would only read four pages that evening before falling asleep, but as he did so, his last thought was of himself as Big Brother, keeping his own electronic eye on things around the world. As the full throes of slumber enveloped him, he thought about the text, and the hidden sub-text too. What he didn't know was that in prying just a little too far into something that did not concern him, he was about to become involved in something that he would wish he was not.

26

The door closed with a soft click, which still managed to slice the synthetic air being pumped around the upper floors of the Bloomfield Police Headquarters. Jim, with his back to the door, let out a long, depressed sigh, and moved away from the door, lest the bodies on the other side of the door should sense his relief that the conversation that he had endured for the last twenty minutes or so was at an end.

The dialogue had not gone well from the start. Someone with infinite knowledge and understanding, plus access to and inclination to watch the mortuary's security cameras, had picked up on Jim's little visit to inspect the remains of Saul Omoku and discuss his feelings with Jessica Quinn, the pathologist. Whoever had shopped him really needed to get out more, he thought to himself. He was not bothered to find out who had informed his superiors; that they had went against the every principles of brotherhood which he felt held the force together, and he hoped that the person in question was thoroughly ashamed of himself.

Despite his best efforts to explain his hunch that the artwork he discovered and the murders were in some way connected, his starched superiors had politely pointed out that whilst able to display initiative and a keen eye for detail, White had not sat any formal exams to progress into the Criminal Investigation Department, and that in light of this detail, he needed to remember his place, and not pursue any 'personal crusades' in order to sublimate the fact that he was not authorised to do any investigative work unless asked by a senior officer. He had continued to express his views, but they had unfortunately fallen on deaf ears, with a final warning that if he was seen attending any other clandestine meetings, he would face further, more harrowing dialogues and run the risk of disciplinary measures. Nobody, he was told, liked a loose cannon on the team.

Team, he thought. *Now there's a funny word to have used in this conversation.* He was incensed that they had mentioned team work at all, as they were clearly unable to accept the views of others themselves, and had probably been upstairs for long enough to forget what a true team was. It made him sick to the stomach. What was worse, he was thinking of the possible effect that his meeting with Jessica might have on her own career. It was bad enough to have been chastised after his unblemished service, but if he was going to have to carry the guilt of a friend suffering at his hand, then that was going to be a very difficult thing to deal with.

He reached for his mobile, and rang Jessica immediately. He had to speak to her. There was a couple of seconds' delay as the network connected him, but she answered almost immediately after the first ring had finished.

'Hi,' he stammered, his cheeks reddening despite this being a spoken conversation, 'it's me. Are you all right there? I've just had the biggest arse chewing you've ever seen. I was made to feel like a bloody kid in there. Have you had the same?'

'No, Jim. It was a bit more low-key here. I had a quiet visit from my immediate line manager, who politely asked what had happened. I told him you had been by, and that you were trying to fill in some gaps after the Omoku murder. This seemed to be enough for him. I'm sorry if I dropped you in it, my friend.'

Jim sighed with relief. She was off the hook. 'Listen Jess, I'm just glad that you're okay. I can deal with things at my end. I'm telling you, though, there's more to this case than meets the eye. This art work I found, and the nature of Old man Omoku's death, I mean, there's something there. He was strangled before he was torched, and you've only got to look at the Patel woman and the way in which she died to see that someone out there has a real grudge against people who don't fit in with their idea of a peaceful life. And I also know this. People like these usually re-offend within a short space of time, and things have been known to escalate very quickly. CID wouldn't even entertain any ideas I had, they're so far up their own backsides. They acted like I wasn't even there.'

'So what are you going to do, Jim?' Jessica enquired. The question hung in the air, and Jim pondered it for a moment, although he didn't need to. He already knew which course of action he was going to follow.

'Well, Jessica, if you can keep this under your hat, I'm going to do a bit more digging. There are a few people that I need to talk to around the place. There's something about this artwork that I saw on a bus stop in town that's been playing on my mind. And, if CID won't listen to me now, maybe they will when I've got enough evidence on the connection between the art and the murders for them to open their eyes, sit up and take notice.'

'Okay Jim, mum's the word as far as I'm concerned. But promise me you'll be careful. If you're right, these people aren't choirboys.'

'Believe me, nobody reckons that more than me. Speak soon.'

'Bye Jim.' The line went dead.

Jim felt uplifted by the conversation he had just held, which had been far more productive than the one before. He not only knew what he was going to do (and blow the consequences), but in the instant he finished talking, he knew where he was going to start digging. With his helmet under his arm, he made his way downstairs and onto the street. He couldn't believe he had been so stupid. The graffiti had been a cut above the usual scrawls and tags that adorned walls, bus shelters and similar areas. This was different. It was art. And if you wanted art of that standard, then the chances were that the best place to find an artist in Bloomfield was Art College. It was pretty thin, but then again, Jim had solved many of the town's mysteries on his hunches. *Screw CID,* he thought. *I'll do it my way anyway.*

27

Saturday afternoons were a real treat for people watchers in Bloomfield. The town had its own pulse, and it was almost indefinitely throbbing each weekend with the sounds of children laughing, sports fans making their way to and from their beloved grounds or pubs whilst their teams played, and shoppers enjoying lengthy lunches and spells in one of the many small outlets that blistered the streets.

The recreation ground (or simply The Rec) was no exception, and the noise level on this day far exceeded its usual threshold. To an outsider, it would seem that the circus was in town; the hollers of workmen, combined with the roar of heavy machinery and power tools, would give anyone that impression. However, although the occasional circus was to be expected, the activity on the recreational field was for an entirely different purpose. As the tents arose like atolls, one by one, they gave the impression of grandeur that only accompanied visited from those with a bigger agenda.

And indeed a bigger agenda it was, for this was to be the setting of the Bloomfield Festival of World Culture. As grand as the title, the local dignitaries and politicians were having a field day with this event, labelling it as a major milestone in the town's efforts to bring the enormous multicultural community together. It was to be one of the biggest events of its kind.

Promising food, drink, and performances from the world's wealth of resources, the organisers had already sold twenty five thousand tickets, and the capacity of forty thousand was expected to be reached. The town of Bloomfield had never seen the likes of this extravaganza, and there was a general buzz of excitement about the way in which things had been developing. The recreational ground was awash with life, and the shells of marquees, smaller tents and stalls would soon be surrounded and filled with bodies, and much to the mayor's delight, it would all be captured on camera. Logistically, of course, it was proving to be a nightmare, and although security was going to be tight, at present there was only a skeleton crew of security staff on site. They were predominantly tied up with ensuring that the resources were safe at night, and it was going to be a few days before the security in the daytime was to be stepped up.

It was for this reason that nobody paid the slightest bit of attention to the lone figure walking in through the gates, carrying what appeared to be a medium sized, silver suitcase. Nobody cared that he had walked straight in, and into the maelstrom of workers and officials who were busy trying to ensure that things were as they should be in the tight time schedule that they had been given. And if they saw him with his luggage, they were certainly far too busy to ask what it was.

The courier looked around, and smiled to himself. He had found what he was looking for. A mobile broadcasting station, housed in an articulated lorry, was parked in the very heart of the grounds, its array of dishes and antennae reaching upwards to the very satellites that would spread their signals anywhere in a matter of seconds. He made his way over to the lorry, and found that the area around it was partly sheltered by another lorry, belonging to one of the many firms that had been charged with erecting big-top style tents around the expansive field. He made his way over, without coming across a single person. *They must be otherwise engaged*, he thought to himself. Slowing down, but not enough to draw attention to himself, he realised that to an onlooker, it would not seem out of the ordinary to onlookers to see a silver suitcase such as his next to a broadcasting station; there were many items of equipment such as cameras or sound recording devices which were kept in such cases. *Whoever has made this package had done their homework*, he deduced.   With a cursory glance around, he quickly ducked under the lorry, and dragged the case with him, careful not to knock it as he went on any protruding rocks and stones.

Reaching the front section of the trailer, he spotted the ideal resting place for the package. There was an almost hidden space above the petrol tank, and the case slid easily into the recess that the huge diesel tank sat into. The deliverer quickly appraised his chances of his cargo being discovered, and it dawned on him that this lorry was completely blocked in, and would be one of the very last vehicles to leave the field when the canvas village was dismantled in a few days' time. Nobody would be moving this lorry, and it was a sound place to place the payload. Additionally, the diesel in the tank would make a very nice accelerator indeed when the explosives were detonated. *Selleck was going to be very happy with the way things have transpired. I may even get a promotion up the ranks for this*, he smiled to himself.

Suddenly, he froze, a sudden chill making him physically shiver. Voices. Two people, their legs visible from his vantage point, were walking along the side of the vehicle. They reached a place adjacent to the driver's door, and one of them began to climb into the cab of the truck. *Oh no, Oh no, Oh no. Please don't drive away. Don't let me have got it wrong. I'm a dead man if you drive away.* There was no noise from the engine though. As quickly as he had climbed up, the driver was disembarking, muttering about the fact that he was always leaving his cigarettes in stupid places. They walked on, oblivious to the stowaway and the package so close by. The man exhaled, and realised that he had been holding his breath for what had seemed an eternity. He drew breath quickly, and felt his heart rate slow to something resembling a normal rate. With the main part of his task done, only one thing remained to be undertaken now. Pulling a small remote from inside his jacket, he read the instructions that had been given to him. Amidst the peripheral noise and industry, he turned on the signal receiver. A light flashed to show him that this had been done, as the instructions indicated that it would. Next, the device would need to be armed....

Happy with the outcome, the man slid out from underneath the lorry, and as nonchalantly as he had done upon his arrival, he walked out through the main gates, having made no contact with anyone. Passing a local transport café, he decided that a small celebration was in order before he reported his success in placing the device to Selleck. Fifteen minutes later, as he used a slice of bread to mop the egg yolk from his plate, he flicked open his cell phone, autodialed Selleck, and in the hustle of the café relayed a brief message in a code that had been agreed previously. You could never be too careful, he thought. With a final swipe of his bread, he cleared his plate and sat back. Across the road from where he sat, the tents continued to rise, and soon enough, in days to come, the crowds would arrive. Then things would really get interesting.

28

The doorbell rang with a quiet clang that roused Nick from his sleep. He drifted out of his bedroom in an ethereal state as fast as he could, and made his way to his front door, where he could see the silhouette of his brother against the frosted glass. He had always regretted getting the wooden door, as he felt it prohibited him from genuinely ignoring people he didn't want to see. Not that he felt that about his brother, but there were times, like this morning, when he felt that he could have done without the interruption.

Just to annoy Matt, he put the chain on before opening the door. It had the desired effect.

'Open the door you idiot. I've got coffee and bagels.'

'Hmmm. Have you got some I.D? There have been a lot of people posing as gas inspectors around here lately.' He stifled a smile, imagining his brother as a gas inspector. He seemed to be unimaginable as anything other than a teacher, and had been for the last several years.

Matt hid his own mirth, and replied honestly. 'You're going to need a health inspector if you're not careful. Open the bloody door before I die of cold out here. It's bloody Sunday morning. Don't piss about.'

Nick crumbled, closing the door and re-opening it to let his brother in. The instant that the door opened, the waft of fresh coffee from a nearby franchise, mingled with the smell of the bacon emanating from the bagel wrappers, made Nick realise what Sunday mornings were for. A fleeting wish for a male interest magazine to round off the perfect morning was forced to the back of his consciousness, and a mental note was made to try to fulfil that part of his destiny later on. Although, his last effort at buying such a publication turned to disaster, when the woman behind the counter at the newsagent's shop had to fetch her daughter due to her inability to read the price on the cover. Her daughter, looking not unlike many of the models inside the magazine, had appeared immediately and looked at Nick with a mixture of surprise and mild interest. Her smile said it all, and Nick left the shop hoping that she would forget him as soon as the next sad bastard came along.

Matt forewent any invite to move into the living area and did so anyway, plonking himself heavily on Nick's ample sofa. His feet came to rest on the coffee table, and he proceeded to empty the food parcel, sharing its contents.

'How did it go last night then?' Matt asked his brother.

'Pretty shit really. Stayed in and played on my computer.' He deliberately didn't give any more information, especially on the website and what he had found out so far. He tried to divert the conversation back to Matt, as he had an uncanny knack of spotting when Nick was hiding something. 'You?' he tentatively offered.

'Pretty much the same really. Didn't feel much like going out. Was absolutely bored shitless.'

'No Sara then?' Nick asked flatly. He was not prying. He figured out that Matt was in deep enough with this girl now to talk about her as a partner or as an 'acquaintance' as he saw fit. Matt took the cue in his stride.

'Nah, she had some family stuff to look after or something. Anyway, we've seen a fair bit of each other over the last few days, and I think it's healthy to have a bit of time to ourselves.' Matt took a bite of his bagel, closing his eyes as his mouth tasted the smoked bacon inside.

'So,' Nick continued, 'it's pretty serious then? Do I need to go out and buy a hat?' He expected to be told to go forth and multiply at this point, but instead, and slightly surprisingly, Matt spoke sensibly.

'Well, between you and me amigo, and don't tell mum about this, I would safely say that we feel pretty close right now, but I don't feel that either one of us wants to get the sneakers on and dash down the aisle just yet. We've both got enough baggage to last us a lifetime.' Matt looked up from the coffee table, and right into his brother's eyes. Nick knew how painful Matt's own divorce had been some years earlier from his wife, Andrea, and even though they were on great terms still, he knew deep down that the whole affair (and it was an affair on her part that had killed any hopes of a lasting marriage for Matt) had ripped a considerable amount of self-respect and faith in the opposite sex out of his brother.

While they pondered this for a moment, Matt spotted the piece of paper on the coffee table, and absentmindedly opened it.

'What's the ISBN number for? You buying someone a book?'

'Very funny, you cretin. Nah. You may or may not believe this, but I've been doing a lot of reading lately. Just finished *Nineteen Eight Four,* actually. This is for the next book in my new library.....sorry, what did you just say?'

'About what?'

'ISBN.' Nick's heart rate increased a little.

'I was asking why you'd written the ISBN number of a book down.'

'Oh yes,' he muttered nonchalantly, 'it's just another Orwell book. *Down And Out In Paris And London.*'

'I've read that. Great book. Glad to see you're getting into this reading lark. I've got some more of his books at home if you'd like.'

It was a fucking ISBN number all along. It's a reference to a book! Nick realised that Matt's voice was tuning out, as he imagined what this text could be. Of course, it could be entirely innocent, and may mean nothing at all. The whole episode could merely be kids trying to be mysterious with each other. God only knew the stunts that he and Matt had pulled in their time. However, his little mission could wait for the moment. He brought himself back to earth briefly, and looked at his brother, smiling.

Matt looked at his brother sardonically. 'Hang on. You read a book, which had no car chases, no gratuitous use of semi-automatic weaponry of any kind, and you actually enjoyed it?'

'Uh-huh.'

'I'm telling mum.' They looked at each other for a fraction of a second, each assimilating the last statement to the full, and then burst into laughter at the mere thought of one of the siblings running to their mother. What was even funnier was the probable reaction from their mother, Martha. At the age of sixty, they could both imagine her rolling her eyes in exasperation at the fact that they were still telling tales on each other, even at their age.

Nick took another bite from his bagel, enjoying the malleability of the rind between his molars. He finished his mouthful, then placed his bagel on the coffee table, replacing it in his hand with his coffee. He smelled the coffee, savouring the bitterness as he took a mouthful. Matt caught his eye, and could see that Nick was waiting to say something, but he knew that he was struggling to get it out. He decided to put Nick out of his misery.

'Come on, spit it out. You look like a Tourette's sufferer in a wedding ceremony. You've been dying to ask me something. What is it?'

Nick smiled weakly, and simply came out with it. 'I was just wondering how it was going with Sara. You've been seeing her a while now. What's the deal there bro?' Matt looked at the fireplace and its mock wooden surround, contemplating how to answer. He decided to go for the direct approach.

'Well, I'll be honest Nick. Don't laugh, but I really feel something for her. You know, it's been a while since the divorce, but there's just something about her. Even as I'm talking to you now, I can smell her on my clothes. It's like she's permeated everything, but in a good way. She doesn't mind that I don't listen that well during conversations when the television is on. She likes the way that I fastidiously move my peas around my plate when eating a Sunday roast, and she laughs at my jokes, mate. I haven't felt about anyone like this since Andrea.' He was referring, of course, to his ex-wife, who unfortunately had decided to enjoy the company of her immediate line manager at work, thus ending the deepest relationship Matt's life had experienced to that point. Nick could tell from Matt's demeanour that he was deadly serious, and his boyish foolery had been momentarily pushed to the recesses of his mind whilst he articulated his thoughts.

Matt continued, and Nick paid him the courtesy of listening intently. God only knew he had listened to Nick's troubles and angst enough times. 'I love being around her, and I don't want to stop. John Baker has already had a chat about how I spend my evenings, and although he was clear that he'd cut my testicles off if I brought the school down by getting a rep as a lothario amongst parents, he didn't exactly try to put a stop to things either. In fact, he led me to believe that I should go for it, based on his own understanding of relationships and where the strongest feelings can appear. And do you know what?'

'No, what?'

'I thought I had it cracked. But…..'

'But what? It sounds pretty straightforward to me. You like her, she likes you. That's for certain. I saw her looking at you in the pub. It looks pretty real to her as well

I think. You seem on a bit of a downer. Have you argued or something?' Nick hoped he was wrong. Matt deserved better.

Matt seemed to become a little distant for a fraction of a second, but quickly brought himself back into the conversation. 'The thing is chief, there's been a development.'

'Oh yeah? What sort? Oh fuck, she's not preggers is she? You arsehole.'

'Shut up. Not even I'm that daft to think I was ready for that right now. It seems like there may be some baggage involved.'

Nick didn't seem to think there was a problem. 'So what? Aren't we all carrying a suitcase, or at least a small vanity case around? You're both grown-ups for God's sake.'

'It's not like that. I had a visitor a few nights ago. I was burgled.' Matt shifted in his seat, his bagel now cold on the table in front of him. He nursed his coffee in his hands, protecting it from the cold air that surrounded it.

'Jesus.'

'I don't think so. This had the look of professionals about it. They also left me a message.'

'What?' Nick genuinely did not understand what was going on here.

'They left me a message. The burglars. Written in shit, on my wall.'

Nick's eyes opened wide as he visualised and processed this information. Although he was inclined not to believe his brother at the best of times, due to his unrelenting ability to wind him up like a clockwork toy, this was too incredulous to be anything other than true.

'They did what? What kind of message?'

'It simply said one word. *Cease.* I spent ages just thinking about what that could mean, and it led me to one thing. This new relationship. And what was worse, Sara told me that her own ex was the type of guy who not only treated her like shit while they were married, but he was also a bit tasty with his temper. It looks like if it is this guy, he's really capable of messing the whole thing up.' His face took a stern look, and he added one last statement. 'I don't want that to happen, and I won't let that happen. I'm telling you straight, my brother, if he even looks like getting heavy, I'm going to mess his shit up properly.'

Nick looked at his brother's eyes, and saw in them something that he had never really seen before. He saw genuine menace. He knew that Matt could be very persuasive when he wanted to be, but he also knew that he had a good heart, and that it would take something very serious for him to put himself before others. He was a teacher, for God's sake. Matt sat for a moment, in silence, as if digesting the information he had just let forth to his brother. He then steeled himself, and sat upright in his chair.

'I think I need to pay this bloke a visit of my own.' He rose from his chair, and motioned for the door. Nick immediately shot out of his seat, and placed himself gently between Matt and the door.

'Easy, tiger. Listen to me. John Wayne is dead, remember? There's no need for heroics here. This guy seems like he means business. I don't think that you should go messing around with people like these. Surely it must be better to leave things as they are and hope he goes away?'

'No, Nick. Do you know? I was set on some time ago now in the street by some idiots from the neighbourhood. I was out for a fucking walk, and they decided based on the fact that I was alone, that they could try and take what was mine. Well, at the risk of sounding like some vigilante or something, I'm not happy with that. Who the hell is this bloke to tell me who I can and can't spend my time with? It's always the people like us who get shat on from a great height, and I'm not going to settle for that. This time, I'm going to stand up for myself.' He stood there, resolute.

'But what are you going to do mate? I know you. I've got the scars to prove I know you well enough.' Nick was genuinely worried about his brother, and did not hide that fact at all. He loved him too much.

'Look. I'm not going to burst in there with my six guns blazing, if that's what you mean. I'm not that daft. But know this, Nick. However hard this bloke thinks he is, and however much muscle he has at his disposal, he doesn't know who I am at all. And if he's used to people rolling over, then wait till he gets a load of me. I'll see you later. Oh, one more thing.'

'What's that?'

'I think I'd look good in a cowboy hat.'

Nick saw his brother to the door, and he closed it gently behind him. He went back to the living room, and flopped down onto the sofa, his legs popping up onto the table in front of him. He had not liked the tone of his brother's voice. It had disturbed him more than anything else, by virtue of the fact that he knew him to be a relatively peaceful character, more inclined to do good deeds than bad. But there was something in the way that he was talking that not only told him how crazy he was about Sara, but that at this particular moment in time, he would be prepared to take on a probable psychopath to ensure that he could carry on seeing her. He hoped in his heart that Matt would be able to hold his temper and try his best to be as polite as possible with this guy. However, at the back of his mind, he also knew that Matt, underneath his caring exterior, was hard as nails, and this guy, whoever he was, needed to be just as careful.

29

It was common practice in schools as a Head Teacher (or Principal, depending on which side of the pond one lived on), to make sure that at any cost, one's private activities should not be encroached upon. Some Head Teachers led far too busy a social life to be bothered with things relating to school, and it was often only in the most serious of circumstances that they were happy to be bothered. The variety of hobbies and interests that they held were great. Some opted for music, others for drama; some fished, some loved to cook. Others with more exotic tastes belonged to the swinging set, and enjoyed sharing far more than their educational expertise. In all cases, however, the simplest rules applied to ensuring that they were not interrupted. The most important of these rules was, of course, to ensure that more than one person had keys to the school in the case of an emergency, or usually, a false alarm. The caretaker (or site manager, environmental adjustor, or grounds technician if being overly p.c.) was one of course. However, sometimes the head would entrust his or her keys to the school with their senior staff, allowing them to not only be available if they lived close to the school (as most Heads did not), but also to come and go as they pleased if they wanted to work at weekends. It is a common myth that teachers work from nine till three-thirty each day. The reality was that most, even the ones who only did a touch more than the bare minimum, were usually in at eight and sometimes did not leave until seven at night, only to go home, eat, sleep, then do it all over again the next day, sometimes opting to work at home as well.

Matt was one of the mythical guardians of the school silverware, and he was about to betray the trust that had been given to him by not only using his status to gain entry at an improper time, but by performing an illegal act while he was there. This did not sit lightly with Matt, who was well aware of the gravity of the situation. If anyone were to find out that he had done what he was about to do, he would face the most serious consequences. However, on the way to school from his flat in the early hours of the evening, he had pondered this fate and had decided that Sara was worth taking the risk for.

As the night fell with leaden speed, he took out his bunch of keys and turned the huge deadlock in the front door of the school. The smell of wood polish filled his nostrils, and his ears were filled with the dampened tones of the alarm system as his body broke through the myriad of invisible laser beams, which stood on sentry tirelessly each night, hoping that someone or something would break the monotony of the inky hush. Matt knew that he had to act swiftly, and enter his alarm code into the system to deactivate the alarm before the ninety second grace period was over. He made his way, abnormally quietly, to the panel and entered his four digit code. He knew full well that the system would recognise him by his code, but if asked, he would say that he had forgotten some books and had returned for them. It was still early enough for this not to be a problem.

Once this action had been completed, he made his way in the darkness into Sheila's office, and turned on her monitor. With her computer subjected to various backups and protective procedures via the county's remote server, she had been instructed to not switch it off, merely turn off her monitor to conserve energy as it used exactly the same amount of electricity on standby as it did when switched on. With this in mind, Matt hoped that Sheila's forgiving nature and unsuspecting mind would help him further. He found himself to be correct, and smiled at her mentally, as if she were in the room. She had left herself logged in to the school's information management system, which housed the hundreds of personal details on the children and their families. From assessment data collected by teachers to medical records, it was all here.

Matt knew that just with the alarm, anyone would be able to see from the event log on the computer that he had logged on using his password, but with Sheila still logged on, he assumed that nobody would be any the wiser to the fact that he had accessed any of the highly confidential information enclosed in the digital vaults.

The cursor stared at him, waiting to be moved. He took it up on its offer and clicked on the icon of a child. A menu appeared prompting Matt to enter the surname of a child. He typed in Sara's surname, Moyes. Immediately the names of two children came up on screen. One was Ashleigh, and the other belonged to an older child in school. Matt clicked on Ashleigh's name, and the screen changed, to a tabulated screen where the user could choose form many options for contacts, medical information and so on. Matt called up the tab which allowed the user to see any emergency contacts. He assumed that Sara's ex-husband would still be on the system. Husbands, wives and partners changed very frequently, and he knew for a fact that often names would not be removed when necessary, due to time constraints or plain forgetfulness. He was right for a second time, as the piece of information he required winked at him on the screen. He made a mental note of it, and made sure that he returned to the screen as he had seen it on his arrival that evening. He turned off the monitor, and in doing so, suddenly realised that he was completely enveloped in darkness momentarily. For some reason, this disturbed him greatly. The school that was so busy during the day was now completely devoid of life, apart from the pigeons in the rafters outside. He heard a shout outside, as some teenagers skated past, and he rose to leave. He took a look over his shoulder, as a chill swept through him. It was not the first time he had been the only one left behind at school, and he always managed to frighten himself by imagining burglars or violent attackers lurking in the darkness. This was suddenly exacerbated by the realisation that he had been burgled, and he quickly re-set the alarm and left the building as quickly as he could. He jogged to his car as nonchalantly as possible, lest anyone were watching him from the nearby houses. He locked the door, started the car on its second attempt, and smiled as he left the car park. He had the address he was looking for. It was time to pay a home visit.

30

The first thing that Matt noticed about the house was that it had the outward appearance of one that had deliberately been allowed to decay. The normal replenishment activities such as replacing weather boards and loose tiles had not been undertaken with any real conviction, and it looked as if the only work that had been done to any exterior part of this house had been done with the sole intention of making it watertight. It was as if whoever lived here had enjoyed seeing it decay, as a punishment to the previous owners. Given the present occupier, Matt did not rule this possibility out.

Approaching the door, he could feel the tension in his shoulders, and he took several long lungfuls of air to help calm himself. There were no two ways about this, he was genuinely anxious about the possible outcomes of his actions; he did not think for a minute that Sara would be at risk, given that this guy Selleck had gone to so much trouble to warn him off. If that were the case he would never entertain what he was doing right now. However, if he were to become aggressive tonight, then Matt had to be prepared to stand and fight his corner. He was not averse to that sort of behaviour, and had certainly been no slouch in the past when faced with a situation where he had to decide between the actions of fight or flight. He could, of course, get what he wanted, which was to be left alone to carry on unopposed in seeing Sara. This was not, he feared, the most likely outcome, and deep down he was sure of this. Anyone who was willing to write in faeces on his wall was probably not the type of person who could be reasoned with over a cup of tea. The third outcome worried Matt even more, though. There was always the possibility that this could spark the beginning of a more sinister campaign against the Greaves cause, and he certainly felt that he could do without any repetition of the burglary, or worse.

'What the fuck are you doing, Greaves,' he said in soliloquy as he took the final steps through the front gate and up to the front door, its flaking paint baring the wood underneath, like bare bone under the rotting flesh of a carcass. He looked for the bell, and found it in the shape of an antique twist-style affair that bore no need for batteries, relying on the simple twist mechanism to rattle the bell on the inside. It was surprisingly loud, and Matt realised absentmindedly that there was indeed no substitute for something that was truly well made, and if it wasn't broken, then there really was no need to fix it.

When no answer came, he tried again, secretly hoping that the house was empty, and that this was, after all, a stupid idea. Silence prevailed, and he turned his back on the front door, all the while hoping that secretly this would be the end of it, and that somewhere, inside, eyes watched him, realising their mistake. His hopes were shattered as his hand touched the latch on the gate. A bolt was heard sliding out of its receptacle with a heavy grating noise, and then the door opened slowly.

'Hello. Can I help you?' It was a very frail, whisker of a woman, and Matt marvelled at the fact that she had the strength to open the door at all. Her hair, thinning slightly in places, betrayed her otherwise youthful face, as its greyness, almost bleached white with age, enveloped her face in pity.

'Hello,' Matt coughed through a raspy, shaky throat, 'I was hoping to find John Selleck. Does he live here?'

'Yes, he does, but he's not in right now. I'm his mother. Can I help you? You're not from the social, are you?' She waited for the answer patiently, as if expecting the answer to be yes. *How protective a mother is of her child*, thought Matt. Whatever Selleck was doing, she knew about it and was willing to protect him, not even realising that were he from the Social Welfare Department, she would have already made things worse by offering the possibility that there was something to hide and that they were expected.

'No, I'm not. I'm sort of a friend of his. I was hoping to have a chat. When will he be back?'

'Well, he went out some time ago. He didn't tell me where, but my guess is he won't be long in coming back. It's almost tea time.' She looked behind her, as if reminding herself that she had to attend to something relating to this tea. Matt took his cue.

'I'm sorry, I didn't realise that you were in the middle of something. I'll come back later.' He motioned to go, but she jumped in quickly to stop him from leaving.

'Well, you are a friend, so why don't you stay? John really won't be long. We don't often get his friends coming around. That hasn't happened since he was a little boy, and even then that wasn't often. I'll put the kettle on. You can wait in the warmth of our living room. Please come in.'

It seemed so much more than a convivial offer to Matt. The whole business of tea time and the way the words dripped from her tongue, and the idea of him having a friend around to play, it was almost as if..........as if he were trapped in some bizarre version of a childhood. Or, Matt thought worryingly, that was the way Selleck had chosen to stay, in order to hide away from the responsibilities of adulthood. With almost certainty, this seemed as if he was being begged to stay, but very politely.

'I'd love to come in for a while,' he said.

Moving into the hallway, he was prompted to relieve himself of his coat, where it was stored in a small, quaint cupboard underneath the peeling banister of the staircase, which seemed to look down on the house with malevolence for a crime it had once committed. Matt was ushered into a living room with two comfy armchairs, and a small two-seater sofa. Looking around the room, Matt immediately saw that time really had stood still, and that if he were to travel back to the sixties, this room would be identical in every way, save for the tarnished ceiling, which had yellowed with age.

'I'm Matt, by the way. What's your name?' Matt offered with a smile.

'Edith, but the women down at the day centre call me Eddie, as I always win at cards. Just like Fast Eddie, you know?' She smiled at her reference to the famous character from 'The Hustler.' Matt loved that film, and warmed inside knowing that he was not the only one to appreciate good things.

'Yes, I've seen that film. I'll remember not to challenge you to a game of Whist.'

'That's probably for the best. I'm a demon you know. Tea or coffee?'

'Tea will be fine, thanks.' Matt sat back in his chair, and suddenly remembered why he was there. The joviality and warmth of Selleck's mother had made him relax completely, and when he suddenly thought of his core purpose in being there, his blood pressure quickly returned to its original state. He fought the urge to make his excuses and leave, and before long, Eddie had returned with a wooden tray. It was adorned with a china teapot, and cups which had clearly been brought out due to his being there. Matt accepted his cup of tea, helped himself to two perfectly formed sugar lumps, and then stirred them, ensuring not to make too much noise a she did so. Eddie watched him intently, waiting for him to finish his task. She instigated further conversation when she was sure that he was ready.

'So do you know my John from school? You look a bit younger than him.' She was canny all right. *Nothing wrong with this one's marbles*, Matt surmised.

'I know him from school, yes. We were in different years though. I bumped into him the other day and decided to pay him a visit. To catch up, you know.'

'That's nice dear. John's not really had any friends since school. He went out with his father a bit, but..............' She did not finish the sentence, much to Matt's annoyance. It would be good to know a bit more about the enemy, to put him at an advantage. He did not have to wait long. Edith spoke on.

'He spends most of his time these days in the box room, looking at his collection. I wish he'd go out more really. All he seems to do is go out every once in a while. It's always late at night as well. Still, I'm not his keeper.'

'Collection?' Matt interceded carefully, to keep her talking. 'What does he collect?' An image of skulls, daggers and instruments of death sprang to mind quickly.

'He collects things, dear, from the war. He buys a lot of them from the....the.... *interdet*, I think. He's always bringing bits back from places or having them delivered. Don't know how he manages to store them all upstairs.' She took a sip from her tea, and Matt did the same. It tasted so much better from a china cup. It was so much more refined than his mugs.

Matt smiled at her innocence in mixing her words. Mind you, *into debt* was probably about right. He was extremely intrigued, though. His quarry that evening, the man who had possibly done so vile a thing in the sanctity of his home, was into collecting memorabilia from an era when aggression and forcing others to comply was seen as morally wrong, but acceptable depending on which side you were on. This would explain a lot if it was indeed proven that Selleck was responsible for the burglary. And it might explain his attitude to another encroaching on his territory. He decided to try and learn more about John Selleck.

'Is it a big collection? How long has John been at it? It sounds as if he's serious about it.' Matt tried his best to hide his hope that he would be granted a free show of the collection of the century. He looked at Eddie, trying his best to look genuinely interested but not overly keen to get into the shrine to death and suffering. He almost cried out when she put down her cup, slowly pushed herself out of the chair she had sat down in and said 'Why don't you come and take a look? I'm sure that John wouldn't mind, seeing that you're a friend and all. Let's go up. I'll go and get the key to the room. John doesn't think I know where it is, but I've seen where he keeps it. I'm sure it's only for my safety. I can't imagine that he's got anything to hide.' She scuttled off hurryingly, and when she returned, Matt was already on his feet, his cup empty.

They climbed the staircase slowly, as Eddie led the way. The steps groaned under her feet, the wood protesting against the need to support her one more time. Matt counted a creak on every single step, and was glad to get to the summit, and onto the carpeted landing. At the end of the narrow hallway, past two closed doors which could only have been bedrooms, she slowed, and fed the key into the shiny golden lock, a clear anachronism when compared to everything else in the house. She turned the key, and pushed the door open. The bottom of the door scraped with a swish against the pile of the carpet, and Matt noticed before he saw anything else that the carpet was almost brand new in this room. The rest throughout had been almost threadbare. This room was clearly John's pride and joy. When Matt looked up from the carpet, his eyes opened wide. Partly with awe at the sheer magnitude of the collection of items before him, but partly because he was genuinely scared in his realisation that someone who had a collection of this size would certainly have the patience to play a waiting game for anything that they wanted in life. Matt began to soak in his surroundings, and took another step closer into the room. Eddie, standing behind Greaves, closed the door. Matt snapped his head around, but there was no malice or sinister agenda behind the act; she was merely making room for the two of them to stand and look. And look they did.

Adorning the walls and shelves in the room was a huge selection of antique artefacts, which would not look out of place in any war museum. There were uniforms, of both the German and Allied varieties. A stash of hats adorned a hat stand in the corner, and there were gas masks in and out of their boxes and receptacles, including what Matt recognised to be an infants' gas mask, which had been designed to completely cover the body of the baby or toddler, and into which air could be pumped from the outside. All around there were bullet boxes, bayonets and knives, and in one corner, there were maybe a dozen rifles, some with their firing pins taken out, but worryingly, some with them still in. Matt knew enough about replicas and antiques to know that generally they would have them removed when bought through legitimate sources. It was the near wall, though, that caught Matt's eye. Or rather, the one piece of equipment that was designed to draw anyone's attention away from everything else. It was as if it were mesmerising Matt, encouraging him to lift it from the wall and touch it, and to fire it one more time. He immediately recognised it as a Luger pistol. Black and shining, it had been carefully restored to its former glory. Without a blemish, it adorned the wall, suspended by a soft bracket. The ration books and personal papers of citizens probably long dead paled into insignificance, and Matt reached out a hand, unable to resist the metallic, icy lure of the cold killing weapon. As his fingers brushed against the grip, he thought of whether this had been only ceremonial, or whether it had fulfilled its purpose. He also questioned if it had fulfilled its destiny, then how many times. On a tiny shelf underneath the gun lay a single magazine. It shone with oil, and the smell of it invaded Matt's senses without his permission. The cartridges visible inside that magazine sent a silent chill through Matt, as he wondered why anyone would want to keep a loaded antique weapon in full view as a centrepiece to a collection. With everything that had happened, he paled at the thought that this man was potentially unhinged, and his presence in the house of the man who was doing a very good job of scaring him suddenly became farcical. Matt realised that this man was probably not going to entertain any suggestions from him, and given his hobby, he was more than likely going to carry on doing exactly what he wanted. Besides, who was going to argue with this guy? He had never seen him, but at that particular moment, he was presented with images of hateful skin-headed yobs, and snarling blonde-haired thugs wearing the attire present in the room before him. He envisaged momentarily boots raining down on him, and cheers as he was subjected to further humiliation from faceless attackers.

He realised that he was sweating, and the coldness of the perspiration brought him back from his visions. He knew instinctively that it was time to go. He had seen enough. He turned to Eddie, and opened his mouth to speak. He coughed to clear his throat, which had begun to close with anxiety, then smiled at the sweet old lady, who seemed to be looking at him quizzically.

'Listen, Eddie, I'm going to have to go. Sorry to have to do this, but I've realised that I'm late for another appointment. I hope that you don't...' But it was too late. Too late for him, anyway. Downstairs, the door had opened with a jangle of keys. And whoever was there had heard him talking. The sound of very quick, heavy footsteps came next on the crippled stairs, and then they stopped outside the door to the box room. Matt stopped breathing again, his feelings outside the front door magnified by a hundred. With the added urgency of someone desperate to find out who was behind it, the door swished once again on the carpet, and for what was not to be the first time, Matt Greaves stood face to face with John Selleck.

31

The plushness of the carpet suddenly seemed to hold Matt in his place, and its thick pile seemed to want to curl itself around his ankles, as if it had been permeated by the evil that seemed to infiltrate every room of the house. His feet became lead, and he found himself transfixed on the figure before him, his hazel eyes meeting those of Selleck. Although Matt was petrified, he did not avert his gaze, for he felt that to do so would relinquish a tiny amount of ground to someone he most definitely did not want to relinquish it to; his ego prevented him from granting him the tiniest leeway, despite the fact that his throat had become dry enough to make him cough, which he did involuntarily.

His counterpart, however, did not flinch at all, and held Matt's stare in silence. His blue eyes sliced the air around him, and his own stare drilled into Greaves, as if all the hatred in the world had been stored up until that very moment in time. His thin lips, pale and insignificant in his pallid face, gave Matt the impression of some sort of spectral monster, as the lack of any colour at the bottom of his face drew the attention towards the eyes, and what may lie behind them. Matt could guess what was behind them at that moment.

Contrary to Matt's conception of how much time had passed in silence, it was but a few seconds. Eddie, embarrassed at being caught in her son's sanctuary, decided to hide her own feelings by smiling and talking to her offspring.

'Hello dear. We've got a visitor tonight. Your friend Matt. He said he knew you from school. We were just...'

'I know, Mother.' He approached Matt, and in the tiny room he seemed to tower over him even more. He moved alongside him and in a movement which completely took Matt by surprise, he put his arm around him, pulling him towards his hulking frame and holding him there. 'Matt and I go back a long way. We share some of the same friends. Don't we, Matt?' He gently squeezed his arm, and Matt could feel the pinch of his enormous fingers through his clothes beginning to make his skin burn with the sheer pressure. He knew that Selleck was trying not to alarm his mother with the situation, and decided that the best course of action, for the time being, was to play along. It was also the best chance he had of getting out of the house in one piece.

'That's right Eddie. We seem to have shared quite a lot together.' He shrugged his shoulder gently, and Selleck relaxed his grip slightly. He took advantage of the release, and moved over to the doorway. Selleck pre-empted any movement towards the stairs and motioned towards his mother.

'Mum, there's no point in us having visitors if we can't have a nice cup of tea together. Any chance of you putting the kettle on? I'll show Matt some more of my collection while you do it. Stay here, Matt.' He led his mother to the stairs, and as he did so, he brushed past Matt as if he were invisible, but at the last moment, he smiled a horrifying smile which matt read immediately. *I'll be back to deal with you in a minute.* His footsteps reached the stairs, and through the doorway, he could see Selleck bend down from his hulking height and gently kiss his mother on the cheek. Matt shivered, and felt the hair on his neck bristle, partly with fear but now with something else, too. He began to feel revulsion for this man, a serious distaste for everything that he was seeing. He quickly thought of his options, and his thoughts turned to Sara. Whatever was going to happen, he would not let her down. He felt his slouch disappear, and for the first time in years, he felt himself stand tall, his back straight and chest solid under his shirt. Where he was frightened before, he was suddenly overcome with a steely determination to see whatever was happening here through to the end, and to let this man know exactly who *he* was dealing with, should the need arise. He looked down at his feet on the carpet, and suddenly noticed that he had absentmindedly made a fist. He opened it, and allowed himself a smile of his own, as an homage to the fact that on at least one level, he might be able to compete with this guy.

He saw Eddie make her way down to the kitchen, and Selleck turn towards the box room. Matt knew this wasn't going to be easy, and with each step that the monstrosity of a man took, his heart rate accelerated. By the time he came through the door, he could feel his pulse throbbing at an incredible rate, and he knew instinctively his physical appearance was one of a frightened man. He made himself as tall as he could, and braced himself for what was about to come.

Selleck came in through the door, and closed it behind him. Matt knew he had nowhere to go, and he knew that the only option that he had was going to be to front up to this man and tell him who he was, that he knew who Selleck was, and what his intentions were. Selleck, though, was seemingly intent on beating Matt to it, and broke the silence as they faced each other amongst the trophies of death.

'You know, for an educated man, you're not too bright, are you?' He finished his opening gambit, and waited for a reply.

'And for a thug, I thought you'd at least be living in a place of your own, not with your mother.' Touché.

Selleck opened his eyes wide, and deliberately lowered his voice when he next spoke, so that there was absolutely no danger of anyone but the two of them hearing what was being said through the paper-thin walls of the house.

'So what the hell do you want? We both know we've never moved in the same circles, and we never will. Nice try with my mother though. She always was gullible. You can tell her anything, that one, and she'll believe it.'

'You know why I'm here. You broke into my house and left me that message. By the way, the guys who analysed your shit said that you needed to eat more fibre.' Although it was probably foolish, Matt began to relax a little, and felt that he was more than capable of standing up to Selleck in a battle of wits.

'I'm afraid I don't know what you're on about there, mate. Somebody got a beef with you? I can understand why after this little stunt you pulled tonight. So whatever's happened, you think it was me? Why would you think that?' He smiled, although there was absolutely no warmth behind what was on display.

Matt felt his blood pressure go up a gear, and his fuse, already lit, was beginning to run short. 'I'll tell you why I think it was you. I spoke to Sara.'

'That little slag? I haven't...'

That was the last straw for Matt. He lunged at Selleck, and this was clearly not expected, for as Matt grabbed the lapels of his denim jacket, he toppled backwards slightly, his back hitting the wall. His head came to rest for a second next to the Luger pistol, and his eyes momentarily focused on it. But only for an instant. His hands shot up, and clamped themselves around Matt's wrists. He tried to break Matt's grip, but to his surprise they would not be freed from his jacket. Instead, Matt remained steadfast, and Selleck saw a look in the eyes of the man daring to challenge him that he had not seen for a long time. It was the look of someone who was capable of something more than his appearance suggested. The icy blue eyes met the steely hazel of Matt, and it was the teacher who took his turn to speak in a whisper. What came out was as cold as anything that Selleck could muster.

'I'm only going to say this once, so you'd better listen. Firstly, don't *ever* use words like that in front of me again to describe Sara. Secondly, I'm not going to bullshit you. You broke into *my* house, and desecrated it with that god-awful message. I didn't like that one bit. You might be used to getting your own way, but believe me, I'm not your mother. You're going to have to try a lot harder to scare me off. At the end of the day, I see worse people than you every day at work, so don't think that with a few trinkets you can make me think that you're somebody. And finally, I don't give a shit about your jealousy. I'm going to continue seeing Sara, and that's final.' Selleck tried to struggle, but even with his massive frame, Matt had planted his feet so squarely that it was impossible to move. Matt continued.

'So here's the deal. Whoever you are, you don't fucking scare me. And now that we've met, if I even get a sniff that you're going to be bothering me, I'm not going to be bothering with the police. It's *you* that is going to have to start looking over your shoulder. Remember that.' And with that, he relinquished his grip on Selleck. His face was purple, and the huge man opened his mouth to speak, but Matt had seen enough for one evening. He had already turned his back on Selleck and was making his way downstairs before his lumbering frame had made it to the first step downwards. Taking the steps in twos to catch Greaves, he moved nimbly for a tall man, and as incensed as he was, he was desperate to make sure that this man did not leave with the upper hand. He reached the hall, and was about to enjoy the feel of Matt's collar when Eddie appeared from the kitchen carrying a tray.

'Here you are, boys. Tea all round.' She stood there, seeming very small with the solitary light from the kitchen illuminating her from behind. Matt turned, and so did Selleck. They both suddenly realised that this was where this meeting truly had to end. They cast a glance at each other, which communicated that they had both been committed to memory, and then it was Matt who spoke.

'I'm sorry Eddie, but I've suddenly realised that I have something else on. I'm going to have to call back another time. Isn't that right, John?' He looked directly at

Selleck, and knew that there would be no more threats tonight. He did not want to upset his mother at any cost, it seemed. It was as if he wanted to hang on to the dichotomous nature of his existence for as long as he could, without his mother discovering that he had a darker side.

'Yeah, mum. Sorry.' He opened the door, and Matt stepped out into the freezing night air outside. At least, he thought it was the ambient temperature. It could, he entertained, quite easily have been the chill from what had transpired that was making him feel this way. Selleck watched him walk up the path, and shut the gate behind him.

'He was a very nice boy, you know. He was really charming.' Chirped Eddie, the tray still in her hands. Through the steam from the teapot, she heard her son reply.

'Yeah, mum. A real charmer. We'll be seeing more of him, for sure.' He relieved her of the tray, and together they made their way back into the kitchen. 'For sure,' he repeated under his breath before filling his mouth.

∗∗∗∗∗∗∗∗∗∗∗

That evening, as Matt walked home through the streets, he prayed that his actions did not make things worse for him and Sara. He knew that he shouldn't have even been there really, let alone react in the way that he did to his petty jibe. His temper had already gotten the better of him on many occasions before, and although it made his relationship with this brother memorable, he baulked at the idea of what he had just done to a man he had never even met before. The last time he had done that had been during his rugby days (apart from the mugging incident a short while earlier that month), when it was deemed acceptable to use controlled aggression. However, there was nothing controlled about his behaviour tonight. He had snapped, pure and simple. He did allow himself some comfort in that he had only reacted because he felt something very strong for Sara, but on another level, he knew that this might not wash with her. He was actually dreading telling her of this, and had entertained not doing so, but his conscience had been very clear in informing him that there were going to be no secrets from Sara. After all, it was secrets that had ruined it for him and Andrea when they were married. He would ring her in the morning, and come clean. He reached his front door, and as if with renewed enthusiasm for doing so, he checked over his shoulder before he entered his polished hallway and climbed the stairs to his flat, which thankfully, for tonight at least, was still locked. When on the other side of the door, he returned it to its previous state, and fell into bed. He was asleep within minutes, having exhausted himself with his adrenaline-fuelled activities. He didn't remember dreaming.

32

'Harry, it's me.' Selleck waited for his voice to be recognised, and then came the reply.

'John, how's it going? Everything all right there? How's that mother of yours? Still keeping you in check is she? Always liked her, you know. If I was only a few years older... .' He chuckled to himself, but Selleck quickly steered the conversation away from his mother. He didn't like anyone talking about her, not even in jest.

'Whatever, Harry. Listen, I need you to do me a favour. I need someone to be given a message from me. You up for it?'

'How much?' Harry enquired. Nothing came for free when muscle was involved.

'The usual. Same as last time with those other two, only this time I want the guy brought to me. I'll do the honours myself. I just need someone to soften him up a bit before he meets me.' Selleck, unbeknownst to the man on the other end of the phone line, was smiling as he said this, and he could feel the excitement building inside him at the anticipation of what he was going to do to this Greaves bloke.

There was a moment's pause as Harry counted his potential earnings from the venture, then agreed to take part. Selleck was relieved, as quality men like Harry were hard to find these days. Harry had grown up with Selleck, and he shared the same beliefs on who should and should not be allowed to walk the streets. As younger men, they roamed the streets together, content to pick fights with anyone who did not fit the mould of a national citizen. Always sober when they attacked their victims, they were always shrewd enough to choose their moments carefully, out of as many prying eyes as possible, enabling them to avoid prosecution down to the surprise nature of their muggings and other attacks.

His full name was Harry Planter, and he was the type of person who found it very easy to blend into the background in any environment. Average height, weight and build, his only distinguishing feature was a larger-than-average mole on his neck, which he constantly vowed he would see to at the first available opportunity. A family man, with a teenage boy, he always felt it was his moral obligation to protect the ones he loved, and whenever he turned on the news these days, all he seemed to hear were tales of another sack load of refugees who were going to burden the country and take up jobs that could be taken by people like his own son, Bradley. He had been extremely happy when John had told him about the New Dawn movement, as this seemed the perfect vehicle for him to demonstrate his commitment to his crusade. Additionally, to be offered money by his friend for the equivalent of taking out the trash, was even better. He awakened from his premature retirement into his thoughts and replied to the affirmative.

'What's the address? And when do you want me to pick this guy up?'
Selleck gave him Matt's address, and thought carefully about the timescale involved. His lips narrowed to a curling smile when he saw that he could fit the pieces of his jigsaw together nicely. *Very nicely indeed*, he thought. He could see his master plan come to fruition at the Cultural Festival, and at the same time rid himself of the one thing that was bothering him more than anything else. He realised at that moment that he wasn't interested in reconciliation with Sara or her brat of a child. That ship had sailed. However, his pride and Matt Greaves had now left him no option but to gain revenge for stealing what was once his. As far as he was concerned, Sara and that family were now damaged goods, which meant that nobody was entitled to time with them unless he gave his permission. Any outsider looking in would have suggested that it was no different to a child having his balloons stolen, but to Selleck he was being totally

rational. This was, after all, the way the world turned every day while he had his eyes open. He also came to the conclusion during his moment of contemplation about the whole affair that Sara needed to be dealt with as well, just in case she went to the police. He would not have to resort to as drastic a measure as he was about to with Greaves, but she perhaps needed to see him made an example of, as a reminder that going to the police was not on. Measures could be put in place to make sure that she didn't know where she was witnessing Greaves's education, so he surmised that full deniability would always be an option.

'I need you to do me an extra favour too Harry. I need you to make another pickup. And both of them will need to be done on Friday night.'

'Right you are John. Don't worry. I'll do exactly what you want, mate.' Selleck smiled to himself at Planter's last statement. They always did.

33

The air was crisp, and a silver sheen shrouded the lawns in front of him as Jim White cut his way through the early morning dew, his tyres throwing off minute droplets of water in distaste as they carried him along the tarmac. Jim often cycled at this time, and as his legs began to burn through the faster than average pace he had set for himself, he wondered (with his eyes carefully on the road ahead), whether his stroke of common sense in the early hours of the previous morning would pay him some dividend today. He could not believe the simplicity of the idea really.

Since finding the artwork, his thoughts had continually been drawn to something relating to what he had seen. He had seen many examples of graffiti over the years, in every shape and form. He had sometimes caught the guilty parties, and usually a caution had done the trick. The culture, however, was changing and 'tagging' had become a pastime for many youths, who insisted on blemishing newly painted buildings, trains and walls with their own unique motif at every available opportunity, claiming the virgin space as a trophy to parade to their friends.

However, it had leapt out at Jim in the darkness that the very fact that the artwork existed was not what was concerning him; it would not be the last time that the streets paid homage to its aspiring artists. It was the *quality* of the work which interested him. Whichever way that Jim looked at the incident, there was no getting away from the fact that the work itself was of a very acceptable standard. So much better than the rest, in fact, that there was every possibility that it had been drawn by someone with exceedingly high skill levels. Narrowing it down, Jim thought of the profile of the protagonist. *Old man? Not likely. Too cold at night time to be wandering the streets. But how young? They've got to be under twenty five. They've also got to be doing this for a living, or at least drawing seriously outside of their normal working day with a mind to others seeing their work.*

Then a possibility struck him sharply, and made him actually sit up in bed. His wife had stirred, murmuring softly, then resumed her dreams. What if this guy was a student? What if he was that good because he had a natural gift? The logical solution to Jim was that he would most likely look to developing his talent further. And, the only place close enough for a young man to do this would be the local college, St. Paul's. An opportunity presented itself to him immediately. Firstly, it was his day off tomorrow. Secondly, this would afford him some anonymity and he would be invisible to his superiors, who had clearly warned him off this line of investigation. He closed his eyes and smiled to himself. He would check out the college tomorrow morning, and he would put his intuition to the test.

****

Jim loved the morning more than any other time of the day, and as he inhaled the crisp air, he quickened his pace on his bicycle, hoping that his hunch would prove to be correct. He loved the feeling of his legs carrying him forward, and he loved the sensation of being his own power supply, and the well-being that this offered him. His destination soon presented itself to him, as an enormous spire came into view before any other feature of the main building, streaking into the sky in desperation to escape the sprawling gothic features below it. Swerving to avoid some pedestrians who had ventured out into the road without looking, he meandered up the path, towards the cycle shelters that were already half-full at eight thirty in the morning. Locking his bicycle, he decided to stand back for a while and watch. Without his uniform on, he guessed he could at least mingle in with the lecturers and occasional mature students, if not the masses. His days of raging against the machine were long past, and he smiled as multitudes of young people began to swarm through the grounds in preparation for their lectures. The diversity was enormous, as the college itself was famed for its varied curriculum of qualifications and areas of study, ranging from car to quantum mechanics, and anywhere in between. As if trying to outdo each other in their efforts to maintain individuality, they had unwittingly created another section of society, their differences in appearance marking their solidarity to the outside world, where buying a suit and getting a job were the ultimate hardship, along with getting a good haircut.

Jim overheard some students as they went past, bragging of their conquests the night before, down at the students' union. Jim remembers his own days as a young man, and the years he spent as an honours student in London. He had decided to study economics, and it was not until much later that he had embarked on a career in the police. The student union, with its subsidised beer and abundance of girls with a penchant for parties and pints, was where he spent many of his evenings, and in another life, he had spent too many drunken nights in the nearby halls of residence (girls' wing), building up his own stash of memories to take to the grave with him. Promiscuity was not frowned upon, and in fact the increase in sexual awareness of the nineteen eighties had allowed him to fill his boots with as much as he could metaphorically carry. His grant, awarded to him by the Education Authority at the time because his father was unemployed, was spent predominantly on beer, but he often wondered on the percentage that actually went on protection. Ironically, he got his pepper spray for free these days, but that was not the type of protection that he was thinking about.

Entering the lobby at last, he looked around for an information desk, and he was eventually pointed in the direction of the Arts block. Not wanting to frighten anybody, he had decided against saying who he was, instead opting for another story of how he wanted to tap into local talent for a new logo for his business. He would be able to carry this alibi for some distance, as there were not many people who would question his choice of profession at this level of enquiry. He had specifically asked for the graphic design department, as he was sure that anyone with an ability to design a logo would be best suited to a career in this field.

He was amazed in the end at how quickly he could speak to people, and he thought that the police could certainly benefit in a few lessons in how to operate smoothly. He waited patiently outside the Dean's office, until he was allowed to enter the modern office with clean lines and streamlined furniture, which seemed an anachronism in the gothic surrounds.

'Mr. White. I'm Peter North, Dean of the Design Faculty. Nice to meet you.'

'Likewise. Thanks for seeing me.' Jim put on his best smile and air of approachability, which was not difficult.

'I understand you're looking to use someone from our student body to provide a logo for you. That's an interesting concept. Not many people have done that before here.' North looked at Jim, expecting him to respond. Jim complied, knowing fully that North was testing the water to see if there were any ulterior motives before he allowed the process to take place. Jim was quietly impressed by the attitudes towards the safety of the students.

'Yes.' Jim replied. 'I'm definitely interested. I think in things like this, we need to keep things local. There's a whole lot of talent out there, and you won't believe it, but I've even got some examples ready of the quality of artwork that I'm going to need. Maybe you would be able to advise me on whether you have anyone who might be able to help.' Jim pulled out the digital images of the New Dawn logo out, and spread them onto the table. North's reaction was instantaneous.

'This is graffiti, Mr. White.'

'Yes, it is. I like the lines. Don't you? I thought it was of a very high standard as I walked past it. It's just an example, but I like the cleanliness and simplicity of the work. Would you agree?'

North nodded after talking another close look. 'Ignoring the subject matter, it's clear to see that this person has got some ability in design. Indeed, my guess is that they would probably have spent some time designing these images beforehand. This is not improvisation.' He chuckled to himself for Jim's benefit. 'You may even have the artist who performed this act of graffiti here as we speak.'

Jim managed a chuckle, thinking to himself that if North had looked a bit deeper into his eyes, he would have realised that he had just hit the nail on the head and exposed him for the charlatan he was. North paused to think for a moment, and then impressed Jim with his insight into the students under his care.

'I'd say, honestly Mr. White.....'

'Please, Jim.'

'Okay, Jim. And you must call me Peter. I'd say, honestly, that if you want to get some serious results, and if you're a serious business, there are probably three students who would stand out at the moment. Rather than trawl through them all, would you accept my recommendations on these three?'

'Of course,' replied Jim, not wanting to admit that he wanted as wide a field as possible, 'You're the boss. Would I be able to meet with them? In your presence, of course.' Jim understood the need for security and safeguarding, and there were simply too many wackos out there to allow any students to meet with individuals in private without supervision, despite being over eighteen.

'Well, you're in luck today Jim. The three students I've got in mind are final year students, and they're all in lectures today if I remember rightly. They might not be in the same rooms, but they're certainly on the premises. Unless, of course, they follow my own path through higher education, which frankly involved as much time in front of the television and chasing girls as it did attending lectures. I called it character building.' They met eyes and laughed together. Jim confirmed that his own pathway to enlightenment was equally as fun-filled. He liked this guy. He seemed to still have that glint in his eye which said he wasn't bowing down to commercialism and adulthood just yet, and that he still had a few tricks up his sleeve.

Jim followed North along the spotless corridors of the faculty building, and was led to a common room, where he waited for a few minutes. While enjoying a cup of coffee from the vending machine, the silence was interrupted by the door clicking open and North reappearing, with three people in tow. Two, both young women of around twenty one years of age, looked way too fresh to be the type to be outside scrawling graffiti over bus shelters. The third, however, immediately struck a chord with Jim. He looked slightly tired, but not through late night partying. He had seen that look before; it was the kind of look that people had when they had been worrying about something for a long period of time.

'Guys, this is Jim White, who is currently working in the business sector, and on the lookout for a bright spark to carry his company forward into the future through their development of a new logo. Actually, Jim,' said North, 'I don't recall you saying what your company actually did…'

Jim smiled, and instantly diffused the situation. 'You're right, Peter, I didn't. I actually own a company called Business Solutions Limited, and my work involves assisting small businesses to improve their image, in order that they can always seem competitive, even when they are not.' He laughed, and the others smiled with him. They all seemed to grasp, maybe through personal experience, that not everyone was the perfect entrepreneur. He was not concerned about lying in this way; nobody would check in the first instance, and even if they did, he would be long gone and not likely to return once he had received the information he needed, should it exist. He was sure it did, though, looking at the candidates in front of him. Well, one of them, anyway.

The next fifteen minutes or so were spent in small talk, getting to know the three young people in front of him. The two girls, one an Asian named Lily Hong, and the other a Londoner named Jessica Waugh, seemed very pleasant, and displayed that industrious nature and innocence that immediately discounted them from any theory that Jim might have been harbouring about them. The third, however, was a definite from the start, and Jim felt mildly smug in his knowledge that his intuition was going to pay off. Sam Kettering would fit into the category that Jim referred to as 'Rebellious Able.' Often mild on the outside, there more often than not lurked a high intelligence, which often left one feeling frustrated with the world around them. It often led these individuals to commit acts which were, in their minds, the only ones which could satisfy someone of such a high intelligence. Sam could be more than able of creating the artwork in question, and equally as motivated to display it around the town.

Jim was able to say goodbye to the two young girls, once he had taken a cursory look at their portfolios, pretending to be interested in their comments on style and how well they were able to follow a design brief. He thanked them for their time, and they left, a little dejected to have not been offered a million-pound contract there and then, but nevertheless no worse off. Sam sat on the leather sofa quietly, his eyes clearly demonstrating a curiosity for the unknown, and also abject fatigue.

'Well, Sam,' said Jim, 'it's just us then. I liked your work.'

'Thanks a lot. Nice to hear it.' *Nice kid, thought White.*

'If you don't mind, I'd like to show you some art work that we were thinking of. We've been looking at how to connect a particular small business with the local community, and of course if we are going to do that, we need to look at the make-up of that community. I've been out and about, and have taken some photos some ideas that might be springboards to new concepts. Have a look at these.'

Jim spread the digital images over the table where they sat again, just as he had done with North. As he did so, Jim looked at Kettering, his disposition masking the intensity with which he was staring at Sam. His eyes were burning into him, analysing every tic, as a poker player would when ascertaining his opponent's weaknesses and strengths. There was no bluff to come, though. As the pictures fell onto the table one by one, Sam's face changed. To Peter North, this was indistinguishable, however Jim did not miss the subtle shift in facial muscles and an ever-so-slight narrowing of the eyes. Jim immediately knew that it was Sam who had graced the town with the illustrations, who had blighted Broomfield's walls and spaces with these monstrosities, in order to publicise whatever cause he was shat particular moment.

'This is what I'm looking for.' Stated Jim in a cool voice, looking directly at Sam.

'What?' Came the reply. Sam looked almost startled.

'This style. It's what I'm looking for in the new logos. I think that the lines are really cool. It's simple. It's hard-hitting, and that's what this particular company needs. It wants to portray the image of being very forward-thinking, and the artwork here is one hundred per cent in line with what they would be looking for.'

Jim laughed out loud, and in a very jocular fashion looked Sam right in the eye and said 'Ideally, I'd like to be talking with the scallywag that tagged all of these buildings right now, to ask him to do the job. You don't know him, do you? Maybe you could put in a good word. His laughter was, of course, put on, and his comment was meant to sound like a joke. Jim was the only one in the room who knew how heavily loaded the statement was, and he remained the only one laughing for a few seconds, until Sam joined him in the laughter, with his own quiet snorts seeming just a fraction too strained and put on to be genuine. Jim had definitely touched a nerve.

'I'm afraid I don't know him, but if I did, with my hand on my heart, I wouldn't want him on board.'

'Why not?' asked Jim in response.

'Anyone who goes around wasting perfectly good talent on graffiti will obviously lack the skills to be professional. I, however, do possess those skills, and I can guarantee you that whatever you see here, I can do better. Much better.'

I bet you could, thought Jim to himself. He smiled at the lad's attempts to cover his tracks. It was written all over his face. Jim had come across many good liars in his time, and he had come across even more poor ones. Any good lie was one with a modicum of truth to it. That was always the case. However, in order to be a good liar, one had to be able to convince oneself that the lie was a truth; even if you knew that what you were saying was blatantly not true, in order to be able to convince someone that it was, you had to believe it yourself momentarily. That's why, in his opinion, even the people who get away with crimes for years got found out. They simply stopped believing their own half-truths, and as a result got sloppy. The only difference was how long it took to get that way. In Sam's case, it was about eleven minutes.

'I'll tell you what, then,' said Jim to the young man in front of him, 'if you think you're up to it, and if you think that you could emulate this style for my client, we'd be interested in giving you a go. I'll need to contact them for their full brief, but when they do, I'd like to bring you in so that the clients can meet you. They normally arrange a car and all that. Would you be happy to give me your address so that I can sort that out for you? We can sort it out another time if you like, but it would kill two birds with one stone and save me the hassle of doing it later....'

'It's ok. That's no problem.' Sam scribbled his address and postcode onto a piece of paper, along with his home and mobile phone number. He handed it across the table to Jim. *Like taking candy from a baby,* he thought.

After saying thank you to Sam, and letting him know that he would be in touch very soon, he turned to Peter North and did the same. Thanking him for his assistance, he kept up the small talk as he was ushered to the door, and was surprised to find out that students these days were mostly having to borrow up to nine thousand pounds a year on their tuition fees. He winced at this, imagining the number of parents who were having to sacrifice lots in order to help their children out, despite the fact that everyone borrowed money these days.

Leaving the building and eventually the grounds of the college, he proceeded to the cycle racks, and it was only a matter of minutes before he was gliding along again, his only immediate thoughts directed at avoiding youngsters as they flittered along the walkways and across his path. He smiled as he compared the students to bacteria; they multiplied quickly, they had no real direction when collected together, and only every so often did they amaze everyone by demonstrating what they could absorb through osmosis.

He hit the road, and then his thoughts turned to more pressing matters. He put his hand into his pocket as he pedalled, and felt the piece of paper in there, with Sam's address and phone numbers upon it. Although the phone numbers could be triangulated and Sam's whereabouts monitored quite easily by the police, it was the address that was of more immediate importance. It was time, Jim decided, to embark on a bit of old-school police work, and go on a bit of a stake-out. It was time to pay more attention to how some of the youth around town were spending their evenings.

34

It was one of those Wednesday afternoons, with the sun trying its best to forge a path through the windows in the late afternoon, which Matt hated. It wasn't the children; he loved the fact that they were now very settled into the routines of the class, and knew that he had the very highest expectations of them. He had taken the trouble to explain very carefully the definition of the zone of proximal learning (the place that we get to when we are producing our very best work and concentrating at a level conducive to the very highest outcomes etc.) and the children had responded very well to this chat. They were in the zone right now, and with five minutes to go, they actually moaned when Matt told them that it was time to pack up in readiness for departing to their homes once more, or 'home time' as it was known. Matt always felt a tinge of sadness at the end of the day. Not because he was one of those teachers who saw the children as their own, and missed them greatly. Not at all. He felt that was too creepy and anyone who thought that way needed some sort of break from teaching. It was, in fact, due to the point that he knew where all of these children were going at the end of the day, and quite simply, for some of them, school was a break from events and feelings that no child should have to witness. For some, it was beatings, for some, it was neglect (and other forms of abuse), and for some, it was loneliness, or the burden of caring for another. Poor sods, he thought.

He realised that he, too, had lost track of time whilst chaperoning his thoughts, and hurried the children along in their clearing up. With a smile and a laugh, he dismissed the children.

'Young man,' he addressed a stick of a boy named Adam, 'can I ask you a favour?' Matt had chosen Adam as he had proven quite difficult at times, due to a mixture of poor upbringing, lack of boundaries at home and simply not enough love, it seemed.

'Yes, of course, Mr. Greaves.' Came the reply. Adam was already smiling. He knew that Matt was going to make him laugh. Sometimes, he didn't even have to say anything at all.

'You've been sickeningly good today, Adam. As a result of your truly wonderful behaviour, I am going to trust you to do a very special job for me tomorrow. But I am only asking you because I know that you will follow my instructions to the letter as you are so ace. Do you accept my offer?'

'Yeah, all right.' Adam's face lit up at the praise. Matt knew this might be the only such positive comment that he would hear till he returned to school tomorrow.

'Splendid. Here are your instructions. Mr. Greaves is going to be teaching you using the computers tomorrow as part of your Design Technology work this term. However, I'm going to need you to go and ask Mrs. Pilkington in the office to order me some things from her catalogue. Quickly, go and get a piece of paper to write these things down.' Adam quickly proceeded to the paper tray, and then the pencil box on his table, and returned promptly as the children were making their way out of class.

'Ready? Write these things down.' The list grew quickly, and Matt reeled off his list of items as seriously as he could. It read:

- A cursor for the computer
- A box of sparks for the spark plugs
- A cartridge of white ink for the printer
- 10 metres of fallopian tube
- Some ice making solution

'Now, Adam, do you think you'll be able to do that for me? All you have to do is give the list to Mrs. Pilkington and she'll do the rest.' Matt turned away, a smile beginning to form on his face as he thought about Sheila's reaction to this list.

'I'll do it first thing in the morning, Mr. Greaves.'

'Oh. There's one more thing to add to the list, please.'

'What is it?' asked Adam, grabbing his pencil.

'A matabubu. I forgot that.

'What's a matabubu?' asked Adam, his face scrunched at the odd sounding piece of equipment.

'Nothing, Yogi.' *Old school rules*, matt grinned to himself. *Old school rules.*

****

Despite his light-hearted end to the day, and the prospect of another episode from Sheila when she read Adam's letter in the morning, matt still felt the burden of recent events weigh heavily on his shoulders. He couldn't shake it. The feelings of rage that had been awakened in him at Selleck's house had left him worrying that it could consume him, and take everyone around him down as well. He had always had the temper, and his touch paper could be short at times, but the incidents where someone had lit it had become so intermittent, that he could not really remember the last time that he had felt so incensed. As he left the school building, and headed for his car, he came to the conclusion that he needed to make a brief stop at The Arthur to enjoy the solitude and isolation of his own thoughts for a while. He knew that the only people likely to be in there were a handful of alcoholics who posed no trouble at all to Keith each day, as they filled themselves up with what he liked to call the milk of amnesia. Not that Keith couldn't handle himself, anyway. Matt had seen him see off local idiots many a time. He opened his car door, screwed his eyes tight as he turned the ignition key, and hoped for the best. The engine cried a little that it was not being allowed to sit there for eternity, then gave up complaining and spluttered into life, its tip-tap voice giving Matt hope that when he got old, maybe he, too, could hold on as long before having to go to the scrap heap.

He was correct in his assumption that The Arthur would be the place to offer him the cocoon of silence that he needed at that particular moment. Opting for the lounge as opposed to the bar, there was nobody at all in there. Not even the landlord, which was slightly unnerving. In this community, there were only too many people who would have helped themselves to the contents of the till while Keith wasn't looking. There was a huge problem in Bloomfield with opportunistic thefts, and Matt pondered the fact that with alcohol, the temptation would be too much for many to resist.

As he considered this, right on cue, Keith appeared from the bar into the Lounge, and seemed surprised to find Greaves sitting on a high stool. Indeed, he was more of an evening patron, and wasn't really much one for afternoon drinking. This was possibly why Keith looked concerned as he poured Matt a pint of lager (without asking what he wanted) and rested it on the bar in front of him. Matt looked up from the bar cloth upon which his drink rested, and smiled at Keith. He motioned to get his wallet out of his pocket, but Keith put his hand up as if to protest.

'Put your money away from now, mate. That's a new lager. Let's call it quality control.' Matt smiled wider, and thanked Keith for his generosity.

'Now,' stated Keith, 'what's a well-respected teacher from the local school doing in the local pub only half an hour after chucking the children out for the night? We don't see you in here too often.' Keith remained standing, with one hand caressing a beer pump that stood next to the sleek lager pump that he had just used to fill the equally slender pint glass in front of Greaves.

Matt took a medium-sized mouthful of beer, enjoyed the taste of the hops for a second, and swallowed, relishing the ice-cold feel as it made its way to his stomach. He instantly felt the beneficial warmth begin to spread as the lager began to do its job. Right now, though, it was more psychological than physiological, although Matt was hoping that he would also be able to feel these effects too. He was in the mood for a few more. He was not averse to leaving the car in the car park overnight (who would steal it, anyway?) and walking home, and thought maybe this would be the way forward. He realised that he had not yet answered Keith, and that he was waiting for an answer.

'Keith, can I ask you a question? We are friends, aren't we?'

'Of course.' Keith said in a lower tone that supported what he had said.

Matt followed the contours of his glass as he spoke, in the way that one would follow the contours of a beautiful woman without her knowing it; starting at the top, working downwards. 'I think I might be in a spot of bother, pal.' He looked over his shoulder, checking to see whether he was now in company or not. The lounge remained deserted.

'Oh yeah? How so?'

'You remember Sara, the girl that I've been out with a few times?'

'Christ, you haven't got her pregnant, have you? I'd have thought that you'd have had more sense than that, you daft..........'

'No, Keith, it's nothing like that. Jesus.' They both laughed at the prospect of Matt having those sorts of difficulties. 'It's....different. Worse, I think.'

Keith, sensing that Matt was really in the need of at least someone to listen to him, released his grip on the beer pump, leaned over to his left, and slid another high stool over to a point opposite Matt. He reached up, grabbed a glass from one of the shelves, and reached underneath the bar. Matt heard a faint clink, as if bottles were being shifted around, and then Keith pulled up onto the bar a dusty, faded bottle of what looked like liquid tar. Matt recognised it immediately. It was a bottle of Loch Dhu, a single malt that he knew to have been reviled all over the world whilst in production, and heralded by some, due to the huge amounts of spirit caramel added during its birth, as the worst whisky ever made. Like most things in life, though, as soon as production stopped, it became incredibly sought after by the same purists who slated it, in order that they had something to discuss at their pretentious dinner parties. Largely sold to Americans in the present day, the dwindling stocks meant that bottled could now go for anything in advance of two hundred and fifty pounds a bottle and upwards. And Keith had a bottle. Keith gestured to Matt, and he nodded in agreement that he would like a shot, too. Another glass appeared, and a no-nonsense shot filled it. They clinked glasses, downed their respective shots, and Keith immediately refilled both tumblers, stationing the bottle between them for both to help themselves too.

'Go on then.'

'Well,' began Matt, 'I didn't know that Sara had an ex.'

'So?' Keith was straight to the point. 'Lots of people have an ex, Matt.'

'The thing is, not all of them are psychos with a fetish for Nazi memorabilia, and with enough of a screw loose to frighten even the hardiest of guys. Do you know a guy named John Selleck, Keith?'

Keith was mid-way to another shot entering his mouth when his ears registered the name. His hand stopped its arc towards his mouth, and he placed the whisky glass back onto the bar in front of him. The gesture in itself made Matt stare at him. Keith returned the stare, and with his hands clasped in front of him on the bar, he spoke in an even lower tone, as if to ensure that the very walls themselves did not hear what was being discussed.

'I've been here a few years now, Greavsie, and in that time I've seen many people come and go through those doors behind you. I've seen fights, tears, laughter, and I've even seen some people enter and leave this world in this very lounge. Some would say that this pub is the hub in this community. Ever read a book by George Eliot named *Silas Marner?*' Matt shook his head. 'There's a scene in it where Silas, the central character, goes to the inn one night, and the scene is painted beautifully by the author (Mary Ann Evans in real life) where social status is measured by their proximity to the fire. Silas is near the exit, illustrating where he stood in the community.'

'So what are you saying mate?' Matt was puzzled where this was going. He couldn't make the connection between what Keith was saying and his predicament.

'I'll tell you where I'm going with this. The answer to your question is yes. I do know John Selleck. And working here, I get to know snippets of information about everyone who lives around here. Even you. But if what you are telling me is that you are in some sort of trouble with Selleck, then you need to be careful. Not a bit careful, but incredibly careful, mate. This guy is not your average ex, as you say.'

Matt was sitting upright now, and he realised that he was hanging on every word that Keith was saying. His landlord obviously knew a lot about this character, or at least more than he did, and he was not going to move until he had heard every last word. 'What is it that you know, Keith?'

'Remember, it's only what I've heard over the years, and when you rely on drunks and partygoers for your information, there's always a risk that intelligence isn't always sound.' Matt noted mentally that it was an unusual turn of phrase for a publican.

'It's all right, Keith. I understand. The information would be useful though.'

'Well, what I do know is that as usual, the behaviour of children has a lot to do with the parents who brought them up. In order to understand John Selleck better, you've got to go back a bit further. To his father, Ray, to be precise. Some of the old codgers who drink in here often get a bit loose-lipped after too much navy rum, and on three separate occasions that I remember to date, all three of these guys, when they started on about the old days, commented on how soft the youngsters were these days. Where it gets interesting is when I tell you that as a benchmark, they all used Ray Selleck as a barometer for how hard or soft someone was. It turns out that this guy was made of nails, and had a fearsome reputation in this community.'

Matt reached to the whisky bottle, and downed what was left in his tumbler. He filled it up again, but not until he had taken a gulp of lager to soothe the passage of the black whisky to his gut. After a momentary pause to drink himself, Keith continued with his half of the dialogue.

'As I was saying, he was well known around here. Having worked hard all his life in the steel industry, working his fingers to the bone each day, he took a wife....'

'I've met her. Edith. Eddie. Nice enough.'

'Yes, nice enough by all accounts. A saint, if you ask me. Given what she went through. It appeared that Ray was a bit tasty with his fists at home, and liked to show Edith who was the boss on a regular basis. She simply took it, though. Not one of these old storytellers mentioned her doing anything about it. Anyway, Ray must have taken a long, hard, look at himself one day, and decided that he was pretty sick of earning an honest living, because he suddenly became Bloomfield's go-to guy. Know what I mean?' Keith waited for a response. Matt nodded his head. Every community probably had a member who could get anything for the right price.

'Apparently it started out very small, with shoplifted goods that Ray had purloined himself. Pretty soon, though, the laws of supply and demand took over, and Ray whipped together a bunch of hard guys to spread the empire a little. You name it, he did it. Van robberies, warehouses, you name it. Plenty of his men were caught, but for some reason they never squealed on Ray. He was as clean as a whistle. There were rumours, though.'

'Rumours? What kind of rumours?' Enquired Matt.

'Scary ones. About guys who threatened to spill the beans on ray. Thought they could stand up to him. One sticks in my mind, though. A man named Pete Trimble. Got fed up with it all, and Ray's demands on all of the men, so decided that he would retire from the profession. After telling Ray about his intentions, and after being told that he was no longer needed, Pete got up one day, kissed his wife goodbye, and left for work. He was never seen again. The very quiet rumours were that he had been taken somewhere very quiet, beaten in front of the rest of the gang as an example, and then his throat slit from ear to ear. The message being sent out was that if you were in, you were in until you were told otherwise.'

'Jesus.' Matt wasn't surprised to hear that someone with clear issues had a parent or two with psychotic or sociopathic tendencies. It just escaped his lips as he was beginning to get a picture of Selleck through his father's actions. 'So what about his son?'

'Well, in the nineteen eighties, Selleck Junior was born. Dad was getting on a bit by then, but lots of people had their children late. Selleck reached the tender age of around twelve, when his father simply died one day, and the story goes that the boy brought him his tea on a tray every day in a cloth armchair in the living room. On this day, though, he arrived to find his father dead in the chair, stone cold, having suffered a massive heart attack. Of course, the stories were out there about the beatings and torment that Ray's son, John, endured along with this mother, and there's no telling what he had been subjected to along with the beatings, of course.'

Matt was slowly going white. He could see the ever-familiar pattern of self-fulfilling prophecy befalling someone, and the old adage of *if the cap fits, wear it*. He waited for the next instalment from Keith, which began again with a question.

'You want to know how John Selleck turned into a name that people only whisper? Well, it's simple, really. As he got older, he must have picked up on the stories surrounding his father, and may have been provoked by his past experiences to achieve the power that his father had. Apparently, though, John Selleck's notoriety came from a different avenue. Instead of being the go-to guy for material things, this bloke's been the one to go to if you needed favours doing.'

'What kind of favours?' Although Matt knew the answer to this question totally. Keith leaned back, then forward again.

'The kind of dirty favours that are needed when people feel that they have no alternatives. The kind that leave your hands, but not your conscience, clean. Let me ask you, now. What trouble are you in with this guy then?'

Mat sighed, and then it poured out of him. The relationship with Sara. the fact that Ashleigh is his daughter in his class at school; the incident at his flat. They all came out, and this time it was Keith's turn to be mesmerised by the account so far. The recount terminated with the events at Selleck's house, and Matt's reaction physically to Selleck. He informed Keith of his feelings for Sara, and how he felt that he needed to protect her and her daughter from Selleck. He described the room full of the memorabilia, and the feeling of dread that this instilled into him. All the time, Keith listened patiently, his eyes visibly indicating that he was actively listening to every word. When Matt had finished, he took a long gulp of his lager, draining the glass. Keith noticed that Matt's knuckles were almost white, he was gripping the glass so tightly.

'So, what do you think?' was all that Matt could think of to say. He felt drained. He didn't know whether there was any advice to be given in this circumstance.

'I'll tell you what I think, Matt. I think that this guy is trouble. It would be no use to say to you to walk away from Sara, because I know that you're not the type of person to do such a thing when you feel the way you do. And, quite rightly, too. Why can't you be happy too? But I will say this. The way I look at it, you've got only got a trio of options. The first is to stay quiet, and hope that Selleck goes away. Attention seekers often stop their behaviour if they are ignored. He's not a child, though. The second option would be to remove yourself and the girls from the situation, but then again, why should you? That would give the bully the power that he craved, and then there would be the possibility that he would never let go of the bone. Thirdly, you could confront him again, and try to explain the situation calmly from your point of view. The only thing with that approach is that he's already had one chat with you, which didn't go too well because you invaded his home, and then stood up to him on his own turf. Basically, whichever way you look at it, you're going to have to be looking over your shoulder for the immediate future.'

'I know, I know.' Whispered Matt, resigned to the fact that this was going to get much worse before it got better. 'Thanks for listening Keith.'

'Listen, this guy is no choirboy. If he's anything like his father, he's going to get others to do his dirty work for him, and he's going to try and keep his own sorry arse as clean as possible. Be very careful. How well protected are you?'

'I'm not tooled up, if that's what you mean. That's not my style. I'm not a fucking gangster, Keith.'

Even though the very thought of carrying a gun or alternative weapon turned on Matt, he would have been ashamed to admit that he was entertaining thoughts, while alone, of what he would do to Selleck or any of his minions, were he given the chance. Especially, he continued to muse, should there never be any chance of anyone finding out. Having already been subjected to a mugging only recently, he was well aware of the potential for disaster in Bloomfield, and the Singh family would always have a lasting reminder of what was out there. However, a gun was a coward's way out for Matt, and as he felt things escalating in his head, and as he foresaw potential encounters with Selleck, he knew that to resort to such avenues would not only incriminate him, but place him on a par with the man who was currently the lowest common denominator in Matt's existence. *He was above that, and would always strive to be, for the sake of everyone around him.*

Matt drained his whisky, followed immediately by the remains of his lager, which had now lost its fizz slightly, reminding him strangely of countryside holidays when his parents were together, and adolescent binges on local flat cider. Thanking Keith, he moved off his stool, comforted by the slight dizziness and hollow feeling in his legs, induced by the Loch Dhu. He opened his mobile as he stepped into the open air, and thought of calling Sara. He realised that he was being selfish in doing so, as he was listening to primal urges in his head, and not thinking with the clarity that he usually demonstrated. He closed it again, and sauntered homewards, stopping briefly to look at a long, white turd that was next to the corner of the wall surrounding the car park at the pub. *You don't see white dogshit anymore*, he pondered, and laughed to himself that with all of this going on, he had chosen this to monopolise his thoughts at that particular moment.

Inside the pub, Keith was still sat alone on his stool. The whole pub was still empty; indeed, there were times during the middle of the week when he would not see anyone at all until seven or eight. Keith had poured himself another shot, but had returned the bottle to its bed. Although he was partial to a drop or two from time to time, he knew that he had to remain at least semi-coherent, whether there were any customers or not, as there were always opportunities for more colourful characters to present challenges to the relative serenity that most of the patrons expected when they visited. Keith took a second to think about the conversation that he had just participated in, and spared a thought for Matt personally. He had a lot of time for both him and his brother. They tended to brighten up the place when they were there, and they were well thought of in the community of locals who came regularly to enjoy the company and banter. To hear that he had seemingly fallen in love, and that this had resulted in pressure from a man who obviously had more than just one screw loose, filled him with more than a touch of sadness. There were so many bigots, alcoholics, abusers, trustees of modern chemistry, and people to whom the world owed a living that the balance seemed to be perched precariously towards the negative. Keith glanced over his shoulder towards the huge, ornate mirror that allowed him to keep a watchful eye on the place while his back was turned. Hidden away behind a bottle of Galliano (nobody ever seemed to drink that anymore) was a faded photograph, showing Keith and three of his old army buddies, nursing their weapons and grinning whilst the harsh terrain of the Falkland Islands tried to claw its way towards the skies behind them. He thought of his motives for enlisting, namely to help people, whilst at the same time saving his own skin from what could have been a life wasted with the wrong people, in the wrong places. He let his eyes linger on the photograph for a while, remembering how he served his country, and the feeling of camaraderie that still existed as a member of the 3rd Parachute Regiment. Not many people knew that he had served, and it was nothing he felt he needed to brag about. Along with the happy, hilarious and sometimes incredibly infantile times that were had, were the horror stories. The stories that one did not tell one's grandchildren around the fire on Christmas Day whilst relatives tutted and braced themselves for another onslaught of flowery storytelling for anyone who would listen.

Keith took himself back to one particular place, on the eleventh of June nineteen eighty two. Mount Longdon, precisely. His eyes began to well with tears as he retraced his steps to his position, moving forward in formation to advance on sniper positions that had been identified. Well trained and armed with his SLR rifle and plenty of spare ammunition, as well as phosphorous grenades and fragmentation grenades also, he felt secure in the knowledge that he stood a very good chance in combat, and would be able to do the job he was asked to do.

He suddenly closed his eyes, recalling the enemy gunfire, and the realisation that the enemy ground troops were much closer than anticipated. What should have been an engagement of firepower quickly became a bloodbath at close quarters, with few men spared the atrocity of going hand-to-hand with someone nearby. Although his regiment, backed with their 105 millimetre gunfire, were victorious that day, and although superior training and skill overcame inexperience, he would never forget the young soldier straddling him, trying to bury his knife into Keith, and his look of surprise, then pain, then resignation as the bullet from Keith's Browning Hi-Power nine millimetre semi-automatic pistol entered his body just under his third rib, and exited through his neck, after being deflected by his right shoulder blade. Without time for a eulogy, he regained his composure and continued to advance, the enemy back in his sights once more. A lengthy battle, he was to see many of his friends killed or seriously wounded that day. Rumours abounded afterwards regarding the Argentinians' use of American mercenaries during the battle, and their subsequent execution on the battlefield once captured. He didn't know about how true those rumours were, but he did know that of the fifty men captured, not all of them would have received the best care after their surrender.

Keith snapped back to reality, and the photograph blurred quickly into focus as he opened his eyes and they adjusted once more to their surroundings. He glanced from the photograph to the hallway, and the stairs leading to his spacious upstairs dwelling. He preferred to live above the pub for security reasons, and it meant that he cut down dramatically on travel. He moaned continuously about taxation and duty, and this was his way of off-setting it. He followed the stairs upwards in his mind's eye, and into his bedroom, where at the back of his wardrobe, behind his winter coats, stood a gun locker, bolted to the wall through the back of the wardrobe. He opened it mentally, and pictured his own personal souvenirs from the war. Black as night, and cleaned regularly, the FN-FAL light automatic rifle stood proudly to attention, just a she did all those years ago. With two well-oiled ammunition clips (each holding twenty rounds of 7.62 NATO rounds) next to it, it was always ready for action. Next to the clips, a specially made box held the almost-new Browning semi-automatic pistol that he claimed as his own after the harrowing conflict on Mount Longdon. Having broken down the rifle and stored it secretly, it was down to the good will of a quartermaster sergeant returning from duty with him that he was able to receive both weapons as souvenirs. He could not believe how easy it was, and shook his head.

The stark reality of his ownership of these weapons was that he would probably never, ever, see them used, however he was glad that he could lay his hands on them. As the door opened in the bar area, and as a group of finely-groomed young twenty-somethings sauntered in with hilarious laughter all around them, Keith pictured Matt, his plight and possible solutions. *You can never be too careful*, he thought as he smiled at his first guests of the evening. The music started from the jukebox, and as the first coins of the evening were quickly gulped by the pool table, Keith returned to solid ground. He just hoped that Matt was grounded enough to realise exactly how much trouble he was in.

35

As the evening wore on, and as the sun set over the anguished grey buildings in Bloomfield, the oasis in the concrete desert that was the recreation ground was awash with people, all intent on ensuring that their own micro-managed activity was undertaken to its perfect solution. Signs were lifted, stalls erected, and security protocols put in place to ensure that the visitors expected on Saturday were exempt and immune from the intentions of those who might want to exercise their right to demonstrate their own personal plight at any given moment. The occasional professional argument could be heard, usually resolved one way or another, and as the sun finally said goodbye to the world, and the moon began her shift, fewer people remained visible. Tired, listless individuals trudged their way home, or to their temporary accommodation while the festival was going on, watched as always by the unseen, hidden hordes of animals that inhabited the locality alongside the temporary invaders.

Turdus merula, or the common blackbird, was one of these locals on this particular evening. With his glossy black plumage, he sat atop an oak tree, preening himself after a particularly aggressive encounter with a lesser suitor to his chosen mate. Delicately pushing his feathers back into their rightful place, he used his beak to adjust his void of feathers accordingly. Seemingly satisfied with his handiwork, he cocked his head, unsure about the noise he was hearing. He chirruped a warning to others around him, and remained still. He was confused, as this noise had been interfering with his hearing for some time, although his perception of time was far distorted from that of the humans he was sharing his space with at present. Hearing in different frequencies, the constant sound, whilst not leading to any immediate event, was unknown, and the unknown was no friend of the blackbird. He called to his mate, who answered after some seconds, and locating the noise, he flew to a space alongside her. Together, they leaped from the tree, and effortlessly began to rise into the evening air. As they left the area to find safety elsewhere from the unknown noises, the male dived towards a square, steel beast that threatened his territory below. At the last moment, he gained altitude, and was gone.

The steel beast, however, remained motionless, staring into the rapidly fading daylight, watching over its own territory with its cold, lifeless eyes. Its wheels remained motionless, planted on the grass below as if trying to take root and leave the park devoid of space to allow nature to grow. Occasionally, the operator would return and enter the beast, stroking it from within, allowing it to wake but not granting permission for it to move anywhere.

What neither the blackbird, nor the operator of the steel beast, had managed to recognise, was that beneath its belly, lay a metal briefcase. Inside that very briefcase, known only to a handful of people, a clock was ticking. The blackbird had been fortunate. The contents of the briefcase, were it in the immediate vicinity when it exploded, would have sealed the territorial debate once and for all. The noise that had so confused the little bird was a carrier frequency for the detonator, and with the push of one button, it would end the signal, and detonate the contents of the briefcase. A failsafe mechanism inside the case would ensure that if the signal was not broken, and as long as the device was armed, the clock would do the job of the remote detonator, were it to fail. Some way off in the distance, an arrogant fox came into view of the eyes of the steel beast. It stopped, as if starting a battle of wits against the great ferrous beast, then thought better of it. As quickly as it had arrived, it vanished into the liquid night.

36

It had been a tough day, and Nick was relieved to have finally turned the key in his own door. He digested quickly the fact that he had been feeling the pressure at work these days, and where he usually used to gobble that sort of pressure up, he was now spending a lot more time analysing the day's events on the way home, and this was unlike the Nick of old. He thought maybe that his new love of reading might well have opened up a door in him to a new layer of sensitivity. It pleased him to be even considering this, as it meant that he was affected by the books that he was reading. Enough to try and make that connection, anyway. This made him feel easier in himself about the day he had witnessed, and the problems he had encountered, and he came to the conclusion that after a beer and a shower, and a bite to eat, his problems wouldn't seem so important. *Anyway,* he thought, looking at his laptop, *we've got another job tonight, you and I.* He was referring to the book that he had bought, subsequent to the last discussion he had held with his brother. As soon as possible, he had looked up the ISBN number, and had seen that the reference number was indeed for a book; it referred specifically to a text entitled *Molloy's Guide To The Law And Jurisprudence.* Official in its appearance, Nick was intelligent enough to know that it was a text for the use and reference of law students and graduates. Friends of his in the profession often had very similar books on their shelves, and in many cases, many volumes adorned their collections, highlighting legal precedents that had been set, in order to assist them in dealing with cases in the present. It was currently on his coffee table, where he had left it on the day of purchase, and with work so very busy, and with so many private clients waiting for results from him, his little side project had been forced to take a back seat. However, tonight was the night when Nick would try to answer his own questions regarding the secret code on the New Dawn message board. He laughed; it was probably going to be some teenager's idea of fun, and he was probably going to unlock the secret to where the coolest skate park was. Nevertheless, this had aroused Nick's curiosity, and like his brother, he was tenacious to say the least. He knew he had lots of faults, but nobody could criticize Nick for never finishing a job. That wasn't in his nature.

He got undressed, and enjoyed the warmth of the water in the shower as he simply stood there for a while, watching the droplets of warm water fall from him as rain would from a broken gutter. He watched the water escape into the drain, and he wondered when the next time would be when that very same water would be used by someone else, if at all. He snapped his thoughts back into gear, and cleaned himself thoroughly, loving the scent of his expensive shower gel. He turned off the shower, and used a luxurious towel to pad the water from his body, before addressing the more difficult areas of his body in need of drying more aggressively. Feeling his skin tingle, he slipped on his underwear, and then his dressing gown. He wasn't going anywhere. He was in for the night. Slipping on some flip flops, he padded his way back into the living room, and made his way immediately to the kitchen, where his tea awaited him, in the form of leftover spaghetti Bolognese from the day before, and a crisp salad to accompany it. He helped himself to an ice-cold bottle of Sapporo lager, and enjoyed the feel of it snaking its way downwards to his stomach as his food warmed in the microwave.

He relished his meal, and when he had eaten enough, he pushed his plate to one side on the coffee table, and jumped up to put some music on. He, like his brother, was a fan of the nineteen eighties, and although he never told any of his friends, he had an extensive collection of vinyl records that would be the envy of any collector. Although his cavalier approach to spending had ensured that a brand new, state-of-the-art mp3 and cd player had pride of place in his living room, he headed for the opposite corner, where his guilty pleasure stood, beckoning. The tower hi-fi system from circa nineteen eighty nine stood proudly, it's turntable atop a class door, which housed a double cassette deck and built-in amplifier. All the rage back then, the sound quality was surprisingly good on his Hitachi outfit, and with modifications he had made to the stylus of the record player, and the speakers also, it was a really classy system when the right music was played. Looking at a shelf above the stereo unit, Nick pulled down an original eighties' copy of the Dire Straits album, *Brothers in Arms*. Removing the record from the sleeve, and taking the white dust sleeve from the LP, he placed it on the turntable, started it at thirty three and a third revolutions per minute, and gently placed the stylus on the title track. He instinctively knew where to place it, and when he cranked the volume up to around half way, he quickly ran to the sofa for a minute. This was his favourite part.

There was something, in his mind, about a vinyl record that set it way apart from a cd or mp3. Each album, once owned, became a living thing, with its own idiosyncrasies and minute voices that talked to you in the form of scratches. One got to know every scratch, every crackle, as if they were there deliberately to personalise the experience for every listener on behalf of the band. Nick liked this, and listened for the tiny symphony of crackles which pre-empted the build up to one of the most iconic saxophone solos of all time. As it started, Nick opened his eyes (for he had closed them) and picked up his new book. Flicking through the pages, he had no real interest in its contents. He was, however, far more interested in how it related to the New Dawn website that he had entered without permission. As he had thought before, even if it was some teenager's idea of fun, it would be an achievement to know that he had invaded this world uninvited, and shared the secrets that had been left there.

Using his laptop and the code that his programme had found, he used his computer's browsing history to call up the website, and easily entered the site once more. The same ISBN number blinked at him, but this time, he knew what it meant. He turned his attention to the other numbers below.

65-12-8

35-14-13

125-22-1

The list continued. More triplets. More numbers teasing him in threes, laughing at him until he worked out their secret. Nick was no fool, though; there had been many a time when |Matt had marvelled at Nick's insights into many things, although he would not usually have congratulated his brother openly. Underneath his seemingly rebellious exterior, there was an incredibly resourceful mind, and Nick was maybe a little too modest about his abilities in many areas. He might not have had the most thrilling of times at school, or in further education for that matter, but he did have resolve, and a very good general knowledge. And on this occasion, it was this knowledge that was going to help him.

Nick tuned out of the music for a moment, and even though absentmindedly singing the words, he was in a tunnel of sorts. An imaginary one between himself and his screen. He forced himself to look at the facts before him.

1. The numbers on the screen were in triplets.
2. They were directly related to the book he held in his hand.
3. Therefore, there must be a law of three that applied to this book.

Nick's new love of reading had led him to develop an understanding of how books were written, and he had enjoyed researching how books and stories had developed through history. He searched his limited knowledge bank, and trawled his memories for anything to do with the number three. He came up with the following:

The Three Little Pigs

The Three Billy Goats Gruff

The Three Musketeers (he discounted this as there were four)

'Three men walk into a bar.....'

He thought about it. The rule of three. *The rule of three.* To his knowledge, authors often employed the rule of three when writing. Children's books were a prime example of this rule. Pigs, billy goats, princes, suitors, three wishes, three chances to guess Rumpelstiltskin's name. Three of everything. All nick had to do, he thought, was to guess which triplet was important. He thought, and thought again, then thought some more (which in itself was a rule of three). And then it dawned on him. *Surely, it can't be that simple.*

Nick opened up a new tab on his internet browser, and in his search engine he typed

'Wartime code breaking.'

There, in front of him, were thousands of potential links to codebreaking during the war. However, it was only one link he was hoping to see. Never one for giving up, the fact that he did not see his desired result anywhere on the first three pages did not deter him. This was often the case, as many people paid huge sums of money to people like him to ensure that their sites and articles were optimized within the search engines to be near the top of the list. The fourth page, however, made him smile, when he saw what he was looking for. There, in bold letters, was the link to his answer:

The Arnold Cipher

Nick clicked on it, and as an homage to himself, he reached forward and finished the remaining mouthfuls of his beer. He leaped up and quickly opened another, flinging the cap onto the kitchen worktop.

Nick resumed his seated position, and scanned the article in front of him. The reliability of this particular article could well have bene suspect, as its contents had been uploaded and added to by several people, each with their own opinions. However, it was safe to say that this was pretty accurate, as Nick had read of this before. Of course, he had to know it, as it was his memory of the code that prompted him to look for it. He read the bare bones of it, and nodded all the while.

The article basically told of the story of the American Revolution, and Benedict Arnold, the once successful military leader, who wrote several letters to John André (Aide De Camp of Sir Henry Clinton, the British Commander-In-Chief). His treacherous activities marked him as one of the most infamous traitors to the American cause, but for Nick, it was *how* it happened that left him with a warm feeling that was not connected to his dinner, or the beer for that matter.

In order that communications would not be intercepted, a code was invented using a book entitled 'Blackstone's Commentaries On The Laws Of England.' Nick raised his eyebrows at this and grinned a little, due to the fact that whoever had created this code knew enough about the story to pay their own homage to it, in choosing the Molloy text instead, and sticking to the legal theme. Nick read on to affirm what he thought was true; Arnold and André had used the exact same code in the late nineteenth century. It was very simple. Using the chosen text, the first number in the triplet was the page, the next was the line, and the next was the word. As long as the text was kept a secret, nobody could ever decipher the data, even if they knew how the code worked; the possible list of texts was almost endless.

But Nick *did* know the text. And as a result of this, he was about to be let into someone's secrets. He took his book, and began deciphering the code, one triplet at a time. He began with a smile on his face, hoping that the message really was from one teenager to his friends, and pertained to something petty and ridiculous. However, after only a couple of sentences, the smile was gone from his face, and when he had completely finished, he picked himself up from the sofa, walked back into the bathroom, and vomited.

****

It was some time before Nick emerged from the bathroom. He had been visibly shaken by his findings that evening, and when he came back to the sofa, there was a part of him that did not even want to look at the computer screen in front of him. Forcing himself, he stared at the page, then down at the piece of paper that he had used to transcribe the message. He just could not believe what he was reading. He read it aloud to himself, as if to justify that it was, indeed, actually there. It read:

Our land is awash with foreign invaders who must be sent home. We will send a message to all of these invaders who steal, rob, beg and share the same streets with us when they have no right. This message will be written in their blood, and will be written when they are not expecting it. The clock is already ticking for them, and soon the fire will take them back to the dark where they belong. Tomorrow, eye nine seven on. New dawn will come for them.

Nick thought about the extremes and what these words could mean when related to the acts of those who behaved in extreme ways. He only had to look back to 9/11 to see the ultimate act of terrorism that could be motivated by hate, and race, and possibly religion. This, however, seemed to draw towards hatred of race, and whoever wrote this clearly had a deep hatred of anyone who was not like them. Nick remembered switching on the news a few days earlier, and blanching at the sight of mass graves in the middle east, where yet another faction was proving its point to the world.

Two things were bothering Nick deeply, and he resolved to solve the first problem immediately. The jigsaw of this puzzle wasn't complete by a long way, but the last sentence eluded him. *Eye nine seven on.* Nick thought once again of possibilities for this statement. He began with a thought on mythological lines. Was there a monster with nine eyes? Different countries had lots of myths. He searched, however quickly discounted this theory after only finding one reference to nine eyes, which was the Japanese mythical talisman of herbal medicine, *Hakutaku.* Nick saw no connection at all. He tried another tack, and wrote each word down individually, to see if anything was possibly right in front of him without him realising it. He took his pen, and scribbled his thought down.

Eye, see, eyes, ayes have it, aye, high.

Nine, nine lives, number, cat o' nine tails,

Seven - lucky number, seven sisters, seven bells, seven shades of shit, seven stars

Nick stopped there, as the preposition 'on' seemingly only meant that something was on top of another thing, or that it was going ahead, as far as he could think. He went back to the start, and the word *eye*. He took his pencil and subconsciously chewed the end while he racked his brain to come up with something tangible. He wrote again:

Eye - I, aye, eye nine, eye number nine, I9

He stopped. I9. *Could be a grid reference*, he thought. He imagined a giant game of battleships, just like he used to play with Matt when they went on holidays. They could never afford to buy the expensive games, but their father was always full of great ideas when he was alive, and showed them how to set up a grid with x and y coordinates alphanumerically. They would draw their battleships in secret, and then would call out reference points one at a time, until one of them had located all of the other's battleships. He reminisced the hours of fun that they had, and strangely that took him to exactly the same cider spree that Matt had considered himself. Nick shook his head, and came back to reality.

He went back to his internet browser, and typed it in. *19*. The resulting hits and links were numerous. Most of them were related to the employment eligibility form in the United States. He skipped over these, and this accounted for five or six pages, interspersed with articles related to cars, sports franchises and the suchlike. He decided to narrow his search, and added *UK to his search parameters.* This brought far fewer hits, and as he scrolled through, he began to realise that he might be pursuing a dead end. He sat back, and threw his pencil onto the coffee table. It bounced against the laptop, and landed on the keyboard. It drew his eye to the laptop again immediately, and to the very last link on that particular page. It was a hyperlink to the LWA (London Water Authority), but more specifically their museum. Nick didn't even think that there would be a museum. However, there was something in the blurb underneath the link that made nick sit up straight and stare, unblinking, at the screen. Nick scanned it, picking out the key words:

19

Water authority

Tunnel system

Bloomfield

1960s

Nick clicked on the article, and for the next five minutes or so he had a quick history lesson, the main topic being the sewer system around London in the Sixties, and the need to change it as the population grew around the suburbs. Nick read with interest that a pioneering maze of tunnels was built underground in many areas, but amongst the first to successfully handle the expansion was I9, named after its nine miles or so of tunnels that were dug under Bloomfield, with nobody knowing due to the new tunnelling technology that had been developed since the end of the Second World War, and the expansion of the London Underground.

Nick re-examined his scribbles, and looked again at the last sentence of the message that he had translated using the Arnold cipher. *Eye nine seven on.*

Nick saw that it could actually make sense. He looked at the date of the latest update to the message board and it had been repeated that very same day. Nick thought about possible meanings once more. Could this be a message to others who shared the same sympathies as the author? It was a bit out there, Nick considered, but plausible. Farfetched, but plausible. If time was accurate, then that could mean that some sort of meeting was going to take place tomorrow (Friday night) around or in I9 (wherever that was in Bloomfield), between the author of this message (if he was for real) and others who followed or agreed with the ideology (if it existed). Nick thought about going to the police and reporting his find, but then thought about two things; firstly, incrimination upon himself as he had technically hacked this website. Secondly, the distinct possibility that he was being subjected to a hoax. That would make his actions a waste of police time, and would double any punishment he received.

He crossed his fingers, linking his hands, and held both palms behind his head. He decided that he would at least check at first if I9 still existed, and if it did, whether it would be possible to see for himself if any meeting was going ahead. If so, it would take one anonymous phone call to the police, and any plans, real or otherwise, would go up in smoke. Nick searched the internet for plans of I9, but every search method he employed came back negative. He became frustrated, until he stood up, and walked around his living room with an air of extreme frustration, occasionally kicking the sofa, or slapping his hands on the wall as a sign of dismay at his lack of progress.

Eventually, he returned to his seat, but not until he had visited his bedroom, and had fetched from a small digital safe a silver memory stick. Plugging it into his laptop, he closed down all of his browsers, and initiated the program that was installed on it. *Right. If you're not public knowledge, then I'll have a look at what's hidden behind door number one.*

Within twenty minutes, Nick had located the servers belonging to the water board, and had circumvented their security protocols with ease, although he was impressed with the fact that they had tried their best to install some high quality firewalls and security systems to prevent people like him from gaining access. Within thirty, he had downloaded the schematics he needed, and within forty minutes he was invisible once again, with any trace of a hack completely eradicated, plus the record of the downloaded documents. Nick felt a wave of smugness wash over him, and deep down he knew that he was good, possibly better than most of his peers when it came to acquiring information that wasn't strictly legal. There was one thing, though, that he felt set him apart. He did possess a conscience, which forbade him from simply hacking into the banks and filling his bank accounts with cash. Not only was it way too risky, even for someone like him, but he would rather ask for a payment from a client, as it made him feel that he was still doing a job of work using the skills he possessed.

Nick looked at the digital schematics in front of him, and he specifically wanted to look at possible entrances to the underground maintenance system, if they still existed. When he located them, he couldn't believe where they actually were. He had crossed that very spot many times, and clearly knew the concrete structure that symbolised the entranceway, however he had no idea in all the years that he had traversed that land of its purpose. He now knew what it was, and he congratulated the owners for keeping it a secret for so long.

He closed down his laptop, and stared at the wall. His eyes were drawn to a glass vase that his mother, Martha, had given him when he moved in. It was full of odds and ends, such as ballpoint pens and paper clips, happy together in their inanimate huddle. He liked the random nature of the items in there. He looked at the remnants of his food, and then stood up. Walking to the kitchen area, he knew what he had to do. He would not tell the police; he would follow his original plan, and check out the entrance to see if anyone was indeed coming or going. He could, after all, have been wrong, he thought. If there was any truth to the matter, and people were meeting, he would call the police, and they could investigate. There would be no harm to him, but he could be doing somebody a great service if his suspicions were correct.

Nick began running the kitchen taps to wash up. There was no need for a dishwasher, as he rarely had more than two or three items to clean. As he saw the bubbles rise, glistening in the hue of his kitchen light, he knew that he was doing the right thing, and although in his heart he felt that he was running a huge risk of looking a fool, based on a complete hypothesis, there was a part of him that hoped that he did see someone, and that would be a huge thrill. He smiled to himself. *You never saw Columbo doing his own washing up.*

37

Jim loved Fridays. He especially loved Fridays when the sun was shining. This particular day was turning out to be fantastic. His shift had gone extremely smoothly, and he put this down to the fact that he knew his community, and his high visibility in the community helped enormously in being approachable, whilst also a deterrent to the antisocial behaviour and crime that was everywhere, if you looked hard enough. He relished what Friday offered; people stepped into an alternative world of pessimism and hope, and were visibly lightened by the fact that they had free time to socialise with their friends and do what human beings did best, communicate. Some let off steam, some courted their future mates, and some simply loved to talk about anything that came to mind. Some relied on alcohol to grease the wheels a bit, but on the whole, Friday was a day of happiness and positivity that made Jim enjoy not only his job, but his life as a whole. God knows there were days he rued ever joining the police.

He was just enjoying the sound of children's laughter somewhere in the distance, when his breast pocket vibrated. It wasn't his work phone though, which doubled up as his walkie-talkie. It was his personal mobile. He found this intriguing, as he had absolutely no idea who could be ringing him on his personal phone during work hours; his wife knew only too well what personal calls could do to a policeman if his or her phone were to go off at the wrong moment.

Pulling the phone out of his breast pocket, he smiled when he saw who it was.

'Jessica, hi. How's it going there?' It was Jessica Quinn, the pathologist and Jim's close friend. He was always glad to hear from Jessica, but he was thrilled that she was ringing him now, as she had been extremely helpful and willing to cooperate with Jim in his own investigations, which were not, at this moment, sanctioned. He respected the fact that she would be jeopardising her career by even telephoning him.

'Hi Jim. I'm fine, thanks. Are you out and about?'

'I'm on the beat at the moment, Jessica, but there's always time for you, of course. Are you winning today?'

'As usual,' she offered, 'I'm up to my neck in customers, and have no-one to talk to. I wish they could be a bit more animated sometimes.' They both laughed at that statement, as they both imagined her clients actually being able to talk with her. *It certainly would make her job a lot easier*, he thought. He stopped for a moment from his walking, and sat down on a rusty, metallic park bench with wooden slats, which allowed pedestrians to enjoy a moment's rest next to a children's play park. Neither had any business being where they were, but Jim relished the brief rest, and time to talk with Jessica. When she spoke next, her voice was hushed, as if the cadavers in her company were going to tell tales on who she was communicating with.

'Jim, I can't talk for long, and I could probably get into a lot of trouble for this, but I needed to share something with you.' She paused for a response, in case Jim didn't want her to continue. He told her to go on. 'Knowing you reasonably well, I thought that you'd not be able to let go of your more, let's say, private investigation of late. I also know that you've been warned off this case by CID. For both those reasons, and because I love the danger, I've decided to share some information with you that I shouldn't.'

Jim listened intently to every word that Jessica spoke carefully, and when she told him of her intentions, he interjected quickly.

'Jessica, I'm really grateful that you want to help, but I couldn't live with myself if you got into serious trouble for helping me. Please know that I won't be offended if you don't tell me anything.'

'Jim,' she said quietly, 'I think we both know that we go back too far together to mess about. You're one of the best friends I have, and I'm sure you'd do the same thing for me if I were ever in need. Wouldn't you?'

This was a no brainer. Jim would do anything for her, given their friendship and how it had grown over the years. Indeed, if it wasn't for the fact that he had met his beautiful wife, Sue, he knew in his heart that somehow, there was a distinct possibility that the feelings he had been carrying for Jessica would have been reciprocated, and he could very well have been with her now.

'Of course.' He replied without hesitation.

'Well, shut up then and listen. Remember Saul Okomu?'

'The poor bastard who got strangled and then lit up?' Jim couldn't believe he had just described the poor man's death in this way, but the mere thought of what had happened was incensing him and bringing him down to their level, whoever *they* were.

'The very same. Well, it seems that the wonders of science have come up trumps again, although how useful the science is will depend on you.'

Jim was intrigued now, and wanted to cut to the chase. He murmured a grunt to beckon Jessica to continue.

'It seems that whoever strangled poor Saul was a soldier. But not just any soldier.'

'What do you mean?' enquired Jim. 'Why not just any soldier?'

Jessica steeled herself on the other end of the line, mentally putting her words into order so that she could explain to Jim in layman's terms exactly what she meant. She didn't have long, after all. 'It's like this, Jim. You know how thorough I am. I'm not happy if I haven't done a job properly. Well, I decided to have another look at Saul's body, and tried to picture the scene. If I asked you how Saul was strangled, what would be your response?'

Jim thought about this for a moment, and pictured it in his mind's eye. The most likely method would have been from behind, with the perpetrator having to initiate some form of arm lock around Saul's neck. It was amazing on how strong somebody could be when their body and mind realised that it was under attack in any way. He knew that although usually switched off, the brain's amygdala would trigger what was commonly known as the 'Fight or flight' reaction. In Saul's case, he would have been prompted to resist the pressure on his throat, and free himself to enable his body to function properly and maintain the basic body functions. In extreme cases, Jim had witnessed people under extreme anxiety become almost super human, and whoever had strangled him would have had to have had a pretty decent grip. Saul was not a small man to begin with, but with the right incentive, he could have put up quite a struggle. The reverse choke hold, or rear naked choke hold as it was also known, would be the most likely option, as it was almost impossible to get out of, and would render the recipient unconscious or worse in a very short space of time. He verbalised this to Jessica.

'I concur, Jim. Something like that would be very effective. Obviously, then, I looked for signs of struggle, and fibre samples under the chin, and around the back of the head, where the contact points would have been. It came up empty, because of the charring after the body was ignited with the accelerant. In this case, it was good, old fashioned petrol. It burned hot, and scarred heavily, leaving a heavy, waxy burn on the outside which would essentially destroy pretty much all material residue left behind.'

Jim smiled at the last statement, and knew that this very clever scientist had found something. 'Pretty much?'

243

'Yes. Pretty much. But not *all*. Here's what happened. Your auntie Jess decided to look a bit closer, and I took off one or two of the top layers of cauterised fat from around Saul's neck. You like pork?'

'Er, yes?' answered Jim. He didn't know where she was going with this.

'Thought so.' She replied. 'You strike me as the type of guy who would go for the chops at a barbecue. Anyway, you know that sometimes, after you've barbecued, you get the odd stray pig's hair that still manages to find its way into your mouth?'

'Actually, I do. There's always one of the little blighters.' Jim was now on the path with Jessica. He understood her logic.

'Well, this is down to the skin or flesh folding from the outside, and then being effectively sealed as the fat is burned and caramelised on the outside. It sounds gross, but the natural oils and sugars that exist burn, and the fat melts, but sometimes, depending on the heat involved, the crust that is formed prevents the inner layers from burning too. It's a bit like a seasoned frying pan. Anyway, I found a single fibre buried underneath the outer, charred skin and fat around Saul's throat.'

Jim laughed out loud. It was possible that she had cracked this mystery, especially if this fibre was hair, and matched the DNA of an existing criminal. He crossed everything in the hope that he was right.

'It's a hair, right?'

'Wrong. Here's the thing. When I slapped it under the microscope and analysed it, I had already separated, cleaned and mounted it, so I knew that whatever was under there was the real deal. But for a while, I couldn't quite understand what was happening. You see, it appeared at first that Okomu had been killed by a sheep.'

'Eh? A sheep? Surely there was some sort of mistake, Jess. Even I'm not going to believe that one.' Jim was somewhere between frustration and laughter, and needed Jess to get to the point, although he would never be that rude to her as to say that.

'Hold your horses, Jim. Of course it wasn't done by a sheep, but it transpires that the single fibre, less than four millimetres in length, were from an overcoat.'

'Any idea what kind? It's not uncommon for people to have woolly overcoats, Jess.' Jim's frustration was growing even further. Jess seemed to sense this, and carried on.

'It took some research, and I had to go back to real basics here and search all of the databases I had access to, in order to find what I could about this fibre. And I eventually found what I was looking for on the INTERPOL database. Jim, this sheep's wool was predominantly used on military overcoats. German military overcoats to be precise. They only really used wool from one particular breed of sheep. They tried others, but in the end decided to use the wool from the German Whiteheaded Mutton. It was a fast grower, a large breed and had a high fecundity. Ideal really.'

'So are you saying that whoever killed Saul was a German soldier?' Jim knew that if this was so, it could be over. There could be hundreds of thousands of possible matches. It would be futile to try and prove that one person was responsible, when there were so many coats in existence.

'No, Jim. This person had a German military overcoat on, but it was an old one. A very old one, in fact.'

'How old?'

'World War Two.' Jessica could almost hear the cogs turn as Jim went through his mental list of anyone that could be connected in any way. He knew of a couple of old boys who collected a few trinkets here and there, but in terms of apparel, even the army surplus store in town would not go back that far. This type of apparel was usually to be found in museums, not on somebody's back. *Whoever owned this piece of clothing was going to be either a serious collector, or a serious nutcase*, he decided.

'Well,' Jim responded, that's amazing, Jess. I'm racking my brains to think of anyone who might own something like that, but so far I can't think of anyone. Shame, that.' He truly was disappointed. More often than not, he knew that arrests and convictions were the result of hard work and research, not the television-fuelled kind of pathways that sensationalised police work and made everyone believe that there was usually a car chase or Mexican stand-off involved between the officers (usually armed) and some corrupt politician or businessman.

'Hang on, Jim. I'm not finished.'

Jim readied himself for another batch of information to assimilate. His brain was hurting a little. He was glad he had sat down. 'Okay, Jess. Go for it.'

'Well, I took the initiative after this find, and received consent from Reena Singh's family to have another look at her body. It took some persuading, but when I had another look at her body, you'll never guess what I found, my old chum.'

'Let me guess, another fibre?'

'Spot on. It matched the first. Now, to me, unless there are suddenly a load of clowns with homicidal tendencies in World War Two overcoats roaming the streets of Bloomfield.........'

'We are most likely looking for one person who committed both crimes. Jessica, you are a star. Are CID onto this?'

'Of course they are, Jim. I've shared this with them, every word. I'm not stupid. They're the good guys too, remember. I just thought you might want to know. You've got your ear to the ground. I'm sure that a good policeman like yourself would inform them if you knew anything. Am I right?'

'Yes you are. And yes, I will. As I said, you're a star, and one of the brightest. And prettiest.' He immediately regretted having said this. Neither of them spoke of their past any more. They simply accepted the present and looked forward to the future. There was a moment's silence, then Jess broke it.

'Take care, Jim. Stay out of trouble.' The line went dead, and Jim replaced his mobile phone into his breast pocket once more. He stood, and continued his beat. There were now lots of things whirring around his consciousness like Catherine wheels, ignited by the information he had just received. Part of his mind was still searching his own grey matter for anyone who might have mentioned or worn such an overcoat. The search results were blank, and he parked that thought. It would have to wait, although it was going to be crucial to this case ever being solved and the families of the victims getting any sort of closure. His mind's eye fell on Sam Kettering next. He had been intrigued greatly by the young man, and his gut was telling him that both his demeanour when they met, and his portfolio of art work, were way too quirky for him *not* to be involved in this in any way. He didn't know why, but he didn't believe that Sam was responsible for those murders. He had looked in the eyes of murderers before, and he didn't see the arrogance, or the distance, that murderers often displayed. He seemed too honest, too uncorrupted. He had delayed his intention to perform an old-school stakeout on Sam, as he had found himself buried in the minutiae of his regular police work and needed to take care of that, for fear of anyone finding out of his desire to dig deeper into the murders. He was resolute, but he still had to pay the bills. However, after the conversation with Quinn, and the twisting feeling in his stomach that was seldom wrong, he felt that the time had come to do exactly that. He would be finished on his shift soon enough. He would go home, get changed, take what he needed, and head off. It might be a long night, but one way or another, he might possibly make sense of Sam, and his involvement, and really make a difference. With his thumbs tucked neatly into his stab vest, he continued on his way around the village he loved, hoping that his presence was all that would be needed to safeguard those that he had sworn to protect.

38

Matt was nearly drunk. He looked at his hand in front of him, and giggled to himself as he reached for the door in front of him. He just about managed to get a proper hold of it, and then urged his brain to communicate with his legs. With what seemed like the speed of a second class letter, his legs responded to the request from his brain (in a language they didn't quite understand), and moved themselves forward, one at a time, as they had once been instructed to do when they were much younger.

Stepping out into the crisp, fresh night air, Matt looked up at the stars. Around Bloomfield, there were usually less stars to be seen than in the countryside, due to a mixture of both light and traffic pollution from the cars and other vehicles around the suburb, plus the general pollution that came from living near a big city like London. Tonight, though, seemed different. For some reason, his alcohol-clouded eyes were able to focus on more than just the major constellations, and he easily located his absolute favourite, Cassiopeia. Named after a vain and boastful queen in Greek mythology, he loved everything about it, and had done since his childhood, when his father used to sit him down at night with a pair of binoculars to find the constellations, telling him of each one in as much detail as he knew. From its distinctive 'W' shape, to the fact that it contained a mysterious star-making nebula (or dust cloud) named 'The Pacman Nebula,' he loved it all, and smiled as he spotted it in the sky. He located his other favourite, Orion's Belt, which was quite literally supposed to symbolise the belt of the great hunter. Also known as the Three Kings, or Three Sisters, it really comprised the three bright stars Alnitak, Alnilam and Mintaka. However, it wasn't the three stars themselves that he loved so much. It was the fact that in all of the potential chaos of space and its unchartered horizons, somebody (or something) had allowed sense to be made from it, in terms of the meaning that had been derived by someone as much in the dark as anyone else. *That was it. It was the sense that could be made from seemingly impossible and implausible scenes.*

Matt looked at the woman stood next to him, and that sentiment rang truer than ever before. Here was he, this complicated, chaotic, mess of a man, struggling to perform to the best of his ability on many levels. Sara had come along, and in a very short space of time, he felt she had begun to bring some sort of order and peace from the maelstrom within him. Looking back over the years, and especially at his failed marriage to Andrea, the very successful personal assistant to a corporate executive, it suddenly made sense. He could never, *never* have been truly happy with her, as their existence together only brought further chaos and antagonism with it, whether over the concept of children together, or general compatibility at the end of the day. But looking at Sara, with her natural beauty, her innocent charm and her grounded approach to, well, everything, he could only admire her more than any other woman he knew or had ever been intimate with. He wondered if this was what love was. He knew it was potentially impossible to define, by virtue of its subjective nature, but when he felt this overwhelmed, he was convinced it had to be.

He snapped his mind back to his surroundings, and to Sara, who was doing a very proficient job of supporting Matt as he tried to suck in the fresh air. She was in a far better state than he, and he knew it. He did love cutting loose on Friday, though.

'Hey you, are you sure you can't come back to mine? Just look at what you'll be missing if you don't.' He struck his best bodybuilder pose, and allowed his face to go purple through the strain of holding it.

'As tempting as watching you shit yourself actually is, I'm going to have to pass, you utter clown. Mum has Ashleigh, and she's got another appointment in the morning, and can't have her longer than about eight thirty. Sorry, but the gun show will simply have to wait till another night.' She was genuinely disappointed, but both of them knew that family came first. Sara had been impressed with Matt since their relationship had become physical, in that he never pushed her to do anything she didn't want to do, and was extremely sensitive to her role as a mother. She presumed this was tied in to the fact that he was a teacher and promoted family values at first, but when he had given her the potted version of his own family history, she realised it was nothing to do with that; he was simply a very caring man who seemingly had no objection to doing the right thing by Sara and Ashleigh. She hadn't told him yet, but in her eyes, this was very, very cool and made him all the more attractive.

'My lady, that's absolutely fine. Given that it appears that I have drunk a little too much, I fear that I will be of very little use in the physical department tonight anyway, and I feel that any attempt to woo you in our customary fashion would be akin to playing snooker with a rope.' Matt knew that as a couple, they were now past the 'not breaking wind' stage, and also the stage whereby it was normal to be as crude as they liked in front of each other (within limits). Matt had found out at quite an early stage that Sara was not unaccustomed to the odd more colourful metaphor, and he was very comfortable with that. This feeling was however superseded by the fact that she had an incredibly dry and quick sense of humour, and she was not afraid to use it on weaker mortals, but never in a horrible way. She was, like him, extremely self-deprecating, and always took what she gave out in very good spirits. Matt knew he was onto a good thing, and although he did his best to play it cool, he recognised he was now trying to make it through every single day without Sara seeing through him for what he believed he really was – a charlatan.

Together, they moved slowly, arms interlocked, until they reached Sara's home for the night. Her mother's house was dark when they reached the door, which Sara always took for a good sign. It meant that there were no mystery illnesses or tantrums that would have kept Ashleigh awake as often happened in the past when she went out in the earlier days before Matt. She had seen a change in this respect, and was loving the fact that it was most likely down to the relationship that Greaves had built with her daughter. He never pretended to be her father, but gave her more affection and quiet guidance than her biological father ever had.

'Well,' Sara whispered, 'this is me.'

'Yes, it is. Thanks for a fantastic night again Sara. Once again, your quiz mastery and karaoke skills have made my life complete.' They had come last in the quiz, and Sara had inadvertently emptied the bar of any stragglers at the end of the night with her rendition of 'Bohemian Rhapsody.'

'I do try and please.' She replied, pulling Matt closer. Their lips met, tenderly, and to Matt, the kiss seemed to last forever. He opened his eyes, and looked right into Sara's eyes.

'Listen, Sara, there's something I think I need to say to you.' Matt was not smiling. Sara immediately thought he was going to call the whole thing off, and her look of fright was clearly visible on her own countenance, because Matt suddenly smiled.

'Don't worry. It's nothing horrible. Well, I hope not anyway.'

'Thank fuck for that. Sorry. Didn't mean to say fuck. Shit!' She knew she was on the verge of making a fool of herself. Matt cut in, and she knew when he opened his mouth that he didn't care that she had used an expletive.

'I think I love you Sara. I don't know if I know what that is, but I think I do. The thing is, I've never been so happy, and...'

This time, it was she who cut his speech short. She said nothing, but pulled herself to within an inch, and then kissed him hard on the mouth. They enjoyed that kiss for a long time, and when they separated, Matt could see in the darkness that Sara had tears in her eyes. This brought his own tears, especially when Sara quietly whispered the words that made Matt want to explode with unbridled joy.

'I love you too. I have done from the moment we met that night. It's so hard for me to say that, but believe me I do. I do, I do.' She turned, unlocked the door, gave Matt a quick kiss on the cheek, and then closed the door quietly. Behind the door, he was sure he could hear her laughing.

The rest of the walk home, although slow, felt like he was drifting through the clouds, like some sort of ethereal being. It was partly down to the drink, but he was ecstatic to know that this time, it was mostly down to the fact that she had not only accepted his proclamation, but had made her own statement of intent to him too. He couldn't fathom it out. She was perfect. She was way too good for him, and she still liked him. *Don't screw it up, Greavsie.* He gave himself this advice over and over in his head, as if the mere repetition would program his brain to undertake every activity to make sure that this happened.

He suddenly realised that he was only a few metres from his front door, and shook his head slightly at the absence from his journey home that his thoughts of Sara had given him. He smiled to himself, and looked forward to what could be the rest of his life in this sort of happiness. His keys jingled and jangled as he searched for the correct one to allow him access, and as he singled out the small, golden key, he was suddenly distracted by a noise from the alleyway opposite.

Matt was not afraid of the dark, and the crash of what seemed like metal bins followed by the sounds of an animal whimpering were too much for his curiosity to bear. Crossing the street, he stopped at the aperture to the alley, squinting into the darkness to see if he could make anything out. It was too dark, so he took a few steps further in, towards the only two bins lining the walls at that particular moment. As he approached, he realised that it was now deathly silent, and the normal night time noises of revellers making their own way home, plus the whine of diesel engines on local minicabs, were non-existent. He approached slower, just in case the animal that had whimpered was hurt. He knew from experience what injured animals could do, and had the scars to prove it from a previous dog bite many years ago.

The blanket of silence that protected the sleep of those nearby was scythed by the frenzied crash of the bins exploding outwards, and Matt was momentarily given the fright of his life by the unknown. He reeled backwards, almost losing his footing, and then straightened as the stray dog scampered away into the light of the street, carrying what appeared to be the carcass of a chicken.

Regaining his breath, Matt smiled, then began to laugh as he realised how it would have looked to any bystander. However, by the time the rising chuckle had begun to escape his lips, his world had gone black, and he had fallen to the floor in an unconscious heap. Behind him, and towering over his own comatose carcass, stood two men. Two men who, in the dead of night, calmly put away their coshes, and roughly carried Matt into the light of the street. Ignoring the immediate danger of publicity, they opened the back doors of a vintage Mark One Ford Transit, and bundled the dead weight into the harsh, bare interior. Closing the doors gently, the larger of the two gentlemen turned to the smaller and asked a simple question.

'Where to?'

Harry Planter simply retorted with 'I-9. Someone has plans for this poor fuck. He's not going to know what hit him.' They entered the van, and with Harry behind the wheel, he lit a cigarette, and steered Matt's carriage into the night. As it disappeared into the distance, a dog emerged, carrying the chicken in its mouth. It stopped in the middle of the road, sniffed the air, and returned to the darkness of the alleyway to resume its meal in privacy.

39

The night surrounded Nick's car like a death shroud, and although there was absolutely nothing out of the ordinary to note, Nick felt a surge of adrenalin as he sat in his car for the first forty five minutes upon arriving at his destination. Having acquired the schematics for I-9 via his own means, he had envisaged a very spy-worthy set of events out in his head, even culminating with the possibility of him foiling the evil megalomaniac, rescuing the girl, and generally kicking ass (even though there wasn't a violent bone in his body, and he wouldn't know what to do with his fists even if he were presented the opportunity).

Nick realised that he was completely out of his depth in even venturing out to undertake such surveillance, and that he had absolutely no clue as to whether he was conspicuous or otherwise in his jeans, hoodie and Nike trainers. He wondered whether he should have opted for the more traditional black clothing for this type of caper, but without realising it, he had been quite near the mark, with his ability to hide in plain sight. His resources for the evening were quite simple; sustenance in the shape of some crisps, and oddly a flask of hot Bovril. This was a last minute addition, and one he was not ashamed of. Secondly, warm clothing to enable him to remain inside the car if it got colder, without drawing attention to himself by turning the car heaters on with the engine running. Lastly, he had brought along his Swiss Army penknife, a present from Matt, just in case he was called upon to be resourceful. He was no McGyver (a television hero from his childhood, who could make a sub-machine gun out of a paper clip and two pieces of Sellotape, it seemed), but he thought in the worst case scenario, if there really was something sinister going on, then he was better off being prepared than not. Frankly, if he were to get into any sort of physical bother, he knew that the knife would be as useful to him as a chocolate fireguard.

Like most adrenaline-fuelled activities, once it has worn off, there is always the low period that follows. Nick was soon experiencing this, having seen, heard and felt absolutely nothing for what turned out to be a very long time. Any police detective worth their salt would have told Nick that stakeouts were nothing like the movies really. Required to secrete themselves for days on end to get the evidence required, the officers involved were often bored, tired, and fed up. However good the intelligence supporting the need for a stakeout, the forces of good always relied on the fact that the perpetrators of crime were planning to follow their instructions and visit the site sooner, rather than later. This often did not go quite to plan, which could lead to severe frustration, constant shift changes, and wasted resources, both human and otherwise.

Nick looked at his watch, and realised that he had been sitting in the car for nearly three hours straight. He became mesmerised by the luminous face momentarily, and allowed the glare from it to burn its way onto his retina. He looked away, smiling at the negative image he now saw in front of him as he looked into the night sky. *Eye nine seven on.* Had he totally misread this? His initial feelings of smugness were now not so prevalent, and were quickly being faced with resignation and regret that he had even taken it upon himself to poke his nose in where it was not wanted, just to satisfy his idle curiosity.

'Jesus, Nick. What a complete arsehole you are.' he said to himself, looking around his car and seeing the remnants of his crisps, and the horizontal flask of Bovril, which he had been very glad to have taken in the end. Its beefy warmth had indeed kept the cold at bay.

He banged both his palms on the steering wheel in anger, and bowed his head till it rested on them. He turned his head to one side, as if repulsed by them, and allowed his stare to extend beyond his own reflection in the side window, to the outside night, and into the scrub land opposite. He snapped himself out of his stupor, and had already plotted the course in his head to the Arthur, plus his first order upon arrival within a fraction of a second afterwards. He reached downwards, gripped the ignition key and turned it to the first position, and then the second. His dashboard lit up. He was about to turn it to the final position and start the engine, when his rear view mirror alerted him with a silent flash. Something had turned the corner a few hundred yards behind him in the distance. He could clearly see the twin lamps of what appeared to be a large car grinning at him, growing larger with every second.

Nick instinctively killed the ignition and slid downwards in his seat. He didn't really know what else to do in the circumstances, but from his vantage point some metres away from the twin gates and their shroud of corrugated iron, he was sure he'd be spotted in the headlights if he remained at anything resembling a normal height.

He used the electric wing mirror adjuster to improve his ability to see what was going on, and his heart skipped a beat when the van slowed to a halt adjacent to the rusty gates, and two men emerged from what Nick recognised as an original Ford Transit van, painted white, with its twin circular headlights surrounded by chrome, and its trademark smiling radiator grille at the front. Nick noticed that it was in pristine condition, and a recent television programme containing various car auctions had shown one going for around thirteen thousand pounds. Nick noticed almost absentmindedly that this one had a number plate from around nineteen seventy. Even in the darkness, it was clear that this was in pristine condition, and the thought crossed Nick's mind that whoever owned it was clearly paid enough from what they did to purchase and maintain it in the condition it sat in currently, with the engine ticking over like a Swiss watch.

Nick surmised next that the business in question had to be deliveries, as the two men appeared from the back end of the van with what appeared to be a really heavy sack, made from canvas, and with a knot tied in the top to prevent its contents from falling out. At that moment, a new list of potential fillings for the sack formed in Nick's mind. *Potatoes? Other vegetables?* That couldn't be possible. Why would anyone have potatoes delivered to this address? Unless there was a secret cookery club taking place that nobody ever spoke about, and which needed the secrecy of an encrypted website, that was never going to be an option.

His eyes widened at the next thought. He tried to ignore the thought, but it simply would not leave his consciousness, no matter how hard he tried. *A body? What if it was a body?* Nick almost laughed out loud at the silliness of what he was contemplating.

'Fuck, Nick,' he sneered to himself quietly, 'come off it, this isn't a gangster movie. This is real life, for fuck's sake.'

However, the events unfolding before him could not have been more similar to a gangster movie if he had written it himself. Here were two men, looking like they were frankly up to no good, carrying what appeared to be a sack containing goods which looked very much shaped like a body. This was most definitely not good. It was beginning to appear that he could well have stumbled upon something very worthy of its own secret web pages and codes. He knew that he was almost definitely out of his league now, and that even if it turned out to be nothing and made him look foolish, he was going to have to report this to somebody as soon as possible.

This was not going to be easy, as it was way after ten o'clock now, and besides the fact that he would have to make a phone call in his car, and draw attention to himself, he was not sure how he was even going to describe what he was seeing without anyone laughing at him. He didn't mind feeling a fool, but it would be better if he had some more evidence first before rushing in head first.

The gates had now opened, and the two men had taken their cargo inside the gates. The gates were left ajar, and the engine was still running in the van, so Nick presumed that this was going to be a very quick drop off. He snapped to action, and decided that he was going to go in for a closer look, a least to an entrance where this mysterious cargo might have been taken. If there was any evidence that it had been a body that had been carried in, then he promised himself he would not go any further, and would call the police from there.

With a final, lengthy check ahead, Nick quietly opened the car door, and slid himself out silently. He envisioned every movement he made as cat-like, and in his mind's eye he pictured himself moving like a young Sean Connery, who had reputedly been awarded the role as James Bond due to the fact that he, too, was thought to move like a panther. The stark reality was that despite his best efforts to conceal himself and not give his position away through sight or sound, he would not have been discovered anyway, as the streets were completely deserted. Nick recognised the absolute lack of audible call sign from anywhere, and this heightened his tension slightly, as he slipped through the open gate and into the darker, more ominous surroundings inside the compound.

It is a widely considered misconception that our eyes adjust quickly to the darkness around us. When we turn off our lights at night, it seems like only minutes before we are able to recognise our surroundings and see what we believe is to the best of our ability. This, however, is not the case. The reality of the situation is much different. Light familiarisation actually happens in two different stages. Firstly, the pupils dilate, to allow any light available to flood the eye. Then, once this has happened, the light sensitive rods adjust over many minutes, often up to several hours. Soldiers are made aware of this as part of their basic training, as many of their activities often take place under the cover of darkness. For the average human being and civilian, though, the rapid adjustment in the first few minutes leaves us thinking that we have fully developed our night vision, without realising that our eyes will continue to improve as time progresses, albeit by smaller amounts over greater amounts of time.

Nick, being a civilian, and completely naïve to the inner workings of the human eye, succumbed to the identical perception of his night vision, and as he crept, stooped, through the compound stretching out in front of him, he was completely unaware of his exact surroundings and the topography of the ground that he was covering. He was aware that in the darkness, he was walking across a mixture of rough concrete floor, which definitely had coarse chippings mixed into it, as he periodically would catch the toe of his trainers on them, causing him to slow his movement, without quite tripping over. The concrete intermittently gave way to patches of rough, uneven brush, with overgrown grasses of indeterminate species, and the occasional piles of rubble and other detritus, flotsam and jetsam that one would expect to see in an unused, desolate working space, which was now devoid of the daily hustle and bustle one would witness were it occupied by any business. As his eyes grew accustomed, he could not see the two men who had entered the complex before him, but could see a narrow, slightly worn pathway, which had recently been covered by one or more people. People whom, he assumed, could have been carrying a third person. A third person wrapped in a tied sack. He tried to make sense of the distances he was covering, and he made a brief connection to driving at night, and the difference in depth perception whilst doing so.

Abruptly, he stopped in his tracks, his brain informing his legs that he needed to appraise himself further of his surroundings before he could continue moving them.

Adjacent to a huge cable reel, he crouched in its relative shelter, and opened his eyes even wider, as if the very fact he had done so would bear relevance to the width of his pupils.

All was silent. There were various outbuildings, all made of concrete with asbestos roofs, and all without any visible doors, or hinges where they once could have been. This led Nick to believe that although empty, they must have once been lump stores, where stones, cement, or other ballast would have been piled, for easy collection and transfer into awaiting lorries or other receptacles. None of these structures seemed capable of housing any entrances to anywhere, and they all looked as if they had bene ignored for years. To make them look this old and disused would have taken some fabrication. Nick extended his gaze to a wider field of vision, and was instantly met with another outhouse, which took his interest and yanked it up, shaking it and forcing him to stare intently through the cloak of grey that surrounded him.

There, at a distance of around fifty metres away, stood a different kind of building. Dilapidated, yes, but in a different kind of way. Its windows, like the eyes of a house that a child would draw, stared into the darkness in a row of five or six sections, and their frames were, even in the darkness, able to display that they had been neglected, covered in a jacket of rust and corrosion. However, Nick noticed almost immediately, even in the low light, that something was wrong. Not wrong, exactly, but there appeared to be an anachronism. Like a wristwatch on one of the disciples at the last supper. The penny dropped, and Nick's heart rate increased considerably as the realisation set in. *The windows. They all have glass panes, and they are all intact.* It would be impossible in Bloomfield, even under lock and key, for glass panes such as these, in these numbers, to be completely untouched. Similarly, Nick noticed that the grey brick of the building was completely devoid of any graffiti whatsoever. In a society where 'tagging' had been taken to new, dangerous extremes, and where disaffected teenagers and young adults regularly risked life and limb to display their call signs on any bare surface, there should be no earthly reason for any building in a derelict site to be this spotless. *Jesus, Nick. There has to be a reason for this. But what? Is it because the kids have been scared off? Are they too worried of the consequences of such actions to even come near the place?*

Nick felt his curiosity burning a hole in him, and he took a moment for his stomach to settle before engaging his feet to carry him closer to the offending building. As he approached, his mind filled in the many blanks that were clearly visible, in terms of what he was going to find when he reached his destination, and also in terms of how much danger he could actually be in, were his ideas on the contents of the sack to be correct. He reached the corner of the glazed outhouse, and flattened his back against the grey, cold brick wall. At that particular moment, he could have been pressed against a glacier, as the cold of the brick in the night air, coupled with the rush of adrenaline around his veins, had made him feel like a Siberian winter. It focused his senses to the point of catching his breath, and summoning his energy, he swivelled around to face the entrance to the building, and potentially a confrontation with the two men whom he had been trying to observe.

He was met with the cold, laconic stare from the glass window panels, and nothing more. Nick's senses burned, and he searched them for any evidence that he was in danger, so that he could activate his brain's natural flight reaction. His hand suddenly sent a pain receptor to his brain, and he looked down, to find that he was gripping his Swiss army knife in his pocket, so tightly that it had hurt his palm. He released his grip on it, and removed his cold hand from the right pocket of his hoodie.

Like the windows, the door of the building was rusted, and again, similarly, in each six-foot metal frame, stood an almost pristine pane of glass. Untouched by vandals, uncracked, and looking as if it had only recently been fitted. Nick placed his hand on the left-hand door, which was slightly ajar, and cold to the touch also. It was as if cold was a metaphor for foreboding evil, and it had channelled as much as possible from the surroundings as a warning to all around.

In the stillness of the night, Nick peeled back the door, and stepped inside the threshold of the building. It swallowed him slowly, and inside, Nick could just about make out a couple of old, wooden desks, just like Matt's teacher's desk at school. Two plastic garden chairs had been placed behind each one, and apart from that, the only other visible feature of the room was a heavy, solid, metal door, looking as if it had been borrowed from a submarine, or maybe a warship. It was slightly ajar, and Nick's breathing instantly stopped when through a sliver in the doorway, a very faint light suddenly appeared. Wavy, and flickering, it instantly presented itself as torchlight to Nick, and he suddenly became flooded with realism in relation to his predicament. He needed to run. Immediately. His brain had already sent the messages to his legs to turn and run, but they were interrupted by something incredibly strange that permeated his consciousness before engaging in flight.

The hinges on the door.

They should have screamed in protest in the silent night.

They were silent as the night itself.

That means that they had been oiled.

That means someone is keeping them quiet.

And that means someone is down there.

Run.

As this thought process finally kicked in, he felt his legs burst into action and begin to turn him around, out of the situation, and back to the relative safety of his car and the arms of the Metropolitan Police, who were clearly far better equipped to investigate such matters. He never got the chance to complete his turn, as his adrenaline was replaced by a sharp prod behind his ear, and as he turned around, his heart literally skipped a beat as he realised that he was staring into the barrel of a charcoal-black revolver. Not shiny and alluring like the guns in the movies; this was a battered, well-used model that had clearly seen better days, but had undoubtedly been fired before. In his fossilized state, Nick tried to block out instantly the thought of how many lives it might have taken. He was still concentrating on the gun, when a lightning movement made the arm holding it recede, and explode forward and across his temple in a narrow arc. Nick did not have time for his automatic defences to kick into action. The room simply went black, and he fell to the floor, unconscious. It was not a heavy blow, as it went; he would not be unconscious for long. However, it was enough to send him into a void which would ensure his new captors enough time to do what they wanted with him. And that was to bind his arms behind his back, and tape his mouth with duct tape. It was just as well that Nick did not have any breathing issues. They did not bother to check this. Not out of malice, but simply as they did not have any knowledge that this was what they needed to do.

The two men, of roughly the same age, and of indeterminate feature, stood over Nick's prone figure and smiled. This was going to earn them some serious brownie points. They picked Nick's limp body up between them, and left the solitude and peace of the night. The entry building swallowed them whole, and did not stop to chew.

40

Jim White smiled to himself, and realised that Julie was going to kill him. Not literally, of course, but when she had asked where he was going, and he had replied that he was going out for a few hours '...to follow up on something he'd seen,' she had sighed heavily, and reminded him that he was not an investigative officer, and that he should stay in with her and enjoy an early night. As he turned his back to leave the house, she had smiled, knowing full well that it would take a team of wild horses to keep him from going out to follow his heart, and his very astute nose, to get answers to his questions. She felt no shame in thanking Jim for keeping her safe, and she knew he loved the fact that she was open about in valuing what he did for the family, and the community, each day.

'Make sure you take your scarf. It's chilly tonight.' He remembered her shouting in what was, to this day, the sexiest voice in the whole, wide world.

Jim had already lifted his scarf and woolly hat from the pegs next to the front door, and turned to Julie as he opened the door.

'I won't be long, gorgeous.' Was all he had said before closing the door behind him and climbing into his run-of-the-mill, highly inconspicuous, boring family saloon. Reliable and trustworthy (like himself), it turned over first time, and without hesitation or any procrastination, he was out of the drive, with one of Julie's boy bands chirping away quietly in the background.

Jim noticed that the night was a clear one, and for that reason he was going to have to make sure that he didn't spend too long out of the car if he could help it. He didn't mind the cold, however he felt that for what he had in mind tonight, the less sign he gave away the better, and his hot breath escaping like steam from a kettle was not going to afford him any sympathy, should his hunch be correct, and tonight's quarry be more attuned to the fact that they were being tailed than he believed they were.

It seemed like no time at all before he had reached his destination. Like most streets in Bloomfield, there was nothing special about this particular street. It could and would be described as modern suburbia in any society. A range of almost identical houses, not old, not new, bearing just enough wear and tear from the elements to tell a casual observer that the people who dwelled here had possibly more interesting things to think about than the upkeep of their houses for the neighbours. Lawns, where visible, showed some care, but the overall décor and paintwork belied a slight lack of attention, and a general low-level neglect that often illustrated the plight of the working man. *I'll do it at the weekend.*

Cosgrove Close was silent, and Jim had taken every precaution that any nosey neighbours, and good citizens, would not be noticing him this evening. He had parked in Primrose avenue, perpendicular to Cosgrove Close, and had only left himself enough of a vantage point to see the front door from an oblique angle. Not that it mattered. There was only one way in, and one way out. And Jim was hoping that tonight, his hunch would pay off, and he would see someone coming out. He had parked in what would have been the shade of an enormous Beech tree that had taken root some years ago in the grass verge alongside the pavement, and it was so in need of trimming, that to the naked eye, the shadows and reflections on the windscreen made it almost impossible to determine whether there was anyone actually in the car or not. Jim preferred the perception to be not. He knew most of the inhabitants, either through his day-to-day professional life, or through social connections, and he did not want anyone to be saying hello tonight.

He looked at his watch, and it was now way past midnight. Closer to one o'clock. Jim, however, did not let this deter him from his quest. Neither the time, nor the fact that Julie would be worrying about him, made him veer from the path he had chosen tonight. Since his meeting at the college with Sam Kettering, and his decision to see where he was spending his evenings, Jim was convinced in his heart that Sam had been hiding something when they had spoken, under the ruse of him wanting an able artist for a corporate re-branding. If there was one thing that Jim knew, it was people. And especially their faces. He was a very good poker player, and it was his ability to know people's ticks and tells (signs that they are bluffing or holding good hands) that meant that he had developed quite the reputation for himself amongst the group of friends he met with regularly to play, eat, and socialise without the pressure of high stakes. It wasn't about the money for him; he was more interested in the calculation, patience and sheer bravado that were sometimes required to help him win.

There were many, many ways in which a person could be seen to be lying. Sam had demonstrated quite a few of the signs that were convincing enough to find Jim where he was at such a late hour. Firstly, Sam had touched his nose. A lot. This was often attributed to a rush of adrenaline to the capillaries in the nose, making them itch. Others attributed it to a subconscious need to hide. Either way, Jim noticed it. Secondly, Jim had noticed a micro-expression in Sam, whereby his eyebrows had raised towards his forehead, creating creases in his forehead. This was widely appreciated as a sign of untruth, especially in interrogation. Thirdly, Sam had, on occasion, looked up, and to the right, when he was talking. In right handed people, when they were making things up and fabricating or embellishing stories, they looked in this direction. It was the opposite for left-handed people. Jim had not shown any recognition to this fact when Sam had spoken and answered his questions, but it was clear as day to him that Sam was clearly hiding something. Jim knew that one could not rely solely on facial expression and nervous ticks alone, so that was why he was chancing his luck on Sam, in the hope that he would be able to shed a little light on the graffiti, and maybe help Jim get a little perspective on what the symbolism was in the icons that had cropped up in several places over town.

Jim loved it when he was right. He was never smug, but he really loved being correct, especially when in relation to a hunch. It affirmed his confidence in himself. Jim was very patient, but had conceded defeat to his stomach, and was just into his second cup of coffee, accompanied by his second Wagon Wheel (which he couldn't help noticing had gone much smaller over the years), when a movement in the corner of his vision took his attention away from the chocolate and marshmallow in his hand, and onto the street. He slid like a python into his seat, hoping it would ingest him enough and not betray his position or purpose.

From the nondescript, slightly unkempt, and badly painted house, emerged Sam Kettering. He was wheeling his bicycle, and he was making every effort to not wake anybody at home while he was leaving. Jim couldn't help but notice that for someone who was cycling at night, he was dressed rather darkly. Black jogging trousers, a black shell suit top, and black trainers, betrayed the fashion sense of his peers, who were all sporting either white polo shirts and trainers with skinny jeans these days, or lurid pinks and reds to accompany their well-groomed hairstyles. Sam flicked on the lights at the front and rear of his cycle, but the beams seemed to be sucked up by the darkness in his attire, and they appeared to only suggest that they were willing to do their job for him that evening.

Sam mounted his bicycle, and quickly picked up speed as he cruised out of his cul-de-sac, and past Jim's car without so much as a blink in his direction. Jim noticed his almost vacant body language, as if her were on auto-pilot. It was as if he had something weighing on his mind, and Jim vowed to try to follow him to his destination, in order to see what it was.

The movies make tailing somebody seem very easy. Anyone watching a film would think that there were only two rules. Firstly, stay two cars behind, and secondly, don't get seen. The reality of this was far different, though. Surveillance by car is based on the premise that *if you can see them, they can see you.* This means that if the movies were correct, everyone following would be in a black Cadillac or shiny vehicle of some description, be wearing dark glasses, and would be visible upon closer inspection only two cars away. The trick was to remain far enough back to not be seen, whilst second guessing the route they would be taking, based on previous surveillance from afar. *Afar.* That was the key. Jim was worried tonight, as he did not have the luxury of traffic to disguise him, and in the quitter streets of Bloomfield, he may as well don his high-visibility vest and leave his hand on the horn permanently, if he did not play it very carefully indeed.

Which is exactly what he did from the start. In his mind, he thought of the potential avenues that Sam would take, based on his desire to be inconspicuous, and based on the fact that he had previously been up to some potentially clandestine activities, away from the main roads and C.C.T.V. cameras. He counted carefully the number of potential corners Sam might take before turning on the ignition, and then pulled away smoothly and quietly, hoping to ensure that he did not stumble on Sam. If Sam had the remotest idea that somebody was being followed, he could either adopt an anti-surveillance route (ASR), or simply pull over, upon which act the game, if that was what it was, would be over for Jim.

And so the game continued. Sam cycled on, the deserted streets affording him a clear route through Bloomfield. Cutting through suburbia, he must have been enjoying the ride, because when he eventually arrived at his destination, Jim realised that he had not taken the most direct route, but had taken a much more convoluted one, the reasons for which could only have been whimsical.

Jim's saloon car came to a ticking stop at the corner of what seemed to be a deserted street, except for a lone bicycle propped just inside a set of large, metal, barred gates, which had deliberately been left ajar. They were reasonably functional, and Jim noticed that the locking mechanism, comprising a sliding bolt and padlock, was well worn, shiny, and smooth. He could see as much, even in the shroud of darkness and street lighting that was spitting its pitiful rays around this chasm of a street. He noticed, also, the sporty hatchback across the road from the gates, and he felt that this was out of place for this area, at this time of night. His first thought was that there were probably youngsters making desperate love in there, unable to find anywhere safer to display their affections for each other. He usually told them to move on, instead of creating a fuss; he was their age once, after all. He decided to investigate.

There were, of course, no teenagers inside the car. It was Nick's vehicle and it was, of course, unoccupied, as it was as yet unknown to Jim that its owner had recently been taken underground, to a fate as yet equally as dubious. Jim quietly peered into the passenger window at the front, and he saw some paraphernalia that slightly disturbed him. Firstly, the flask, which indicated that somebody had either been out previously, and had needed a flask, or had been at that very spot, using it as sustenance during the activity that they were undertaking, which probably involved a whole lot of surveillance, in his head. He had brought his own energy supplies to his own stakeout after all.

From the car, he looked across the road to the open gates. They had not moved in the last five minutes, and stood resolute, defiant to anyone who dared to try to break down their defences when closed and locked. Jim was no fool when it came to his own patch, and there was no place in Bloomfield that he did not have at least the bare minimum of information about. He knew that this particular property belonged to the Water Authority, or at least it did belong to them. He knew that it had been disused for some years now, due to larger, more efficient premises being built to cope with the increased demand on the water supply as population grew. But he also knew that in all his recent years on the force, he had not once been called to an incident of graffiti, criminal damage, or anything else for that matter. He found that hugely interesting, as he had spent considerable time in the local primary schools proactively policing, often without being asked to do so, in the hope that he could convey the messages regarding crime and consequences to the young people of Bloomfield. The messages, he thought, that they really wanted to hear, not the ones that his superiors, or the government, wanted conveyed due to their statistics. He would speak to them about the real and present danger of abduction, grooming online, and also the dangers of venturing onto building sites, and business properties just like this one. It was this fact that interested his curiosity in his own abilities; he knew he was good, but he wasn't *that* good. There should have been at least one or two idiots around who would have taken one look at the pristine, blank stone and wanted to tag it with indecipherable nonsense. There was a singular reason why nobody at all had visited this site. Usually, it was complacency, or sometimes pride in one's neighbourhood which led to unwritten laws of where one could and could not commit crimes of vandalism; secondly, and in this case more probably, the potential criminals had been scared off. Sometimes through legend, but sometimes more directly, word was enough to make anyone, young or old, go somewhere else to ply their trade.

Jim looked down at his feet. They were used to pounding the pavements, his bicycle pedals, and occasionally running at speed. He curled the corner of his mouth up as he questioned whether they were built for stealth. He agreed with his conscience that on this occasion, they were. He was acutely aware that in following Sam Kettering into the old, disused depot and any one of its buildings or underground corridors (for he knew they existed, but not from first-hand experience) was trespassing. He was not on duty, and his superiors would most definitely have questioned his motives, even if he were. It was likely they would not allow him to progress, but he was convinced in his mind that Sam was up to no good. And that meant that he would be doing Sam, himself, his profession and the community an injustice if he did not go ant take a very small look around to investigate whether there was any criminal activity afoot. He thought of what he would do if discovered, and he decided that he would pretend that he had simply seen the open gate and the bicycle, and had come in to check that nobody had been injured.

He crossed the road, and the ferrous jaws of the complex stood before him, grinning, with a black opening just wide enough for his whole body to walk through without his shoulders touching either gate. He did just that. It reminded him of entering a graveyard. To him, it didn't matter how busy the world was outside, the moment that one entered a graveyard, it acted as a shield to the world outside. The peace that surrounded the buried, and their own air of secrecy, made it impossible not to notice this. In a similar way, he noticed that despite the peaceful stillness of night outside the gates, once inside the threshold, there was no mistaking the almost vacuous silence, that some might equate to the immeasurable void of space.

Jim used his rapidly developing night vision to look for signs that Sam had been on a known path. He didn't have to look far for signs of movement, but it puzzled him that as an amateur boy scout, it was not difficult to see that there was more than one set of footprints on the dusty pathway, and all of them had been made quite recently. He used his senses in union to determine whether anyone was active on site or not. He assumed not, as his peripheral vision highlighted a multitude of rats, busy at work, foraging and industriously asserting their rights over anything edible.

Crouched slightly, he used his visible knowledge of cover to secure a relatively secluded journey to the end of the tracks as they stood. He was left standing outside a bleak, grey, foreboding outhouse, with what appeared to be a set of ancient, metallic doors at its front end. His sharp intellect jabbed him like his pencil with the fact that there were panes of untouched glass in them, and that this went against their age. He noted this in his mental notepad, and gently pulled one of them, after another listen for signs of human occupation. Nothing. He grimaced as he pulled the door, in anticipation of the rusty scream of the hinges, but it never came.

Noticing the desks inside, facing each other like stags during rutting season, he sat on one quietly, noticing the chairs behind each one.

'This is a sentry house.' He whispered to himself. 'Now why, oh why, would anyone require sentries when it's deserted, Jimbo?'

He reached into his jacket pocket, and produced a tiny Mag-Lite torch. There were others available on the market, but he was a stickler for the fact that in some cases, one got what they paid for. Jim had made sure that this model had been given a makeover, and he had inserted a red filter over the lens. He was glad of this, for when he turned it on, he was still able to shed light on his path ahead, without drawing undue attention to himself should anyone be watching from anywhere close by.

The floor of the outhouse was dusty, and Jim immediately became aroused intellectually by the patterns he could see. There were footprints, but also elongated, strangulated furrows in the dirt. The kind that could have been made by something being dragged. *Sam maybe? Or was he dragging something down there?*

Jim thought once again about his options. Like Nick only a short while before, Jim realised that the most sensible course of action would be to simply retrace his steps, and phone the police with his suspicions. He would get into trouble for following Sam without authorisation, as this was a breach of his human rights, but it was still the most sensible path to follow. There was also another thought in Jim's mind, though, which kept him rooted to the spot. *What if Sam, or anybody else for that matter, were in immediate danger? Who knows what could be happening to them, and if I could get a little closer, I would be able to maybe at least help them, if it was possible to do so.*

Jim used his torch to find the door at the back of the outhouse, and with the red, soft beam cutting through the darkness, he slowly, and silently, made his way through the door after opening it, and was surprised to see the steps leading downwards into the belly of Bloomfield. After testing the steps to see if they creaked in the middle, and finding that they didn't, he progressed downwards, not really knowing what he was going to find. Behind him, in the blackness outside, a single cloud covered the moon, and the resulting shadow forced one of the army of rats to momentarily look upwards, before continuing about its business of looking for more detritus to eat. What that particular rodent didn't know was that around fifteen to twenty metres below him, there was enough living human detritus to feed them all.

41

Selleck surveyed his domain, as it was set out in front of him. He was seated in an expansive, well-lit room, adorned with lots of his favourite pieces from World War Two. Behind him, a huge, original Swastika lay draped over the wall, which had allegedly been displayed in the Cretan capital, Heraklion, during the occupation. Some said that the battles fought in and around Crete, and the huge effort by the Cretan resistance with their Spartan weapons over rough terrain, were instrumental in sealing the fate of the Nazis in their whole war effort, due to the enormous amount of resources that were needed to sustain such an occupation in an island that was in parts barren, desolate, impossible to navigate and an ideal hiding place for the resistance. To this day, museums around the island never let tourists and nationals forget the sacrifice and determination of the islanders. It was the idea of the sacrifice that prompted Selleck to pursue that particular item, as he was sure that in order to push his own agenda, this particular omelette could not be made without breaking some eggs.

He looked around the room, and tried to take in the gaze of every man present around him, waiting for him to speak. He had specifically asked them to attend so that he could address them, as his hero addressed the masses all those year ago. As they stood there, with their drinks in hand, he knew he would soon be able to tell them of the glorious adventure that was going to begin in less than a day's time. As he gazed around the sea of heads, he was acutely aware that there were two other reasons why he was so excited. Everything was converging as planned, and there was a bonus to boot.

The seat that Selleck sat upon was no ordinary seat. One of four, this had been the property of none other than Heinrich Himmler himself. Beautifully carved and ornate, it had been presented to him on behalf of his staff, and it was the handiwork of

Karl Maria Willigut that had caught Selleck's eye when he had come across this item on one of his many internet auction sites specialising in memorabilia. Draped in the chair, as a throw would cover the sofa, his bulk filled the chair more than the original recipient ever could, and when he thought of the price he had paid for the item (just over twelve thousand pounds), he smiled widely, knowing that were he to sell it now, it would fetch over ten times that amount.

He called his adoring, and partly intimidated audience to silence. The throng assembled stopped what they were doing in a wave, and the silence fell quickly, all heads turned towards him, awaiting his next words. They were an odd mixture who had been recruited either by word of mouth, or directly by Selleck, recognising their specific talents. Amongst them were many professionals; plumbers, carpenters, accountants, lawyers, ground workers, retail assistants, and almost any other profession that one could imagine. Selleck had been very astute in his recruitment. Through it, and his use of favours and sometimes veiled threat, he was able to acquire goods and services for next to nothing, for the promise of a cash payment here, and protection or a problem solved elsewhere. In fact, the majority of work that had been undertaken in his I-9 complex had been done for a song. The actual cost was probably still ticking over into hundreds of thousands of pounds, but he had done it for only a fraction of that.

'Although a strange time to be talking to you tonight, the time is most definitely right for us. For too long, those of us who follow our cause have witnessed a disease spreading in our midst.' Some of the crowd murmured their agreement, whilst the rest remained transfixed on Selleck and his enormous frame. Even whilst seated, he was an imposing presence. He remained seated, and everyone remained glued to him. Some intrigued by the preamble that was taking shape in such a melodramatic way.

'For decades, we have seen our beautiful land poisoned by those wishing to call themselves natives of our land. This land, which was denied the right to have been ruled by the greatest race on Earth in the two Great Wars. There was a very simple philosophy behind their approach to empire building. If you were not pure, you were to be taken away and made an example of.' Selleck was warming up now to the task of motivating the mostly-male mob, and placing his hands on each arm of the ornate wooden chair, heaved himself in a swift movement up and out of his seated position, bypassing the wooden desk he was behind and moving to the front of the slightly raised floor that provided him with a natural stage on which to perform.

'You have been chosen to enjoy the benefits of our elite club because you believe in the principles that made the Nazi party the most successful proponents of cleansing, ever. In doing so, you have chosen to believe in me. You have served our purpose well, some of you for several years now. Like most long-term campaigns, we were forced to start small, due to limited resources and a membership that needed to grow. Well, I am now able to tell you that I have managed to bring us into the daylight. The new dawn that we have been waiting for, and which named us, is to be upon us. Please look closely at this, and admire the fruits of your labours.'

There was a quiet murmur as those at the back moved forward, to gain a better view of the enormous flat screen monitor that was mounted on the wall. Sleek, black, and expensive (but not to Selleck), it clung to the wall with invisible fingers, and silently came to life when he clicked the appropriate button on the elongated, gleaming remote that had been awaiting his caress on his equally impressive contemporary desk. Upon awakening, he pressed another button, which was directly linked to his sleek laptop computer, on a shelf under his desk. It was lined up with hand-held camera footage, which came to life and began to show movement once activated.

As soon as it started, the audience recognised the venue within which the scenes were being played out. The footage was of the Recreation Ground, or Rec to everyone who was local to Bloomfield. With its sprawling expanses of greenery, each member of the New Dawn movement had, at some point, enjoyed the shelter of the trees there, whether as a playground, a drinking spot, or a secluded outdoor bedroom for late night drunken sex. The pairs of eyes glued to the screen seemed unblinking to Selleck as he watched his captive audience, and he smiled to himself, as if he were able to see his reflection, and he were conspiring with it. He knew he had their full attention.

'You've been patient. You've put up with the foul stench and poison that the Pakis, the Darkies and the Coons have spread around the place for way too long. We've tried to send messages to them, but they wouldn't listen to us. Well, keep your eyes on the screen, and you'll know what I mean when I say that I have made arrangements for a message that every single person will sit up and listen to tomorrow.'

The images on the screen, although shaky due to the motion of the person holding the camera, moved along from the entrance gates, into an area awash with outside broadcast vehicles, articulated lorries resting their heavy bulk on boards to protect the living grassland underneath. A myriad of cables meandered like rivers flowing to their respective seas, and amongst them all, the camera quietly progressed, the shaky tremors of what could have been nervous hands resonating through the screen and displaying their reticence to be filming to everyone. Selleck did not register this as a possible cause of poor picture, or indeed a worry; he watched his audience, silenced in anticipation of what was to come. He then turned his head to the screen once more, for the coup d'état.

The camera holder had made his way precariously between two sleek vehicles that were clearly designed for two purposes only. Either an outside broadcast, or for a very conspicuous surveillance operation. The satellite dish on the roof of one of the vehicles was a testament to the fact that these vehicles were there as they possessed serious power, and as such were very valuable. Sleek, black body panels adorned both, and the pair of vehicles, although identical in make, were both adorned with the logos of different broadcasting companies. Both with a huge share of the broadcasting market, they could easily afford to use only the very best in equipment.

The camera and its driver stopped at the front of one of the lorries, and the lens panned left and right, as if a first-person view from a Cyclops was being recorded. It was if the cameraman was checking the way for possible perils, and having done so, it moved onwards towards the main stage, which was a huge, circular affair, raised at a height of around three metres from floor level, and protected by low-level fencing at its edge. It had been designed to be erected and dismantled with ease, and was actually on its way to Hyde Park immediately after the festival, to be used for another outdoor concert that had been scheduled.

The point of view moved onwards to the far side of the centre stage, where more vehicles of the same stature sat in judgement over the proceedings, and all the while, the people around Selleck stood transfixed, almost impatient for the final destination to present itself. Which it did after approximately thirty seconds more. The surrounds came to a standstill in the periphery, and searching in unison with the cameraman's eyes, the lens moved slowly to, and then fro, until in the half-light, its quarry was spotted. The zoom was used to move the focus inwards, and an audible gasp was omitted from the crowd when they allowed their collective pennies to drop. They immediately understood what the clichéd silver briefcase symbolised to Selleck, and what its contents were capable of. The throng of people had no idea as to where the man who had been proclaimed their leader had acquired such a device, however they did realise, almost in unison, that this revelation had taken their involvement to an entirely new height.

In Selleck's mind, he, too, understood that the very act of even showing them this footage was cementing their commitment to the cause. For them not to report this act, made them accessories to the crime, inasmuch as they were failing to take action to prevent an act of terrorism. The laws of the land were very clear on this. To him, it was an acid test of their commitment to him. They knew what the consequences of reporting them would be, and this was the real measure of their loyalty to him, as far as he was concerned. In a roundabout sort of way, he mused he would actually respect anyone who reported him, and he would give them the deference they deserved, right to the point where he would cut them open like the proverbial tin of beans. He expected they wouldn't.

Some of the crowd began to feel uneasy at the thought they knew such information. A very small minority began to feel fear rising in them, as they worked out the possible repercussions of telling anyone, and what this now meant to everyone in the room, whether they liked it or not. Their organisation was based around taking and not giving, and for some of those present who were intelligent enough to rationalise what had just transpired, they realised that they had just had something extremely important taken away from them. Their right to choose to engage or not.

Selleck changed his attention quickly, allowing his huge frame to make its way to the space in front of the desk, where two bodies lay, in differing states of animation. The first was Greaves; his body lay limp and motionless, propped with his back against the desk, head slumped as if in prayer for the dead. His body was almost motionless, apart from the shallow breathing emanating from his nose, and from around the impromptu gag that had been fashioned from an old handkerchief. Upon Greaves's head lay a lump, angry and purple, deepening by the minute as the bruise under his scalp came into clearer focus. That was the gift from harry Planter, who had done exactly as he was told, and had enjoyed the process of collecting Greaves and relocating him to I-9.

The other seated figure, bound and gagged also, was Sara. She had been denied the luxury of being knocked unconscious, and in her mind she truly wished that she could be where Greaves was now, despite the pain that he would feel when he awakened. She found Selleck abhorrent to even look at, and the images that surrounded her now made her feel physically sick. Her hands, bound at the rear with hard, plastic cable ties, were protesting heavily at the thought of being held in that position indefinitely, and her arms were beginning to lose feeling. She knew that Selleck would not care about that. More worryingly, though, was the fact that the man she had fallen in love with was next to her, with both their fates as yet unknown. She had always felt that in her heart, Selleck was not the type to kill anyone, although he had, in the past, been heavy handed with her and Ashleigh. As with most mothers subjected to domestic violence, she had tried her best to protect her daughter, through any means necessary. Sleepovers, trips away where possible, and clubs and activities had meant that she had spent more time out of the home environment after school than indoors, and she had relished these chances without really realising the true reason. However, she had been subjected to her ex-husband's torment, in both emotional and physical abuse, and it was this that eventually led her to flee permanently and start again, although it was clear that she had not moved far enough away, as she was now jeopardising her family and Matt, who was only responsible for loving both her, and Ashleigh. She did not like to hear that people hated one another; she truly believed that about the man stood towering over her at that moment though.

'Tonight will be the start of our ultimate power over the disease that is spreading through our society, and I hope that you all realise that this act, this pathway, will eventually persuade everyone in this country that we are not to be poisoned like this. I want you to go home now, and relish the opportunity to watch this unfold tomorrow. Everyone at this so-called 'festival' will go about their business, but when I press this switch...' He held aloft a device which was somewhere between a remote control and a computer joystick, only sleek and black, '....everyone will know the business that we are in, and our true intent.'

Sara looked on, aghast at what she was witnessing. *You really are crazy*, she thought. Selleck continued his closing speech, ignoring the two of them at the foot of the desk and stretching his arms out as he spoke. 'The order of the day will be maximum disruption. Our message will be clear at the venue. However, I urge you to do what you do best, and that is to cause havoc. As soon as this happens, I want you to join together as brothers with a common cause. I want you all to choose a target. Corner shops, houses, youth clubs, wherever you see the disease. I want you to leave your mark, too, in whatever way you see fit to do so. Now, you've had your orders. I trust that you'll all do what you're told. This is a momentous occasion for the New Dawn, and whoever plays their part in the cleansing process will know first-hand what it is like to eradicate a disease, just as many before us have done and failed. Even the greatest minds could not accomplish this mission in its entirety, and although we have a long way to go, this message will be given to everyone that we are now a force to be reckoned with.'

Sara looked up through her tears, and wished the very life could be taken from the maniac in front of her. Her vision cloudy with tears of shame and hate for her ex-husband and what he stood for, she searched around aimlessly, that she might find an object of some sort that she could use against him, or that she could later use to free herself. Her search was in vain.

Selleck dismissed all but three of his minions. Harry Planter, whom Selleck intended to remain with him throughout the rest of this dark adventure (due to his loyalty), and two lesser assistants, who were relatively new, yet made up for their inexperience with youthful strength, ignorance, and for some reason, an undying need to impress Selleck.

One, Jason Grantham, stood tall, lean and muscular, a regular user of the gym and all-round fitness fanatic. He exuded strength, and fancied himself as a local scrapper. Indeed, he had won Selleck a few pounds in unlicensed fights, using his brute strength to pulverise weaker opponents. His trademark shaved head, and tattooed neck, were designed to instil fear in those who stood against him, and his opinionated nature often meant that he came across those who felt they had to do so.

The other, Michael Flattery (known to his friends as Feet of Flames due to his name resembling that of a renowned Irish dancer of a similar name) stood equally as tall, but emitted a different kind of raw energy that Selleck had picked up and tapped into almost immediately after being introduced to him. His Irish descendants had left him with the strength of a grizzly bear, which was unusual, given his tall, but lean frame, and this he attributed to his upbringing of hearty food, fresh air outdoors and casual beatings by his father, which he believed made him the 'man' he was. There was hardly an ounce of fat on his body, and his lean arms enticed the muscles attached to his bones to strain at the short-sleeved shirt that he had chosen to cover them with. His bright red hair, curly and long, exploded from his scalp in protest at something unknown, and his naturally ruddy complexion let others feel that he was constantly trying to calm down after a harrowing bout of exercise.

'Harry, you two as well, I need you to do me a favour if you'd be so kind.' The words themselves sounded as if they could possibly be used in a polite way by someone who was used to using such niceties, however there was no such feeling intended, and all three of the men facing him knew that they had no option but to follow his instructions. He remained at the front of the table, and turned his body in the general direction of Sara and Greaves, who was yet to awaken from his induced slumber. He didn't make eye contact with her as he spoke, although he did enough to make her scrutinise him very carefully. She was worried about what was coming next for both herself and her partner.

'It seems that we have some guests, lads. I'm sorry to say that they weren't really invited, but now seeing as they're here, it would be rude of us not to welcome them to our little party, wouldn't it?' He smiled a false, contrived smile, which dripped from his teeth and fought to escape the rest of his face. His three servants smiled back, not really enjoying Selleck's tone, but paying attention nevertheless.

He bent down now, his breath warm and fetid on Sara's face. She tried to move her head away, but Matt's body and the desk meant that there was no escape.

'I'm going to leave you here, you little bitch. I want you to watch our moment of triumph with me. When I send my message, and after the fun begins, I'm going to turn the clock back, and you and I are going to have a little fun I think. I'm sure there's a little romance left in you.' Sara recognised his intentions, and the tears streamed from her face. She began to writhe fiercely in order to loosen her bonds, but it was to no purpose. She screamed through her gag, and started coughing as a result.

'Sssssssssh.' He put his finger gently on her lips, or rather, where her lips would be were her mouth not full of the dirty rag that had been used to stem her talking and screaming. 'Save your energy, my love. You're going to need it for when….' He trailed off, as the door to the assembly room opened hurriedly, and two men, followed by a third, came in with yet another unconscious, unwilling visitor. Sara looked on in horror as Nick's body was unceremoniously brought to the front of the desk, and dumped against it like a sack of coal being unloaded from a lorry.

Selleck looked puzzled at first, but when he looked at Nick's face in closer detail, he broke into a grin. It turned into a chuckle, and then a grating, booming laugh, which travelled to the corners of the room, and which made Sara's blood curdle in her veins.

'Well, if it isn't our resident computer expert, and brother to this piece of shit who's also out for the count. It seems that being nosey and poking your fucking nose in where it's not wanted runs in the family, doesn't it?' He stopped, his cogs beginning to turn mentally. His smile dipped briefly, as he processed potential reasons as to why he would be there at that particular moment. 'Oh dear. I think that we might have a bit of a problem here, lads.'

'Why's that, John?' Planter asked, almost as if he had been told to enquire at that particular moment.

'I'll tell you why, Harry, me old mate. Mr. Greaves (senior) here, is here because he thinks he's a fucking hard nut, and can lord it over everyone else, even when he's handling damaged goods. He's going to get what's coming to him, that's for sure.' He made sure that he stared directly at Sara when he made that statement. It received the required response. He continued. 'His brother, though, is a slightly more troublesome matter. He's most definitely got the ability to see places using his knowledge of computers that most other people can't. It's no secret that he does favours for the right people. Nobody does things like that without somebody dodgy knowing about it. And the thing is, anyone who does anything tasty knows me. Ergo sum, I know about it all.

If you want anything deleted, added, changed electronically, then this clever sod's your man. Now, I've got a funny feeling in my gut that he's bene poking his nose into our website. How did he get into it? How did he even know it existed? Who knows? We'll find out soon enough. We have our ways of asking people to tell us what they know. You can try if you like, lads.'

Selleck bent down again, and got even closer to Sara this time. 'Your boyfriend has inadvertently got his brother in the shit. We've got a website, you see. There's no point not telling you now, as you've seen everything. But if this wanker has hacked our website, then I'm afraid that doesn't look too good for him, does it? We can't really have any Tom, Dick or Harry blabbing around town now, can we? If he can do it without knowing we existed, the filth will probably not be far behind. We're going to have to close it down, and it's that sort of inconvenience that really gets under my skin. And you know what happens when things get under my skin. I'm going to have to deal with all of you. The only thing is, when shall I do it?'

He tapped his cheek childishly, in pretence of thought on the matter. Sara whimpered, knowing that their fate was sealed, and barring a miracle, he would not be listening to any pleas for clemency anytime soon. She knew from days gone past that he was ignorant to any requests to see reason, because in his eyes, he was the most reasonable man in the world.

Selleck's eyes suddenly became impassive, as if he had grown extremely weary of the conversation, and he turned back to his three willing servants, who seemed to hang on every word he uttered.

'Right. You two. Take these two fuckers down to room one oh one. I'll be along in a while, and I'll find out exactly what they know and don't know about what we've been doing, especially our technology expert here. Not that I care. I'm going to be disposing of them afterwards anyway.' His face beamed, as a new idea came to fruition. 'In fact, our teacher friend here might even be the one who pushes the button when the time is right. Congratulations, Greavsie, in the near future, you're going to become a wanted terrorist. Today keeps getting better and better. In the meantime, I'll keep Miss World here with me, so that I can keep a nice little eye on her. Might even start my celebrations early.'

Sara closed her eyes, but it was no use. As Matt and Nick were taken away from her, and out of the Assembly Room, to have their own private fates decided, she knew not only what Selleck was truly capable of now, but that the image of their unconscious bodies was going to be the last image she ever registered of the man she loved, and his intuitive, but helpless brother. The tears escaped their prison, and she was powerless to resist.

42

Through the blackness, and through the haze of awakening, it was Matt who was the first to open his eyes first. Slowly, the light entering his eyes registered with his brain and he began to perceive images of his surroundings. Hi strange thought was to liken his awakening to an energy saving bulb being brought to life at home, and as the images cleared, the stark light of a single fluorescent strip above him painted everything in his vicinity a dull, grey colour. He tried to lift his hand to check a stabbing pain at the back of his head, but found that he could not raise either hand, as they had been cable tied to the leg of a metal chair which was affixed to the floor, and which he butted up against. He realised that the seat itself was digging into his back, and it was this final discomfort that made his anger explode, and he writhed furiously, trying to free himself from his bonds.

Mat had no idea where he was. The absence of windows in his current surroundings meant that he had no sense of place or time, and he frantically cast his mind back to the last thing he could remember. He saw the alleyway, the darkness, and then nothing. He surmised that whoever had taken him, had done so at that time, under the cover of darkness. That was all he could envision though; that, and the fact that it almost certainly had something to do with John Selleck. He felt his blood pressure rise again at the mere thought of him, and he writhed automatically again, as if his freedom meant that he was going to seek him out and wring the life from him.

Matt forced himself to calm down as best he could, but this was not easy, as there were many thoughts of all of his loved ones running through his brain at that moment. Additionally, he was naturally afraid for his own safety, and his body's natural adrenaline kick that would accompany this stressful situation had increased his heart rate to a race. He closed his eyes again, tried to block out the pain, and did his best to clear his mind for a moment. This helped, and he felt his pulse slow in his neck and in his wrists, which were beginning to tingle due to their restriction.

He opened his eyes again, blinking against the sterile light, and turned his head to see his surroundings, as far as he could. As he did, his heart froze momentarily, and then his pulse blasted upwards once again. He cried out in anguish through the gag that had been applied to him, and as he struggled to free himself, tears began to flow down his cheeks. There, perpendicular to him in the solitary chair adorning what must have been some sort of maintenance office, was his brother, Nick. Bound, gagged, and not moving at all. He could just about make out a trickle of dried blood on Nick's neck, which must have been from the blow that put him in his own state of unconsciousness.

Matt studied his surroundings. He realised that he had one immediate mission, and that was to free himself in order to help his brother. Whatever came next was going to have to be prioritised, if he had a chance to do so. He looked at the fabric of the room that held him; sparse, with only a table and chairs, all of which were bolted to the floor. An old, rusty filing cabinet in the corner might have told a story or two at one time in history, but it certainly wasn't going to be in use at that particular moment in time. It was falling to pieces.

Matt listened intently for any signs of life outside. The door was a thick, heavy fire door, without a glass panel. He could not see, or hear, anything that warned him of his captors' presence. He took that as an opportunity to try to rouse his brother.

'Nick! Wake up! It's Matt!' Nothing came in response. Matt tried again, only this time, a little louder than his whispered shout. The urgency remained.

'Nick, wake up pal! Wake up, come on!' He found an air of desperation creeping in to his mind, and began to feel his ire rising once again, when he knew deep inside that what he needed to do was focus, and not waste energy on the things which he could not control at that particular moment in time. He shifted in his seat, and tried to see if the chair would move, lift, or be persuaded to topple. That was not going to work, he realised, after a good minute of strenuous movement. He then tried standing, but realised that his hands could not move far enough up the leg of the chair as it was blocked by what seemed like an outcrop of rust, which appeared to have bubbled and provided his hands with the obstacle in front of them. He sat back down hastily, as his legs were beginning to hurt in the crouched position.

However, Matt realised that this could be an opportunity, rather than a hindrance. He moved his arms up once again, and although he had to squat, he found that by rubbing the cable tie against the rusted patch, it scuffed the hard-wearing plastic, and when he felt the makeshift shackle with his finger, it was definitely wearing down. He was just beginning to get started on a more vigorous approach when the door opened quickly, and there in front of him stood Selleck, looking huge from such a recessed position. Without a single word, he approached Matt directly from the front, and unleashed a savage backhand slap across his face, which brought blackness into the periphery of Matt's vision, and forced him to sit down on his bottom. Not out of courtesy or doing as he was told, but because his legs had momentarily lost their strength due to the ferocity of the blow he had been dealt. When his vision returned to colour, it was Selleck who beat Greaves to the first words.

'You think you're some sort of a tough guy, don't you? Look at you, though. You're weak. A real piece of shit. You're nothing. Nothing!' he lifted his hand again to strike Matt, but stopped when he saw that Matt hadn't flinched, as most other men in his position would. Selleck was used to pleading, begging, and offers of the world when he was inflicting pain, but he was genuinely intrigued with Matt's apparent lack of fear of him. Matt drew a shaky, deep breath, and spoke himself.

'You're the piece of shit. You fucking coward. Take off this cable tie. Free my hands, and then we'll see who the better man is. Go on, let's see.'

Selleck contemplated letting him loose, just for the fun of it, and looked into Matt's eyes as he stared up from the floor at him. Matt's eyes held a steely determination that was new to him. Nobody ever gave Selleck that look. They always looked away. Scared of him. *This one though*, he thought, *this one doesn't even care who I am.*

'I think I'll leave you where you are for now, son.' He replied flatly.

'I'm not your fucking son.' Matt's voice escaped from his throat like gravel death.

'Well, whatever you are, you're not going to be able to be so mouthy soon enough. I've got a couple of lads out here who are just dying, and I mean *dying*, to teach you a lesson. Just soften you up a bit. I'll just let you know, I'm going to take care of you personally, and your meddling brother too, but I'm going to watch my bomb go off in the Rec first. When that's done, though, I'm going to take great delight in choking the last breath out of you. You think you can just take what's mine, and get away with it? You think you can come into my own house, and try to tell me to back off? Well, here's just a reminder of who *I* am, you little twat. Oh, and by the way, when I leave here, I'm going to go back to where I came from, and I'm going to remind Sara of what a real man feels like.'

He unleashed another smack, this time on the other cheek. It reverberated through Matt's skull, and his vision blurred once again. Fighting off nausea and unconsciousness, he spat out some blood that had begun to seep from a molar which had been loosened inside his mouth, and looked directly at Selleck once more. The gravel in his vocal chords returned with a vengeance, and Selleck had no choice but to listen, as this was not in any way put on for his effect. This was from his heart, and he meant every syllable.

'Listen to me, you complete sack of shit. I don't give a flying fuck who you are, or what you're going to do. All I'm saying is, whatever you're planning to do to me, you'd better make sure that you kill me doing it. Because if you don't, and if you hurt even one hair on Sara's head, I'm going to be coming after you. Here, today, now, or in the future, whatever happens, you're not even going to see me coming. I'm going to find you, and I'm going to rip your throat out with my bare hands. It's me who's going to watch you take your last breath. And I'm going to be smiling while you, and your pantomime of a show here, crash down around your thick fucking skull. It's you who doesn't understand the most obvious thing about what's going on here. Right now, there's a huge difference between you and me. At this immediate moment in time, I don't care whether I live or die, as long as I get my hands on you for long enough for YOU to feel what a real man is like. And I mean in how I inflict pain on you. Look into my eyes, and tell me what you see. I'm giving you a chance to walk away while you still can. You have no fucking idea what I'm capable of. Free me, and I promise you I'm going to give you an idea.'

Selleck seemed to ignore Matt's comments, and merely stepped outside, summoning Grantham and Flattery in to the room with a gesture of his head.

'If the skinny one wakes up, then he gets the same treatment as this one. But in the meantime, give this wanker a taste of his own medicine, and teach *him* a thing or two. Remember all those times you got shouted at by your teacher? Well, here's your chance to get your own back. He used to be a teacher. Just soften him up though. I'm going to be finishing him off when the time is right.' Matt noticed the emphasis on the past tense, and smiled as the first in a series of blows and kicks began to rain down on him. He continued to smile until the curtains fell on his sobriety once more, and he was left, slumped, to await his ultimate fate.

43

Jim was no coward, but he had spent a long time hiding since he had decided to enter the old, seemingly abandoned facility. He had not been given much of a choice. Upon entering the dark maze of tunnels and corridors, he had not gone far before his ears had picked up the sound of human movement approaching. Choosing a nearby alcove, dark and recessed, and containing some old display screens similar to those used at trade fairs, he had secreted himself, waiting for the hustle and bustle of the unknown inhabitants to die down before   deciding to venture out into the dull, unwelcoming light of the myriad of passageways. In his mind, Jim envisaged the tunnels to be akin to those deployed in Vietnam during the war in the last century. He knew that they were nowhere near similar in reality, but the feelings coursing through him at that particular moment were enough to make him empathise with any soldier who had been asked to investigate tunnels underground. They might not be booby trapped with hand grenades or other delights (he knew poisonous snakes were also left behind by the Viet Cong soldiers during the Tet Offensive), but the fear of the unknown around every corner was making him feel very uncomfortable. As a result, he found another temporary hiding place in a similar alcove, and checked his cell phone for any signs of signal, just in case he needed to call anyone as a direct result of what he found in the immediate future. He was surprised to find that even in this subterranean hideaway, he still had one bar of signal. *Modern technology*, he thought to himself. *A few years ago, I'd have been scouting around outside for a phone box.*

At any given time, it is a certainty that somebody is thinking that if anything can go wrong with technology, it will, and usually at the most inopportune moment. A writer, upon entering the last page of a modern novel, will find that their computer suddenly shuts down; a mechanic, at a crucial stage of a repair, will find that their highly delicate instrument will cease to be helpful. Anyone who has tried to take an important call on a mobile phone in the countryside will have felt degrees of irritation at being cut off due to lack of signal. On this occasion, it was Jim's phone that let him down, but not because it had failed to work, but because it worked at the wrong moment. And when his phone decided to chirp, Jim immediately wished that he had not been 'lucky' enough to have had even one bar of signal on his phone.

From his alcove, whilst checking his phone for signs of life, he had heard footsteps approaching. His better-than-average hearing had picked up the sounds of approaching feet. In trainers probably, due to the muted padding that accompanied each step. Jim surmised that whoever owned the trainers was quite large, because each footstep sounded to him like a slap from a flat foot, rather than the more delicate tread of someone with higher arches.

He flattened himself against the wall, but realised that the strip light on the ceiling of the main corridor was too close to afford any real amount of shade, bar a wedge of darkness deep in the recesses of his hiding place. He knew that if anyone were to look sideways as they walked past, they would immediately find him hiding there, and would probably raise an alarm. If anyone was up to no good, he'd be in it up to his neck, and beyond. He instinctively pressed himself up to the side wall, hoping that the pedestrian would walk straight past, and miss him totally as the alcove would be long past his field of vision before noticing that there was a person trying to look invisible in there.

Jim couldn't help it, but held his breath as the footsteps, now sounding like thunder, entered Jim's immediate space, and a lumbering giant of a man strode past. Jim knew that three of this guy's steps would see him past the alcove, and he counted as he traversed the opening. *One, two…….*

As Jim's tongue formed the beginning of the next number, his phone chirruped. In a similar tone to Morse code, his phone beeped its pattern, alerting Jim of his incoming call. Jim's blood froze in his veins, and he did not have time to see who the caller was, as his eyes were instinctively drawn to the passing man's features as he stopped, turned around, and gazed directly at Jim. He knew that he had been rumbled, and Jim tried to fathom out his choice before the hypothalamus in his brain made the decision for him, and enlisted the help of the sympathetic nervous system to make his physical moves for him, and the adrenal-cortical system kicked his bloodstream into life to fuel his muscles, which were already tensed.

Time seemed to stand still for Jim at this point, and he seemed to study the man's features forever. Rugged creases in the forehead; a scar on the left cheek, which had been made by a blade of some sort, by the looks of it; muscular arms, that could squeeze the life out of a bear, probably. These were not encouraging signs. He looked some more, drawn to the man's lips and mouth, which soften gave away a person's intentions long before they opened their mouth to speak. It had already started to snarl, and that was enough for Jim. His defence mechanism sprang into life, and he did something that he had not done for many, many years. He lunged at the man, and made the first move in what could be his only chance of survival if this had been allowed to. He would never beat a man like this in a fist fight, so he had to rely on the element of surprise. Jim was no slouch, but even he knew that when facing an assailant, the best option is only to use self-defence to allow you enough time to run away. Nobody ever wins a fight. The movies had a lot to answer for, really.

Jim's fist, which had been clenched almost immediately upon knowing that he was being spotted, came around and lashed the unsuspecting man in the face, in a continuous movement that had been started with a forward step of Jim's left foot.

Rotating his hips, he let fly with a straight drive that connected perfectly with his opponent's nose. There was a sickening crunch of gristle and bone merging, and the man immediately shrieked n agony as his own brain told him that he was hurting.

However, to Jim's dismay, this unknown assailant was aware of what that sort of pain felt like, and he refused to go down. In reality, many would have, but not this one. He was too big, experienced and ugly to simply go down. With blood now streaming from his nose, he used his sleeve to wipe it away, smearing his cheek in a trail of claret. He used the other hand to quickly wipe his eyes, the victims of involuntary tears. Irrespective of whatever anyone says, if you are hit hard enough in the face, you will shed a tear. Then, he did something more frightening than not going down. He smiled, and began to square up, his arms rising to something resembling a boxing guard. There would be no more surprise blows to the head.

Jim thought fast, and in a quick movement, stepped inside the guard, seriously invading the man's intimate space. With his nose broken, the man instinctively suspected another barrage of blows, and raised his guard whilst preparing to strike himself. It was at this point that Jim brought up his knee, and with every ounce of his strength, planted it into the soft, yielding space between his legs. The man shrieked again, and crumpled to the floor, gasping for breath. Jim positioned himself behind the man, now helpless, and with both arms, put him into a choke hold. Using one arm as leverage for another to block the blood supply to the brain, and cause blackout. The man's arms flailed, his own bodily defences struggling to cope with the barrage of pain signals, and the fact that he was about to be rendered unconscious.

From that position, Jim knew that he was in control, and sat back, his victim helpless. Being careful not to kill him, once unconscious, Jim let go, and reached into his pockets. His hand appeared holding a cable tie of his own, and he thanked himself that he had tried to think about worst-case scenarios when he had been preparing his stakeout earlier. In his coat pocket, there were two sets of handcuffs. He had brought them too, but figured that as this poor guy would be out for the next fifteen to twenty minutes, the cable tie would suffice. He would gag him, and that would buy him extra time to find out exactly what he was dealing with, and escape if necessary. He blanched as his mind

He realised suddenly that he did not have time, relatively speaking, to dawdle in the middle of a corridor, in an environment where so far, one hundred percent of those using it were hostile. He was a man of action, so picked up the unconscious man, dragged him into the alcove, and hid him as best he could behind a couple of old office chairs that had been abandoned a very long time before being used. He made sure he was propped up, as he didn't want the poor soul to suffocate on any blood that may still be dripping down his throat. He wasn't sorry at all for what he had done, no matter how far out of character violence was for him; he didn't want to unnecessarily hurt anyone though.

He was faced with the choice of going on, or trying to find his way back out and contacting the police to come and investigate. Despite his head telling him that he needed to escape, his heart, and his curiosity, made him choose to proceed. He decided that if there were any nefarious acts going on, then he would be able to give first-hand evidence of what he saw (he had his phone after all to take pictures), and then he would get out of there as fast as his legs could carry him, before his opponent awoke and notified somebody of the intruder's presence. Looking around at his feet, he noticed a piece of old, rusty scaffold tubing on the ground, adjacent to the back wall. *If I'm going to be scrapping, I'll be needing this*, he decided. He picked it up, and just out of interest, checked his phone before moving on into the darkness, to see who had rung him. It was

Jessica Quinn, the pathologist and scene of crime officer who had initially spoken to him about the murders and the strange nature surrounding the fibres that had been found. He didn't have time to respond, and made a mental note that if he made it out in one piece, he would remember to call. He replaced the phone in his pocket, tightened his grip on the section of pipe in his hand, and in the most delicate steps possible for him, he proceeded down the corridor.

His adrenaline flowing, he proceeded forwards, and downwards. He felt the temperature change as the corridors moved downwards, Dampness surrounded him as he breathed, and on occasion, his breath could be seen in the deathly light. All had gone quiet, and he heard no more footsteps, no talking, and he began to believe that there were no more people to be found in this dank hellhole. He soon came to see that there was a pattern to the corridors, and a similar rhythm to the alcoves that he had hidden in, with varying degrees of success. He checked his watch. It was now just after seven o'clock in the morning, and when he realised this, he became aware of how tired he was. Adrenaline was keeping him going, but when it finally wore off, he was going to be dead on his feet.

He came to the end of a corridor, and took a flight of stairs leading downwards once more. He waited at the double doors at the base of the flight of steps, and peeked through the glass panels on the doors for any signs of life. Nothing. Moving through, he noticed a room on the far left ahead, with a shaft of light scything its way into the darkness of the corridor. This particular walkway was not as well lit, and it was almost in total darkness, apart from a single bulb or flickering strip of white here and there. It was not as well maintained, that was for sure.

He slowed down long before he reached the doorway. He had forced himself to decide what he would do if anyone exited the room, and he had decided that he would have to make an immediate decision and risk assessment once he realised how many potential threats there were. He figured that if there were one or two, and they were of the same temperament as his previous obstacle, then he would probably face the music and try and use the scaffold pipe and his training as best he could; any more than two, and he would have to scarper. He wasn't going to be able to cope with more, especially if they were the same size as the man who lay unconscious a bit further back.

He pressed his back against the cold, unforgiving wall adjacent to the doorway, and listened. Nothing. He crouched down, and turned his body to get a closer look. He peeped quickly, figuring that lower down, nobody would expect to see someone peering into the doorway. The room was indeed empty, apart from a desk, chair, and a coat stand in the corner. Strangely, his eyes remained on this, as it was adorned and being kept warm by a grey overcoat. A *huge* grey overcoat that would have been made for a man of considerable size and presence, by the looks of it. Jim turned his head once more, and looked up and down the corridor. All was still silent. Gazing slowly back into the lit room, he was once more taken with the coat. Something was tugging at his thoughts, telling him to inspect it further. He couldn't quite remember why. His hands found themselves in his own coat pockets, and when he came into contact with his phone, the pieces clicked into place. Jessica had called him. Jessica had told him about the overcoat and the fibres. The fibres from the vintage army coat. The fibres that had been found on the two corpses. *Could this be the coat?*

Jim realised that he needed to snap into action. If the coat was here which held the fibres, then it was safe to assume that maybe the murderer was here too. This had just become very real to Jim, even after his altercation. It had just moved to a new level of seriousness, and he knew that his prime directive was now to get in there, take some samples of the fibres, and get the hell out of there and back to the police. It was time for his amateur detective work to end, and for the serious matter of protocol to be instigated. He threw caution to the wind and stood up, and walked in, covering his corners just to be on the safe side. There was nobody there and the room was vacant.

As well as the handcuffs in his pockets, Jim was lucky enough to have some doggy bags, which he often carried with him when he was out. He hated dog mess, and became frustrated as a dog owner himself when he saw other users acting irresponsibly. He walked quickly over to the coat, and opening up a bag, used his penknife to scrape as many of the coarse fibres from the coat as possible in the time he had allocated himself. He tried not to touch the fibres, as not to contaminate them with his own DNA or other possible sources of contamination, and tied the bag, placing it too in his pocket.

He reached the doorway, turned left to carry on his journey in silence, but his first few steps were the only ones he took, as the corridor, angular at the end, delivered sounds to his ears which gave him a feeling of dread which enveloped him totally, and which made his stomach toss like the sea in a storm. The sounds were coming from a room just beyond the angular turn in the walkway, and they were clearly the sounds of anguish, and those attached to physical violence. Somebody was being subjected to a beating. Jim could not make out how many assailants, or indeed victims, there were, but he was sure that there were at least two assailants, as he could hear the voices of two people, chortling, and sometimes grunting, in between the blows that they must have been delivering.

Jim was faced with a division in his emotions. On the one hand, having just dispatched one of the people involved in whatever this whole thing was, his rising anger wanted him to save whoever was at the receiving end of the physical attack, and teach these bullies a lesson they might never forget. His sense of self-preservation was telling him to turn and run, and not look back. *You've got away with it so far, Jimbo. Don't push your luck.* Against the wall once more, as if camouflaging himself into the dilapidated paintwork on the bare brick walls, he felt like crumbling, just as they were. He punched the wall in anger, stopping himself from doing it twice in case he was discovered due to the noise. *I can't leave them. What if they die? What if they're innocent? I can't allow that to happen. I just can't,* he pleaded with himself.

That was enough for him to make the decision he needed to. He pushed ahead, around the corner carefully, after checking for signs of life in the distance. The darker corridor afforded him a shroud within which to progress, and once again, solitary shafts of light in the distance pierced the darkness, harvesting it like a scythe. Outside the room, an old set of drawers on castors had been placed against the wall, but it was clear that it had no purpose, and was only there as a remnant. It was worn, yellow, and held nothing by the looks of it. Jim saw it as the perfect hiding place, from where he could sneak a look inside the room, and the business that was being conducted there. He crouched down, and although it hurt his knees, he stayed in that position and walked, with his bottom almost dragging on the ground, knees bent, clicking with each step. He reached the drawers, and took a deep breath. He knew that the vantage point would put him at risk, but it would also afford him a clear vista of what was happening, and would help him (or force him) to choose his next course of action. He peered around the edge of the apparatus, and in an instant, he wished he hadn't. His eyes filled with tears at the image before him. And especially when he realised that he knew who one of the battered, bloody recipients of this torture was. Jim realised that it was Matt Greaves, the school teacher who had been burgled a short while back. His face was a mess, and the two youngsters who were doling out punishment in turn didn't look like they were letting up. Greaves was, astonishingly, still just about conscious. One of the young thugs, with dark hair and muscle to help him on his way, landed a punch squarely on

Matt's right cheek. Matt's head swivelled to take the blow, as he couldn't use his hands. Jim noticed he had been bound. His anger rose. He heard Matt spit at the attackers in defiance, then use what appeared to be his diminishing energy to speak.

'Is that the best you can do? You hit like a fucking girl. Go back and tell your boss that he needs to look at his recruitment policy. There clearly has to be a shortage of hard men these days.' He chortled to himself.

'Funny. Real funny.' Replied the red-haired accomplice. Jim noticed that he was squaring up for a punch, and he watched in horror as he landed it on the opposite cheek, as if the two were playing a game of tag with Matt's head. Matt clearly felt that, but managed to stay conscious. Slowly, his grimace turned into a smile, and he spoke again, his voice muted slightly by his cheek, which was swelling due to the blows being administered. His gag had been removed and rested on his belly.

'Go get some more men, and watch you don't hit your vagina on the door on your way out. While you're there, have a check to see if your boyfriend hasn't broken a nail.' He laughed directly at his adversary. Jim couldn't help but admire his gall in the face of what was happening to him. He had seen many people in pressure situations, subjected to many horrible things, but they all reacted differently. Only a minority ever stood up to their adversity with bare-faced cheek and went out fighting. Jim was full of admiration for Greaves at that moment in time, and the bruises on the unconscious form of the young man next to Matt also indicated that they both were being subjected to this treatment. It was quite possible that the younger of the two had not been able to withstand as much as Matt was currently proving he could.

Jim felt another emotion stir inside him, and it didn't take long for the rage within his stomach to surface. He could physically feel his face turn purple, and he soon realised that the heat emanating from every pore was involuntary, and connected only to the immediate need for retribution for what he had been witnessing. He stepped out from behind the storage unit, and walked straight into the room, where Flattery and Grantham were stood, their backs turned to him in unconscious defiance.

What happened next took years in Jim's mind, but only a matter of seconds in Greaves's vision, which had begun to blur savagely due to exhaustion and the cumulative effect of the blows raining mercilessly down in him. He was disoriented, and at first he could not even comprehend that somebody was in the room, but when he heard the whistle from the doorway, he knew that there was indeed another person who had introduced themselves to proceedings. Matt thought that his captors had heeded his advice and brought another friend along, and he began to feel smug in what would probably be his last moments, that he had withstood the punishment that they had doled out. He knew he would not be able to take the strength of three men on, not without his free arms to defend himself.

Jim whistled, not wanting the two young men to not see him coming. His rage was such that he was prepared to take them both on, face to face, without agenda other than to inflict the same pain as they had done to their two prisoners.

'What the......?' was all that Grantham could manage to get out, before there was a metallic thunk on his right temple, and his legs buckled. The scaffold pole had done its job, and the henchman was unconscious before he hit the floor. He fell forward, landing on his face, breaking his nose with a quiet, sickening crunch.

Flattery, turning around fully now, made the mistake of looking at his partner and his prone features, when he should have immediately attacked Jim while his posture was of balance. However, Jim had steadied himself, and with a scream, Flattery charged at him, but Jim was too wary of what might happen. Jim, in slow motion, thought how predictable the haymaker was that Flattery had thrown, and with all the time in the world, Jim lifted the length of scaffold pole to face height in front of him horizontally with both hands, and met Flattery's closed fist, where at least three of his fingers immediately broke below the first knuckle. He screamed again, but this time in pain, and used his other hand to instinctively cradle his broken fingers.

Big mistake, Jim thought to himself. With Flattery's guard momentarily down, Jim stepped to the side, and with considerable speed arced a huge upward slice with his makeshift weapon, which caught Flattery in the sweet spot under the cleft of his chin. His eyes fluttered briefly, but then he too succumbed to the call of his slumber, and he fell backwards, smashing his head on the floor as he fell like a sawn tree. Jim noticed that a trickle of blood had appeared on the floor behind Flattery, but he made an immediate assessment that he didn't care, and moved straight away to Greaves's vicinity, where he managed a smile to the bruised, beaten individual.

'Hi Mr. Greaves. It's Jim. Jim White. The copper who met you the other night. Remember me?'

'Course I do, Jim. I must say, I'm glad that you're here. I don't know how much longer I could have played with those two fuckers before it would have turned serious.' He smiled a sore smile at Jim, who couldn't help but grin at his attempt at humour, even in the gravest of situations. Greaves wasn't totally without his faculties, though. 'Any chance you can get us out of these bindings? There could be more of those idiots along at any moment. It's Matt, by the way. Call me Matt. This twat next to me is my little brother, Nick. He never did have a very large pain threshold. Poor sod.'

'Jesus, of course.' Jim took his penknife out of his pocket, and sliced the bindings on the two men's hands. Nick stirred, but did not awaken fully. Matt turned to Jim, his hands flopped lifelessly by his sides.

'I can't…..I can't feel my hands and arms yet. Can you check he's all right? Please. I don't care about me, I……'

'Matt, it's fine. Of course. Just sit still for a minute. I don't envy you your pins and needles when your blood returns though. Chin up, mate.' He immediately moved over to Nick, and began gently tapping him on the face to try and rouse him, calling his name to illicit a response. It was not long before he had answered groggily, and there was a huge sense of relief from both Jim and Matt when he eventually opened his eyes. It took Nick some time to refocus his vision, and he was very shaky on his feet, but it appeared that he was going to be okay. Matt made a note (without regarding himself) to keep an eye for signs of concussion, and shook his arms, which had now begun to feel like his own, apart from the multitude of virtual needles jabbing into his skin and flesh with every movement he made, due to the return of blood to his extremities and the re-awakening of his nervous system.

'We need to get out of here, and fast, Matt. What the hell are you doing in here, anyway?' Jim enquired tentatively. Part of him didn't want to know the answer, but he knew in his heart that he needed to find out the truth about Matt, and know whether his last acts were wasted. If Matt and his brother were up to no good, and were no better than the thugs that he had just seen off, then he would probably give them the same treatment.

'You might not believe this, but I think this is some sort of underground right-wing movement of some description. There's a guy. Real arsehole. Name's Selleck, John Selleck. He's in charge down here. Well, it seems that way, anyway.' He stood, and moved his arms around as he spoke to revive them fully. Jim realised that he was quite well built, and he was quite impressed with how sprightly he was, given the beating he had endured until his intervention.

'What?' Jim was incredulous.

'I know, it sounds farfetched, but this guy is for real, believe me. He's some sort of neo-Nazi nutjob. I've been round to his house. To try and sort something out with him. I didn't realise, but I've been dating his ex, and he was trying to intimidate me. I mean, us. He's really not right, Jim. He thinks he's fucking Hitler or something. I've got a bad feeling about this.'

'Why's your brother here? What have you done to end up here, Nick?'

Nick, shaky but already standing, pulled up a dilapidated plastic chair, and plonked his body down heavily on it. He was fatigued from the beating, and he genuinely didn't look in good enough shape to be even sitting, let alone standing upright. His arms shook as he supported his weight on his arms in order to sit down. Jim figured he was going into shock. He pulled off his jacket, and gave it to Nick.

'Here, put this on. You're going into shock, Nick. That's what the shaking is. Your body's been running on adrenaline for a while. It does this when you're coming down off that rush. You're cold, right?'

'Thanks. I am. Bloody freezing.' He gladly accepted the advice, and the jacket. He donned it, wincing as his own biceps protested at their previous prison. Nick didn't wait for anyone else to speak. 'Listen, there's something else. Jim, Matt's right. This guy is crazy. It's much worse, though. He's been planning an act of terror. A bomb by the sounds of it. I'm a computer programmer, and through no fault of my own, I came across a secret website that was written in code using page and line references from a chosen text. It's.....'

'The Arnold Cipher.' Jim finished his sentence for him. 'I know. I'm a bit of an amateur detective, and have come across this in cases of old. Anyway, carry on. Sorry to interrupt.' Jim knelt down himself while listening to Nick, almost as if the act of doing so helped his ears and eyes to focus more effectively. Nick smiled at him, acknowledging his apology, and continued.

'The website took a bit of finding, but it basically highlights the meeting times and dates for these clowns, and there's a pretty detailed, albeit cryptic, message board too. There's a lot of talk on it from the guy who simply calls himself 'S' on there about something called the cleansing, but he also mentions that there's a surprise awaiting the partygoers at the festival in town tomorrow. I can only assume that it's a bomb.' Nick looked at his brother, and Matt met his gaze in return. Matt opened his eyes wide, as if to wake himself up as fully as possible.

'Anything else?' He enquired.

'That's all I can remember. Surely that's enough to be worrying about though?'

'You're not wrong, little brother. What's worrying me more, though, is that if this bastard has got me and you, and Jim if we're not quick about you two leaving, then he will probably have got his hands on Sara too. Jesus, Sara….' His head dropped, then snapped up quickly. 'I've got to find her. If she's here, god only knows what the sick little twat will do to her. I can't let that happen.' He moved towards the door. Jim momentarily blocked his path, and placed his hand on Matt's shoulder. Matt stopped, looked down at Jim's hand, and spoke quietly. 'If you're looking to stop me, I'm really sorry, Jim, but that really isn't going to happen. I really don't want to argue about it. I'm begging you, please. Don't let us fall out over this. *I'm doing this.*'

Their eyes met, and even though Jim was trying to safeguard Greaves, he knew that from the look in his eyes, it was futile. He lowered his hand.

'You're going to need a weapon of some kind. Here.' He offered his makeshift metal cosh. Matt smiled weakly.

'No thanks, Jim. You keep it. You need to get Nick out of this shithole, and as fast as you can. You're going to need to phone your buddies and get them down here, and be sharp, if you're going to be a hero and save the lives of lots of innocent people.'

'What about you? What are you going to do if you find him? This seems to be a pretty big place, you know. And what if he has your partner? What will you do?'

Matt's eyes met Jim's directly, and Jim knew that the battered, exhausted man before him was as serious as any man had ever been in what came out of his mouth. Matt seemed to think about the exact words very carefully, in order for there to be no ambiguity whatsoever.

'If I find him, and he's alone, I'm sorry to say that he's going to experience a more Victorian style education. Read what you want into that. If he has Sara, then he's still going to experience that, but I'm going to have to extoll the virtues of treating women nicely too, which may or may not take a while, as he's so far behind the times in his awareness of what women want.' He paused again, and not for effect. He was making sure he spoke with crystal clarity. 'Either way, he's going down, or I'm going to die trying.' With that, he turned through the doorway, paused as if sniffing the air to catch a scent of Selleck's presence, and was gone. The room fell silent.

Jim, realising that he had just condoned an act of violence form Matt, tried not to think about that as he prioritised his next actions. Firstly, he was going to get Nick out. He looked in quite bad shape, and was definitely going to need looking at by the medics. Before that, though, he was going to need to contact the police and let them know about what he had been told, no matter how farfetched it was. He knew that he had been warned off the graffiti in the town by his superiors, and he had been told not to allow himself to give in to his fantasies as a detective. He knew he would now be in quite a lot of trouble after ignoring those instructions, but there were, after all, the lives of lots of innocent people at risk, and he was going to have to be quick if this threat was real. Far right-wing efforts were under close scrutiny, and Jim realised that Matt would himself have had instructions on what schools needed to be doing to prevent radicalisation of young people. This, it seemed, was demonstrating that more needed to be done. Much more.

'Come on, Nick, let's go. If we come across any more of these characters, do you think you have it in you to see them off? Here. You take this, just in case.' He offered Nick the scaffold pole. Unlike his sibling, Nick took it gladly, gripped it tightly, and then together, they began to soft-shoe themselves back towards the sunlight. It would not be an easy task, as every corner would hold a challenge in the shape of unforeseen company, but they had to push on, and fast.

'What about these two clowns?' Nick enquired, looking down at the still figures of Grantham and Flattery.

'Don't worry. I was always taught to be prepared. Here. You take this, and I'll sort the other one out. Quick.' He tossed a pair of cuffs from his pocket.

Nick grinned and immediately set to work. Within a minute and a half, both of the young assailants were handcuffed, gagged with the old gags that had been used to silence Matt and his brother, and only when they had taken a final, incredulous look at the scene around them, did they proceed towards the light, and out of the dank hell they had witnessed.

44

Sara tried to turn her head from Selleck's grip, but his sizeable hand simply locked onto her jaw and turned her head both ways playfully as he spoke in a quiet, calm, but dreadful tone.

'Look at you. Damaged goods. No wonder you ended up with a school teacher. Nancy boy like him probably felt sorry for your little sob story. Single mother, making ends meet. Probably made him feel good to give you charity.' He smiled, and his fetid breath cascaded into Sara's nose, filling her with revulsion.

'He's more man than you'll ever be, and ever were. You're nothing but a lousy piece of shit, who can't get it up. What have you done with them? If you've harmed him, I'll....'

'You'll what, my pretty? Kill me? I can't see that happening, love. Not in your lifetime, anyway. Which, by the way, won't be very long, once I've enjoyed seeing my little present set the ethnic world on fire at The Rec. Don't worry, though. I'll make sure that your boyfriend gets to watch you have one last nice time with me, before I send him and his idiot brother on their fucking way. I don't know what's more exciting. Knowing I'm going to get to end all three of you, or deciding which way to do it.' Sara didn't know whether it was intentional or subliminal, but she realised that he had been holding his crotch while he spoke to her. His hand still held her face, but he quickly released it with a sharp twist, which brought tears to Sara's eyes once more.

She was tied to a sturdy plastic and steel chair, and had been gagged, just as matt and Nick had been, although she had managed to spit out the binding on her mouth, which was being humoured for the time being. Through her exertion to wriggle free from her bindings and also Selleck's proximity, her hair had matted to her forehead, giving her the appearance of a street urchin, with the distressed look that did nothing to hide the emotional and physical stress she had bene put under. She had absolutely no idea of the time, but she knew that she had been incarcerated for some hours, as she had developed a massive urge to relieve her bladder, and she knew that there was no point in mentioning this to Selleck, as he would revel in seeing her compromised in that way.

'Did you know, that during the Second World War, the Nazis were extremely inventive during their ethnic cleansing? Open heart surgery without anaesthetic, piercings in extremely painful but non-lethal areas, and there were some exponents of interrogation who were extremely adept at carving their victims. It sometimes took their victims days to die, and in the most painful of ways.' Selleck rubbed his chin, like a fairy tale giant, although his intentions were only ever visualised in the very earliest fairy tales, which had been used to frighten children away from danger areas. He appalled Sara with his dreamy appearance, which was obviously due to his excitement towards hurting others.

'Whatever you do, you'd better kill me, you fucker, because if you don't, I swear I'll make you pay for what you've done.' She felt the tears welling again, but in sympathy for Matt and Nick, and the prospect of what the future would hold for them.

Selleck didn't register her words, only returned her stare with one of his own. Cold and callous, the only thing visible was the truth in his character. He was nothing if not honest about who he was. There was a time, he thought to himself, that he cared about Sara and their child. There was a time when he believed that she would bend to his will, like everyone else did, but when she resisted, that was the straw that broke the camel's back for him. He had tolerated much from her, and was willing to allow her the freedom to go out occasionally, and try to be independent, when he really knew in his heart that it was he who was in total control of her destiny. And that of the girl, too. Now, there was nothing but revulsion for the woman who he looked at in front of him.

He thought her pathetic, weak, and she was thoroughly deserving of everything that she had coming to her. *Everything*. He immediately found his revulsion spill over, and his anger drove him back to her face, where he lifted the gag roughly, and forced it back into her mouth. She resisted, but it was no use; the foul rag was replaced, and she was silenced. His rage was as yet unabated though, and he found it all too easy to go back to the old days of living together. He raised his hand, expecting her to turn her head, as she had often done in the past to prepare herself for contact. Instead, though, she remained resolute, and stared right at him, into his eyes, and this unnerved him. *Just like that pathetic teacher looked at me*, he mused, and unleashed a back-handed swipe across her cheekbone. She immediately lost consciousness. The blow would have felled most men, and she was simply not strong enough to endure what he had just administered. *Just like old times*, he recalled with a fond smile. Towering over her, he felt the surge of superiority within him, and knew that there was, at that moment in time, nobody who could touch him. At his finest moment, with the whole world about to sit up and know him, he was totally convinced that he was invincible.

45

It was eight o'clock, and the weather showed promise of cooperation. The sun began to elope over the morning rooftops, and search out its victims in the crisp air. High above, in the branches of trees that had witnessed countless events, and that could tell a myriad of stories, squirrels went about their business, their heightened senses allowing them the luxury of seeing life in slow motion around them, their reactions lightning fast, their balance steadfast. One such creature, a large, grey female, stopped her quest for food, and alighted on the wobbling, swaying tip of a large oak branch, curious as to the nature of the noises heard below. Her acute hearing drew her attention to a metallic, scraping sound, and her keen eyesight was pinned on the gates to The Rec, which at that moment were being opened by the security guard.

Michael Burns was good at what he did. He possessed a rare quality for someone in the security business. He genuinely cared about his job, and took pride in what he did. It was safe to say that there were many people in his line of work, earning very little comparatively, whose attitude reflected their remuneration. He was not one of these people. At the tender age of twenty eight, he had never excelled academically. He made up for it in enthusiasm, however, and it was his fervour for getting the job done, coupled with his personality, that gave others the feeling that they wanted him to do well, and wanted to help him to do so. He loved his job, and to date, had never, ever had to confront anyone at night whilst he was in charge of security at The Rec, and he was proud of the fact that he was well known in his position with young and old alike. A mutual respect between user and venue existed, and it was this respect that filtered through to Michael, and the job that he undertook in an area that was more than a challenge at times.

His keys played their usual symphony on his retractable lanyard, as he walked backwards with the large, heavy gate. He repeated the process with the opposite side, and welcomed the throng of professionals who had come to work that day at the festival. From camera crew, lighting and sound engineers, to reporters and journalists representing the huge variety of media covering the event, they had all decided to make sure that they were at the venue early to undertake their duties and play whatever part they had in the smooth running of the day and its coverage.

Burns smiled as the people, especially the locals, began to pour in. Advance ticket sales had meant that thousands of people had arrived to spectate early, and to grab the best vantage points next to the stages that were to hold their favourite acts in music, dance and other artistic forms. Many of the visitors were in buoyant mood, smiling and greeting him as they came in, relishing the prospect of the day ahead, and many of them relishing the ethos of the special day and its meaning for everyone in attendance.

As some of the crowd filtered towards the visitors' gates to purchase tickets or be admitted to the inner circle where the stages and vendors would be, and as the professionals filtered through security with their passes, Michael smiled to himself. They were going to have a wonderful treat, and his presence there was going to help them feel safe, and forget whatever troubles they might have in their ordinary working lives, if indeed they did work. He turned his back on the gates and began to make his way back towards the inner field where the main action would be kicking off at around nine o'clock that morning. He knew it would be full from the very start, and he and the rest of the safety wardens would have their work cut out to ensure that everything ran smoothly for everyone. Many were volunteers, and had needed special training as it was the first event of this kind they would be attending. He smiled again, knowing that he had been allowed to line manage all of the volunteers, and was being paid double his usual rate for that privilege. He began to think of the various items he would buy with the extra cash, but decided that he would be putting it towards his new motorbike, as he had recently passed his motorcycle test and his eye was set on a particularly fetching Japanese model with all the trimmings. He chuckled to himself as he pictured himself atop his new vehicle in the future, and the sprawling countryside welcoming him freely as the wind howled around him on his travels. He liked the thought of that.

The Rec steadily filled, and with each second that passed, the sea of people grew as visitors and staff brought the venue to life, giving it a fluid pulse that throbbed. The stalls began to open, and vendors began to peddle their trades. Food, crafts and trinkets were exchanged for money, and within half an hour of the gates opening, the aroma of cooking food from all over the world filled the air, enticing even more to sample what was on offer. Large groups of people, young and old, laughed and joked with each other as they settled in for the day. The excitement filled the atmosphere, and those enjoying it threw away their cares, suspended their disbelief and emptied their minds momentarily, hoping only for the good times to continue.

And all the while, in a quiet, shaded spot underneath a behemoth of the road, stood a solitary, silver case. Nothing special to look at, but sleek in design. Many existed, but only this one, today, carried its special, singular cargo, its only purposes being carnage, mayhem, and the extinguishing of innocent life. From the outside, to an observer, it meant only that someone had been careless and forgetful, but in the inside, its contents were the result of care and attention to detail, and were a testament to everything that was negative in relation to modern technology. As it sat, motionless, awaiting its wake-up call, a large, brown spider, adorned with colourful markings to ward off predators, moved with gossamer feet up the polished exterior, and rested a while, impervious to the knowledge that others had regarding the horrors that lay within its confines. It remained in shadow, and ignored the happy noises that escalated as the headcount multiplied. It would soon be time to awaken.

46

Selleck sat in his chair, his face contorted with delight at the scenes of the packed venue. He looked on with a huge smile emanating from his face, even though he was repulsed by what he thought was the scar on the face of society in front of him. He felt sick at the sight of the alien races, mixing with the pure-bred Anglo-Saxons on the wide screen television before his very eyes. He was too ignorant to even think of the fact that Anglo-Saxons, by very nature, were created through foreign intervention and invasion, but continued with his musings on each and every single race that poured through the gates and into The Rec, under their pretence of harmony and satisfaction with the existence they were living.

Two objects adorned his line of vision on the sprawling desk in front of him. One was the remote control that he used for the television. Black, shiny, and served its purpose, like most of the people under his command. The remaining object was the *other* remote. It stared at him, beckoning him, taunting him to rouse it from its slumber and send its deadly message across town to where its servant was waiting to follow its command. Selleck's fingers twitched, akin to a gunslinger in the old Spaghetti Westerns. He felt himself at that moment to be faced off with all of those varied faces on the television. Them against him. They, armed with their very existence and their way of life, poisoning society with their long game. He, armed with the remote control, and with one push of the button, his response to their philosophy.

He cast an incidental glance downwards to where Sara still lay, semi unconscious. She was stirring, but remained silent. Maybe she was doing it to avoid another blow, he considered. That would make no difference to him, he knew. If he wanted to attack her again, there was nothing she or anybody else could do, and that he was the only one with the power to change things, to control the direction of proceedings. He felt this power surge through his veins once again, and reached for the remote detonator. He did not switch it on, as he did not want to risk wearing its battery and therefore its potency down at all. He practiced the motion, though. He used a dummy motion of his thumb to flick the power button to the 'on' position, and then the same thumb to feign a push of the button that would detonate the device. He instinctively looked up at the screen, imagining those people scattering, screaming hysterically, covered in the remains of their loved ones and strangers. *Not long now.* He replaced the remote to its original place on the table, and resumed his occupation with the images on the screen. It was all coming together. He remained seated, patiently, and felt the clock ticking ever backwards in his head. *Not long now.*

47

Matt succumbed to a strange thought as he crept through the darkness in his search for Sara and Selleck. His anger, determination and sheer frustration at not knowing where he was had made him furious, and he felt the adrenaline surge through his veins once again as he wondered what the most dangerous creature was on the planet. He knew that the hippo caused more deaths than lions each year, and he knew that sharks paled into insignificance when compared to them. Right now, though, he felt that it was he, himself, who took the award. Any wild animal protecting those that were dear to them would be a formidable opponent, but Selleck had fucked with the wrong guy. *If he wanted to see wild, then wait till he gets a load of me.* Matt realised that he didn't care about himself at that moment. His own safety became tertiary to the safety and well-being of Sara, Nick and Jim, to whom he owed a great debt, but also to the people at The Rec, who were going to know terror beyond belief, unless Matt could stop the madman and maniac who was John Selleck. Matt knew that he would die trying, if it meant that they could be safe. He pictured Sara, smiling in his arms, and then Selleck, hurting her with his fists, his feet, and in other ways too horrible to bear.

He quickened his pace. He glanced around him, and could not believe how extensive this maze of tunnels ran underground. He thought it absurd that anyone would build such a facility for any reason, when it could be undertaken above ground. *Maybe that was why it had been abandoned*, he thought to himself. That was of no concern now, though; his concern was to continue along these dank, foreboding corridors until he found his prey. He felt that he had been travelling downwards in a circular motion for some time, and realised that the corridors were in a rough spiral, most likely. He realised that he had not been concentrating on the twists and turns, should he get lost, but he felt no fear or claustrophobia in here, and knew that if he were able, he would make sure that Sara and he would get back to the daylight. He realised at this point, that his thoughts in solitude had led him to ignore his pace, and that he was almost running along. He knew that he needed to have one eye on potential enemies, and that Selleck could have more men here. He slowed slightly, and moved into the darker parts of the corridor wherever possible.

He had begun to despair, though. There was no real sign of occupation, and any rooms he had come across had left him no real sign that anyone had been there. One room, with its door open, had shown only a pornographic magazine as sign that somebody had been there, its pages left open at what might have been the reader's favourite page, before they had been ordered to leave the room. Another held only a small flask, with its cup next to it. Coffee remained in the cup, and it was cold to the touch. The inhabitants of this room had left some time ago.

Matt had begun to feel that he needed to turn around and retrace his steps, as he had maybe missed something. He was considering that maybe he had needed to look at other rooms further back, or that he had missed a turning in the darkness that would have led to a more rational choice of room where Selleck could direct things. His mind was beginning to play tricks on him in the darkness, too. He saw shadows where he knew nobody was there, and his peripheral vision had begun to suggest that every recess held an inhabitant, when his ears convinced him of otherwise.

He rounded a corner, and stopped in his tracks. He had clearly reached the end of the maze downwards, and the spiral literally had stopped in front of him. A single door lay ahead of him in the twilight, and a large, metal door lay slightly ajar. Enough light had pushed its way out of the crack in the door to reveal that the lights were indeed ablaze from within the chamber, but it was not the light that had made Matt freeze where he stood. It was his ears that had warned him to desist his forward motion. Matt could hear something. Voices, or maybe a single voice. The light was flickering slightly, so this led Matt to believe that a television was switched on inside the room. And if the television was left on, somebody was going to be in there watching it. *Or just about to return to the room.* Matt instinctively looked over his shoulder. There was nobody there, and he was still alone in the walkway.

Like a cat in bedroom slippers, he moved like a ghost to the crack in the door. It was a solid, metal door, built to withstand both fire and flood by the looks of it, he thought to himself. The crack on the hinge side of the door was too small to peer through, due to the door's construction and design, and the larger aperture did not grant him any real advantage in knowing the contents of the room behind. There was only one thing he could do, and that was to push the door open far enough to get his head around the door quickly, or to simply enter the room and use the element of surprise.

He thought about simply rushing in, and took a few deep breaths to steady himself in preparation, but then discounted this way forward. He realised that there may be more than one person behind the door or in the room, and if the distance were too great between himself and the occupants, he could be in serious trouble. He considered that they could and probably would be armed, knowing what Selleck had on display at his house, and knowing what he had already been through. He decided to gently push the door open, and hope that it didn't alert anybody to his presence until he could ascertain how many people were there.

He held his breath, and placed his foot against the heavy door. He prayed it was in constant use, and that the hinges wouldn't scream in protest to the force he was about to apply. He exhaled slowly, and at the same time, pushed gently forward. To his surprise, the door glided forward without a sound. He ducked out of sight behind the wall, and waited a full minute before moving again, his fists clenched the whole time.

His heart raced as he moved back into position, and then very slowly, in a crouched position, he guided his head through the open door and looked around.

His eyes were immediately drawn to the corner of the room, where what he saw almost made him scream out in fear. Sara was seated on the floor, in what appeared to be an unconscious state. Her hair matted, her cheeks red and stained with salt from her tears, her head lolled to one side. Matt immediately felt a tear in his eye, and his pulse pounded in his neck and his chest simultaneously. He was on the verge of exploding. He knew his blood pressure was through the roof, and he felt himself grow purple with rage. He dragged his eyes to their next focal point quickly, which was the seated figure of Selleck, his back turned, his head glued in the direction of the television. He knew that Selleck hadn't noticed the door opening, as the door was directly behind him at his six o'clock position, but the volume on the television was also loud enough to block out the glide of the door as it had opened.

Matt knew at that moment that this was going to be his only opportunity to rescue Sara. If Selleck alerted any more of his men in any way, that would be him and her done for. He couldn't afford for that to happen. Behind Selleck, resting on the desk, were two devices, which both looked like remote control devices for the television. Matt immediately joined up the dots to ascertain that his brother was indeed right. There was every likelihood that the act of terror that Selleck was bragging about on his website was indeed a bomb, and the second remote could very well be the detonator. He had just given himself another objective, and before springing into action, he prioritised them internally.

1. Give Selleck the education he deserves for his actions

2. Free Sara

3. Get the detonator to safety and get Sara out of this hellhole

4. Call the police

Matt adjusted his posture from a crouched one, to his full height. He had not taken the cut length of scaffold pole from Jim White, and flexed his fingers open and closed, and then into fists, knowing full well that as it stood, they were the only weapons he was going to need. He took a deep breath, and thought of Sara, his love, and of Ashleigh. He thought of his beloved brother, Nick, and Jim White, who had risked his own life to rescue him. His last immediate thought was of Selleck, and what he was trying to achieve. Knowing that he would give his last breath stopping him, Matt knew that the shoe was now on the other foot. It was he, as the teacher, who was going to be doing what he did best, and that was teaching. And teaching *hard*. Matt stepped through the open door, looked around him at the two figures inside the room, and while the television blared out its messages, closed it behind him with an unheard click. The lesson was going to begin. One way or another, it was time for Selleck to learn his lesson.

48

Jim was lost. He was worried about Nick's physical state, which had deteriorated a little since leaving the room where he and Matt had been kept. He was clearly dehydrated, and was in need of fluids desperately. He was extremely sluggish, but was shivering almost uncontrollably due to his state of shock after the ordeal he had been put through. Jim was doing his best to support him, but he realised that he had possibly taken a wrong turning somewhere along the way, and was worried that although he seemed to be moving upwards, this was not the path he had taken to reach the two brothers. He was never one to panic in times of stress, but he was certainly worried about his travelling companion, and knew that he needed medical attention, and soon. He checked his phone quickly. There was still no signal.

'You all right there, Nick?' Jim asked in a whisper. 'Not far now. We'll be outside soon, pal.'

'I'm all right, Jim. I've been better, but believe me, I've been in worse shape. Usually through drink, but I've definitely felt worse.' His eye met Jim's and they smiled. Jim was comforted, knowing that if Nick could joke, then he wasn't at death's door quite yet. 'By the way, where the fuck are we?'

'You don't miss a trick, do you?' Jim replied. He smirked at the fact that Nick was nobody's fool, and still had the energy to remind Jim of that. He liked that, and he liked his resilience. 'Let's stop for a minute, and take stock. We can't be far from the exit. We're still moving upwards. My guess is that we just need to cut across from one corridor to an adjacent one. I'm not sure if all roads lead to Rome, so maybe we'd better think about finding a link corridor somewhere. I'm sure I came across one on the way down.' He put Nick on the floor for a moment, and relished not having his weight on his own shoulders for a while.

'Jim?' Nick said quietly.

'Yes, young man. What is it?'

'I haven't thanked you properly for getting the pair of us out of there. I thought we were done for, you know. Those bastards gave us a really good going over. I'm not sure how Matt does it, but he can take much more of that type of thing than me. You should have seen the scrapes we used to get into as kids. He never stopped protecting me. Still does. Thank you, Jim. Seriously.'

'Listen. You don't have to thank me for anything. And don't worry about Matt. He seems like the type of guy who can handle himself. I've seen his type before. He could eat nails and spit out rivets, that one. Besides, we're not out of the woods just yet. We need to find that link corridor. I'm worried that if we don't, we might not stop that idiot from doing what he wants. Not that I think your brother.........' Jim stopped, knowing that he had just said the wrong thing.

'It's all right, Jim. I'm sure that Matt will be ok. One way or another. It's Selleck that I'm most worried for. If he really knew what Matt was capable of, he'd have left him well alone long before now. I know you're a policeman and all, but I'm really not sure what's going to happen to him. Matt's temper is as hot as Las Vegas weather. It's the red mist. Once he sees that, nobody's safe if they're on the wrong side of him.'

Jim contemplated those words, and processed the true meaning. Nick was basically explaining that his brother might be capable of taking Selleck's life, if he was driven to it. That was a pretty big statement. However, whilst he didn't doubt Matt's resilience, he did see an air of grace mixed in with the other, raw emotions, and he figured that if push came to shove, matt would exercise that grace and not commit the ultimate atrocity in taking another man's right to breathe. He had done despicable things, but Jim felt that his unwritten oath as a teacher would not allow him to commit that sort of act. That said, Jim knew that matt may be presented with a 'him or me' situation, and he knew fully that the human brain, with its 'fight or flight' mechanism, would lead one person to places they hadn't been before, when faced with adversity.

'Nick, come on, let's get out of here.' He picked up the young man once more, and headed down the corridor, where they were, indeed, soon confronted by an adjoining corridor, with a sturdy fire door at each end. Akin to an airlock on a spaceship, they would be in a veritable no-man's-land once through the first door, but Jim was confident that he would find himself close to the exit once through the other side. His bearings were rarely wrong.

They proceeded carefully and slowly through the first fire door, banging themselves on the door frame due to their walking abreast. Once through, the door's closing mechanism quickly performed its duty, and they did indeed find themselves in a narrow corridor, lined with linoleum, and with an identical door at the other end. They slowly made their way to the exit, and without incident, pulled open the door and progressed their way through. As they left the narrow passage, they could see the circular corridor move away from them, making Nick remember an old version of Roald Dahl's *Charlie and the Chocolate Factory*. He too had walked down a similar corridor, in order to allow the guests to enter their tour of his marvellous factory.

This, however, was where the similarity ended for Nick, as the next ten metres or so brought them to a halt, stopped dead in their tracks as a shadow emerged from one of the side rooms, bathed in half-light, which made his presence even more sinister to the two escapees.

'Morning, gentlemen. Going somewhere, are we?'

It was Harry Planter, and the object he carried in his hands made both Nick and Jim flinch. As if carved by The Devil himself, Planter's gnarled fingers cradled what had once been a baseball bat, but which had transformed over some time into a pitted, yellow, stained harbinger of misery, which had doubtless times caused such harm to his victims that their memories were etched into the grain that carried the varying pigments. Jim quickly inspected it, and wondered how much blood was embossed into it, and from how many different people.

Jim reacted first, by letting go of Nick, who found his knees weaken due to the fright he had just received, and also his fatigue from his previous endeavours. Jim stepped instinctively to stand between Planter and Nick, protecting him, doing his sworn job as a policeman. In his mind, Jim had become two people. One, the law abiding citizen with a sworn duty to protect those who needed it from harm within the laws of the land. The other, he discovered with surprise, was a seething, wild beast, borne out of furious anger and hatred for those who were being put before him.

'As a matter of fact,' Jim sighed, 'we are. We're going that way.' He pointed to a spot behind Planter vaguely, as if he couldn't be bothered to dignify him with a real response. 'And if you don't get out of the way, I'm going to have to do whenever I come across road kill on the road.'

'Oh yeah? And what's that then? Blow it a kiss, you faggot?' Planter's face did not show any emotion, despite the way in which he had spat out his words at Jim.

'No, I kick it out of the way and be on my way, you slimy piece of shit. Your choice.' Jim stood steadfast. He was not running.

'Well,' Planter smiled, 'I'm not sure you're fucking hard enough for that, son.'

'Let's find out.'

Jim made the first move, stepping towards Planter quickly to deliver a swift jab to the face. Planter, however, had years of experience as a boxer, and his pugilistic skills stretched way beyond amateur level. He slipped the punch briefly, with Jim's punch only landing a glancing blow. It was still enough to bring water to his eyes, but he used some deft footwork for a man his age to dance backwards and to the side.

'Not bad, but not good enough, mate. Let's see how you do against my little friend here, shall we?' It was Planter's turn to move now, and he danced from side to side, forcing Jim to dance around his feigned advances. Suddenly, he sidestepped and moved in quickly, jabbing the butt of his weapon into Jim's midriff. Jim was too slow, and took the full force of the blow. Winded, he tried his best not to double with the pain, but it was of no use. Knowing that a head shot would probably come next, he covered his head with an elbow guard, and this thankfully took the sting out of the fierce swipe with the baseball bat. Jim knew he was not going to win this one. He refused to back down, though, and vowed silently that he would give his last breath defending Nick and eliciting their freedom.

'Is that all you've got? Are you a vegetarian?' Jim taunted, keeping his distance momentarily. He could see that Planter was ruffled by this, and he continued. 'I thought you old-school gangsters were supposed to be hard. Maybe I was ill informed.'

'You fucking pansy. I'm going to fucking kill you.' Planter ran at Jim, his bat raised high in the air. Jim rushed forward, moving inside the effective range of the weapon, and slammed his knee into Planter's gut. Planter growled with pain. *That hurt,* Jim thought to himself. *You're not so cocky now, are you?*

Planter then did something totally unexpected. He threw his bat away, behind him, down the corridor. He smiled at Jim, and snarled as he moved forward, closing Jim down and restricting his ability to manoeuvre in the confines of the narrow corridor. It seemed that he was a man of warped principle, but principle nevertheless, and he wanted to prove to Jim that he could take him on his terms, man to man, on an even playing field.

'Right. Let's do this the old fashioned way. Your boyfriend here,' he pointed to Nick as he spoke from his prone position, 'is going to witness how we used to deal with problems back in the day.'

'You can try.' Was all that Jim could think of to say in return. No snappy comebacks like the movie stars would. Just the facts. Jim held his hands up in a fighting guard, and stood his ground. He wasn't going to simply lay down and die. He would need his life taking from him, and he wasn't going to let Planter do that easily. He would have to work for it. He circled around clockwise, and began to dance a little, feigning right and left, provoking a false move from Planter. He was no slouch with his fists, and had undertaken training in both boxing and karate when younger. Although not as flexible as he used to be, he still could look after himself, however had never had to use his skills in all his years on the force to this extent. Not until now. He stepped in, and jabbed Planter twice in the face. A trickle of blood appeared from his nose after the squelch of fist against nose, but the roughened features of Jim's opponent were used to this treatment. Planter unleashed a feigned punch to the head, and followed this with two crushing body shots to the ribs, along with a savage right hook to Jim's cheek.

Jim sailed to the side, disoriented. He fell to one knee, and Planter was immediately on him, using his fist like a hammer on the back of Jim's head. Jim knew he was beaten, and despite his efforts to stand, Planter's weight on his back was too great, and he had no option but to prepare himself for darkness, which was beginning to close in with every shot. His hearing, muffled, picked up Planter's words, distorted by the sound of the blood rushing through his ears.

'I told you, I'm going to end you. Old school. Good night you fucking......' He raised his hand to deal what could have been the final blow to Jim's head, but another sound rang out, and Planter's hand fell down to his side. Jim's foggy vision picked out

Planter simply fall to his knees, his eyes closed, his jaw slack, and his body topple onto Jim's. Jim instinctively pushed him off, leaving him lying on his back next to him. In the silence, Jim saw the slim figure of Nick, holding the length of scaffold pole in his hand. He was trembling, and he dropped the scaffold.

'It was you or him, Jim. I couldn't let that happen. I had to do something. I…'

'It's okay, Nick.' Jim panted, sitting up, supporting his weight as his vision returned slowly with every beat of his heart, which danced a polka inside his ribcage. 'You're right. It was me or him. Thank you, you did the right thing there. Thank you.'

'Is he dead?' Nick enquired.

'If he is, Nick, you saved my life.' Jim looked at Nick, and could see the young man tormented by the fact that he might have taken the life away from another. The fact remained, though, that Nick had saved him from certain death. 'I won't say anything. Nobody will know it was you.' He stood, shakily, and picked up the scaffold pole. Taking Harry Planter's sweater, he feverishly rubbed the pole, cleansing it of any fingerprints that he or Nick might have left on it. 'Don't touch anything. Hang on.'
Jim used his finger to feel for a pulse in Planter's neck. Nick held his own breath, visibly.

'Well?' Nick asked feebly.

'He's alive. He's going to need a skip load of Nurofen when he comes around, but he's going to enjoy a nice, long sleep at your expense. Come on. Let's move this piece of trash somewhere quiet. We can't be far away. Can you walk? Come on, I'll help you.' Jim dragged Planter into the room from where he appeared, and once inside, removed a rusty, metal key from the lock, closed the door, and locked it from the outside. He motioned to help Nick, but Nick held up his hand in protest.

'I'm fine, Jim. I'll walk myself. You've been through it a bit. Let's rock.'

Jim checked his phone again. Still no signal. He was going to need to be outside, he thought. And the quicker, the better. Together, they continued upwards, hoping that soon they would see daylight, and find the help that Matt was probably going to need very, very soon. They both thought of nothing else as they trudged, weaponless, through the murky soup of darkness that followed their every step.

49

With the door closed, Matt advanced slowly towards the desk. He had forgotten about the element of surprise; he *wanted* Selleck to see him. He wanted him to experience fright. He wanted to intimidate him, and let him feel fear. He needed to fear him, because he was going to hurt him. He was going to hurt him badly.

Selleck remained transfixed to the screen, watching the crowds begin to squeeze into the various staged areas, becoming one organism, instead of a thousand separate ones all vying for space. He was clearly mesmerised by the events, and as Matt neared the huge table that separated the two men, he closed in on the detonator.

Matt saw Sara open her eyes, and squint at him, trying to make sense of what she was seeing. Matt put his finger to his lips in a hushing gesture, he didn't want her to spoil the nice little surprise for Selleck. She recognised him, and almost called out to him. Whether to warn him of something, or in relief, she thought against it, obviously heeding his signal. She understood that he wanted to reach a particular spot before introducing himself. Which he did.

'Hello John. You've been a bad boy, and now you're going to have to see sir.'

Selleck spun around in his chair, and the shock of hearing an unfamiliar voice behind him made him jump. Matt couldn't help it, but he could not contain a laugh at his extreme reaction.

'WHAT THE FUCK ARE YOU DOING HERE?' He bellowed. Matt knew that the volume was not through anger, but embarrassment. He had let his guard down, and he knew that Matt and Sara had seen him display shock and fear, albeit for an instant.

'I told you, I'm here to teach you a lesson, you piece of shit. Now, come out here form behind that fucking desk, and let me educate you in what real pain feels like.' Matt moved forward, towards the desk. Selleck stood up, his giant frame blocking out the television screen. Matt stood his ground for a moment. He knew that the best opportunity would be for him to meet Selleck man-to-man in a wider space, and not where he would be restricted in any way. He was acutely aware that Selleck could be armed, or have a gun secreted in his desk, but he was willing to take that chance, and he was prepared to run and dive at Selleck, were he to make any movement to pull any sort of weapon. Despite the beating he had taken, he still felt that he had enough energy to devote to this inhuman monster in front of him.

'I'm going to fucking kill you, and your bitch there! I'm going to rip your fucking heart out and feed it to the dogs. But do you know what? I'm going to keep you alive long enough to see me take her one more time, and long enough for you to watch me use this to blow all of those bastards on the television sky high. Do you know how long I've waited for this? Well, now I'm going to get to waste you, her, and your brother at the same time.' Selleck moved around the table, and out into the space between Greaves and it.

'You're forgetting something, you stupid, pathetic piece of shit. My brother is gone. If I'm free, do you think I left him there on his own? Your boys needed to brush up on covering their backs. They're probably coming around right about now, but they won't be able to help you. And Nick is long gone by now. You see, we've had some help. And right about now, the police will be getting a phone call. They'll be finding out all about this shithole, and the bomb, and the person behind it. It's you who's fucked. Not Sara. And it's you who's going to get to watch. You're going to watch me kick the living shit out of you. So let's do this.'

Selleck's face contorted into a grimace of pure, unadulterated hatred for Greaves. He could see that his plan was unravelling, yet he still wasn't willing to admit it.

'You? You're a fucking disgrace. I'm going to snap you in two.'

'I wasn't always a teacher. You're going down.' Matt saw Selleck's face change momentarily. A new emotion fleeted across it. Fear.

Selleck made the first move. He charged at Matt, hoping to hit him hard with his full weight at chest height. Matt was ready, he sidestepped with incredible agility, and left his foot out to trip Selleck. He accomplished this, and the giant fell forward, onto his front. He wasn't hurt, but Matt loved the fact that he had made him fall.

'Come on, you big cissy. What's the matter? Fell over?' he made a beckoning gesture with his open hand, palm up, beckoning Selleck back to the fight. Selleck hauled himself back onto his feet, and moved towards Greaves, slower this time. Both men had their guard up. This was now a fist fight. Matt was hoping it wold come to this. *This, I know. Welcome to my world, Selleck. Welcome to my childhood.*

Selleck threw a wild haymaker with his right hand, but matt ducked it, unleashing a savage left hook of his own, which connected heavily with the side of Selleck's right cheek. The sound was sickening, but Selleck remained standing. His adrenaline had left him feeling only a fraction of the pain that he would have done under normal circumstances, but the effect of the punch was obvious. He waivered on his feet, and steadied himself.

'Try that again, Mr. Teacher Man.'

'My fucking pleasure.' Replied Matt. He moved around, and with a feint, motioned to give Selleck a jab to the face. When his guard came up, Matt jumped up, and as he moved towards Selleck, threw a punch over his guard, which connected with his forehead. Not much damage, but he'd got through again. When he landed, Matt threw two body hooks in quick succession, *left-right*, followed by another right hook.

Selleck, although taller, with a bigger reach, was slow, and Matt was willing to exploit this.

Selleck threw a straight cross, and Matt instinctively knew what to do. He parried the punch with his left hand, throwing Selleck's balance off to the left, and stepping outside the outstretched right arm, delivered a huge elbow cross to his opponent's cheek. Selleck grunted, and stepped sideways with the force of the blow. He punched back wildly with his left hand, hoping to connect somewhere, but Matt ducked this punch also, and with Selleck's weight now transferred to the right, he posted a powerful right hook to the left cheek, which sent him the other way.

Selleck stared at Matt in disbelief. How could this guy be beating him? He looked at Matt, who simply grinned at him, and beckoned him once more towards him.

My god, the bewildered giant thought, *he's enjoying this. He's not scared of me.* Selleck thought of another plan. He rushed at Matt, and grabbed him by the back of the head. He hugged him in close in a bear hug, and began to squeeze. He would squeeze the life out of his combatant.

Matt realised his arms weren't able to move. He would have to think quickly. He knew there was only one thing for it, given the circumstances. He snapped his head forward, his forehead connecting squarely with Selleck's nose. It exploded in front of his eyes, and Matt knew that there was no way that he would able to keep the bear hug going with that mess of a face. He was right. Selleck screamed in pain, and blood spurted out of his nose and down his face. He did, indeed, let go, but not until he had unleashed a rage-fuelled right-handed driver, that caught matt on the chin. Matt felt that one, and the crunch that accompanied it inside his mouth, plus the searing pain, made Matt realise that he'd been dealt some damage. He felt the coppery taste of blood and new that one of his teeth had been loosened by the connection. He felt himself move backwards, and felt the cold wall against his back. Selleck did not relent, realising that he had momentarily stolen back the advantage, and got in close, delivering a stomach blow which, although not the hardest he had ever experienced, still made Matt's legs buckle, and he slid down the wall, onto his bottom momentarily. He tried to breathe, but couldn't fill his lungs properly.

He thought this could mean his demise, but instead, Selleck ran to the table shakily, and snatched the remote detonator from the table, bringing it back to Matt. Towering over Matt now, Selleck regained some of his composure, and he swaggered falsely to Matt, waving the object.

'You think you can win? Here, just look at the screen there you bastard. See what I've orchestrated. It's going to be wonderful.'

'You're crazy. You're fucking insane. Don't do it, Selleck.' Matt said flatly, without wanting to give him the feeling that he was begging. He had regained his breath back, and he knew he could stand again, but this was unknown to Selleck, as he had flicked on the detonator, and seeing its red light took him to a new level. He stood proudly, as if at an altar, delivering a sermon, and positioned himself so that both Sara and Matt could witness the act of pushing the button.

'You get to share this with me. You get to witness the first message that the New Dawn is here. I'm going to kill you both soon, but at least you get to see my handiwork.' He raised the detonator aloft, like a chalice to the gods, and depressed the switch with his thumb.

'NO!' Sara screamed. Matt simply watched the screen in horror.

But nothing happened.

Selleck pressed the switch again. Nothing

He pressed it again, and again. Nothing

Matt didn't need another chance. He sprang up like a gazelle, and covered the space between him and Selleck in a fraction of a second. He rugby tackled Selleck, cutting in half with a body-on-body contact so fierce, it made the giant look like a giant letter 'U' in mid-air. Selleck hit the ground on his back, hard. Matt was the first to move, and struggled on top of Selleck, and straddled his chest. He began to rain the blows down on Selleck, and spoke with each one. Selleck's arms were pinned, and he couldn't move. He rode each punch, but Matt knew they were hurting. They were the hardest blows he could muster, given the circumstances and his fatigue.

'YOU....HAVE....NO...IDEA...WHO...YOU'RE...DEALING...WITH. YOU'VE...FUCKED...WITH...THE...WRONG...GUY! FUCK...YOU!'

The last blow he delivered seemed to be the final straw for Selleck, and the weak smile he had spread across his face seemed to fade. His eyes appeared to glass over, and his head suddenly flopped to one side. His eyes half closed. *Job done*, Matt thought. He clambered from Selleck's chest, and made his way immediately to Sara. She was cable tied to the chair, and Matt quickly moved back to the table to look in the drawers for a knife to cut her free with. He didn't find one, but did find a Luger pistol and a pair of scissors. Just to be on the safe side, he held the pistol in his hand, and located the magazine release button. He released the magazine, and checked the chamber to see if there was a round in there. He knew to do that from memory. His father had been a member of a local gun club in his youth, and he had remembered watching him with his own automatic pistol, that he used for target shooting. A single round escaped onto the floor. Matt kept the magazine, in case, and threw the gun back into the drawer. He picked up the scissors, and ran back to Sara, where he sliced her bindings. Her arms were numb, and she couldn't move them. She had soiled herself due to the length of her incarceration, but neither of them cared. Matt flung his arms around her, and the tears flowed freely down her cheeks as he kissed her head.

'Thank you, Matt. Jesus, thank you for rescuing me. He would have done such horrible things to me. I was so worried about you as well. He would have killed you.' She sobbed uncontrollably, and he pulled her close again. His own tears welling.

'Not on my watch. As long as there's a hole in my arse, I'd always have found a way to come and get you. I wasn't going to lose you. I'm never going to lose you.' It was his turn to let his emotions out briefly, and she hugged him, as if they had just invented it.

'God I love you, Greavsie.'

'Obviously. I am irresistible to all women, and some men, after all.' They both found a second to laugh.

'What are you going to do now? Why didn't the bomb go off, Matt?'

Matt brought himself back down to Earth, and realised that he had work to do.

'I assume we are too far underground, and the signal couldn't find is way to its destination. Lots of walkie-talkies, things like that, they often work on a line-of-sight basis and can't find their way through lots of obstacles. Ground being one of them. Obviously, if it was a satellite system, it might be different, but that's my best guess. Either way, we'd better get the detonator, and this piece of........' He turned and pointed at Selleck. Or rather, the space where he was laid out a minute earlier.

The prone figure had disappeared, and so had the detonator. Matt leapt to his feet and ran. His only mission now was to stop him from getting to daylight.

50

Nick cried out with relief as he saw what appeared to be a shaft of daylight piercing the darkness of the corridor, as they rounded what turned out to be the last corner they would face that morning. Jim, although silent, shared Nick's joy at what was going to be a welcome respite from the subterranean hell that they had witnessed, and the physical trauma that they had endured together. Their energy seemed to be returning as they took each of the steps upwards into what was the administration office that Jim had encountered, and he noted that it looked completely different in the stark daylight. They both blinked furiously as the light strangled their senses, and Nick took a second to perch on the corner of one of the old, dilapidated desks that stood there.

Jim lifted up his hand in a silent, swift motion, not dissimilar to one that a marine commando would use in the jungle to silently warn his team of approaching danger. There was no immediate danger to Jim's senses, but he suddenly realised that there still could be company somewhere, and the last thing he needed was to have to engage any more of what would appear to be stragglers. He simply didn't have the capacity. He knew that. He decided that caution was the best option. He also knew that he needed to call the police as quickly as possible, and he did not want to miss that opportunity due to having alerted anyone nearby to their presence. The police would do their job better with the element of surprise and stealth on their side. They would be sending armed officers, and they would never want to draw attention to themselves unnecessarily or create panic.

Jim quietly nosed around the immediate outside areas, and ascertained quickly that the facility was deserted, apart from those left inside. He took out his phone, and dialled the direct line to the station. He was put immediately through to the switchboard, and after a succinct, but informative call, he disconnected, having informed them of everything that was in his knowledge and understanding.

Jim knew that he was going to be in trouble, as he had previously been warned away from investigating the artwork around Bloomfield, but he could not see how he could be sanctioned heavily, if it had led to hundreds of lives being saved, and the eradication of the threat of a terrorist act being carried out on domestic soil.

'They're on their way. To here with armed officers, and also to The Rec. It's going to have to be evacuated, but they will have a detailed plan in place for evacuation and emergency. As much of a shame as it is for everyone, they'll be glad to be out of danger. I just hope that we're not too late.' He looked at Nick and waited for a response.

'I need to go back in. For Matt. I can't leave him in there, Jim.'

'That's a negative on that one. You can't do that. The armed officers won't want additional civilians in there when they sweep the facility, especially if there's a terrorist threat. There have been too many incidents of mistaken identity and near misses for them to have to worry about that. They've got a description of both Selleck and Matt. They'll know who they're looking for in there. They need to keep it simple. Come on. We'll need to get out of the way.' He motioned for Nick to follow him.

Nick grudgingly agreed to Jim's theory on what needed to be done, and with a cursory glance down the stairs behind him, he followed Jim. They made their way across the scrubland, and to the front gates, where Nick's car remained, untouched. He seemed relieved at that, Jim regarded.

In the distance, they soon heard the sirens. They sat on the pavement, against the fence in plain view, in non-threatening poses. The last thing they needed was for the armed response policemen to see them as a threat. There was every possibility that they would be bound for their own protection due to the nature of the report called in, but they didn't want to risk being counted in with the rest of the hoodlums below, however many there were.

The sirens stopped in the distance, and after a couple of minutes, all of the vehicles that were rushing to the scene converged at once. Both ends of the access road were cordoned off, and Nick and Jim were greeted, cuffed, and marched to the end of the road, where Jim explained who he was, and that he was the person who had called in the incident and the threat. Nick was separated from him, and after a brief interview, remained cuffed, but was taken to the nearest ambulance under supervision to receive medical treatment. The police were incredibly methodical, and spent some considerable time debriefing Jim on the layout of the facility, the prospective numbers of people inside the facility, who they were, and what they were doing. The officer in charge of proceedings, a sergeant named Richard Hillard, exchanged information with the armed response team, whose heckler and Koch MP5 rifles were clean, loaded and ready for action. Their side arms remained in their holsters, but all of the officers looked super-focused, and ready for action. From their separate vantage points, both Nick and Jim realised how lucky they were to have such a rapid response team available, that were so professional in their approach.

In situations like these, identified as dynamic responses, they had already been granted urgent firearms authority. This had come from the delegated Inspector. In turn, the delegated Inspector had received confirmed authority from the Superintendent. Once satisfied that they had enough information, the practicality and controlled urgency of the situation took over and they moved to the gate of the facility, in formation, covering all of the angles. With silent signal, and with extreme concentration, they moved inside the gate and to their destination, using all available cover from what they already knew about the site, having used available intelligence. As they disappeared,

Jim looked on, and managed to catch Nick's eye in the distance. Jim's cuffs had been removed, as had Nick's, as they had been deemed safe, and as their gazes met, Jim nodded solemnly, but a nod of support. This was returned, and they realised that whatever happened now, it was completely out of their hands.

51

Some miles away, the organisers at The Rec, including the security firms employed, had been notified within minutes of the possible threat, and had already begun to implement their emergency evacuation plan. The huge crowds, upon hearing through the address system that they were to leave by the nearest exit, did so with mixed reactions. It was better that they did not know of the imminent threat, and the organisers had taken great care not to frighten anyone by mentioning that there was a suspect package. This could only lead to panic and a possible stampede, and they were very direct in communicating that the reason was only a minor precaution but a necessary one. The throng were directed to their muster points, and were happy and calm knowing that their welfare had been taken care of. Once at their muster points, they remained there, under supervision from the wardens, and police as they arrived on scene. Although many people remained inside, the venue was emptying quickly, and would soon be completely safe.

From his vantage point, Michael Burns looked at his array of monitors from the safety of the security control centre, and smiled with satisfaction, knowing that every single person would be evacuated safely. He relished the fact that the processes had been followed to the letter by all of the staff involved, and he revelled in the fact that whatever the issue, the police were already here and able to deal with it effectively. He was still, as such, in the dark regarding the nature of the emergency, but when he saw the white van arrive, adorned with its yellow horizontal stripe, he knew immediately that what was happening was serious. It was the bomb disposal team. His heart raced into his throat, and he immediately urged time to quicken. If there was that sort of threat, then now, more than ever, he needed to ensure that everyone remained professional, and worked together. Within minutes, there was a knock at the door, and he was being introduced to the sergeant in charge, a grey-haired, incredibly calm officer of many years' experience named David Hollander. From the moment that Michael Burns met him, he felt comfortable knowing that they would be in safe hands. What he didn't know, though, was that their destiny was being controlled from elsewhere.

52

Matt was using every available ounce of his strength to close on Selleck. He was breathing hard, due to his injuries sustained during his capture, but he was still mobile, and that was good enough for him. *I'm coming to get you, you bastard, and you're not getting away this time. You're going down. One way or another, you're going down.* His thoughts blurred as he ran, following the fresh footsteps in the dust and dirt that lined the floor. As he ran, he slammed into the doors that stood in his way, and he hoped that if he was gaining, then Selleck would hear him, and know that he was going to be caught. There would be no stopping matt this time. He had held back slightly in front of Sara, his sensibilities preventing him from making him cry like a child. He knew that this time, he was going to catch him, and he *was* going to pay in sweat and blood, and his own tears.

He forged ahead, sprinting through the curved corridors, upwards. Ever upwards. Matt knew that he needed to speed up, and used his thoughts of Sara and Ashleigh to spur him on. He felt his adrenaline surge with those feelings, and he felt he would create a sonic boom, he was moving so fast through the darkness. He smiled to himself, which made him feel uneasy inside. He knew that he should not have felt as if he was looking forward to catching his prey, but he was resolute in the knowledge that he hadn't finished teaching him a lesson.

Matt had already followed the freshest footsteps he could see through a minor corridor that seemed to adjoin concentric circular corridors, and was back on the circular pathway once again. He rounded a corner, and in the distance, he could see shadows moving. *Gotcha!* He thought to himself. Spurred on by the fact that he had made the ground he needed, he pushed ahead, his breathing now beginning to heave under the stress of the chase. He refused to relent, though, and suddenly he saw the heel of a boot, which became a leg, and then the rest of Selleck. He was exhausted, but he had seemingly made it to his destination, as matt could see two small shafts of light up ahead, which were the property of two large fire doors, with push bars attached.

Matt knew that he couldn't allow Selleck to reach the open air outside. *Hell, I might already be too late.* He was gaining at an alarming rate, and Selleck looked behind him, sensing that the footsteps were close behind him.

'Come...here... you... piece...of....' Matt yelled, as he zoomed towards Selleck, who had completely run out of steam, and who was now moving at almost a walking pace. Matt didn't finish his sentence, as he ploughed a tackle into Selleck from behind, hoping to knock the remote detonator out of his right hand. Greaves had spotted it from a distance, and knew he had to obtain it, or put Selleck out of action before he could use it. Either way, Selleck was going to get hurt.

'Get the fuck off me!' Selleck screamed, thrashing.

Matt obliged, but positioned himself between Selleck and the door.

'Come on! Let's see what you've got. Whether you push that button or not, you're going to have to go through me to get out. You're going down. You're getting hurt. COME ON!' Matt raised his guard, and he could see that Selleck was either exhausted, or scared, or both. Matt knew that he had him.

Selleck still refused to admit defeat in any measure, and put the detonator in his pocket, which pleased Matt. It was now out of the way, and it meant that he hadn't depressed the switch. He was going to try and get past him to the safety of the outdoors, and away from any police involvement. Selleck raised his own guard, and lumbered towards matt to engage him. The swagger had gone, and his face was full of hatred as before, but no matter how hard he tried, he could not hide the fact that Matt was worrying him. He was genuinely frightened of losing to him.

Matt didn't hesitate to strike first, and had planned his first foray into defeating Selleck long before this moment; his hand streaked forward, landing a deft punch squarely on Selleck's chin. He thrashed a wild right hand hook in return, but Matt stepped inside to close the gap, raised his arm in an elbow cover, and used his own right hand to blast three quick punches in quick succession into the soft flesh of the giant's belly. Matt heard the wind forced out of him with each punch, and stepped back, towards the door. Selleck took one step forward, tentatively, not knowing what to do. Matt had him scared. He knew he was beaten for speed. He tried to force himself forward again at speed, but Matt was prepared. He parried the first jab downwards with his left hand, and hammered his right in a back-fisted punch straight into Selleck's nose. The nose protested briefly, but then gave up its contents, in a red streak that spewed down his face and onto his shirt. Having already been broken, the pain was excruciating, and the victim of the onslaught howled in agony.

Matt didn't stop there. He used his momentum to use his left fist to start a violent combination of jabs, hooks and body shots that drove Selleck back with each painful connection, and which brought further blood to his face. Matt connected one punch to his eye socket, which immediately began to close, his vision now hugely impeded. He went down on one knee, and took the full force of Matt's boot to the head from the front. He did not go over backwards as expected, but rather soaked up the contact, and with what seemed like inhuman strength, leapt upwards with his fists clenched together, catching matt under the chin. This time it was the turn of the smaller man to be driven backwards, and although he didn't collapse, he did feel his vision blur, and his balance was left reeling. He began to succumb to dizziness. Matt could feel the daylight on his shoulder, and realised that he was close to the door. It was too late, though. Selleck had removed the detonator from his pocket and had armed it once again. The red light stared at Matt, piercing the half-light like a needle.

'Fuck you. You haven't stopped anything.' Selleck bean to laugh. 'In a second, you'll hear the explosion. You'll know I've succeeded, and it's you who'll have lost. Fuck all of you!'

Before Matt had a chance to dive for him, Selleck had charged at him, and the two men collided like asteroids. The huge, toppling mass crashed into the doors, triggering the push-bar mechanism, and the two men tumbled out together in an embrace of hatred, out of the doorway, and down the grass embankment that lay outside. The slid, tumbled and rolled the ten feet or so, until they reached the bottom.

It was Selleck who arose first, but hadn't noticed the company he was keeping.

'ARMED POLICE! DON'T MOVE! GET DOWN ON THE GROUND!' Came the shouts with the controlled aggression that their training had given them.

Matt froze, and realised that only metres away, the police, armed with their semi-automatic rifles, had them trained on the pair of them, waiting for the next move.

Selleck ignored them, and lofted the detonator into the air. He depressed the switch, and Matt waited for the explosion to follow. In slow motion, Greaves thought of the people trapped at The Rec, and the carnage. He thought of the loss of life, and the fact that he had failed to prevent it. He felt tears on his face, instantaneously.

But the explosion never filled the air. What did, however, was a single gunshot. Matt, glued to the detonator, saw Selleck's raised hand jerk backwards, and the detonator, along with half his hand, disintegrate. Specks of blood covered Matt's face, and in the instant this had taken to happen, Matt knew that something had gone wrong with the master plan. Something hadn't worked in the scheme to bring chaos to the world around them.

Selleck fell to his knees, screaming violently at the hole where his fingers used to dwell, and he was immediately surrounded by police. He was crying profusely, the tears a mixture of pain and disappointment in relation to his failure. He couldn't understand why the bomb hadn't detonated. *Pitov promised me. He promised me it would work. That bastard. I shouldn't have trusted him.* He was led away to receive medical attention, and to eventually be arrested. On his way to the ambulance, his hands still bound in opposite directions to make it difficult for him to operate, he realised that a crown had begun to congregate behind the police cordon. A mixture of onlookers stood there, devoid of passion, watching every move that anybody made, storing up as much information as possible. This would inevitably be exaggerated later on, but they revelled in the events unfolding. As Selleck was marched into the ambulance, he noticed a familiar face in the crowd. Two eyes stared at him, unblinking, unwavering from his own countenance. It took a minute to register, but then he realised who it was. It was Sam Kettering. One of his members. The very member that he had trusted to plant the device at The Rec. Through his pain, Selleck tried to make sense of what was happening. *I gave him specific instructions on where to put the device. I told him to leave it under one of the vehicles, preferably one of the bigger ones. I showed him specifically how to arm the bomb, and hell, I even gave him the instructions. It came with instructions, written down by Pitov. You would have to be some sort of idiot not to be able to……..*

Then it struck Selleck like a sledgehammer. He remembered some days ago, down in I-9. He had been made to teach that one a lesson, and had given him the empty chamber treatment. He remembered that he had made him cry, too. He was the one who had been drawing the logo all over town, drawing unnecessary attention to himself. Their eyes remained locked. That is, until Selleck was approached by an armed officer, his body armour making him sweat profusely. He approached Selleck, and ignored his surroundings as he spoke to Selleck.

'Well, Mr. Selleck, it appears that you've been a busy boy. We know who you are, mate. We had an anonymous tip-off a short time ago. Seems like you've been a naughty boy, planting explosive devices in public places. Not sure where you got it from, but I'll bet it wasn't Argos.' The officer was enjoying his one-sided chat with the culprit. He continued. 'The thing is, as well as our anonymous tip-off, we've just received news from The Rec. It's from our bomb disposal unit guys. After they evacuated the festival, one of our officers, a spaniel named Sam, managed to locate your device. He's good like that.' The policeman moved closer, his so every word could be heard. 'Usually, with devices like that, we can put them into a blast tin, to diffuse the blast upwards. Thing was, we didn't know what type of device it was. So we had to use our x-ray equipment. Very sophisticated, like. You getting this. Keeping up?'

Selleck was listening intently. He was hanging on every word, in fact. He didn't know where this story was going. He nodded, slowly, the medic working on his damaged hand now, cleaning the wound briefly.

'Anyway,' the officer continued, 'turned out we had to get the robot in. We had to open it. Ended up using it to cut through the catches on the briefcase to open it. We knew it wasn't rigged after the x-ray. Strange thing, though, that when we got it open, we were all ready to detonate it safely, with the blast going straight up, when we realised that the thing wasn't even armed. It had been set up to accept a signal, but whoever had placed the device, and I'm assuming you, had forgotten to arm it. It was '*The light's on, but nobody home to collect the mail.*' It's a good job that you're going inside, by the looks of it, as you're pretty shit at terrorism mate. Now, get in the car and let's get you fixed up before we start the really hard questions. We're going to be having a long chat. One without coffee.'

Selleck said nothing. Not a single word. He merely walked as directed, bowed his head as not to bang it getting in, and allowed the officer to tap the car for him to be removed. He ignored the onlookers. All except Sam, who took calm delight in producing a piece of paper from his pocket and reading it as the squad car drove past him. It was a piece of paper with very specific instructions written upon it. A how-to, if you will, for arming a device. Sam smiled at Selleck. And Selleck screamed from within the car at Sam. As the car disappeared into the distance, the young artist thought how funny it was that sooner or later, everyone would reach their breaking point, and how funny it always was that what goes around, comes around. Sam began his journey home, knowing full well that there was every likelihood that the police would soon be knocking on his door, so he took incredibly close care on the way home to make sure that each and every square inch of the instructions were burnt with his lighter. He enjoyed watching the ashen remains of the paper float away on the breeze. He knew that each one was like a butterfly, carrying his alibi. Without the instructions, it was going to be his word against Selleck's, and the only people who knew that it was he who had armed the bomb were those two themselves. It was time, he mused, that he took a holiday from the racism business, and maybe started concentrating on his art a bit more. There was more money in that. He whistled as he walked the distance to his home. It was a good tune.

****

At the police station, Jim realised that in layman's terms, he was getting his arse handed to him by his superiors. He was being debriefed, and that was an understatement. He had recounted his story from the start, and was incredibly honest about the fact that he had disobeyed direct orders to leave his amateur detective skills at home. He explained how he had become more and more embroiled in the activities surrounding the graffiti, and how he had begun to believe that in some strange way, the art work, the logos, the slogans, and the killings in town were all connected. He explained about tailing the young Sam Kettering (who would eventually only be cautioned for his membership of the organisation and given community service for his graffiti. He would also be bound over to keep the peace following his admission of membership to the New Dawn Movement) into the I-9 facility, and the events that followed. How he found Matt and Nick tied up, and how he freed them easily so that they could go their separate ways. He did have to come clean, though, about the fibres of the coat, and the ones he had scooped up from the subterranean tunnels. Jessica Quinn would unfortunately be joining him in the stocks, it seems, but he knew her well enough to know she wouldn't mind in the long run. She was a woman of principle.

His Superintendent, and the Inspector present at his debriefing, were very clear on what was going to be the likely outcome of Jim's behaviour. He had, without doubt, disobeyed orders, and had also withheld information connected to an ongoing investigation. That was not good news as far as he was concerned.

'Jim, while the rest of this mess is pieced together, we're going to be suspending you on full pay. You have behaved in an inappropriate way, however it seems that were it not for your actions, we could, in theory, have been looking at a whole different scenario. Whether the bomb was armed or not, the fact remains that the perpetrator of this act has been caught and incarcerated. For that, you do deserve thanks. Your record will not show a commendation, however unofficially, we do extend thanks for your attitude and bravery. What do you think?' The Superintendent, a highly decorated officer named Pete Willard, looked directly at Jim.

'It's a fair decision. I appreciate the thanks, but I'm very sorry for not telling you about the rest. It won't happen again.' He looked at the floor, slightly ashamed of his actions and the way in which he had tarnished his reputation.

His superiors looked at each other, and Willard spoke again.

'Jim, you need to know something. You're probably thinking that Jessica Quinn will be joining you on the naughty step. Well, that's only half-right. She contacted me yesterday to say that the fibres from the coat she found match those found on both Saul Omoku, but also Reena Singh. Omoku had been grabbed from behind, and a fibre had been trapped in the folds of skin in his neck. When he was set on fire, the skin had cauterized, and had trapped the fibre, protecting it. Those fibres have been found In Selleck's house, Jim. He's going down. He's had it. You've stopped a terrorist attack, and helped capture a murderer and kidnapper. This Greaves character has been instrumental, and although we didn't approve of his behaviour in taking the law into his own hands and going after Selleck in the way he did underground, it was clearly self-defence, and he is going to receive an accolade for his actions. It's good PR. It's important to know how grateful we are, but due to your withholding of information, nobody will ever know.' It was Willard's turn to look at the floor.

Jim smiled, and commented that he felt fine about that. He was glad just to be alive, have a job to return to eventually, and he was pleased that Greaves would be recognised. He commented that he felt proud to have associated with a man of such bravery. He was dismissed. On the way out, he took his mobile phone, and made a call. It was to his travel agent. It was about time that he treated Julie to that trip on the Orient Express. He'd always wanted to see Venice.

53

Selleck sang like the proverbial canary. Upon being presented with the evidence against him by the police, he decided that there was really no honour amongst thieves, and took his barrister's advice, admitting that he would be pleading guilty to all of the charges. However, his barrister had informed the crown prosecution service that there was extra information that they were going to be able to provide in relation to the bomb maker. It was made extremely clear that this information was going to be of the utmost importance, and that if it was to be divulged, then there would need to be an agreement before the trial that the maximum sentence would have to be reduced. This was agreed.

Selleck eventually went on to inform the police of the origin of his device, and where exactly he had procured it from. He described to the minutiae the café, the hidden rooms, and the workshop downstairs, where he had made his deal. He regaled with abandon the description of the man he bought the device from, but lied and stated that he had no recollection of the man's name. He refused to give up the contact who had facilitated the meeting, saying instead that he had been contacted anonymously via a written letter, which he no longer owned. There was no proof of this, of course, but the police immediately put together an operation to raid the premises in the back streets of London, in the hope that they were able to locate the bomb maker and catch him in the act.

The operation was meticulously planned, and when the armed police eventually raided the café, they were disappointed to find that the café was completely empty, except for a lone, sterile plastic cup on the counter. Selleck's description was accurate, however the rooms downstairs had been torched, and despite the best efforts of the Scene of Crime Officers, they found no evidence of explosives. It was quite possible that the architect of the chaos machines had worked out of these premises, but traces made on ownership only led to dummy companies set up in false names, which although incriminating and suspicious, gave no real results. However, the deal had been made, and as a result, Selleck's guarantee was given; his sentences would all run concurrently, meaning that there was at least a glimmer of hope that he would see daylight as a free man in his lifetime. He was taken to Wormwood Scrubs, the notorious London prison, where he would remain on remand until his trial. Selleck settled for this, and felt that at least he had made some sort of deal. As he spent his first night in his cell, and as the darkness shrouded his new living quarters, he dreamed of becoming the new godfather of Wormwood, and began plotting new schemes to exact revenge on Greaves and his family.

Epilogue – One year later.

The music filtered through the living room, and seemed to reverberate off the walls. It was loud, but Eddie Selleck liked it that way. It reminded her of the better days, when she used to go dancing. She loved to dance. Glenn Miller was her favourite, and it was his version of 'In the Mood' that was now playing for the neighbours, as well as herself. She knew she was a bit deaf, but since her John had left, and she had found herself all alone, she didn't care. She didn't have anyone to talk to any more. Her neighbours didn't really speak to her now, although they had always tended to ignore her. Her music was all she had. She tapped the arm of the chair in perfect time with the swinging beat, and hummed to herself, not that she could hear her voice above the music. She thought of changing the record for something slower, and arose from her chair. As she did so, she noticed a movement at the window. Someone was looking in at the front window!

It dawned on Eddie that she might have missed the doorbell due to the music. *That's what it is. Me and my music.* She left the music playing, but turned it down a little. She shuffled to the front door, her slight frame dwarfed in the hallway. As she opened the door, she was surprised to find two men, not one. Large men. With leather coats, she noticed.

'Hello, may I help you? I'm afraid John isn't here at the moment. He's gone away. He won't be back for a while.' She smiled feebly at her guests.

'It's okay, Mrs. Selleck. We're friends of John. He sent us around to check you were okay.' The tallest of the men spoke very eloquently, and Eddie was immediately taken in by his disarming smile.

'That's nice of him, looking after his mum like that. You'd better come in. I was just about to make a pot of tea. Would you like some?' She stepped aside, beckoning them inside. She was hoping they would say yes. She was simply *dying* to speak to them. To anyone.

'That would be lovely, Eddie. Two sugars, please.' Replied The Smiler.

'Come in, then. Make yourselves at home.'

They did just that. Eddie headed straight for the kitchen, along the patterned hall floor and into the antiquated, aged kitchen. She took hold of the kettle, and filled the teapot once it had boiled. With her back to the door, she produced some biscuits, and laid them on a little plate, adorned with a doily. *Only the best for the visitors.*

She turned around, humming to the last few bars of *In the Mood*. She loved that song. As she turned around, she stopped in her tracks, her jaw open slightly. The Smiler was not smiling. Both he, and his friend, were stood behind her, and both held silenced pistols. She felt a sharp pain in her chest, followed by another one. *Thud, thud*, came the sounds. She immediately felt dizzy, and dropped the tray, its contents spilling over the floor. She toppled forward, landing on top of the tray and fragments of the teapot, and as she lay on the cold floor, she noticed fluid all around her. She was unable to lift her head, but had she been able to, she would have seen the blood around her, and realised that it wasn't the contents of the teapot. In the living room, the next song had started, and as *Moonlight Serenade* filled the air, she remembered how she loved to dance. In her mind, she was still dancing in the summer evening air, when the last bullet entered her skull, and the room went black.

****

Selleck was beginning to settle into prison life. He was pleasantly surprised at how easily, even in this, the harshest of prison environments, he had been able to establish himself as somebody to be left alone, but someone who needed respect. The lesser gangsters and hoodlums had been relatively easy to deal with. Their advances were easily spurned, and there were already tales between inmates of beatings he had given those who had disrespected him. There was even a rumour that one inmate had been forced to hang himself in his cell, rather than face him. Selleck knew this to be untrue, but had never, of course, agreed or denied this. Sometimes, it was better to say nothing at all.

Contrary to the government's reports that contraband was not making its way into prisons, Selleck had made sure that he had created, through his usual favours, a huge supply network for the other inmates. Mobile phones, cigarettes, drugs, and even more outlandish requests to satisfy the other inmates' more creative needs, were not out of bounds for him. He had made friends with some of the guards, and had bribed them sufficiently for them to not only turn a blind eye to the smuggled goods, but also to allow him some say in the duties he performed. He benefitted from the lighter duties, such as the library trolley, or the laundry work. He even looked forward to these duties on some days, as he had realised that too many inmates went crazy, and became institutionalised, when they did not keep themselves active. *This is going to be easy time*, he reminded himself daily.

It was a Thursday, and a particularly rainy one at that. The bleak concrete surroundings of the laundry were not motivating him today, and Selleck blamed this on the weather. He had done quite a lot of reading, and SAD (Seasonal Affective Disorder) was known to him. He often thought of how strongly he was affected by the inclement weather, and it was as if the prison walls were channelling the negativity from outside, through its pores and directly into the psyche of the collective.

Selleck took collection of his wheelie bin full of dirty laundry, and absentmindedly emptied it into the respective washers. One for linen, one for uniforms, and so on. He could do this with his eyes closed, and although he relished the time out of his cell, he still found it hard to motivate himself on this particular day. Reaching into the bottom of the wheelie bin for the last few pieces, he arose, to be met by three men. From behind. John turned, and looked at the men. He knew most of the faces on his wing, and these were unfamiliar. Indeed, they were completely unknown. Before he had a chance to say anything, they grabbed him, one at each arm. It was not uncommon for inmates to be raped, but he had not been bothered, not since he beat a prospective suitor to within an inch of his life in the shower.

Selleck resisted, and tried to break free from the grip bestowed upon him by his immediate captors.

'What the fuck? Let me go. Now.' Selleck tried his menacing tones, but they went unanswered. 'Who the fuck are you? What the fuck is this?' he began to panic.

The third man, smaller than the other two, reached into a small holdall, and produced a tablet P.C. Selleck was confused. *What the hell?* His two restrainers marched him backwards. Selleck knew it was futile to resist. He had nowhere near enough strength to break free from these two. The third, quiet, smaller man drew himself near to Selleck, turned on the display, and turned the tablet so that Selleck could share the images. It was unclear at first, but with shocking reality, Selleck realised that the image he was looking at was his mother, Eddie. It was a video, but had been paused, showing her facing the camera, with a tray, upon which were a teapot, a saucer of biscuits, and a doily to garnish the plate. The silent man pressed play.

Selleck watched in horror as his mother, carrying the tray, took two steps, and was shot twice in the chest. He saw her look of surprise, then pain, then shock, followed by her crashing fall onto the kitchen floor.

'NO!' Selleck screamed, tears drowning his eyes. Through the salty drizzle blocking his vision, he forced himself to look at her, screaming again when the third, and final bullet, finished her off. He looked at her frail form, and the mixture of brain, bone and blood mingled with her tea on the floor. He sobbed uncontrollably, and looked directly, forlornly, into the eyes of the man in front of him. He tried to move his arms to wipe his eyes, but he couldn't. They were held steadfast.

The silent man placed the tablet P.C. back into the holdall, and instead, produced an ice pick. Long, sleek and silver in hue, it glimmered in the stark light of the laundry. Selleck thrashed, but the quiet man placed a hand on his head, and made a hushing sound. 'Sssssh.' Selleck was immediately quiet.

'Alexander Pitov says hello, John. He asked me to remind you that a long time ago, he asked you to keep him out of the limelight. You broke that promise. Alexander Pitov wishes you a good journey.'

John Selleck did not have time to protest. With frightening speed, the ice pick flashed in and out. *Snick, snick, snick, snick.* All told, the quiet man stabbed Selleck fourteen times. With every penetration of the weapon, Selleck grew weaker, until his legs gave way, and his captors finally released him. He fell onto the floor, the cold, unforgiving concrete holding him while his lungs filled with blood. Selleck began to feel his breathing become heavier, and he coughed once, producing a pool of blood which spilled onto the floor. He could not struggle; he was too weak, and drowsiness was taking over. He knew he was dying. Tears for his mother trickled down his cheek as his last few breaths escaped, his attackers gone. In the harsh, bewildered light of the prison, John Selleck thought one last thought of himself as King, then closed his eyes and died in a pool of his own blood.

****

Greaves was happy. He was sat at his desk (which was a rarity), and his class were tidying up. He loved Friday. He especially loved Fridays now that he knew that he was going to be spending them with Sara and Ashleigh. He looked at her, as she went about her business helping the other children clear the detritus of the day from their desks and prepare to be dismissed. *You've really come along. You're a wonderful little girl, and I'm going to be giving you everything you deserve in life from now on. Just you wait and see. I love you like you were my own.* He forced himself to stop thinking that thought, for fear that the class would see him crying.

Although both he and Sara were still plagued with the occasional nightmare, things were really picking up. They had moved from Bloomfield, and all three were now living in the town of Shaleford. Sara had managed to find herself a great little job with a firm of estate agents as an administrator, and between them, they were able to purchase a lovely cottage, with three perfect bedrooms, a perfect garden for Ashleigh, and a perfect sofa for them to share at the end of the day. Matt reached behind him, and felt inside his jacket pocket for the package he had purchased for Sara that lunch time. Maybe he would give it to her tonight. All he needed was two minutes of courage. *Maybe.*

Matt thought of his brother, and about how close they had become since the events of a year ago. Nick had sworn to give up his nefarious deeds, and thus far had stuck to his plans, opening his own consultancy firm, helping businesses to deliver anything and everything in terms of digital technology. He wasn't bored, which was good, and matt knew this would be the key to him staying on the straight and narrow. What he did know, though, was that they had started talking like they never had before, and he didn't want that to stop. They seemed to dwell on the good times from their childhood, not the bad, and that would do for him.

Being Matt, he even spared a thought for John Selleck. Unfortunately, it was going to take a while for him to be able to look at Ashleigh without seeing him. However, this was getting better, and Matt never mentioned this to anyone. There was no love lost, obviously, but he was sad to hear that both Selleck and his mother had died in suspicious circumstances. *If you play with fire, you get burned.* He certainly had demonstrated that. And then some.

'Mr. Greaves?' It was Little David, as he was known, for obvious reasons. He really was tiny for his age.

'Yes, Dave, my old chum. What is it?'

'Tell us a joke. Go on.' Little David smiled his best smile. It was irresistible.

'Tell me, Dave. Why did the baker wash his hands?' Matt remained dead pan.

'I don't know.'

'Because he kneaded a poo.'

Little David thought about it, then thought about it some more. 'I don't get it, Mr. Greaves.'

'Don't you worry, Dave. Go home in a minute, and ask your dad to explain it. Be sure to tell him that Mr. Baker told you it though. Okay?' Matt smirked at this. He had, over the years, blamed the head for many a bad joke. He hoped this would continue as long as possible, too.

'David, you'll do no such thing. You tell your dad it was Mrs. Forsyth in Year two. That's an order.' It was John Baker himself. Little David went back to his seat, and John and Matt shared a laugh. John looked around the class, gave a satisfied smile to himself, and then turned to Matt. 'Matt, I've got something I need to ask you. I've been watching you…'

'Oh god, are you stalking me? I needed the money. Those photos are art.'

'Idiot. Listen, and don't interrupt. Off the record, and I mean, off the record, the deputy headship is going to be coming up. Pete Miller's got a new job in an international school in Hong Kong of all places. I think you might want to consider it. You'd make a great addition to the leadership team. What do you think?' John waited patiently for Matt to process the information.

'John, I don't know.'

'Promise me you'll think about it. Please? You'll have to go through the process, but between us, I can't think of anybody better. I think you'll be a very popular choice with everyone.' John was being incredibly sincere, and Matt was genuinely touched.

'All right. I'll think about it John. Thanks.'

Matt looked at his watch, and in high spirits, he dismissed the class, who were genuinely sad to be saying cheerio for the weekend. Once empty, he tidied his own space, made sure his lesson plans were ready for the following Monday, and exited his classroom, gently closing the door behind him. Exiting the school, he approached the gate, and in the distance, saw Sara, leaning on the adjacent fence. She spotted him, and her face broke into a smile. It was infectious, and Matt quickened his pace. He couldn't wait to start the weekend with her, and he didn't care who knew.

With the image of him kissing her in his mind, he stopped just short of the gate, and put his hands up in apology. 'Sorry love. Got to go back. Hang on.'

'What now?' Sara feigned disappointment, and mocked frustration by stamping her feet like a toddler.

'I've got something really, really important to do. Oh, before I go though, how do you fancy getting married?' He pulled out the small box, velvet and beautiful, and walked back towards Sara. *Two minutes of courage. Jesus.*

Sara held Matt's hand, and took the ring from him when he removed it from its receptacle. He placed it on her ring finger. She stared at it briefly, smiled, and turned back to Greaves. He waited. Then waited some more.

'Yeah. Go on then.' She felt her eyes fill with tears, but didn't care. She noticed that Matt's eyes were misty too. They kissed briefly, and hugged, not wanting to let go. However, it was Matt who broke the embrace, and looking into Sara's eyes, softly spoke.

'I promise, I'll only be a second. There's two things I really need to do.'

'What, for god's sake?' Sara cried.

'Well, for starters, I need to tell John Baker that I'm definitely going to be going for the deputy headship. If I'm going to be getting married, I'm going to need to provide a better life for my family, aren't I?' Matt smiled at Sara's reaction. As he walked back, Sara shouted after him.

'And the second thing?'

'I'll just be a minute.' Matt reached into his pocket in the sunshine, and as he made his way back inside, he opened his cheque book. He never had got round to paying Sheila his tea money. He had to start sometime. Especially now that he was a responsible adult. Well, almost.

Printed in Great Britain
by Amazon